Orthokostá

Orthokostá
A Novel

THANASSIS VALTINOS

ΟΡΘΟΚΩΣΤΑ
ΜΥΘΙΣΤΟΡΗΜΑ

ΘΑΝΑΣΗΣ ΒΑΛΤΙΝΟΣ

**TRANSLATED FROM THE GREEK BY JANE
ASSIMAKOPOULOS AND STAVROS DELIGIORGIS**

FOREWORD BY STATHIS N. KALYVAS

YALE UNIVERSITY PRESS ■ NEW HAVEN AND LONDON

A MARGELLOS
WORLD REPUBLIC OF LETTERS BOOK

English translation copyright © 2016 by Yale University.

Originally published as ΟΡΘΟΚΩΣΤΆ: ΜΥΘΙΣΤΟΡΗΜΑ. Copyright © 1994, Agra Publications. Copyright © Hestia Publishers and Thanassis Valtinos, 2007, Athens, Greece.

Maps by Christos Kountouras, 2014; courtesy of Stavros Deligiorgis. Foreword by Stathis N. Kalyvas. Introduction by Stavros Deligiorgis.

Yale University Press books may be purchased in quantity for educational, business, or promotional use. For information, please e-mail sales.press@yale.edu (U.S. office) or sales@yaleup.co.uk (U.K. office).

Set in Electra and Nobel type by Tseng Information Systems, Inc. Printed in the United States of America.

Library of Congress Control Number: 2015959235
ISBN 978-0-300-20999-0 (hardcover : alk. paper)

A catalogue record for this book is available from the British Library.

This paper meets the requirements of ANSI/NISO Z39.48–1992 (Permanence of Paper).

10 9 8 7 6 5 4 3 2 1

CONTENTS

Thanassis Valtinos's *Orthokostá* opens with a brief description of a village in flames. Where are we? Why is this village burning? And why should we care?

Here is a book based on a series of oral recollections that are stitched together into a fragmented, potentially confusing narrative. The reader is quickly assaulted by a profusion of personal and place names, and the narrators confuse dates, contest events, and stress ostensibly extraneous details. Indeed, it is this fragmented and multi-faceted style that makes the narrative so compelling but at the same time so challenging. Hence the necessity of geographical and historical context.

We quickly find out that we are in the district of Kynouria, one of three in the province of Arcadia, which makes up the core of the Peloponnese in Greece. This large peninsula, at the southern end of the Balkans, carries a powerful historical charge, associated with the famous war between Greek city-states that took place between 431 and 404 B.C.E. and was immortalized by Thucydides as the Peloponnesian War. More recently, in the 1820s, the modern Greek state grew out of an uprising that took place primarily in that region. The events described in *Orthokostá* take place at yet another critical historical moment, the 1940s.

The village in question was destroyed in the summer of 1944, when Greece was undergoing a ruthless occupation. Many mountain villages had been targeted by a brutal counterinsurgency campaign, carried out by German troops along with their local allies, who were generally known as Security Battalions. Opposing them was a Resistance guerrilla army, the Greek Popular Liberation Army (ELAS), the largest such group in Greece and under the control of the Communist Party of Greece, via a front organization known as the National Liberation Front (EAM). As a result of this conflict thousands of innocent peasants died and hundreds of villages went up in flames.

At the center of the book is a village named Kastri, Valtinos's ancestral village, along with a constellation of smaller neighboring villages: Ayia Sofia, Karatoula, Mesorrahi, Oria, Rouvali, and Eleohori, this last farther away but closely connected to Kastri. A multitude of other places appear, including the town of Tripolis, capital of Arcadia, and Athens.

It soon becomes apparent in the novel that Kastri was destroyed not by German troops, as one might have expected, but by ELAS, which also had set up one of its detention camps for local civilians in a nearby monastery known as Orthokostá. In fact, many of the book's narrators had been imprisoned and tortured there. The realization that the culprits of these atrocities are Greek Resistance fighters rather than Nazi occupiers comes as a shock and goes a long way toward explaining the book's impact in Greece's intellectual circles at the time of its publication in 1994. *Orthokostá* showcases two of the most controversial, delicate, and until recently suppressed aspects of World War II in Greece: the dark side of the Resistance and the collaboration's grassroots dimension. *Orthokostá* is an account of the vicious internecine Civil War that ravaged Greece during the Occupation, setting neighbors against one another.

Valtinos's political and literary credentials among left-leaning intellectuals were such that *Orthokostá* could not be ignored or dismissed. It attracted considerable attention and critical acclaim. At the same time, however, it also became the target of harsh criticism by a small but vocal minority who accused him of seeking to tarnish the image of the Resistance. The novel's impact went beyond the literary realm to inform debates about public history and collective memory.

To understand why this was so, we should start with a key observation: the main events structuring the stories told throughout the book (the formation of the Security Battalions, the destruction of Kastri, and so on) are real, even though their recounting is highly personal, reflecting each narrator's distinct experience and bias as processed through Valtinos's unique prose. Indeed, at one point a female narrator tells her husband: "Don't say anything you shouldn't." These events are also broadly representative of a range of similar processes that took place during this period across the Peloponnese and in other regions of Greece, particularly in Macedonia, in northern Greece. In these areas, a grassroots armed movement emerged in 1944 to challenge EAM and ELAS, spurring a bloody civil war that went through a variety of forms and permutations, ending only in 1949.

How did we get there? In April 1941 Greece was overrun by Nazi Germany, after having successfully resisted an Italian invasion that began in October 1940. What followed was a triple occupation of the country by Germany, Italy, and Bulgaria—which effectively became a German occupation after Italy capitulated in the autumn of 1943. As in many other European countries conquered by Germany and its allies (as well as many Asian countries conquered by Japan), the Occupation was both brutal and vigorously contested. As the war went on, and Germany's prospects began to dim, Resistance groups emerged throughout Greece to challenge the Axis rule. Initially clandestine, urban, and focused on intelligence gathering and sabotage, the Resistance quickly grew into full-fledged rural insurgencies. Britain was instrumental in encouraging them with financial and military assistance. In particular, Greece and Yugoslavia were priority areas for Britain, and the Special Operations Executive (SOE) was tasked with spurring a "partisan" war in both countries. An unintended effect was the spectacular rise of Communist insurgencies.

Relying on Greece's rough mountain terrain, vigorous patriotic feeling, and tradition of irregular warfare and rural banditry, various guerrilla bands began to emerge starting in 1942. They quickly coalesced into two rival groups, one headed by the Communist Party and the other by demobilized officers of the Greek Army. The Communist-led EAM was more centralized, disciplined, and coordinated than the nationalist bands, and it relied on the strong organizational know-how of its cadres, who had amassed considerable experience through years of clandestine political action. As a result, by the end of 1943, the Communists had destroyed the competition and came to dominate the Resistance. The defeat of the nationalist guerrilla bands in the Peloponnese is recounted by several narrators, most notably in chapters 4, 42, and 44.

The Communist takeover of the Resistance in what was a first instance of civil conflict within the Occupation gave rise to a paradox: villages dominated by a traditionalist, property-owning peasantry found themselves ruled by the Communist Party, a group that had been marginal in Greece's mountain hinterland until then. This paradox was especially pronounced in the Peloponnese, where many peasants had to be coerced into joining EAM and ELAS. Most complied, but several resisted (see, for example, the accounts in chapters 16 and 26). Thus, a second paradox: the emergence of a resistance against the Resistance.

Communist coercion and the opposition it led to suffuse the bulk of the narratives. In this way, *Orthokostá* provides a powerful counterpoint to the much better-known account of a quasi-universal, patriotic resistance against Nazi rule in Greece, and the concomitant description of the repression suffered by the left. Indeed, this is a doubly transgressive account. It sheds light on the dark side of the Greek Resistance, which had been airbrushed to emphasize its heroic dimension, and it brings to the surface the real dimensions of collaboration, and its causes, that had been minimized or even suppressed by both its supporters and foes.

Indeed, the thorny issue of collaboration stands at the core of *Orthokostá*. During the first two years of the Occupation, active collaboration with Axis forces was marginal, limited mainly to fascist ideologues, members of previously repressed ethnic minorities, and opportunists of various kinds. This began to change in 1943. The capitulation of Italy, the rapid spread of the Resistance, and the ineffectiveness of a counterinsurgency based on blind, indiscriminate reprisals convinced the occupiers that they were in urgent need of local assistance. It was at this point that a widespread loathing of the

Communists and their methods came together with the Germans' need for local allies, causing the explosive growth of a new kind of grassroots armed collaboration that reached unprecedented levels, comparable to the reach of ELAS.

This process was fed by a gradual escalation of violence. The destruction of nationalist guerrilla bands and the ensuing repression by the Communists encouraged a grassroots opposition to EAM and ELAS that remained silent so long as it was unarmed. However, when the Germans began to supply the dissidents with weapons in the spring and summer of 1944, this opposition became both vocal and violent. Now areas that had been ruled by EAM came under the control of the occupiers and their collaborators. But this period was brief; almost immediately the Germans began retreating in anticipation of their departure from Greece. It was then that ELAS returned with a vengeance and destroyed the villages that had been disloyal to it such as Kastri.

Nor did this cycle of violence stop with the end of the Occupation. The Communist insurrection in Athens in December 1944 provided the stage for new atrocities, followed by low-intensity warfare in 1945–46, which was accompanied by the persecution, formal and informal, of real and suspected Communists. The Civil War moved into its final phase, often referred to as "the" Greek Civil War, in 1946. Now, however, the main theater of armed action was northern Greece, which explains why this conflict does not appear very much in *Orthokostá*.

When examining the grassroots collaboration, we cannot help but wonder about individual motives. Why would so many people ally with the Germans, who were at best disliked and at worse hated? Some of the narrators provide straightforward answers:

The Battalions weren't formed in Trípolis only. They were in all the towns of the Peloponnese. Those were times of national emergency. No Greek ever liked the Germans. Or wanted to collaborate with them. That's when the Peloponnese Battalions were created. In the spring of 1944. When it was becoming

clear that the Germans were losing the war. And it was also becoming clear how dangerous it would be for anyone who might
find himself at the mercy of ELAS after the German collapse.
After they cleared out. . . . EAM and ELAS were the imminent
danger. They would wipe us all out. Any of us who didn't want
to or wouldn't consent to join them. That's how we saw it—and
that's how it was.

The Battalions were formed later on. As a reaction to everything
that had happened. To the arrests and the executions.

Of course these answers only scratch the surface of a complex
issue. It is fascinating to explore the multiple drivers of what appear
to be straightforward political choices but in reality are multifaceted
processes that include everything from personal disputes and local
vendettas to concerns about survival and safety by a population
caught between two fires:

Take the village of Oriá. They hated anyone from Karátoula, so
much hatred between those two villages.

So I went and enlisted. I owed that time. But that's what always
happens. Where will you get food, where will you sleep? In the
barracks. Wherever they give you food. That was the beginning
of the enlistments. On both sides. That was one reason to enlist.
And the other was safety. In the mountains no one came after
you. You went around, you ate, you drank, you got laid. Otherwise you were a reactionary, and you were hounded. You ended
up in the Battalions. You found a place to lay your head.

The rebels came here, they said, Leave your houses, all of you.
Whoever stays in the village will be executed. And the Germans
dropped leaflets. Stay in your homes, no one will harm you.

This was a world dominated by violence, which was both a cause
of individual choices and behaviors but also their inevitable con-
sequence, taking endless shapes and forms because "a human life

wasn't worth much then, that's how things were." Or as another narrator puts it simply: "Ruthless men."

Violence could be indiscriminate, but more often it was highly personal. Indeed, this was a highly personalized war, which only made it that much more terrifying. We cannot help but shudder at statements like "It was our cousin Paraskevás who marched our brother Kóstas up along the river" or "An exceptional man, a progressive farmer, among the best in the area. And that splendid young man was taken to the detention camp by his own brothers. Who executed him later on."

As is often the case, the mechanism that reproduced and escalated violence was revenge, a central feature of many narratives and a powerful driver of violent behavior in general: "We were young then. We wanted revenge." When it comes to revenge, the narratives that stand out include the terrible first-person description of the ordeal imposed on a rival ("With my brother killed and everything, just like I told you. I was fourteen, fifteen. And that's why I took care of Pavlákos later on. I beat him for one whole day and one night."), or the third-person description of the beating of a Communist by the husband of the pregnant woman he had allegedly condemned to death ("I wish I hadn't seen all that"). It is also striking how revenge transcends geography: escaping to Athens offered no respite, as revenge-seekers followed their enemies and took advantage of the chaotic situation to target and assassinate them. Inevitably, revenge caused counter-revenge, violence led to more violence. Even after the violence stopped, the memory of it shaped people's identities and affected their behavior in lasting ways.

Not everything in the novel is bleak, however. There is a flip side to the revenge narratives, for instance, consisting of accounts of positive reciprocity when people who protected others by erasing a few names from a target list, intervening on someone's behalf, or refusing to denounce someone who victimized them were later protected in a moment of need by those they had helped. The story of Yiórgos and Yeorghía in chapter 2 is particularly moving in this respect.

The violence also has its absurd side. We find it in the story of the young woman who stitched a crown instead of a hammer and sickle on the berets she made for the Communist guerrillas and almost lost her life because of it, the man who was executed by the Germans when they found that the papers he had stuffed into his shoes to blunt the nails holding the soles were EAM leaflets, or the Security Battalion officer who survived many difficult moments only to be assassinated in Athens where he went to pursue his love interest. The pinnacle of absurdity is probably reached when German troops turn out as the liberators of the peasants being held by the guerrillas in the monastery detention camp.

Of course, taking all these complex processes into account does not mean that we need to accept that the choices made by these individuals are morally justified. It is worth stressing here that *Orthokostá* is by no means one-sided. We find in it extensive descriptions of atrocities committed by the Security Battalions (see, for example, chapters 6 and 33), while several narrators provide many qualifications and counterpoints. However, critics who accuse Valtinos of equating understanding with excusing miss the book's point, which is to reveal the intricate universe into which all these people moved and to immerse us in it. On that score, *Orthokostá* is an unmitigated success.

Does its unrelenting focus on this complex reality make *Orthokostá* an amoral account? Quite the opposite. I would argue instead that it is deeply moral. Although no attempt is made to apportion responsibility for the atrocities, several stories contain elements of a "moral economy" shared by most narrators, one that privileges an understanding of individual responsibility embedded in its context, as opposed to a general and abstract judgment. In this view, most people are seen as subject to their own passions and the prevailing social norms, victims of the terrible situation in which they found themselves. It is often hard to blame them, for they are hardly masters of their own volition. Nor, obviously, can they be praised. Yet at the same time certain actions are singled out, either positively or negatively: positively, when people transcend their limitations to perform unexpected good deeds ("He wasn't a die-hard Communist. He would cover for our fellow villagers."); negatively, when individuals transcend them in the opposite direction to commit random or excess violence, as do militiamen such as the Galaxýdis brothers and Kóstas Kotrótsos, who were trigger-happy, looters, "unprincipled drifter[s]," or simply "animal[s]," or the old man who helped the militiamen set a house on fire:

> And on their way up to the square old Yiánnis Prásinos says, Haven't you set it ablaze yet? And he took out his flint lighter. They were going to burn it down one way or another. But old Yiánnis, he gave them his lighter. He tossed it to them from his bench. May God forgive him.

Orthokostá may be read as an account of the Greek Civil War as it was experienced in the villages of Kynouria: it is a fascinating and enlightening one. But it may also be read much more broadly, as an account of the human experience in the midst of extraordinarily harsh circumstances. This latter reading resonates powerfully with journalistic reports from contemporary civil wars and also with Thucydides' description of civil strife in the earlier Peloponnesian War: "Human nature, always ready to offend even where laws exist, showed itself proudly in its true colours, as something incapable of controlling passion, insubordinate to the idea of justice, the enemy to anything superior to itself."

Orthokostá's narrators reassert, via Valtinos, Thucydides' perspective when they offer observations and reflections that encapsulate everlasting, almost biblical, truths:

> It was God's wrath, all that, there's nothing else you can say.

> And may all that never happen again.

Notre histoire est noble et tragique
Comme le masque d'un tyran.

—Guillaume Apollinaire, "Cors de chasse," *Alcools* (1913)

When Thanassis Valtinos first began writing, the literary climate in Greece was not particularly auspicious for fiction. Poetry was the dominant medium of expression, and formidable writers like George Seferis, Odysseas Elytis, Andreas Embirikos, and Yannis Ritsos were in the forefront, giving Greek poetry both national and international acclaim. The appearance in 1963 of Valtinos's novel *Η κάθοδος των εννιά* (The Descent of the Nine), however, set the pace for new forms of expression in prose fiction that had no precedent in terms of immediacy, terseness, and use of controversial subject matter—with the possible exception of the memoirs of the nineteenth-century general Ioannis Makrygiannis (published in 1907). Among Valtinos's contemporaries few had ventured to broach the occulted subject of the 1947–49 Greek Civil War in all its problematical dimensions. And while it was obvious to everybody that Valtinos's first novel dignified the sacrifices made in a lost ideological cause, it was also impossible for anyone to miss the harsh reality imposed by his telegraphic medium: the actual voices of the nine antigovernment rebels who perished through a variety of mishaps in an inhospitable landscape that forever withheld the redemption of the sea.

Valtinos's daring new voice in *The Descent of the Nine* had been preceded by only one Civil War novel worthy of a subject of such political complexity and demanding such self-examination—Stratis Tsirkas's Ακυβέρνητες πολιτείες (Drifting Cities, 1961–65)—and followed by a mere handful of comparable attempts, such as Yannis Beratis's Το Πλατύ ποτάμι (The Wide River, 1946–65), and Aris Alexandrou's Το Κιβώτιο (The Box, 1974). But these were solitary works; Valtinos has been revisiting the Civil War tragedy in cycles over the years, with narratives both long and short, most powerfully Orthokostá (1994). Taken together with Valtinos's other major works, Orthokostá holds pride of place as the most successful testing of the range fiction writing can achieve when plumbing the spaces between language and memory and the shading of the inhuman into the humane. History in the making seems to be the chief end of the present novel, even as its numerous asides imply the impossibility of viewing history divorced from the light of art and thought.

■

Valtinos has sandwiched his narrative between two texts, one ascribed to an eighteenth-century cleric named Isaakios, perhaps the last humanist to project the virtues of ancient Arcadia onto the landscape of the southeastern Peloponnese, the Christian monastery in its middle notwithstanding; and the other an epilogue that debunks the good cleric's utopian opener. Between the extreme sublimation at the outset and the grim realities that have intervened by the end, the novel similarly appears to have two hearts: one beating to the drum taps of the ancient epics, the other to the transport of lyricists like Tyrtaeus, Callinus, and George Seferis.

It would be natural for an explorer of literary texts to want to prospect, upon first leafing through this book, for the presence of any sign promising the joyful experience of poetry—the aspect of any artifact, in other words, that would determine the quality of the time invested in the reading. If the precritical indicators could serve as guides and Orthokostá proved indeed to be the kind of "news that STAYS news," in Ezra Pound's definition, they certainly informed the impact that the book made when it was launched in 1994. A first rather short, page-long chapter, a much longer second, and then a surprising, barely twenty lines long, third must surely have raised intriguing questions regarding the conventions *Orthokostá* embodied. These rough, apperceptive data are the novel's invitational markers—one thinks of the four initial notes of Beethoven's Fifth—and a persistent reminder that the general thrust of the narrative and the relationship of its parts to the whole would need to be viewed on an equal footing with its other, more discursive materials.

Keeping both the content and its organization constantly before the mind's eye is a balancing act few readers of the prose classics, be they by Montaigne or Tolstoy, manage to maintain. *Orthokostá*'s irresistible human representations, its numerous dramatis personae coming slowly and rather mysteriously into focus, have tended to attract more vocal and more articulate responses than the book's structure and its semi-transparent message. The terror that spread throughout the Greek countryside during the fratricidal period, roughly between 1943 and 1946, the appalling suffering it caused, as well as the survivors' stories, would be hard to ignore. The book, however, communicates not long after its curtain raisers that it is as much about the many tortured tales men and women tell as it is about the drama of the disembodied voice-over experiences in its interviews and its surprising shorter but cryptic interjections. The latter, refrain-like sections—without which the book would hardly make sense—serve to reorient the reader away, momentarily, from the chronicles of the direct rightist or leftist depositions and toward a more meditative mode, in effect, toward the enigma of the aesthetic composition of the book as a whole. Shifting between elegy and anecdote, exorcism and self-exculpatory soliloquy, tableau and interview, novella and epiphany, *Orthokostá* exhibits virtuoso syncopation on the one hand and the infinite drama of the themes of the classical canon on the other.

■

The book raised a furor when it first appeared in 1994 for presumably favoring one side of the conflict it portrayed over the other. Is it possible that so many of its critics read past the material in any single account (or the ironies inherent in the succession of any two) in an attempt to mine their subject matter for evidence of the author's— Mr. Thanassis Valtinos of Main Street's—own predilections? Was the medium of the many narratives so transparent and apparently without texture that they took it for raw, uninflected content? The numerous speaking sections of *Orthokostá* were easily construed as the evidentiary grail so many cultural historians are typically in search of. Even the possibility that the *Rashomon* effect might hint at the problematical nature of the novel, a text in the process of serial riddling, took second place to the quest for the oral histories covering the specific three terrible years that preceded the outbreak of the equally terrible Civil War in 1947. The knee-jerk reception of these critics to *Orthokostá*, personal penchants aside, might be explained in part by one legal technicality. Greece was probably the last anti-Axis country in Europe to pass legislation acknowledging that there had been resistance against the World War II Occupation powers. When the belated law was passed in 1984, both conservatives and leftists vehemently denied the other any right to claim participation in the Resistance. All this a full forty years after the withdrawal of the last German troops from Greece and only ten years before the appearance of *Orthokostá*, with its provocative polyphony.

There have indeed been the exceptional readers who sensed an "impersonal" air to the book. They recognized Valtinos's attraction to the slice-of-life, unsentimental folk forms that had informed a large number of his earlier works and to the unself-conscious, unschooled speech patterns of the man in the village coffeehouse, whether in Lesbos (*You Will Find My Bones Under Rain*, 1992) or in the Kastri epicenter of *Orthokostá*. Valtinos's often nameless speakers parallel his own rather oblique presence in the larger story. Starting out as the primary listener to and transcriber of the numerous reminiscences, he comes across at first as the anthropologist's participant observer and only gradually as the native interrogator's amanuensis.

The writer's intermittent visibility in many of the narratives is but the self-ghosting of "Valtinos" the virtual editor who leaves no trace of his hand behind, no hint that he determined the order or form in which the book would greet or confront its readers. As the protagonists' sex and political persuasions become progressively clearer, however, the novel appears to be concerned less with the characters' existential predicaments, and lesser still with Greece's role in the geo-ideological theater of the Balkans in the 1940s. Far from conflating the conventional in art with the historical, *Orthokostá* does not miss a chance to foreground the musicality of its linguistic medium and the logic of its structure. In doing so it appeals on almost every page to the range of its readers' relationships to the craft of literature in general and the concision of poetry in particular.

Gradations of timbre abound. Some sections read like officers' reports to headquarters, others like legal treatises. They are the sections that make use of the purist, katharevousa, idiom by the speakers, who range from schoolteachers to lawyers to Party cadres. Other sections feature the reluctant responses to questions by an unidentified interlocutor. The philosopher Walter Benjamin, in his essay on Nikolai Leskov, observed that survivors of the carnage of World War I, contrary to expectations, were less not more talkative. The chronicler in *Orthokostá*, several times, gives way to the rhapsode, like the unidentified narrator (Homer?) in the *Odyssey* who, at some point, asks his fictional hero, "What did you do next, Odysseus?" The mix of the individual and the supra-individual in the novel suggests that its core of insight and sympathy lies not in the individual stories but rather in their seemingly unedited transcription as oral accounts that somehow reached the domain of the page in the form of an affidavit. Convention and invention are so tightly intertwined in the structure of the book readers may forget to shift from the substance of each first-person point of view to the page's unacknowledged origin. The Aristotelian unities of action, place, and time have been replaced in the novel by a roaming ear that captures inflections and idiosyncratic expressions about incidents beyond count that each chapter introduces with dreadful timing.

The periodic cross-fading of personalities in their relationship to time and the landscape of the Peloponnese underscores Valtinos's implied insistence that he is dealing in uncoached random reports. Somehow, magically, Valtinos's wildly variegated statements exhibit an interconnectedness and relevance to one another reminiscent of wind-blown *papiers trouvés*. Cervantes' hero Don Quixote at some point in the novel that bears his name expresses an irrepressible desire to read every torn piece of paper littering the streets of the city. In practical terms, Valtinos has often acknowledged the same urge. His novel *Data from the Decade of the Sixties* (1989) exhibited a gargantuan appetite for the discarded and found scraps Cervantes writes about. Newspaper clippings, illiterate application forms scavenged from office wastebaskets, and letters of the lovelorn to a Greek Miss Lonelyhearts make up the *Data* "novel." The transitionless linking together of so many sections of *Orthokostá* leaves no doubt that this novel is erected on a more elevated plane and in more closely figured themes than the docu-fantasies of his other books. The apparently unmediated orality in *Orthokostá* exhibits the stark ethopoeia of Aeschylus's *Persians* and Thucydides' unapologetic speeches in the genocidal Melian expedition. Both, like *Orthokostá*, make for fractured readings in times of fractured collectivity.

■

Once past the prefatory utopia Valtinos sets the tone for the kind of communication that has neither Bishop Isaakios's euphuism nor the detachment of its modernist retraction in the finale. The page-long first chapter contains a woman's recollection of the summer wind carrying cinders from houses burning in neighboring villages. She cites the urgency of men's messages to their families to pick up everything and make themselves scarce because bad things are coming their way. The sense of approaching danger, the rumors of violence spreading facelessly like a contagion, is so gripping that one forgets that this is happening in Arcadia, where such things are not supposed to happen. The unthinkable is becoming real. A local can tell that the smoke is not coming from burning vegetation. Houses that had not been bombed by Germans or blown up by Italians are now being torched, one after the other, with the help of a broomstick set afire by a fellow Greek's flint lighter. This man, mentioned by name, even exchanges a quip or two with the members of the committee that was carrying out orders as directed by the Party chapter chairwoman.

Like Hawthorne's "Custom-House" overture to *The Scarlet Letter*, Valtinos's audible hovering in portions of *Orthokostá* ensures, primarily, that its realist frontage does not falter, that its linguistic cast will give pleasure, and that its *apport* to the imagination will be to so conceal art that it will come across as artless. And what better masking of the conventions of the techne in any art than the apparent artlessness in direct voice transcriptions? Valtinos's lifelong contributions to Greek cinema, including widely known collaborations with Theodoros Angelopoulos, may go a long way toward explaining his method: no genre does a better job of obscuring the seams of editing, the splicing and shuffling of "takes," than the documentary. The framing mode of the audio-to-paper transfer is made explicit in other books by Valtinos. A cassette recorder is mentioned in *Deep Blue Almost Black* (1985), and *The Life and Times of Andreas Kordopatis* (1964) is an oral account partially based on an emigrant's journal. Regarding *Orthokostá*, it matters little whether the published material is lifted from "live" recordings or simply "hearsay." Even if Valtinos had done "the police in different voices" (T. S. Eliot's original title for *The Waste Land*) in the forty-nine chapters of *Orthokostá*, this in itself would be no mean feat. Neither Bishop Isaakios's "blurb" on the land around Orthokostá nor the Triple A–like epilogue would lie beyond Valtinos's inventive abilities. In the end both are fictions that serve, each in its own way, to distance the reader from the gore and suffering associated with Orthokostá.

Speakers in the book are either warned, typically by another speaker, not to mention any names, or they suddenly turn silent with an expression that comes close to a gruff, but ambiguous "I'm done talking." The concluding reference to much that is unspeakable in Valtinos often assumes the gravity of historical closure ("The rebel insurrection was over. . . . It was over for good," the Greek verb in this context being a derivative of *catharsis*). Occasionally the account progresses towards a note of exorcism. The parting shots of most of the recorded stories often end with a laconic one-liner ("that bloodshed still hounds him"). The beginnings, on the other hand, tend to be almost always teasers that, by dint of repetition, could as easily apply to the captive audience as to the speaker: "We were arrested when . . ." Once the captivity narrative gets under way, however, the contents are surprising in their immediacy. Both captors and captives, in the hundreds, are ill-equipped for the mountainous terrain, both are chronically undernourished, few attempt to escape their preordained ranks, and both stoically accept the long marches that serve to maintain a supply of men and women hostages to be culled for summary retaliatory executions whenever the captors are attacked.

The oft-intuited dilemma in *Orthokostá*, "damned if you do, damned if you don't," sounds painfully familiar from the ancient historians' accounts of cities destroyed for not choosing neutrality and then destroyed, a second time, for having chosen it. Like all complex epics *Orthokostá* is rich in war paradoxes. Glaucus's meeting with Diomedes in the sixth book of the *Iliad* manages to tinge the action of the entire poem with the possibility of somber ironies ("Go find yourself other Greeks to kill . . .") where one would least expect to find them. In one sense there is little that is peculiarly Peloponnesian in the list of the *Orthokostá* atrocities. The ancient lyricists such as Tyrtaeus and Callinus testify to the opposite. And so do Homer and Sophocles when it comes to orders that the executed not be buried. Were it not for the gods' daily intervention Achilles' punishment of the dead Hector's body in the *Iliad* would have resulted in the same kind of posthumous disfigurement a man in *Orthokostá* suffers at the hands of his torturers. "Mémos's Fields" refers to a spot named for a local official and torture victim who was shot during a march he could not keep up with because of the beatings he had received on the soles of his feet. As with the heroes of antiquity, place names are given to commemorate a victim's tragic death. Walter Benjamin's eighteenth thesis on the art of the storyteller — once again from his essay on Nikolai Leskov—sums up the etiological presentation as one that allows the "voice of nature" to speak, including the dark work of hatred. An anonymous initiative in itself, the naming of Mémos's Fields does not monumentalize the circumstance of victimization, nor is it triumphalist. One corner of the countryside that had been repeatedly crisscrossed by forced marches of hundreds and hundreds of civilian "enemies of the people" now has a voice and a face.

■

Valtinos's speakers come from or go through places that are inseparable from their own and their families' identities. The metaphor, a synecdoche really, is saying, "If you're looking for 'art' it's out there," in a territory of narrowly topical and date-bound, often warring, site-specific states. Allusions to places of birth, mixed in with the speakers' relatives and acquaintances, make *Orthokostá* appear at first to be just another demographic dump of the Greek Civil War and its participants. To the untrained ear they are as superficially unattractive as the four-hundred-line catalogue of ships in the *Iliad*—a 1955 translation omitted them as of no interest to the modern reader!—which enumerates both the European and the Asian expeditionary contingents that participated in the siege of Troy. It is true that the illusionism of the main action in the *Iliad* is momentarily suspended. In its place, and behind the euphony of locations like Sparta, Epidaurus, Mycenae, Euboea, Ithaca—to Valtinos's "Parnon" "Karatoula," "Tripolis," and "Argos"—one notices that Homer's catalogue is also about the families the troops leave behind, the attributes of the locales they come from, the miniature epics of still other alliances and hatreds: in other words of countless other Troys embedded in the framework of the main epos. In *Orthokostá* whole neighborhoods, individual plots of land, and even stone fences are known by their founders' or builders' names. Trajectories of movement through fields or towns are marked by itemized ownerships. The naming rituals of older titles, the degrees of belonging to a family network, or the rituals of christening and mourning that fill the book all build up to the *chora*—a term adopted by the theoretician Jacques Derrida from Plato's *Timaeus* for the matrix of villages that, in this case, mysteriously engender language and social relations. The unfailing rootedness to conditions on the ground of any entries in Valtinos's lists, long or short, adduced by the narrators seems to be saying insistently that whoever touches a man touches a place, cherished or haunted.

Chora can be alarmingly literal as well. In one of the shortest chapters of the book the speaker describes a team of mules loaded with sacks of chestnuts traveling by night. When the animals suddenly freeze in their tracks the muleteer wonders whether they had sensed the macabre past under their hooves. Washington Irving and Balaam's Ass from the book of Numbers converge upon the reader's novelized interviewee, who wonders whether it was "the devil playing tricks, or . . . the smell of blood—three years since Fotiás was killed there." The reader has long sensed that the indirection by which so much information is conveyed to the page is intentional and that possibly the blurry contours and the discontinuous nature of its interludes are so many nudges toward the participatory cast of this fiction, the active connecting of lines of thought and the juxtaposing of the varying gradients of truthfulness (or posing) between the book's two covers. The reader's co-authoring of *Orthokostá* is of the same critical order as that called for by Laurence Sterne's refracted fabulations in *Tristram Shandy* or by Julio Cortázar's Escherian *Hopscotch*.

Valtinos does not divulge the information as to how the first-person reports in the novel came into his possession, or the process by which they lined themselves up for the readable, published version. The documents fascinate from the start by their alternating emphases and changing points of view. Some are prodding investigations while others are tableau-like miniatures of pathos. Even bathos. Take the execution of an emaciated old woman who refuses to betray her son's whereabouts and is killed on the spot. Others read like Norse sagas. *Burnt Njall* is an apt analogue as the wind blows in cinders from burning homes in the vicinity. Homer's retelling of the siege of Meleager's home in the *Iliad* is clearly reenacted here. Meleager dies when his external soul, a log that was saved by his mother from the hearth when he was born, is thrown back into the fire by his mother. *Orthokostá*-like — paralleled by a notorious female rebel leader who stridently demands that her own father and brothers be put to death — Meleager and his household are doomed to die at the hands of none other than his mother's brothers. The opposing sides in the novel burn each other's homes down while also holding separate "courts" in the mountains to judge and hang their rivals. A sizable part of the population is made to choose between forced conscription and summary execution while another beleaguered group prefers volunteering for camps in Germany to being held hostage in the place of relatives who had taken refuge in Athens.

The persona of the non-omniscient narrator whom, for convenience' sake, we can call Valtinos, reappears in later chapters of the book in order to close an epic ring composition and to pose questions that mark him as another local, on intimate terms with various families' histories and, frequently, an acquaintance of the speakers. There are moments when the questions resemble Socrates' maieutic method of facilitating the birthing of a story or Homer's questioning of his hero. The working assumption in *Orthokostá* seems to have been that the integrity of every testimony would be preserved at all stylistic costs and that all "data," commented on or not, would be respected as delivered and as recorded. More narrowly, "style" for Valtinos is the projection of the vividness of the medium he salvaged from the mouths of the protagonists of the novel with as little manipulation as possible. The initially choppy, fragmented phrasing of any one of his speakers occurring anywhere in a section may go on for some time, until a particular idiom explodes that cancels out all the inarticulate fumblings leading up to it and brings with it an unforgettable, often surprising turn of thought. The Greek that the obscure villagers of *Orthokostá* speak, be they in or out of uniform, be they victims or victimizers, communicates an expressive vigor that even under the duress of recollecting the troubled times is nothing short of astounding. The array of the narratives of the novel seems to be saying, Let the people at the receiving end of history talk as they will and two things will emerge simultaneously: on the one hand the kind of local knowledge that the fourteenth- and fifteenth-century chronicles of the Morea—another name for the Peloponnese—or Cyprus, for example, are famous for, and on the other the torrents of live eloquence one associates with Froissart and Xenophon.

■

The chapters are subtly intertwined, and so are the interludes. The withholding, for instance, of a specific detail for hundreds of pages until its significance is made clear in a new, still shifting context affects the reader's sense of time and disbelief. And it affirms Valtinos's sense of the dignity of what would have otherwise been trivial facets of the essentially subjective nature of human experience. Valtinos is so fastidious about not overstating a particular mood he often concludes with aphoristic brevity or by the mere restating of his speakers' last words.

This book may help explain the attraction Valtinos's dry, laconic style holds for his readers. The "intermittency" of the Civil War material with the shorter prose poems, besides serving to return the reader to the life of the senses, reveals a Valtinos constantly on the lookout for the other kinds of life going on even among the ruins. Indeed, there are rich doses of Bakhtinian "novelizing" in *Orthokostá*. Squabbles erupt over a stolen watch. The killing of two ravenous dogs ends in reconciliation. Neighboring villagers who fear a poor citrus fruit crop for that year resign themselves to planting onions. These "gratuitous" minor incidents could be considered as contrastive textures that are inserted in an otherwise torrential series. It is through variations of this kind that Valtinos communicates textual complexity. For lack of a better term they might be called *pauses plastiques*. They appear as a thematic punctuation in the flow of the longer stories. And they also prevent facile symmetries. Cameo-like, they are breathers permitting the continuous exposition to assume the tones of poetry. Predictability is broken up by the subtle associations afforded by the inserts. Beginning with chapter 3, and ending on the last page of the last chapter of the book, these snapshots are the space in which the unnamed participant observer intrudes the least and sometimes even vanishes altogether. From a literary-historical point of view, alternating the modes of a single composition is part of a tradition that reaches back to the Attic playwrights' polyrhythms, the Roman prosimetra, and the Christian liturgy. From Ibn Hazm al-Andalusi's *Dove's Neck Ring About Love* of the tenth century and Rigas Feraeos's *Mismayés* of the eighteenth there is but a short step to *Orthokostá*. The contrapuntal, collagistic *Orthokostá* could not adequately convey a sense of suffering humanity in the round if the uneven chords it struck did not resonate with its readership's familiarity with other more traditional and more modern projects in music, architecture, and the visual arts. Meaning, in the novel, emerges to a far greater extent from its reading than from its writing.

As the short chapters are mounted in the midst of the longer ones they tend to be emblematic of circumstances as well as of states of mind. In a barely four-line section a woman is asked if she remembered the incident of concealing someone inside a storage trunk: "She started to cry. Poor thing, she's an old lady now, all shriveled up." The souls, even of the bravest, as in many of Homer's martial encounters, depart with a whimper. Valtinos's snapshots function much like the linguist Roman Jakobson's continuators, both phatic and evocatory.

Whatever else makes up the chapters of the book is suddenly pushed into the background by the awareness that in the midst of untold calamities a young woman can still be romanced and proposed to by a rebel captain passing through, while another can be coveted by a rightist hothead who can find no other way to be near her except by arresting and re-arresting her; trains are somehow still connecting small townships to county seats; while a handful of naked German soldiers take a dip in a stream of mountainous Arcadia. It is these short, compressed tableaus, in the final analysis, that carry the day. When the agonizing of relatives and friends finally subsides, the last image the last chapter leaves the reader with is of a villager's speculating over a source of fresh water: if his price is not met, the water will be left to lie in its underground resting place. The site of anguish and fear for the reader is relieved by the hint of an element of life ready to gush forth if only the agency of man would not interfere with it. Even the novelist and critic Edward Dahlberg heard, in his essay "Melanctha" from *Can These Bones Live*, the clamor and convulsions of the age for "blood, for human offal," as "a cry for dim and fetal beginnings."

■

The cross-layering of human motivations in *Orthokostá* fast acquires the status of written objects—military operations transparencies, parchment, blotting paper—all in different hands and in different inks rousing the gamut of response from rage and nostalgia to reverie. To the rest of the world the mind of a southeastern Peloponnesian in the early 1940s might well be an enigma. The two pre-forties Greek-American interludes in *Orthokostá* appear, superficially, to have no relation to the burning issues of the Occupation and the ensuing Civil War. But they do offer glimpses of normalcy (and comic relief) in a society where marriages are arranged for some successful emigrants, while other less disciplined returnees lose their entire life earnings to the fiats of crazed nationalists and ideologues in high places. The women also report on their looted households and the shunting from shelter to shelter of clothing, dowry items, and precious sewing machines, the signifiers of feminine dignity, scattered to the four winds by armed bullies who see no contradiction between their actions and their credos.

By not insinuating any known voice in the master narrative and by not damning either of the fratricidal sides, Valtinos allows scenes of desperate choices to speak for themselves. Even as the Greeks commandeer historic monasteries like Orthokostá and Loukou to "process" future victims, the German occupying forces do their own culling of civilians for the labor camps at home. Does the category of a peasant society whose members are forever enmeshed in the cycles of subsistence farming and the rituals of homemaking explain the violent swings of one group to "liberationist" oppression and of its rival to murderous defensiveness? Through the unfolding of the stories themselves Valtinos distances himself enough to let the reader share in the quizzicality of the events. One woman pretends to be an epileptic—a ploy reminiscent of the Hellenistic romances—in order to avoid deportation to Germany. Only a few chapters later, a group of war-weary individuals volunteers to be taken to camps in Germany in order to escape being exterminated at home! The forces at plague, as James Joyce would have put it, would make idiocy of any attempt at generalizing.

Forty years on, during the writing of the book, many of the blood-stained locales in the Peloponnesus were renamed—some even removed—as if chora had been acting the author: revising, crossing out, and rewording the screed on the ground. In keeping with the fragility and transitoriness of power, as quoted from the book of Psalms in the epigraph of *Orthokostá*, Valtinos's sobering conclusion closely parallels George Seferis's poem "The King of Asine." When the "things of this world" are said and done (and turned to dust)—Asine being in the Argolis prefecture, only a few miles north of Orthokostá—some Mycenaean-age *turannos*'s mask of beaten gold may still survive and give back a tinny sound when a pebble is dropped on it.

A novel is the onset of a new creation. During the fourteenth-century Plague in Florence, and a generation before Chaucer, Giovanni Boccaccio arranged for his storytellers' brigade, some of whom are related to each other, just as some of the *Orthokostá* characters are, to meet in the church of Santa Maria Novella. And just like the *Decameron* and the *Canterbury Tales* before it, *Orthokostá* is an organ diapason drowning out all the personalist, jejune readings and rewritings of our times, as Derek Walcott's *Omeros* would have put it, which achieve little else besides making literature as guilty as history.

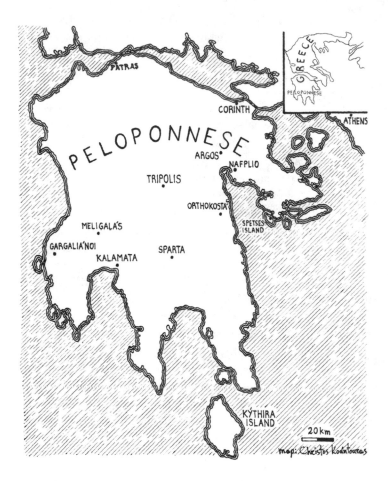

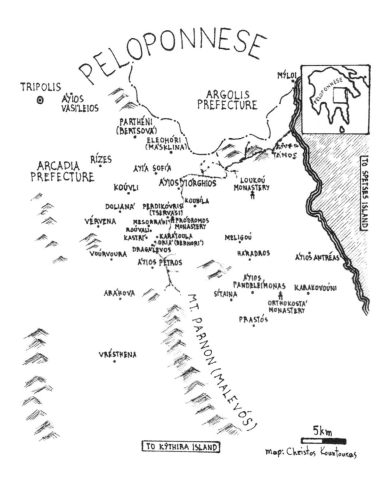

Orthokostá

Thou shalt dash them in pieces like a potter's vessel.

—Psalm 2:9

In the shadow of Mount Malevós,[1] at its foothills and not too far from Orióntas Province, there stands a monastery called Orthokostá celebrating the Ninth-day Feast of the Dormition of the Virgin.[2] It was erected in early Christian times but was destroyed and looted around the year 1724 by Saracens, who repeatedly raided and pillaged the region of Tsakoniá[3] from all sides. The monastery was immediately rebuilt upon the still visible ruins by a monk named Barnábas Kaf-soxyliótis, who truly led a hermit's life, equal unto an angel, and was erudite in both secular and holy learning. And although at present the monastery has lapsed from its former beauty, it is once again flour-ishing, inhabited by approximately sixty monks who busy themselves regularly with all manner of agricultural tasks and most of the arts. Its verdant gardens boast a variety of fruit trees, while in the Foúska plain below, which is especially hospitable to olive groves, wheat, bar-ley, beans, and other vegetables are grown, and even vineyards yield-ing rich vintages of mirth-inducing wine of cinnamon color. The river Mégas, descending from Mount Malevós and fed by so many streams it becomes torrential, runs through the valley. One might almost say that the entire well-being of the monastery depends on it. On the left bank of the river and along the length of the hills there is a vein of lead and silver that remains to this day unexploited. According to a belief that is hard to confirm, the underground course of this vein can be clearly traced if every year, on the morning of August 23 before dawn, one stands silently, facing east, on the upper balcony of the monas-tery. From this same balcony the eye can see as far as the Sea of Náf-

plion bounded to the north by the peak of Mount Karakovoúni, to the south by the Cape of Saint Andréas, and to the east across the sea reaching well beyond the island of Spétses. A lower mountain range encircles the area from Cape Karakovoúni all the way to that of Saint Andréas and, extending three or four miles out from the sea, it shelters the Foúska plain from the Northerlies, which may well be the cause of the heat waves during the summer. The grounds around the monastery are delightfully wooded and green the year round in any weather, its ice-cold, crystal-clear, healthful waters bestowing great delight and refreshment upon its guests.

ISAÁKIOS, BISHOP OF RHÉON AND PRASTÓS
An Account of the Country of Prasiae and Thyreátis

Chapter 1

All day long the wind carried ashes down toward us. But it was quiet. In the evening we sat out in front of the house, and the men saw five people heading out from the Makrís property and going off. They went down a ways to a clearing, and they saw two of them going into the Koúros gorge, and the other three going up toward Masklinéki Vigla.[1] The men came back, they said, Something's up, we're clearing out because they're going to arrest us tonight. They'll kill us. And they left right then and there. They told us women, Collect your things, get the animals out tomorrow, away from Koubíla, don't leave anything behind. Because something's up. They left, and we left in the morning, break of day. Me, the shepherds' wives, and my sister-in-law, Yiórgos's wife. Yiórgos the lawyer. She'd come there from Trípolis, they had Yiórgos in the detention camp, they'd arrested him. We gathered up the goats from Lákka. Tsioúlos's widow was there, Lioú.[2] She tried to catch some hens to take with her, she had a rooster, it got away from her. She says, Let's not be too long, because the men told us to leave, I'll come back and get it tonight. She went back that night, but the rooster wasn't in the coop. They go out looking, she had her two eldest children with her, ten, eleven years old, they see feathers down on the threshing floor. Lioú says, That brute, he killed our rooster.

Chapter 2

The next day they took *me* in. That's when it was. I'd come from Kastrí. I left with Paraskeví that evening. The men sent me to check the house, and so I wouldn't be alone I stayed with your girls, Iríni. At your place. I went out to the square to go to your house, I see a lot of people. Where the Telephone Company is now. They're saying, They burned down Ayiasofiá[1] last night. There was killing and the like. I leave, I go to Chrónis's pharmacy. He says, Yeorghía, they saw your brothers in Másklina.[2] I didn't know a thing. What are you talking about, Lámbros? I started crying. I went up to your house. Yiórgos Haloúlos was there. He was with Anthí. Pavlákos was there, down at the butcher's. At Goúnas's. In the doorway. And he gave me a look, like that. Nikólas did. I go find Yiórgos and Anthí. They were talking about me. I was terrified after Lámbros told me about my brothers, that they'd seen them in Másklina. Because I was the one would pay for it. Don't worry, Yiórgos Haloúlos tells me. We were just talking about you, to see where to hide you. Well, anyway. Anthí takes me, and we go to the shack, you know, the shack, Iríni. To see if I could stay there. I tell Anthí. I was a young girl, in the prime of my youth. I tell her, Anthí, honey, that Pavlákos fellow was giving me the eye. Sly-like, you know. That son of a bitch, says Anthí. That son of a bitch. Don't pay him any mind. Later on I understood why he was looking at me. That night Pótis Lenghéris comes by. Who doesn't know anything yet. I was still with the girls. He says, They want you at the office. The office was at Mángas's house. They want to question you, he says. He takes me there. Mángas's house was just a few steps away. We go inside. I see the Koutsoyiánnis family from Douminá. Relatives of the others who'd left with our brothers. It must have been evening. The sun must have set. Stávros Koutsoyiánnis, his son Yiórgos and Vasílis Koutsoyiánnis's wife. I started crying. I also saw some villagers from Ayiasofiá. They'd arrested them the same day. The day after they burned down their village. It was July, because we were harvesting. And there I am crying. Your father comes in, the girls had fixed me something to eat. He brought me eggs with potatoes.

—Was Pavlákos there?

—When I went he wasn't there yet. The other men were there. Kléarhos, Velissaróyiannis,[3] Mavromantilás. They were the leaders. At night they got us and took us to Ayiopétro.[4] The girls come in, Anthí—no not Anthí, Sotiría, she brings me a blanket. She puts it right in my hand. And there I was in these sandals. They said they were taking us to Ayiopétro for questioning. They take us there, they shove us in some cellar dungeon. The next day they move us. They put us in line to send us off to the detention camp. As we're going there, Pavlákos comes along. There were about twenty of us. Lyghítsos's wife Eléni was there.

—Is Eléni alive?

—She is, she's in Athens. Pavlákos comes over, he comes up next to me. He says, When they question you say that you're willing to work for the Organization.[5] That was his advice to me.

—Pavlákos may have been whatever he was, but he wasn't a die-hard Communist. He would cover for our fellow villagers. He was the one who helped Kalosynátos escape.

—Yes, but let me continue now. And as we were about to get started, Pavlákos says, Wait, I have to announce something to you. Just this minute, he says, they went to Koubíla to burn down the Makrís family's houses, his exact words, and to take in the rest of the family, and they didn't find anyone. They'd left for Másklina. They went to the Germans. And Kléarhos said, Looks like they were traitors.

—Didn't he say anything to tip you off, all he did was make that announcement?

—That's why they arrested her. That's how her brothers left. But she didn't start it right.

—How my brothers left is another story. I'm telling how they arrested me.

—They arrested you, that's why they arrested you.

—They took us to the detention camp. We go inside. The balconies are packed full. Yiórgos Kontós from Karakovoúni. Mítsos Kapetanéas, Chrístos Petrákos, Nikólas's brother, Dímos Kokkiniás, Thanásis Grigorákis, someone named Theodorópoulos from Dolianá, and Panayotoúros. Let me try and remember them.

—Themistoklís?

—Themistoklís and I went to the detention camp together. With his brother Chrístos.

—They had Chrístos in the detention camp too?

—They did. They beat him something awful.

—Which Chrístos?

—Anagnostákos. Themistoklís's brother.

—Did they beat him too?

—They did. Don't interrupt me, because I'm going to tell it all. He's dead now. We went there, we go in. I was lost, there were so many people. We lie right down. I lay out the one blanket your sisters had given me. I lie down and pass out. They come in, Get up, Chrysanthe says to me, get up, it's nighttime. I get up, they take us up to the cells. Going up, on the stairs I see Nikítas Braílas with his mother. I start crying. A man named Yiorgátsis comes in, worked at the detention camp. I don't know where he was from. Girl, you should have cried those tears for your brothers. For my brothers, so they wouldn't leave for Másklina. They take us upstairs, the cells are all full. They take us out on a balcony. Me, Lyghítsos's wife Eléni, a couple of women from Ayiasofiá, and one from Tegéa, a young girl. I put the blanket in front of us on the railing. And we waited. Vasílis Tóyias comes by. He tells me.

—Tóyias was there?

—He was the camp commander. Tóyias from Mesorráhi. He was killed. And Stratís Karadímas. The General, we could say. He came in, he put a fright in me, We'll cut off your hair, you.[6] Why cut off my hair, just put a bullet in me. And Tóyias says to me, No, you're a hostage, we're holding you because of your brothers. We'll cut the hair off the other women. Thirty-six days I was a hostage. I wouldn't eat. They'd give us watery soup with flies in it and a tiny piece of bread. Like a piece of *antídoron*.[7] They'd tell us: Any of you don't eat your bread, you take it with you. I didn't eat. I was going out the door one day. Why don't you take your bread with you, the General asks me. You think we give a damn that you don't eat? I didn't answer him. Then that Tóyias gave us a speech. They gathered us in the church. And this is what he said, I heard every word of it. Like for example, if Makrís, Yeorghía's father, does anything for the Germans right now, of course his daughter will pay for it. He said that in his speech. Three days later they took me to be questioned. There was a hunchback there in a large cell, with firearms in it. He says to me, Come over here, are you going to tell us the truth or do you want to go to the hole. I got scared. I didn't know about holes, didn't know what they were and what they did. I found that out later there. But I was scared. Very scared. He was a deformed man, that interrogator, a hunchback. He says, Who were your brothers with, what was their relation with the Germans? I say, Our men were at home, they didn't have relations with anyone. They arrested me in Kastrí, and I found out that they left. I don't know what happened in between. He says, Did they say anything in defense of the Germans? In our house, I say, never. Never heard any talk like that. And he says, If we give you a gun now will you go and kill your brothers who went with the Germans? I say, No, I won't go. Why, you afraid of the blood? I am, and especially of my brothers' blood. He kept trying to get me on his side. One hour of questioning. It was crazy. Finally he says to me, If we give you a position will you work? Yes, if you give me one, I say. I mean, if we send you to a hospital. I say, If you send me there I'll go. And then when they sent us to Prastós and Lyghítsos's wife Eléni came down with typhus, they put me in charge of her care, I had her, and I had Themistoklís. His care was different, rubdowns and salves for Themistoklís.

   — To the village of Prastós?

—To the village of Prastós.

—They took Themistoklís there?

—And then they took us up to the mountains. They made Panayótis, Iraklís's brother, play the clarinet. And they danced. Well, anyway. It's all a muddle.

—And when the Germans came they took you.

—When the Germans came we went and gave ourselves up. But
we had got some water earlier. There was a drinking fountain. Look,
girls, down there down by the wild pears, one of them said. We got
water. Someone, a tall man, says, Who's that girl, and Vasílis Tóyias
said, She and her whole family are in deep with the Security Battalions.[8] About me. We took the water, and on the road the man who had
asked about me stopped us. He tells us, I'm Alímonos, and he turns to
me, he tells me, I killed Ioannítzis from your village over there. Right
there, he says to me. He showed me a hillside. A beautiful hillside.
His head is planted under a pear tree. That's what he said. Then I was
really frightened. They took us farther up. It was hot. We tell Panayótis, Play a song. I told him that. To cheer us up. I will, he says. But
first I'll play a funeral dirge. We all gave a shudder. No, no, Panayótis,
don't do that. I don't remember if he played anything. And that night,
at twelve o'clock, they killed him. They kept them behind, they sent
us away. The men took us there, the rebels, along the way they began
to talk. What are you saying, what's going on? Nothing, stay close
to us. It was pitch dark. They took us to those shepherds. I couldn't
reap grain. I didn't know how. They wouldn't give me anything to
eat. Chrysanthe went and reaped the grain for me. Later we saw the
Germans. They were swimming in the stream. We gave ourselves up;
they took us back to Orthokostá. Kalabakóyiannis comes in, he tells
us, Tonight they killed Braílas's mother, and Maraskés, and Themistoklís. And Panayótis Polítis. They were killing them all night, and
that woman from Trípolis, they smashed in her head with the butt
of a gun, left her dead on the spot. I got out safe. From Orthokostá
they took us to Leonídio. I went to the school, the Boínis sisters were
in there. Prisoners. Alexandra and the other one. They were crying. I
ask, What's wrong with them, someone tells me, They found out their

brothers were killed. I felt sorry for them, I went over to them, I say, Don't cry, girls. I said that like a good Christian, they didn't answer me. I go outside, I run into Iraklís Polítis. Yeorghía, are the Boínis girls in there? No, I tell him, and he didn't go in. He believed me. We went to the seafront. There were people in line waiting to get into the caïques. Lots of people. From the Orthokostá detention camp, people the rebels had taken to Xerokámpi. I found Tasía Kambýlis there and Matína Lymbéris, Chía's sister, I found Tasía's brother Stamátis. Iraklís comes in angry as can be, I could kill you now, Yeorghía, in front of your brother, who cares? Just because I hadn't given away the Boínis sisters. Go away, I tell him, get away from me, leave me alone. And then I see those very women, they're escorting them somewhere. They took them away, and they disappeared among the vegetable plots. They took them. Much later I learned they had executed one of them. From Leonídio we went to Náfplion. And from Náfplion up to Eleohóri. To Másklina. They come and tell me, They want you. They had taken someone in. My aunt tells me, You'd better go in case it's someone innocent and they kill him for no reason. I go out into the street, Chrysanthe tells me, It's that man. The one who told me at the detention camp I should be crying those tears for my brothers. Well, there he was again, right there in front of me. Lígdas says to me, We're counting on you. Lígdas from the Security Battalions. As we're talking I hear a voice coming from downstairs at the school. They were holding him in the basement. Hey, Yeorghía, it's me. Who's that? Yiórgos, don't you remember me? Oh, Yiórgos, it's you. You're holding *him* prisoner, I say. In the end, they let the man go free. The next day we get on the train to go to Trípolis. Our parents stay up in Eleohóri. They stayed with our uncles. Kákos Barbitsiótis was on the train. So was the man they'd let go. He says to him, You should light a candle for this woman as long as you live. Because now you'd be hanging from a plane tree, at the hands of those Germans. We went to Trípolis. The Germans left, the Security Battalions left, they went to Spétses. Then the rebels came in. One day there's a knock on our door. Someone says, I want Yeorghía. It was him. He says, If they harm you, if they bother you in any way, you let me know immediately. I'll be at the jail. I'm a guard. He was grateful for my kindness to him. But nothing happened to us. No one bothered us. Except for that man who wanted to marry me.

—Was he in the detention camp?

—He passed through once. A kapetánios.⁹ Kapetán Farmákis. And he saw me, and he came to Trípolis looking for me. He found out where I was, got directions, and he came looking for me. To marry me. And he was so insistent. He'd come in one door and I'd be out the other. I'd go to Aryíris's place. To Yiórgos's, and hide. I can't, I'd tell them, I just can't. And there he'd be again. Asking for my hand. He finally gave up.

Chapter 3

They burned down Ayiasofiá around harvest time. We were still
in Koubíla. We didn't go up there, how could we go there, but all
night long we heard the crackling of the fire. And the smell of the
smoke kept coming down to us, making us choke. We found out later
that Anghelís Lambíris's mother had stayed behind. The man with
the blacksmith shop. The others had gotten out and gone across from
there. The kapetanaíoi[1] show up. Where is your son, where's your son?
She says, What do you want with him, dear man, an invalid with six
children. He was missing an eye. Lost it in Albania.[2] He knows how to
hide, they say. They pressed her to say where he was but she wouldn't
tell. With the villagers watching from the distance. And as she stood
there leaning up against the wall they shot her, and that's how they
found her. Standing, just as she'd been. She didn't fall down. She was
propped up on her cane, she was thin, she didn't fall down. And they
found her there dead.

Chapter 4

His brother Kyriákos was killed that day. They had gone down to Stólos to look around. The Stólos villages. Most likely his own fault. He had an Italian rifle. He tried to do something, and the rifle went off and killed him. Well, Mihális took that loss very personally. On that same day they had brought Tsígris to Trípolis. He was a commissioned major, from the Reserves I think. He belonged to ELAS.[1] The ELAS Reserves. They arrested him, brought him in, and he was in Lýras's custody. I worked in Lýras's office. The 2nd Bureau. Lýras was a captain and a graduate of the Army Cadets Academy; at the time he was chief of Intelligence for the 2nd Gendarmes Corps Headquarters. Under Papadóngonas,[2] that is. The 2nd Gendarmes Corps Headquarters. That was its official title. Lýras was from Ayios Andréas, or rather from Karakovoúni. A fellow villager, and among the first to come down. Why I had come there is a different story. At any rate, it was all uncharted waters for me. The Battalions weren't formed in Trípolis only. They were in all the towns of the Peloponnese. Those were times of national emergency. No Greek ever liked the Germans. Or wanted to collaborate with them. That's when the Peloponnese Battalions were created. In the spring of 1944. When it was becoming clear that the Germans were losing the war. And it was also becoming clear how dangerous it would be for anyone who might find himself at the mercy of ELAS after the German collapse. After they cleared out. And that's precisely where things led for them. Inevitably. The push had started, however, very early on. At a time when no one suspected anything. After the Albanian front had crumbled. The first seeds of doubt were sown. They kept saying that only the reservists had fought. That the commissioned officers were only interested in their stripes. This is all lies, of course. I should know. I served in the critical center of the theater of operations. The 13th Regiment of the 11th Division. I was at the most forward point of the front. Toward Beráti. And that's where we came under the German onslaught. Immediately the 11th Division—ours, that is—and the 13th Regiment where I was serving were issued an urgent order to leave. I was in the 2nd Machine Gun Battery of the 2nd Battalion. Platoon officer. We had to leave urgently and get to Katára to establish a line of defense. To cover the rear of the Epirus Corps. The corps that was already operating in Albania, so as not to be outflanked by the Germans. We arrived at Katára, where we had to set up our line of defense. Just above Metsovo, exactly at Prophítis Ilías.[3] But everyone could already see that it was hopeless. Thousands of soldiers and officers were marching in from western Macedonia toward Yiánnina. An army in disarray. We were right on that line when the armistice was signed. We stayed in Prophítis Ilías until Easter. Luftwaffe planes were flying overhead. They bombed Yiánnina. The armistice was signed there, at Bodonási. Archbishop Spyrídon arrived, accompanied by Generals Bákos and Tsolákoglou.[4] They signed the armistice with the Germans. And I was one of the last to arrive at Kastrí. And that's how it all ended. And then of course they started saying, The reservists did all the fighting, the COs just looked after their stripes. From that far back. There was Yiánnis Velissáris, who was no leftist and no anarchist either. He was just an objector. To everything. If our group had only trusted him, Kyreléis and the rest, they would have had him join up. He wouldn't have ended up where he did. Like so many others whose isolation pushed them over to the opposite side. Yiánnis was a good man. We were close friends, and I thought it was a terrible misfortune that he was executed. I was now back in the army. A lieutenant at that time and on a manhunt for Aris.[5] I was in Tríkala, with the 1st Tríkala Battalion of the National Guard. Velouhiótis was already in disfavor with the KKE.[6] He'd had a falling-out with the Central Committee and they expelled him. He had disagreed about the Várkiza Treaty and all that.[7] Well, he was trying to get papers so he could leave for Yugo-slavia. He was just hanging around waiting for them. We had a pla-toon stationed in Kalambáka, up in Kourtsoúfiani. The platoon leader let us know that Aris, with about forty men, had gone up to Mount Kóziakas. Kóziakas is right next to Tríkala. At Pýli we had another platoon. Pýli, at the foot of Kóziakas. The Portaïkós River runs right by there. It's about fifteen kilometers away from Tríkala. We had a platoon over there with a second lieutenant. They had got hold of some firearms, the kind that were easy to get back then. They had formed teams to defend themselves, and also to get back at ELAS. To get even with them. Well, the Pýli second lieutenant sent us a mes-sage. Second Lieutenant Nikoláou of the Reserves. He had heard that Aris was spotted at Týrna, a village on the slopes of Kóziakas. This was his message to the Battalion: Am setting out with my platoon in pur-suit of Velouhiótis. Send backup and food. He's going after Aris. Let him go. Half the National Guardsmen we had then were leftists. They were half-and-half. They were 10 percent, at the very least. They joined up on purpose so they could get arms. At any rate, the base commander sends Nikoláou a message to turn back. But he was al-ready advancing through the Ágrafa Mountains. A region where no government had ever set foot. An unwritten law. Since the time of Katsantónis.[8] He had to get back to base because they were all afraid Aris would cut them to pieces. He even sent an officer to Pýli, but he didn't get there in time, and he was reluctant to go on. The base com-mander sent a second envoy, same story. So at around midnight they come and wake *me* up. Get up, the commander wants you. I go over to their headquarters. Lieutenant, I'm sending you on a mission. What's going on? Here's the story. It's Nikoláou. He needs to turn back right away. But, Sir. No buts; I'm assigning a sergeant to your detail who knows the terrain. All right, I say. But in my opinion the outcome of this operation is very uncertain. They gave me a Jeep and I made it to Pýli. The sergeant and I each had a tommy gun. We went to Pýli. Pýli was fortified to the teeth. They had learned that Aris was prowling about in the area. They had posted double patrols all around. Made up of locals. Armed civilians. We went inside, and I say, I'm looking for Dervénagas. Dervénagas was in charge of those teams. He later became an MP. He was from Pýli himself. He's asleep, they tell me, We shouldn't wake him. Pýli had been burned down by the Germans. Everyone there was living in rundown shacks. They wake Dervénagas, What's going on, Second Lieutenant? I tell him, I need to find Nikoláou. He knew that Nikoláou had left in the morning. He asks me, How will you get through the lines? My men let you through and you got in all right. But the men from Mouzáki are out there. That's Mouzáki, by Kardítsa. They'll try to stop you. I tell him, If I managed to get in, I'll find a way out. Okay, he says, If you want to go, go. He didn't tell me anything about the situation. That Aris was somewhere around there. I didn't know that then. So I took my sergeant and we got going. Just the two of us. No car this time. We exited Pýli. We came to a ravine. In the area near Kóziakas. Wooded terrain. The river and the road down below. A mule path. We kept moving forward. We found our way by the light of the moon. I kept hoping that that idiot Nikoláou would notice that no reinforcements were sent and turn back. But we kept on. Just before dawn a grenade exploded in the distance. There was a bridge there, I was told later on. We came to the road and waited. It got quiet. We kept going, we had no choice. Day was breaking, the wind brought us the sounds of shuffling feet. We took cover. I thought to myself, Maybe it's Nikoláou coming back. It was him, all right. I saw him. He was walking ahead of the others. He was startled by our being there. There we were with our tommy guns in hand. I tell him, I ought to bash you one, you clown, you. By morning we were at Pýli. The cold was unbearable. They'd put out large pots, the patrols came down and gathered there to get something warm to drink and so on. Dervénagas shows up. He tells me, You're back. I am. Are you ever lucky, if you only knew, poor man, where you've just been. Aris was right there near you all along. Across from Týrna. A soldier threw that grenade as a warning. The National Guard was full of leftists. I already said that. In the meantime our Battalion was replaced. There was a general of the High Command, Avramídis, and Pangoútsos had complained to him. Pangoútsos of the Agrarian Party. He collaborated with the left. He set up an organization, brought in some farmers, farmers that Soúrlas's[9] groups wouldn't give free rein to. So he complained. He cabled the Communist newspaper *Rizospástis,* which wrote it up on the editorial page, and Avramídis was furious. He was an officer of democratic persuasions. Plastíras was prime minister at the time. And he ordered the replacement of our battalion. We had to go down to Lárissa. Then various other units closed in on Aris. Did his own men execute him or did he kill himself, no one knows. The whole story is still murky. The fact remains that he expected the Office of the Prefecture to okay his leaving for Yugoslavia. So we went south to Lárissa. We spent all the time until the fall of 1946 in Lárissa and in Vólos. Then came the plebiscite.[10] And later on, when the rebellion started and the first skirmishes had occurred at Litóchoro and Pontokerasiá,[11] our battalion had already been disbanded. The National Guard was disbanded, units of regulars were now being formed, and conscripts were being drafted. Hard times were beginning and all that came with them. The courts-martial and all that. Yiánnis was tried and convicted in Trípolis. I didn't hear about his execution until later. His uncle Mítsos Kapetanéas, his mother's brother, had tried to get him to reconsider. There was still the chance to renounce his former allegiance at the time. But Yiánnis was hardheaded. He was the kind of man who would never compromise. And his sacrifice was a waste. A lively character, and kind too. He could even have proved useful. Though he did us great harm, me and my brother. Aside from burning down our home, he had denounced us and cursed us as traitors and criminals. When, in fact, he could have become one of us. But the spirit of dissention had prevailed. I could see that there was a deliberate priming of the ground from that time on. Just after I got back from the Albanian front. At any rate, I stayed in Kastrí until 1943. The summer of '43, when we had gotten our core group together. When Márkos Ioannítzis arrived. Then things started going wrong. Márkos was extremely naive when it came to conspiracies. Although he knew full well that the opposite side wanted to monopolize everything. One evening we got together at Réppas's house, and he was going on and on. Talking openly. I remember Harís Lenghéris getting all tearful. Or pretending to. He took me aside. Please, teach me to become a fighter. As the oldest of a twelve-member family he'd never been to boot camp. Haroúlis[12] Lenghéris, the notorious Communist. I'm trying to say that Márkos didn't cover his back. He had come equipped with military maps, he had become a member of the Peloponnese Resistance network. He had men in many different places. On his last night, before leaving for the hills of Mount Parnon, we met just below the square. At Ayía Paraskeví. At the chapel. At night. We were all there, me, my first cousin Márkos Mávros, Chrístos Haloúlis, Kóstas Kyreléis, the whole group. About ten of us. And he gave us our final instructions. He assigned the Laconía sector to me. I was to meet a certain justice of the peace in Gýthio. That was the first leg, the other would be the Sykiá airfield, in Moláous. There was someone at the airfield whose name I don't remember. Mántis, I think. But a disabled vet, at any rate. From these two I would gather information, among other things. He tells me, You'll get started as soon as I come back from Mount Parnon. That's when you'll contact them. He never came back. He had gone to Mount Parnon to meet the British. To convince them to reinforce *him* too. And he ran into Látsis and someone else. Communists he knew. And they're the ones who killed him. In the meantime he had connected our local cell with RO, the Radical Organization of Athens. Twice I had carried information memos to Athens. The memos were assembled by officers in Trípolis. I dropped these off at a side street off Agámon Square. Chrístos Frángos, from Kastrí, had a pastry shop there. I think he was a waiter. RO was trying to get the British to make supply drops in the area around Mount Parnon. And to create a cell operating a wireless radio. So that we could make use of Stámos Triantafýllis's forces. And Kontalónis's too. Kontalónis I knew from my school days in Trípolis. He was a second lieutenant, a Cadet Academy graduate. He had formed a group but fell into the clutches of the Communists. Of Leventákis and the others. He had started out as a royalist. We were hoping he would work with us. But of course there was nothing he could do then. He was already in the stranglehold of the Leventákis-Prekezés group. Later on he changed sides. They persuaded him to attack a small German unit. They were driving to Aráhova to get potatoes. To Aráhova in Laconía. And he attacked them. They were an easy target. There were either three or four Germans, they'd left their weapons in the truck. But that was his mission, to attack. The Germans burned down the village. That's what drove the villagers of Aráhova up to the mountains. Our group, through the RO liaison, was expecting to be supplied by sea. I went to reconnoiter a submarine approach. Márkos had given me a map of the region. I set out from Kastrí. But we were under close surveillance. By Magoúlis and some others. I took Ilías Darláras as my muleteer. His house was below ours. He was Galioúris's brother-in-law. He took me at night as far as Meligoú and left me there. I went down to Astros. I met Yiórgos Stratigópoulos there, a law student. He was from Ayios Andréas. His mother was from Kastrí. He was a leftist, but he worked with us. Exceptional fellow. I found him at Astros. We went to Ayios Andréas together. I did my reconnaissance. Coordinates and all. I noted everything on the map, so we could ask to be supplied from the Middle East Command. We went back to Astros. I delegated Níkos Farmakoulídas to set up the submarine reception. And since my being there seemed strange, I let it be known, confidentially, that Níkos was in the process of arranging a marriage for me. That was soon to take place. I went back to Kastrí on a truck, a gasogene truck. Yiórghis Réppas was driving it. There were no other means of transportation then. I found it by chance. It was summer. It must have been June. Late June. Because we had picked apricots as we drove through the fields. And they weren't ripe yet. We arrived at Kastrí, I sent my report to Athens. With the point where the submarine could approach and its coordinates. But all of this, the drops and everything, was controlled from Cairo. Paradrops were made to groups favored by the British. And they wouldn't reinforce leaderless or isolated groups. They made drops to Zérvas,[13] and also to ELAS. The reason given for canceling the shipment to us of supplies, mainly munitions, was that the sub's point of approach was not clearly designated. The response soon came. The coordinates were not precise enough, they had to be accompanied by a particular landmark, a special feature of the location. Then it occurred to me that there was a windmill there. I instantly put together a second memo. Just beyond the rocky shore there is a sandy beach, its coordinates being such and such, and at a distance of two hundred meters a very visible windmill stands alone. No doubt about it, a submarine could reach that spot, if it wanted to. But of course all this was just an excuse. In the meantime, Kóstas Kyreléis had left Kastrí and gone up to Mount Taygetus. And I'm now alone as a local overseer. Yiannakópoulos[14] was there at Mount Taygetus. Katsaréas was there. Vrettákos was there. And also Stámos Triantafýllis. ELAS wouldn't let him operate on Mount Parnon. All this in 1943, in the summer. And that was when the Yiannakópoulos pact with the Communists was signed. The Brits had intervened. Tavernarákis was up there too, as liaison with the SMA.[15] I don't know exactly why or how, but they decided to have a joint command. To merge, that is. Yiannakópoulos was a colonel. There were officers from Sparta and from Messinía. There were units there, regular divisions. There were rebels there. Vanghélis Mílis from Karátoula. He had joined Kóstas Kyreléis's group. And someone named Diamantoúros from Voúrvoura. Lots of men. Spirited young men. And when the pact was made public, we were shocked. It was just like the Communists, whenever they couldn't dominate an organization, they absorbed it. They would oust the leaders and then absorb the organization. The officers up there reacted; they knew this was the end. That they were at the mercy of ELAS. And they considered Yiannakópoulos's action treasonous. But Yiannakópoulos had no choice. He was pressured by the British. That was their policy. Had he refused the merger, ELAS would have attacked and wiped him out. Then they began celebrating, as if there were no more problems. As if unity had been achieved. And of course for them there was no problem. At about that time Italy collapsed. At Kastrí we heard about Badoglio's capitulation on the radio. We had no weapons in Kastrí. Just a few pistols. I owned a Lebel myself. We used Yiánnis Moúntros's house by the cemetery as storage space. We stocked about twenty pairs of boots that had been sent to us from Athens. We kept them there, and we would give them out to the men going to Mount Taygetus. That's also where I kept the Lebel. We had no weapons, even though everybody thought we did. Oh, those men from Kastrí, they're so well armed, and so on. When I heard about the capitulation I thought it would be a golden opportunity for us to get weapons from the Italians. The bridges along the railroad line were guarded by Italians. At Eleohóri. From Andrítsa, all the way to Parthéni, the bridges were guarded by Italians. So I got the group together, Yiórgos Kyreléis, Chrístos Haloúlos, Thanásis Kosmás. About ten men. Chrístos and Kokkiniás also. Ready and willing. Vasílis Biniáris. Brave men. We went down to Eleohóri with only our pistols. We had nothing else. But with our pistols displayed prominently on our belts. We were counting now on the low morale of the Italians. And I made contact with them. We could have disarmed some of those guards, but we didn't want to give grounds for reprisals against the village. What we wanted was to quietly win over the Italians to our side. To get them to come over to our side with their arms. I promised we would secure food for them. And also a way to escape. We could send them anywhere they wanted. In exchange for their arms. The Italians in Eleohóri told me that the decision could only be made by the commander in charge of all the guards, an Italian Army captain. Who was in Andrítsa. I don't remember if he was stationed there or if he was there by chance. I called him on the phone. He spoke passable Greek. I explained the situation to him. I tell him, The Germans are coming any minute now. What will you do? We'll defend ourselves, he tells me. You can't be serious. The Germans will storm you with everything they've got, and you intend to defend yourselves? What's the point? Defend what? I tell him, I'm asking you to surrender your arms and follow us. We'll guarantee your safety to the best of our ability. If you stay put, your fate is certain. He insisted, We'll defend ourselves. And in any case, if we do what you suggest, we'll only surrender to an armed unit. And to officers in full uniform. In other words he wanted to ensure that all conventions were observed. That their honor was preserved. I tell him, That's ridiculous. We men here *are* a group. Two officers from the Reserves, and ten citizen soldiers. And we are requesting your arms to mount our resistance against the Germans. Well, he refused. He tells me, It can't be done. So we went to Saint

Mámas hill. From there I sent out an echelon to Andrítsa under Chrístos Haloúlos. To try and change his mind. And even to threaten him. We stayed at Saint Mámas until dawn. They went there, they came back empty-handed. So we went back to Eleohóri at daybreak, to the village square. Then the EAM deputy arrives. He hands me a note. They had gotten in touch with Kastrí. They were afraid that as soon as we went down there we'd get our hands on some arms. This would be dangerous for them. Afraid we'd form a force they couldn't control. They were trying like mad to prevent this. They sent me that note asking me to desist from any attempt at disarming the Italians. Because now that the various Taygetus organizations had merged, the whole case was under the jurisdiction of the Central Committee. And so on and so forth. Saying I have no right to act independently. The note came from Kastrí, from Kléarhos Aryiríou. They had gotten in touch with Kastrí from Eleohóri, and Kastrí sent me the note immediately. I laughed. The situation was ridiculous. Ridiculous and sad. Because it had been resolved by itself. We went back. And we were now on standby. After Italy's capitulation there was a general expectation that an Allied landing in Greece would follow. We thought the Germans would be leaving in a month. This conviction was widespread. That in one month the Germans would leave Greece. That the Allies would land in the Balkans. And of course these hopes were all tied up with the problem of our survival. We could all see it clearly now. EAM and ELAS were the imminent danger. They would wipe us all out. Any of us who didn't want to or wouldn't consent to join them. That's how we saw it—and that's how it was. At any rate, we stayed in Kastrí. In a state of uncertainty. Under the watchful eye of Magoúlis and the rest. And then I receive a message from Trípolis. My cousin Mihális Tepeghiózis arrived from there during the night. He came there as a liaison. I was being called to Artemísion. One unit from Taygetus had escaped and gone to Artemísion to await air drops. Also a group of officers from Náfplion had gone there. Under Major Christópoulos. They were expecting air drops at Krýa Vrísi. In the Artemísion region. On Mount Hteniás just above Ahladókampos. I left Kastrí at noon. Taking every possible precaution. So I could go down to Ahladókampos via Ayiasofiá. In the message I was also asked to supply information about the possibility of manning groups. And the possibility of arming combat teams. I left exactly at noon and there, just below Mihális Vozíkis's house, I saw Níkos Petrákos. It was just about then that Níkos had returned from Taygetus. He was the first to leave following the Yiannakópoulos agreement. But he and I had been unable to meet and talk comfortably. We were constantly under surveillance. So when I saw him, to avoid arousing suspicion, I whispered to him while looking straight ahead. Níkos, I'm taking off for Artemísion. It's our only hope. He answered, God speed. I went down to Ayiasofiá and met with Yiórghis Antonákos. A distant uncle of mine. We went to see Mihális Lymbéris. Mihális supported our organization. He knew. He was one of ours. He and Vasílis Panayotá-kis from Stólos. Panayotákis was Yiórghis Antonákos's brother-in-law. I filled Mihális in about the situation and started off for Ahladókam-pos by night. Antonákos, myself, and a man named Vanghélis Kan-glís. He came along so he could become a guerrilla up there. We left at night. We reached Ahladókampos at midnight. We went and found Yiórghis Baláskas, an artillery noncommissioned petty officer. Now retired, a colonel. At the Military Geographical Service. He gave us a liaison, he gave us passwords and countersigns. He was in touch with the Artemísion sector. We left the same night, we went to the slopes of Mount Hteniás. Our guide told us to wait there. At daybreak a liaison will come to get you. He left. It was getting light out. We kept looking up toward the mountain ridge, we couldn't see anything moving. Eventually someone appeared off in the distance. Approach-ing very cautiously. He made his way hesitantly over to us, until at last we recognized each other. He was an officer from Néa Kíos in Argo-lís. He says, Don't go on. The ridge has been occupied. ELAS attacked us last night. The battle at Krýa Vrísi had already taken place. They knew supply drops were expected, and they attacked. Lots of dead and wounded. They decimated the unit. They wiped us out, the offi-cer says. Therefore all operations are off. I had a few packs of cigarettes with me. I gave him two and we went our separate ways. We turned around to go back. We had to cross the motorway connecting Ahladókampos with Trípolis, and go down to Andrítsa. But the road was undergoing repairs. The road crews were watched over by German guards. This was another sign that the Germans were about to leave. The road contractors were under orders to deliver all roads within one month. There was a widespread conviction that in one month the Allies would land in the Peloponnese. We reached Andrítsa. I told the others, From this point on may the Lord help us. And I went by train to Trípolis. There I met up with Kóstas Kyreléis. He had just arrived from Taygetus. They'd been decimated. He had gone to Kalamáta and from Kalamáta to Trípolis. So I say to him, Kóstas, what's going on? He tells me, We have to save ourselves by any means possible. In Taygetus our groups had been wiped out. ELAS had prevailed. Vrettákos escaped with his company but was hunted down, and in the end they killed him. Cavalry Captain Vrettákos, no less. So what should we do? I say to him. We'll leave for Athens, he answers. But I had to go up to Kastrí. My brother and sister were there. I had to go there to pick them up. And take whatever we could with us and get out. Me, Yiánnis, and Iphigenia. It was September already, or maybe October. Late October. So I go up to Kastrí. The Communists were all gathered in the square. Magoúlis, Yiórghis Velissáris, Yiánnis Velissáris, all of them. They had noticed my absence. They had learned I'd been gone a few days. It was Magoúlis who greeted me. Sort of smiling, he says to me, From now on we'll all be fighting together. We'll all help to become one organization. I tell him, I have no objection. I never refused to be of service to the common cause. He says to me, You, being an officer, will be in charge of Security. The Security Section meant you were now in their noose. You'd arrest someone here, beat someone there, or do an execution the next day. So they could rope you in, bind you in blood. That was the Organization. Security was the most dangerous section. The most prone to willfulness and brutality. I say, I have no objection. I'll work in whatever capacity you decide. My position, however, is down there. I'd been assigned to Néa Hóra. At Roúvali. That's where I was posted. I say, For me to do a better job I need to be transferred to Kastrí. I need to be here, to have a position at the school. He says, Of course, we'll take care of it. I say, I'll visit the school inspector tomorrow. I'll ask him to have me transferred to Kastrí. He says, We'll help. I say, No. It's better that you don't get involved. So he won't think we're pressuring him. Let me ask him. If he presents difficulties, if he raises objections, then the Organization can intervene. So I'll go down to Trípolis tomorrow. I'd come here to Kastrí to collect whatever I could, to see my brother and sister and then take off. For Athens. Yiánnis Velissáris says, I'll go to Trípolis too. We'll go together. I say, Let's go. I knew immediately what this meant. We went to Trípolis. At noon we met at Antonákos's restaurant. As we'd arranged. He says, Did you get anything done? Unfortunately not. The inspector is away touring the district. I'll have to stay until tomorrow. He looked at me without saying anything. Like he was daydreaming. Then he says, I'll stay too. I haven't finished up here. I realized that things were getting harder. And I went back to the German Kommandantur. Chrístos Haloúlos and I had spent an entire morning there getting permits. You couldn't travel anywhere without them. And it was very hard to have one issued the same day you applied for it. So I went back to their headquarters. It was in a side street, next to the Malliarópoulos school building. I was standing to one side, not on line. And I saw Yiánnis walking by on the opposite sidewalk. By now it was obvious that he was following me. Again he didn't say anything. But he didn't pretend not to see me. On the contrary he stared straight at me. Just like before. What do we do, I ask Chrístos Haloúlos. He says to me, Let's clear out. And we did. He went and found a truck, and we climbed in. We made it, we crossed the Corinth Isthmus. Without permits. We arrived in Athens. That's where the chase really began. Because I'd fooled them and left Kastrí. In Athens I was appointed by the Ministry of Education to a school in Ambelókipi. And I lived down in the Metaxourgheío district[16] at a cousin's, Iosíf Skítzis. Of course, they never left me alone. Dr. Mávros lived in the same neighborhood. He had left too. But much earlier. Menélaos Mávros, twice an MP with the Populist Party, and once with Tourkovasílis. Every noon we met at Yiánnis Moúndros's taverna on Constantinoupóleos Street, at the corner of Ayías Théklas. Me, Mávros, and Daskoliás. A colonel in the

Military Judicial. He was from Eleohóri. Both of them single, by necessity. Of course we were being closely shadowed. As for me, I was looking for contacts so I could leave for the Middle East. On one of my visits to the Ministry regarding my assignment I ran into a colleague working for Panteleímon. Panteleímon, the bishop of Karystía. He used to plan missions that were launched from Kými. He had created this channel. He later became archbishop of the armed forces. Panteleímon Fostínis. He had seen action in Ukraine when the Greek Military Expeditionary sailed there in 1918. To help quash the Bolshevik revolution. So I found this colleague. We met by chance. We had both attended the Trípolis Academy. He tells me, I'll smuggle you out. His sister was at the Red Cross hospital. A patient there. As soon as she's out of the hospital we'll all go to Kými. You *will* get out. In the meantime they stopped a small boat with officers and civilians on board. Among them was Koryzís's daughter. Or so they said. They were all executed. Most likely because someone ratted on them, naturally. So all operations were temporarily suspended. That's when I learned that Stámos Triantafýllis was in Athens. We thought he'd been killed on Taygetus. When my escape via Kými and Çesme became impossible, I found Stámos. But Stámos had money. His family had sold olive oil, and I don't know what else, in Ayios Andréas. The asking price then was seven gold sovereigns, I think. Seven or nine gold sovereigns for someone to escape. They were starting to sell passages to the Middle East. On small sailboats. There were caïques on that route. Stámos paid for his passage and he got out. I didn't have those seven or nine sovereigns. I stayed behind. And in the ten days that followed there were two successive attempts on my life. The first time they shot at me through the window, I was in my room. I escaped by pure chance. From the OPLA.[17] The following day, they came looking for me at Mávros's house. They went to Mávros's address and asked for Dránias. They'd got it all wrong, of course. Or they figured that, because I was scared after having nearly been murdered, I would go and hide there. At any rate, I realized I had run out of options. Next day I packed up my stuff and took off. I went to the Patísia district. Kóstas Kyreléis was in Athens then. With the National Guard. The

Unknown Soldier's Guard. The Battalions, in other words. The Battalions in Athens. When he left Trípolis he went there and enlisted. They had split them up. In the Peloponnese were the so-called Royalist Battalions. Under Papadóngonas. So I went to stay with Kóstas Kyreléis and his brothers. At their house. Yiórgos and Pános. I joined the Battalions later. Chrístos Haloúlos inducted me. It was quite an ordeal, of course. So the Battalions were formed, and we went to Trípolis. The 2nd Gendarmes Corps Headquarters was set up there. Noncommissioned officers as well as reservists. Lýras plus some others. Of course there were a lot of problems. We went to Trípolis on March 31. To the 2nd Gendarmes Corps Headquarters. Operations was housed in Áreos Square. In the County Courthouse. I served in the 2nd Bureau under Captain Lýras. Lýras from Karakovoúni, Kynouría. A priest's son. A good man. Later, as a veteran, he worked with Nikólaos Psaroudákis. They published the bi-weekly newspaper *Christian Democracy*. He wrote articles for them until the end of his life. He had found religion. His father was a priest. The men from Kastrí came down to Trípolis later on. After the big blockade. Kóstas Kotrótsos came into my office. One of those characters who's easily carried away. An unprincipled drifter. He was either a sergeant or a corporal. But he presented himself as second lieutenant. He pulled the same thing later in the Militia. But he was found out and demoted. He walked into my office and said, Come take a look. I went to the balcony. Áreos Square below was full of men arriving from Kastrí. Reporting for duty. They were issued arms. This was after the big blockade, about the end of June that is. Kastrí was burned down in July. About a month later. Our houses had been burned before that. Maybe in May. When exactly they brought Tsígris in I don't remember. It was some time in summer. Lýras interrogated him. He was just a poor soul, nobody special. A regular army officer. An aging colonel. He was in the ELAS Reserves. Perhaps he'd been coerced, or perhaps he was a leftist. So they brought him in. I can't remember the circumstances under which he was arrested either. Lýras interrogated him. It was strongly suggested later that this was a face-saving way for him to surrender. At any rate. Lýras interrogated him. A routine interrogation more or less. Mihális Galaxýdis walked in at some point. He opened the door, cocked his pistol, and *bam, bam, bam,* he shot him three times. One shot grazed me. It hit the wall, ricocheted, and covered me in bits of plaster. Tsígris fell down. We lifted him up. We carried him across the street to the Hotel Maínalon, which was being used as a hospital. He died right there in front of me.

Chapter 5

Take the village of Oriá. They hated anyone from Karátoula, so much hatred between those two villages. And you know what I think. It's one thing to have your differences, to have different interests, but to carry things that far, I mean, why? Why to such extremes? It was our cousin Paraskevás who marched our brother Kóstas up along the river. He took him to Ayios Pétros. It was him, it was Voúlis,[1] and he took in Loukás too. And they beat him. Beat him real bad. Pantelís told me that. I had him working for me, he did two days. That's when they rounded them up. They took them to Dragálevo. They tell them, You have to join the Organization. They say, We won't join. And they gave it to them good. They beat the daylights out of Antonákos—his legs never healed. They beat them so bad. And then someone says to them, I congratulate you for your strong convictions, but now go join the Security Battalions, there's no place for you here. They would capture them, then indoctrinate them, try to make them join the Party. My sister Evrydíki got out, it was Aryiróyiannis who helped her, God rest his soul. Kyriazís's brother-in-law, because he cared for her back then. And he went and got her out, he brought her back. He was killed in Megalópolis. And I had my own narrow escape. They had me make a dozen or so berets. I put the insignia in the front. I was good with my hands then, had been from early on. But with my miserable little brain, I didn't know much, I put two crossing Greek flags and above them, right in the middle, a crown. And all the men who wore those berets, they didn't realize that it should have been a hammer and sickle. At some point the rebels come to the school, the head men.

And the men from Karátoula show up too, in their berets, they go over there. As soon as they see them they say, Hey, look at this, who made these berets, who made them? And there I am in the yard. Our men didn't know what to do, they said, Who knows what will happen now? The priest signals me to leave. He wasn't a priest then. He says, Get out, go hide. I sneak off and leave. Imagine that. I leave, and the others say, The girl didn't know, some old women showed her, they didn't know either. That's how they covered up, somehow they did it, and it was over. I stitched them a flag with a crown. Those rebels wouldn't think twice about it, they'd call you a reactionary, and that was the end. And me a fifteen-year-old girl.

Chapter 6

They arrested us in 1944. At first it was just Chrístos Kaprános, myself, and Stavróyiannis. It was in June. I don't remember the date. It was during the big blockade. We were ordered to leave. Word had got out that the Germans were coming, and we had to leave. We went up to Malevós. Lots of people there. When we got there Dr. Karavítis ordered us to go fetch a lamb from a certain shepherd. Chrístos was superstitious. He believed he was going to die. The thought had gotten into his head. He had dreamt that his sister-in-law was getting married. His brother Charálambos's wife. He saw her as a bride.[1] We went to the shepherd's as the doctor ordered us to. You fellows from Kastrí? he asked. From Kastrí, we answered. And he began apologizing. Saying he'd done us wrong. It was back in 1922. He had killed Menélaos Méngos. Menélaos Méngos was an authorized Singer service dealer, Chrístos's first cousin. He used to travel around the villages on Mount Malevós and repair sewing machines. Spare parts and money in his briefcase. When Chrístos heard this he tells us, I told you, something's not right with me. Imagine coming face-to-face with my cousin's murderer. He slaughtered the lamb, and we took it. Suddenly there was an alarm. The Germans, the Germans. We were at Megáli Lákka. We went someplace else, we hid the lamb. We piled tree branches on top of it in case we got back in time to recover it. We just took out its liver. We wrapped it up in a kerchief. Megáli Lákka was all in bloom, the sage plants in bloom. We split up. Our thirst was getting to us. In the evening we went down to the wells at the village of Sítaina. We spent the night in a ravine. At daybreak we lit a

fire, singed the liver, and ate it. Then we reached the wells. We threw
a rock inside. The water level was low, and we had no way of getting
any out. I was wearing some Greek Army leg wraps. I took them off,
we tied them together, and we tied a kerchief at one end. The one we
had wrapped the lamb liver in. We lowered this until it was soaked
through, then we wrung it into our mouths. Then Chrístos remembered he had his wallet with him. I made a ring around the top with
twigs, and fastened them with some string. It was like a small bucket.
And we'd lower it, we drew up a lot of water, we drank and drank.
We were very thirsty. The following day we left there. We came to a
clearing. So we wouldn't be too close together and be an easy target
we said we'd follow different footpaths. Some Germans appeared up
above coming down from across the way. There would be Greeks
with them, for sure. Did they see us? Or didn't they? They started
machine-gunning. They started throwing hand grenades. At which
point it was every man for himself. I call out to Stavróyiannis, we
threw ourselves into a ravine. There were some shepherds there. But
they didn't bother with shepherds. After that we lost track of Chrístos.
I think he stayed there during the skirmish. They found him there,
killed. Who found him, I don't know. We looked for a way to escape.
We headed for the Sítaina woods. West of there were some high rocks;
we climbed them. We found two rebels hiding there. With the sun
beating down on us all afternoon. And not a drop of water to drink.
The four of us agreed, finally, to slip out of there during the night. To
look for a way out, to escape from the Germans. But things turned out
differently. In the evening, as we were leaving, a patrol heard us. They
fired two flares; we hit the ground. We waited. One rebel comes over,
he points his pistol at us. You stay right here, he says, or I'll kill you.
So we wouldn't cause any trouble. They knew their way around. We
didn't. Okay, we'll stay here. And we spent the night there. We were
parched. We would put out our tongues and lick at the rocks to get
a little moisture. Day broke; the wells were above us. The Germans
had taken possession of them. Yiánnis and I decided to surrender. We
got up, we raised our hands. Luckily for us, they must have been Aus-
trians. *Kom, kom,* they say to us. We understood that they wanted to

know where we were from and all that. We say to them, From Kastrí. *Nichts Kommunist*, I say to them. *Nichts. Nichts Partisán.* We asked for water, they brought us a bucketful. We drank till we burst. Then they took us away. They didn't give us food. A platoon picked us up, we said, That's it. We saw a place where mules were urinating, there were flies swarming around, we thought they had killed people there. At any rate, we kept walking. Them with their machine guns and us up ahead. We spent the night in Sítaina. The next day they took us to Kastánitsa. That's where their headquarters was. And there they interrogated us. Yiánnis didn't have his police ID with him, he had lost it. Mine was in order, it had been officially stamped and approved in Hoúria. Yiánnis didn't have his. Why don't you have it? We left in a hurry, he said. That was the excuse he gave. Then the verdict was announced. We would be taken to Vrésthena, and they would release us there. One more rebel had been added to the force. The same platoon escorts us. On the way the rebel is up ahead. Up ahead with a mule, like a guide.

And at some point he gives them the slip. He leaps down a cliff, there was a ravine below, he runs in there, he disappears. They started strafing the area with their machine guns. They come over to us. A brother of yours? A cousin, says one of them to me. *Nichts*, man, I say to him. *Nichts* cousin of mine. Me from Kastrí, *andere* from Barbítsa. The other man. I was talking about that rebel. But they didn't do anything to us. We arrived at Vrésthena. They tell us, We'll eat, and we'll let you go. But we won't be responsible for you any more. We went and pulled up some potatoes, they washed them, they boiled them. They had a goat with them. They cut it up. They gave us that to eat. Then we left. They let us go. We came to a place where the road turned toward Aráhova. We made it to Aráhova. Different headquarters there. There was a major in command, spoke fluent Greek. He started asking us about Kléarhos, about Velissáris. About everyone in the local chapter of Kastrí. In the end he let us go. Get going, he said. But don't go past the cemetery because there's a guardhouse there. They might kill you. Go by a different road. We headed out, we followed his advice. We took a much lower path. We left. We arrived at the village. We saw the first houses. Stamatáris's house. He received us in person. You're both guilty. That pig. Both guilty. His house was brand new, I had worked on it for him. Door frames, doors. I did the roof too. So we came here. We go and find Vasílis Biniáris. He was also a fugitive, but not in any danger. He had made a deal with Nikólas Petrákos. He had worked it all out, the two of them corresponded and all that. They didn't touch him. Stavróyiannis left, they took him away. I stayed behind. The Security Battalions came. I wasn't in hiding. I slept at home. I see Mihális Galaxýdis, in a rage. Those bastards. Hey you, aren't you a Communist? What could I tell him? Since when was *he* such a patriot? Treating me like a Communist. They arrest me. He was with some other men. Not local men. They lead me over to a car. Someone named Arménis was in the car. A member of the Battalions. I try to climb in too. Another man's gun misfires, it kills Arménis. And they forced me to make his coffin. They carried him up to the shop. On a bench. Blood everywhere. I found planks, I made the coffin. They made us spend the night in the school building. And the next day they took us to Trípolis. But they had us outside. Free for the moment to roam about town. We milled around there in Ayíou Vasilíou Square. Then they took us to Áreos Square. And they interrogated us. Kóstas Dránias from the Military Intelligence Office asked me—well, Okay. I say to him, You know me. It's true that we had been registered in the local organization. Blackmailed into it. Wasn't Kóstas Braílas in the Organization? That's enough, Dránias says to me. No further questions. And they took me downstairs. Mihális Galaxýdis took me there. Now deceased. Down to the basement. All this in the Courthouse. They were holding lots of men there. Like Spýros Roúmelis. Roúmelis was known as Selímos. His brother Yiórghis as Alkyviádis. They killed them. They killed them right before our eyes. They stood them in front of us and executed them. Just a short while later. In an instant, on a Sunday. It seems an order had come in to execute twenty-six men. Because twenty-six of Stoúpas's[2] men had been killed. Somewhere, I don't know. Yiánnis Kotsoríbas was the guard. Also deceased. And Kóstas Lígdas, another one deceased. Lígdas at the women's jail. Both of them from Másklina. Everyone from Másklina is actually from Kas-trí. And some of them from Ayiasofiá too. They're from Karátoula, most of them. Both of them from Másklina. Lígdas protected me then. They were ordered to select prisoners from all the wards. A total of twenty-six. To count them up and take them to where the ambush had been carried out. The execution would take place there. And me, I wanted to go outside. Sergeant, sir, I say to him. Lígdas was a ser-geant. He asked what my name was. Papavasilíou, I say to him. I didn't know him back then. No, you're not coming. I wanted to go outside, I thought they were taking them for chores detail. They took the others down there, and the order was rescinded. Rescinded. They came back later, twenty-six men scared out of their wits. Because they'd realized what was really going on. And they executed them a little later. On Thursday. Wednesday or Thursday. They came in the evening, supposedly to pick out the convicted felons from our midst. They ripped off our insignias. They picked the men they wanted. Well, the rest tomorrow. We'll take care of them tomorrow. Later they brought someone else who was in the hospital. They let him spend the night. Up until four in the morning they were dragging them out-side. They used wire cable to tie them. There was shouting and curs-ing. Where are you taking us with no interrogation? This from Roú-melis, God rest his soul. They had promised not to hurt anyone, and now they were killing people. And they'd picked out women too. Alexandra Boínis. I heard her. Heard her voice in the night. Cursing. Iraklís came the next day. He treated me well. He hugged me be-tween the bars. Don't be afraid, he says. Iraklís Polítis. He hugged me and then he says to us, To save yourselves you need to go to Germany. Nothing else you can do. Myself, Panayótis Gagás, and so many others. Panayótis, Eléni's husband. We left Trípolis before the Feast of the Virgin. But we stopped at various places. We had to. In Corinth we stayed six or seven days. At the Haïdári camp two or three days more. Pótis Lenghéris was in Haïdári too. Pótis Junior. But he didn't go to Germany. People pulled strings back then too. Neither did Gagás. They, and I don't remember who else, didn't go to Germany. It was left for us to make the trip. About twelve hundred of us left

Haïdári. There were very few men from Kastrí. And very few from the villages below Kastrí. There was one man from Ayiórghis.³ A man they called "Gaïdoúras,"⁴ the Donkey. We were taken to Hanau, in the Frankfurt area. At Hanau they picked out two hundred of the less hardy among us for the crematoriums. The Lagerführer said no. We called him Fatso. He was chubby. Let's find work for them, let's improve the meals. Because the food was God-awful. The Lagerführer. We were very fortunate. From the death camp we were ordered to go to Opel. They had Russians there, making mud bricks. About two thousand men. They took us to Opel. A large factory but all bombed out. Also close to Frankfurt. Thirteen kilometers away, on the river Main. Quite a story. There were five of us from the Peloponnese. We went to Wiesbaden afterward. Toward the end. We were liberated in February. February of '45. That's right. The end of February. The Americans bombed us at Wiesbaden. Bombed the camp. There were large wooden shelters there, huge ones. Two bombs per shelter. They thought they were barracks. Fourteen dead. From Wiesbaden we were taken to Biblis. There were other Greeks there. Then the order came to relocate us. There were 800 of us when we started out, and now there were only 130. Some managed to escape. Mítsos Koutsoyiánnis, Eléni Zoumboúlis's husband. A good sort. He had given me a lot of help. I don't know if he's alive. The Americans found us on the road. Near—I don't remember the name of the place. I don't remember. It took me seven months after that to get back. We reached Marseille in August. From Marseilles we went to Naples. The sea was full of mines. We disembarked at Pátras. I met a woman there. Evanghelía. Various state-owned cars arrived to transfer us. Something like the Red Cross. An Englishwoman was in charge, petite and blond. You thought she'd break if you touched her. She drove a monster of a truck. This young thing would get in and rev it up till it trembled. Repatriation service. She tells me, Wait. We're going to give you clothes, food, and money. She had blue eyes, all teary. They wouldn't let you say no. Ten days. For ten days I helped that woman. That Evanghelía. She had just given birth. She was married to someone named Taloúmis from Trípolis. I don't know how she got there. She gave birth to a boy. And that boy is now a civil engineer. Evanghelía, a Cretan. She had a sister, she said she'd like to make me her brother-in-law. She showed me photos. We stayed in Corinth for a day, and that's when she told me this. I tell her, Let's get back to our homes first. Let's see if we find anyone there. Well, anyway. We got out in Corinth to wait for some other cars to come. There I see Iríni Koutsoúmbis and her sister. We were *koumbároi.*[5] Sávvas, they say to me, Sávvas. They saw the woman with the baby. Is this baby yours? I told them the whole story. Taloúmis, they both say at once. Daphne runs off and brings someone. It was Taloúmis's brother. He gave us cigarettes, he asks us if we need anything. He worked in Corinth. Finally we left. Or did we leave Evanghelía there? I don't remember. I think we left her there. I got to the village on September 14. I'll always remember that day. Réppas brought me to Kastrí from Trípolis. His job was transportation. I reached in my pocket to pay him. He says, What are you talking about, Sávvas? Me take money from you?

Chapter 7

Márkos had gone. He'd come down from the mountains. Just in time. When he was a student he'd joined an anti-Metaxás[1] organization. 1936. The year I first went to Athens. We lived on Ayíou Pávlou Street in Patíssia. The students had started this movement, and the Security Police dressed up as priests and whatnot and they caught them — eight of them. They took in a lot of them, they kept eight. Ilías Vlahákis, he's an ophthalmologist now, and our brother Márkos. They had them at Security Headquarters, near Tosítsa Street, one street over from Káningos Square. Stournára. Stournára Street. That's where they had Márkos and the others, and I'd go see them. I'd bring them cigarettes and food wrapped in that day's newspaper, so they could keep up with the news. I don't remember how long they held them. They took them up on the roof — Márkos's hands were swollen like loaves of bread from the beatings. I don't know if he had to drink castor oil too. Maybe he's just not telling. Maniadákis[2] would force them to drink castor oil.[3] And it tore right through them. The Security Police showed up, they arrested him at his house. He had a sore, a boil, on the back of his neck. Then they took them to the Army Transfer Section. Seven of them and Márkos eight, to exile them. 1936. I don't know how I managed it, I'd go and see them. They were covered in lice by then and they would catch them, put them in cigarette boxes and stroll around with them. Then Mavroyiórghis arrived, on the Feast of the Annunciation, I think. There was someone named Anghelétos, served on the police force in Kastrí, my father knew him. Because our house was like some kind of monastery, whoever passed through would get a meal, even strangers. Anghelétos was getting on in years now. A commander. And they pulled it off, in the end Márkos wasn't exiled. But his papers stayed at Security Headquarters, the Italians found them. And that's how our troubles began. We left our house and slept at the Sotíris place. Seven times we evacuated our house. We'd hear that the Italians were coming to burn us down. We'd go upstairs, collect our clothing, our linens, and off we'd run. Well, anyway, during that period the Germans arrived. From the fire to the frying pan. We hid our things. In those so-called shelters. The Sotíris family had a storeroom. No. It was Omorfoúla's winepress behind the wall. We hid our things in there, the whole neighborhood did. Someone gave us away, I don't know how, and we took them to Old Man Sotíris's place. From there, we left a lot behind, we took them to Haroúlis Lenghéris's parents' place. Put them in the cistern. And someone told on us again. We were away. Old Gligóris's wife Stamáta took them, with Theodóti, her sister. Kókkinos's wife. They took them to their own cistern. Some things, not the whole lot. Again someone gave us away, our auntie Sokrátaina,[4] Marinákos's wife, took them. Her husband was my mother's oldest nephew. And her mother-in-law was Mávroyiórgaina's sister. And Aunt Margaríta's. He was a watchman. A field guard. Auntie had an oakwood chest, and she buried it in her yard. Some blankets and two kilim rugs, one piece each, that we women had woven on our loom. And those were saved. Nothing else. The rest Haroúlis snitched about to someone, I don't know who. We had a whole suitcaseful. My father had given me quite a few things. I was a good girl. In fact he wanted to take me to Sýra, he used to travel there to stock up. He had given me a gold sovereign. There weren't any in circulation at that time. And there was also my mother's gold jewelry. She'd got it from her uncle the doctor. A diamond and other things. And embroideries of mine. Whatever Anna Papayiánnis had, I had too. We'd been friends from way back then, friends since childhood. Whatever one of us embroidered, the other did too. Some satins—those were taken by the rebels, from shelter to shelter. The sewing machine stayed at home. And I don't know why, I had taken out Granny's fur-trimmed jacket. I like saying that: Granny. She'd given it to me, I was named after her. Grandma Eléni. When she married Grandpa Márkos, the doctor, her father borrowed two thousand gold drachmas. Back then, in 1800 and something. He was a licensed doctor. She was a priest's daughter. They made her an outfit just like Queen Amalia's. His brother was a tailor for the palace. Grandpa's brother. And his other brother a merchant in Venice, he went back and forth. Anyway, he gave me the fur jacket. I kept it in a sturdy cardboard box along with two embroideries. I'd copied the design from Mrs. Manolópoulos. The wife of the justice of the peace. They had come to Kastrí at that time. She was the only daughter with nine brothers, and they gave her everything. A fantastic dowry. Lace from Cyprus and the like. I had those things at home, I'd left them there along with the sewing machine. And they barged in, Galaxýdis and the others, and someone, I have no idea who, took those things. That's when the blockade started, the big blockade. The rebels said whoever stays in their houses we'll kill. All the men outside. And the Germans said everyone had to stay in their houses. They passed through Voúrvoura, they found sixty or so men in the woods, they killed them all. Their wives came to Athanásis's place to buy black mourning clothes. Four or five women. Ismíni opened up the shop. Maybe Andréas was there too. I was astonished, I went in, I asked, Which of your kinfolk did they kill? My husband, my son, and my father, one of them said. On the same day. Then the Security Battalions came. Mihális Galaxýdis and the others. They found Spýros Roúmelis. I think that's who it was. His shoes had nails in them, and he'd put paper in them so they wouldn't hurt him. They rounded up everyone. They searched them. The papers in Roúmelis's shoes were EAM leaflets. They rounded up all those men in the coffee shop, they took them to Trípolis. And they executed Roúmelis there. They took in Stávros Farmakídis, just a kid, Yiórghis⁵ Kontós's nephew. Mihális Galaxýdis. May God forgive him. And they beat that kid something awful. We were watching from our windows, the square was still unpaved, with all that marble lying there. They kicked him all the way from Mángas's house. Just like a ball. Where did he get all that strength? Kicked him all the way to the edge of the square. And there he whacks him one, knocks him down onto Mákraina's outdoor clay oven. Stood over him and shot him *bam-bam-bam* with his automatic assault rifle. They took him away. I don't remember if it was them, if they took him and threw him in Marinákos's yard. Just below it, in Stelios's wife's field. Or was it us, did we take him there in a sheet? I don't remember how he got there. Then we laid him on a ladder, covered in blood, me, my sister Stella, Kóllias's daughters Dímitra and Stavroúla. The four of us. I think maybe Yeorghía Makrís was there too. We took him to the church, we dug a grave, and we buried him. We went down to the square. Our auntie was there, Petroú,[6] Tatoúlis's wife. Her hands like this behind her, going round like a madwoman. Oh, Eléni. Eléni. What is it, Auntie? We have to go get Mihális, they killed Mihális. Stella went, I couldn't bear to. They found him somewhere near Ayios Panteleímonas with his brains blown out. It was the month of July. Then Galaxýdis and the rest, they tell us, The Germans are setting up base here. And the Security Battalions. We were so angry. Especially me. We said, Let them come, maybe we'll get some peace. Then someone confirmed it. I don't remember who. I went to Papadis's house to find Alexandra Chrónis. Stávros Karvouniáris was there. I went over to ask him. What are you doing here, you whore, you? Me, a whore! What are you doing here? They had someone in a coffin, they were loading him into a car. In the back. And he started to swear at me. Right outside Sávvas Papavasilíou's lumber shop. Sávvas was there, he'd been taken prisoner. Two or three days later, Karvouniáris himself comes round, he says, We're taking you to Trípolis for interrogation. More interrogations. They put us in a truck. He and Spýros Galaxýdis. They put our sewing machine in, and our goat. They put Christina, Stella, and Phaídros in. The old folks stayed behind. They didn't take them. They took us to Trípolis. They took us to Evanthía Makrís's house. They left us there. There were lots of people from Kastrí there. Whoever was in the Security Battalions could come and go freely. I thought about going to the Salivéris's place. I don't remember if I went. And I said, Darn it, why didn't I take a few things with me to give them so they could keep them for me. Granny's fur-trimmed jacket. And give it all to the Salivérises. Maria was a teacher in the

village, we were friends. I don't remember if I went. And I don't know
how some of my clothes turned up there. A black velvet dress. Aunt
Merópi had sent it to me from America. From Alabama. The fur-
trimmed jacket was lost in the end. It was well made—it was wine-
colored, I can still see it. A real dream. Iraklís Polítis came for us, he
tells us, We're going for an interrogation. And he took us to the Gestapo. They interrogated us. At some point in there I tell Iraklís, You
should be ashamed of yourself. He gives me a slap, my ears are still
buzzing. They took us to the county jail. There were two girls named
Haldoúpis there, from Ayios Pétros. One was a teacher. Alexandra
and Nitsa Boínis were there. And Sávvas Papavasilíou from Kastrí.
And Panayótis Gagás, who became Eléni's husband later. A man
called the Donkey from Néa Hóra. Koutsoyiánnis, nicknamed the
Donkey. A woman named Karapanayótis from Trípolis. Father Karapanayótis's niece. A woman named Pítsa, I don't remember her last
name. We were going out to the yard. It was the month of July. We
heard that on the Feast of Saint Paraskeví,[7] they burned down our
house. They had already set the big fire. The rebels. They had burned
down the other village. A hundred and more houses. Galaxýdis was
the one who burned down our house, the women came running—
Aunt Efthymía and I don't know which other women. They took the
holy icons, they took two trunks of my mother's. They saved those.
But very little else. The rebels had taken the other things. They threw
on some gasoline, but they had no matches. It was Spýros Galaxýdis,
he wasn't alone. We were in jail, they told us about it. They couldn't
find matches and they left. They had piled up chairs, tables, some
cabinets. And on their way up to the square old Yiánnis Prásinos says,
Haven't you set it ablaze yet? And he took out his flint lighter. They
were going to burn it down one way or another. But old Yiánnis, he
gave them his lighter. He tossed it to them from his bench. May God
forgive him. Christina and I were in the jail. They had Stella in the
slaughterhouse. And Phaídros in the basement of the Seminary. Why
Phaídros, he was just a kid? He was born in 1929. In 1943 he wasn't
even fourteen. They arrested him at Apáno Ayiánnis.[8] He had a tray
of Turkish Delight and was selling cigarettes. And they decided he

was a liaison. That's where they arrested the poor kid. And they had him in the basement of the Seminary. Stella at the slaughterhouse. And Christina and me in the jail. In three different places. My mother and father came a short time later. Liás Athanasiádis put them up. Athanasiádis Distilleries. He had a big fine house. The Germans had requisitioned two rooms for officers. We stayed in prison until August 5. How many days in all, I can't quite reckon. Every morning, every night, when the gate opened, they would take people to be executed. And our hearts would race and we'd look at each other. Whose turn would it be? We were on the list, they had us written there. We found out later that Kóstas Dránias had come and taken us off the list. One of us was going to be killed. They killed the Haldoúpis woman from Ayios Pétros. One of them. The other they left. We women prisoners had become very close. In a ditch in Ayios Nikólaos, behind the jail, they killed fifty people. A mass shooting. Behind the jail. We could hear the rifle shots. We could hear everything. There was a crossbar, there was a big door, it kept slamming, *bam-bam-bang*. And now at night, with the lights on, you had to say your name, and every morning they took us out and gave us something to drink. A watery broth. When they took us outside we wondered would we go back in or not. On August 5 they let us out of there. The Athanasiádises had made friends with the officers who were staying at their house. They told them they were taking us to Germany. So those officers—one of them was a doctor, I think. They sent us German Deutschmarks through my mother—I had saved those marks but then I threw them away. Stupid. They sent us lots of marks and an address. And they would write their relatives there to pick us up so we didn't fall into the wrong hands. As domestic servants and the like. We were 250 prisoners. Men and women. About 50 women, maybe more. On that day, August 5, everyone from Trípolis had come out to watch. Lined up from the prison to the train station. People on both sides of the road shaking with fear. I spoke to some people, I said hello—nothing. Only Vasílis Máïnas, he came over to me. Now there were guards, marching us along, right-left, right-left, on both sides of us, with their guns, with their bayonets. And Vasílis kept coming over to me, Want anything, Eléni, do you want anything? All the way to the station. He walked up and down, Do any of you want anything? Like that all the way to the station. Asking if we wanted him to bring us anything. He had left Kastrí with the others. The villagers had left, to protect themselves. They put us on the train, so many women. That woman from Ayios Pétros. One of them. They killed the other one. And they killed Alexandra Boínis. And the Karapanayótis girl . . . A girl named Pítsa Birbílis. I just remembered her last name. Birbílis. A lively young woman. We had our picture taken together. A woman named Papadópoulos from Stenós. So many women. I don't remember their names. I had written them all down. We arrived in Corinth. There were Italians there, held prisoner. In the army barracks. They took us off the train, now the Germans were in charge. They took us inside. They gave us some gruel for sustenance. Corinth had no water, we were suffering. The Koutsoúmbis sisters found out about us, they came to see us. They were from Oriá. Iríni, Daphne, and the youngest girl. They brought us a basket of grapes. They called us outside. They were living in Corinth, they had settled there. They were seamstresses, they had opened an atelier. And they were working—they had twenty apprentices. Iríni and Daphne. I don't remember the youngest one's name. They brought us grapes and bread, I think. The Italians were hostages there. But there was one named Amadeo, tall with green eyes. The Germans put them on a train, and they pushed them into the Corinth Canal. But he and only he—that Karapanayótis girl, I don't know how, but she and he became sweethearts, and she managed it so they escaped. A beautiful girl, she fell in love with him, and very high-spirited. They escaped. Later we found out that they killed that Amadeo somewhere. With those green eyes, a real doll. We stayed there until August 15, the Feast of the Virgin.[9] On August 15 they sent us to Haïdári. The train stopped at the grist mills in Athens. Mýloi,[10] they told us. Just outside Athens, before Liósia. That's as far as they took us. The Athens grist mills. I went out to pee, I hid, my sister and I hid behind a freight car. Two or three men were escorting us, we could have gotten away and gone into any house, who would give us away? We would go to the first house we found.

They would hide us. But we thought that they might kill the others back in Trípolis. Phaídros and Stella. So we took our things, it was really hot, we put them on our heads, we had a few pieces of clothing, and we walked all the way to Haïdári. There were Germans there, and someone called Yiánnis. Yiánnis the Devil. They had taken Léla Karayiánnis[11] prisoner. On the day of the Feast of the Virgin. Our relatives in Kifisiá[12] found out, I don't know how, maybe from the Koutsoúmbis sisters, that we were in the Haïdári detention camp, that they were sending us to Germany. They were allowed to bring us one package with nuts, grapes, and the like. They took us inside. We bathed there. Washed ourselves in a huge chamber, fifty women. Our cousin Christina Támbaris sent us the first package. And after a few days, when they said they were sending us away, she sent us clothes. We were seen by doctors. And the doctors were from Sparta. I think they killed them later on. Spartan prisoners. They tell us, You're sisters. Say that one of you has a venereal disease. They don't take those women. And that you're taking such-and-such shots. The doctor in charge is a German. But only one of you, not both will go. You, no you—in the end I was the more insistent one. I was older. Christina and I agreed that she would be the one with venereal disease. She was examined by the doctors. The days passed. It was now September. We learned that they took Léla Karapanayótis and the others and killed them. They were holding the men farther down in a crawl space under barbed wire. Panayótis the Donkey was there. And Panayótis Gagás, and Sávvas Papavasilíou. They made them walk on all fours. One-two on their hands and knees. They had cut off their hair and Panayótis the Donkey—he would put his hands up like this, like you do for the sun, as if they were his hair, and joke with me. We got the package with the clothes from my cousin Christina. I still remember, I still talk about it. It had her only jacket inside. A black fur jacket. Christina Támbaris sent it to me when I was going to Germany. And she sent me some underwear from a relative of hers. Women's clothes. There was a field across from the detention camp, some distance away. The prisoners' relatives would come there. One would hold up a red kerchief, and wave to his relative. Another would open and close an umbrella. Another would hold up a newspaper. Kind of like signals. Those were the visiting hours. Long-distance. In the meantime Christina and I separated. They let her out. Where will you go? To Trípolis, she said. But she ended up in Kifisiá via Corinth. At my mother's brother. Was he still alive? I can't remember. At any rate, my aunt Magdálo was there. His wife. And our cousins. Then one day visitors arrived across from the camp. It was late September, and they called out. Wednesday, everyone on Wednesday. All that shouting. The guards were Italians. *Rat-tat-tat* with their machine guns. The Italians. They were following orders. They hadn't capitulated. Wednesday, everyone on Wednesday. What did that mean? We had a woman at the Camp, a *saltadórissa*,[13] she stole things off moving trucks. Stole things on the run, they arrested her, a real live wire! They arrested her for stealing tires from the Germans and selling them to the Greeks. She sold them on the black market. We had all become friends. And on Wednesday, the following Wednesday, they notify us that they're letting us free. On September 11, I think. We slept. There are many things I've never done. And from that time on I never went back to Orthokostá. I had made a vow, and I never went back there. We left Haïdári. Everyone got out. At any rate, Sávvas Papavasilíou went to Germany. They had sent them off earlier, they were shipping people out. Wednesday, everyone on Wednesday. That shouting, all that noise. And it was Wednesday, and they let us go.

Chapter 8

They said they were bringing them from Orthokostá. I don't
know. Or rather I don't know where they were taking them. Lots
of them. A whole lot of prisoners. I mean, best I can reckon, maybe
as many as 150, maybe 200. Maybe more. They took them through
Galtená. They had my brother-in-law, Yiórghis Aryiríou. The Makrís
sisters told me that they had their brother Nikólas too. Because Nikólas—they had an olive press then and they charged a fee for using
it, like a tax.[1] The rebels. And they claimed that the Makrís family
had hidden quite a few gallons of olive oil, and they hauled them
in for that. Them and the Koutsoyiánnis family. Because they didn't
obey the orders of EAM. They took everything from us. The goats
and the mules too. They didn't leave us anything. Don't know where
they brought those prisoners from. But they passed through Galtená,
they passed through Ayiórghis. Kapetán Kléarhos was with them. He
tells Nikólas Makrís, I don't want to kill the entire prison camp, but
if the Germans force us to we will. Get yourself out of here and go
over to Zoubás's storehouses. Zoubás's storehouses are somewhere
in the area round Mesorráhi. Just down from Másklina. The area is
called Mesorrahiótika. That's where Nikólas was going to. So he left
and went there and yes, he was saved. But the others were saved too.
Because they were bringing the whole campful of prisoners through
Ayiórghis on toward Koubíla and toward Eleohóri, and lots of Germans started moving in. Swarms of them. That's when they killed
Mémos. Kostákis Mémos, the village alderman of Mýloi. Had him
up on a mule, he couldn't walk. What should we do with this one,

said the two men taking him away. And one of them said to the other, Whatever our superior said to do. The head of the detention camp. In other words, Kapetán Kléarhos. And *bam*, they fired one shot with a rifle. Just so he wouldn't slow them down. The woman pulling the mule turned around. She had been pressed into service. Dína, Mítsos Fotópoulos's wife. She turns round, she sees Mémos on the ground and his saddle full of blood. And if she's no longer alive, her children will know about that. Her Dimítris and her Yiánnis will know about that, she must have told them. She told me everything herself. How she turned and saw the blood and how frightened she was. They had taken her from her village to transfer the prisoner. Kostákis Mémos. And today we call that place "Mémos's Fields." Well, anyway, they kept the others moving. They took them to a gorge. Between Ayiaso-fiá and Eleohóri. Today the road to Dolianá runs through there. A big gorge, and up above in many spots big rocks jut out. The prisoners from the camp were hidden there and they had orders to execute them all if they saw Germans coming. But they saw the Germans and they didn't have time, they all just ran off. And those people were saved.

Chapter 9

Anéstis Poúlios was a neighbor of ours. A neighbor of our Aunt Anna's. Anna Mikroliá. My father's sister. She lived on the outskirts of Mesorráhi. As children we used to go there and play with our cousins. Aunt Anna was the one who built the Church of the Transfiguration. A chapel, really. She donated her entire property, and she took up a collection. Gave everything she owned. She went out panhandling too. That's how she built the church. Down there, near Poriá. About five hundred meters from her house. The Church of the Transfiguration. Anéstis lived just above us. A leftist, from the very beginning of the rebel uprising. I couldn't have ended up in worse hands. Anéstis Poúlios, Nikólas Pavlákos, and one of the Tóyias men. Vasílis Tóyias. All of them from Mesorráhi. Papadóngonas came down to Trípolis. In March I think. For the precise dates I'd have to ask my brother. Kóstas was the head of the 2nd Bureau. He could give out information. And help a lot of people regarding pensions. With those so-called certificates of "Recognition" for services rendered.[1] He knows all the details. Regarding Petrákos and Haloúlos, he could provide answers. They were his subordinates. Chrístos Haloúlos was in his office. In the 2nd Bureau. The Intelligence Bureau of the 2nd Gendarmes Corps Headquarters. That was the official designation. And Petrákos was posted somewhere around there. As sergeant major back then. He was killed in 1946 or '47 during some battle at Aíyio, then promoted to second lieutenant post mortem. They say a nephew of his killed him. His sister's child. He had nephews in Aíyio. Or someone who knew him, at any rate. Someone he knew well. An execution, in other words. Kóstas had left for Athens in the fall of 1943. Everybody had left. Chrístos Haloúlos, my brother Kóstas, the Kyreléis men. Anyone who had any kind of involvement with the Resistance. To get away from the pressure on them. The pressure to join EAM was unbearable. After the Yiannakópoulos agreement on Mount Taygetus. Chrístos Haloúlos was killed during the December Uprising in Athens.[2] We left Trípolis for Spétses with Papadóngonas. We were disarmed at Mýloi[3] and we went to Spétses. About eight hundred of us had started out, but only about three hundred arrived there. Most had slipped away. We stayed in Spétses for three or four weeks. Life was quiet. The Koryalénios College buildings were our barracks. Kaloyerópoulos was mayor, a son-in-law of the Hasapoyiánnis family. He came from Astros. He helped us. The local people likewise. They were all right-wing nationalists. The defections continued daily. That's when Chrístos left. Some sort of romantic involvement drew him to Athens. We never saw him again after that. He went to live with his sisters in Athens and was killed during the first days of the December Uprising. Before he had time to find his bearings. To join a group for his own protection. There were several organizations. The royalist X,[4] for instance, and others. It seems he didn't pursue that option, maybe he didn't care to. Love sometimes leads to inertia. I knew the woman in question. We ran into each other some years ago at the Lárissa train station. She recognized me. A little hesitantly. Yiánnis, she called out. She introduced her four sons to me. Four sons, tall as could be. I named one of them after Chrístos, she told me. She was the person who'd drawn him to Athens. And I think he just didn't have the time, or didn't want to join up. They went and arrested him. They took him away, and after that he disappeared. His body was never even found. His sisters claim they recognized his comb on a cadaver. A decomposing cadaver. That was all. Nothing else was found. And it was the same story with Yiánnis Pavlákos. No relation to Nikólas Pavlákos. Maybe a distant relative. Yiánnis was a plant pathologist, one of the best in Greece. He did research for the Kanellópoulos Fertilizer Company. He was from Eleohóri. He was also a trade unionist. All the workers loved him. A great fellow. He was unmarried, his mother was his only relative. Not married. Another one who went to waste. They went and got him from his house in his pajamas. That was in Athens. His mother went looking for him; she found nothing. Back when they took those men hostage and were dragging them toward the town of Króra. He was in that convoy of hostages. We'd go and search in the town dumpsites. I went with his mother, that is, twice. The stench of decomposing bodies still haunts me. At any rate, Papadóngonas had gone down to Trípolis. Kóstas had enlisted. No other men from Kastrí had joined yet. Kóstas was in the 2nd Bureau. And there were some men from the surrounding area, but not many. There was a Yiórgos Yeroyiánnis from Parthéni, an artillery officer. Lýras was in charge of the 2nd Bureau. I think he was from Astros. An army captain. From the Lýras family. Kanákis from Vlahokerasiá. A man called Karatzás, who was later executed, chained up with others, and bound. But I don't remember any other men from Kastrí. Nikólas Petrákos, of course. A noncommissioned officer. Chrístos Haloúlos, also an NCO. And the notorious Kotrótsos, Kotrótsos the animal. He was a sergeant during the Albanian campaign, Reserve Officers Academy. Picked himself up a uniform, pinned a star on it, who would ever check him? He presented himself in Trípolis as a noncommissioned officer. And he roared around on his motorcycle. He was Kóstas Kotrótsos, the big shot, the one and only. Who never left anyone alone. Then something happened that stunned us. The Germans were about to execute some people. They had them in jail. There was a schoolgirl among them. During those months two or three schoolgirls had been executed. People were saying, Papanoútsos is responsible for what was happening to the girls. Papanoútsos, the director of the Teachers Academy. They took those people from the jail and stood them up against the wall. The young girl, in patent-leather shoes and white socks, as if she were going to take communion. The Germans had pressed a Greek platoon into escorting the condemned, as an execution squad. Under reservist Varoutsís, the son of Major Varoutsís from Trípolis. This horrified us. It was one thing for the Germans to do the killing. But not us Greeks. Then something happened that disappointed us beyond words. We would listen to the BBC every day. To get the news. About the expected Allied landing on the coast of the Peloponnese. So one evening we heard that the government in the Middle East had outlawed the Security Battalions. Another great blow to us. One day at about that time Papadóngonas, whether out of obligation or as a political maneuver, congratulated Hitler on having survived the plot against him. He congratulated him, he sent him a cable. We discussed all this. There was a place, like a club. We all met there. I was sometimes in uniform, sometimes not. I had a uniform; I wore it when I went out. The Germans in the neighborhood knew me. They would salute me, and I'd salute back. I had a woman I used to visit, there were restrictions and a curfew. Somehow I had to obtain the password. The password and counter-password. I would get them from Chrístos Haloúlos. Chrístos was in charge of codes; he had the files. Chrístos. A short while later we advanced on Kastrí. But at this point things become blurry. I don't remember exactly why this happened. They had burned down the village. People from Kastrí had made their way down, and we heard about it. The arson took place on the twenty-third or the twenty-fourth of July. After the Feast of Saint Ilías.[5] Right about then. Our houses had been burned down earlier. Probably in May. The first seven of them. But I'm talking about the big fire now. On the following day the Braílas men went there, a small group. They walked into the village, the walls were standing, still smoldering. They were furious. There was no doubt that atrocities had been committed. At any rate, we finally went up to Kastrí. And we went to Astros. In trucks. And three or four cars. There weren't many of us. We spent one day in Astros. We went to Manolákos's store. A large storehouse. The Manolákos brothers, Yiórghis and Grigóris. They were Dr. Konstantínos's brothers-in-law. They had a problem with one of the brothers' children. He had gotten mixed up with the rebel movement. They brought us wine, hard goat cheese, and bread. And we drank. We ate and we drank. Then we left Astros. We didn't stay in Astros, it was a dangerous place. Wide open on all sides. We went up to Xerokámpi, to somewhere near Tarmíri. We posted sentries and spent the night there. There were no Germans with us. There was a detail of theirs in

Kastrí. Arrived there before we did. Because I remember that on our way through I went to their doctor. My knee was swollen, I'd hurt it somewhere. He didn't do anything to me, and of course I couldn't understand what he was saying. He put some iodine on it, dabbed it with iodine. And then we moved on. We knew that there were rebels in Meligoú. Militia units but commanders too. Velissáris, Kléarhos. So the leadership decided to surround Meligoú. We stopped about one kilometer outside the village and sent two teams to encircle it. To block the village exits. And before they even got there, only five minutes after they started, Mihális Galaxýdis climbs into his truck with about ten other men, and going full speed, machine guns in hand and horns at full blast, he rides into Meligoú. He went in and he captured it. Of course no one stayed there to wait for us. They had all taken off. We only found a young girl. She was lighting the oil candles[6] in the church, or pretending to. She wore a kerchief on her head, and a black skirt, but I recognized her. She saw that I'd seen her. She didn't say anything. I didn't either. The girl was innocent. Kléarhos's sister. She was arrested later on. They brought her down here. Antonía, she's Fánis Grigorákis's wife at present. But that's what was happening then. All sorts of trigger-happy characters would do whatever came into their heads. Mihális Galaxýdis was one of them. That's how he killed Tsígris. Tsígris was a regular army colonel. Whom the Communists had taken to better staff their forces. Or perhaps as a front. A Greek Army colonel. He was arrested, or rather the poor man surrendered. To us. He found a face-saving solution, he surrendered. It's well known that this is done. You get yourself arrested so you don't appear to have surrendered. Tsígris. Plytás, and all the officers from Náfplion. The Náfplion garrison. Instead of ending up in their hands, the arms ended up with the Communists. Due to airdrops by the British on Mount Taygetus, and especially the Zíreia Mountains. Airdrops of arms and gold sovereigns. And of course they dropped boots too. Everything was in their hands. So what could Yiannakópoulos and the rest do? They had nothing. And above all no moral support. What could they do? There were lots of officers. Tsígris, Lyritzís. Yes. And my brother Kóstas interrogated Tsígris. On

Papadóngonas's orders. So he could verify certain things. That was Kóstas's job, interrogations. On that same day a Battalions unit set out for Eleohóri-Ayiórghis. It was a routine sortie. Nothing but saber rattling. Now who could they possibly be chasing down there? Possibly, also, to bring back food. There was a shortage of food. Kyriákos Galaxýdis was in that unit too. A former gendarme. A patrol sergeant I think. And he was about to beat this woman, but he didn't beat her, he pushed her with his rifle, an Italian carbine. Vanghélis Farazís's mother. A little old woman. In her house, there was a small staircase leading downstairs. These were quiet people, peaceful as sheep. And Kyriákos kept pushing that old woman. Where have you hidden the oil, where have you hidden the oil? The poor woman was going down the stairs, probably to show him where. How can you hide oil? Kyriákos was all worked up, he wanted that oil. And as he was pushing her with his rifle butt, the rifle went off and killed him. They immediately sent a dispatch to Trípolis. To his brother in Trípolis. He had stayed in Trípolis. He was another violent character, like Kotrótsos. He went around with a revolver, acting like some hotshot. As soon as he hears about this he rushes over to the Intelligence Bureau to kill Tsígris. To take revenge. And he emptied his pistol at him just as Kóstas was interrogating him. One shot, out of all those he fired, hit him. One. That's how Tsígris was executed. By now the Germans knew they'd be leaving, and they begin to hand over their heavy weaponry to us. Artillery and mortars. So we could fortify Trípolis. The Germans. When they saw they were leaving they gave all that to us, plus ammunition. Trípolis was eventually fortified and mined on all sides. All the way out. In other words its defensive fortification was complete. Mines, mortars, and all thirty-six cannons. We had placed them at the important sites, and we waited. There were just about enough of us to make up one regiment. A lot of people. And many locals had enrolled too. Reservists as well as ordinary citizens. The ELAS troops gradually began surrounding us and threatening us over their megaphones. But each time they stormed us they achieved nothing. We were well secured. One sector was taken by Chrístos Haloúlos with Níkos Méngos. Níkos Méngos, a second lieutenant in the Reserves.

He joined the Battalions in its final days. Like so many others. For protection. For self-protection. He was from Eleohóri, an Ionian Bank employee. An okay fellow. He died in Athens, never married. A very good man. Well, those men had secured their sectors well. Barbed wire, mines, heavy weapons. Why, a rabbit couldn't get through there, let alone a man. But of course the rebels had their own methods. The method of drafting civilians. Unarmed civilians. At any rate, we kept on waiting. We'd listen to the radio, I'd got hold of a radio. A cousin of mine had bought it somewhere for me. A large one, dry battery cell. At night we'd tune in to the BBC. We were staying at Vanghélis Psalídas's house. A true "Kolokotrónis" style house. It dated back to the siege of Trípolis.[7] It had a stone fence and a wide entrance so oxcarts could go through. Psalídas was in Athens, now a member of EAM. We stayed at his house and filled it with firewood. When we left, we left behind enough firewood to last two years. We went out and hauled firewood. We said we'd spend the winter there. No. We said nothing, we knew nothing. We just hauled firewood. At the time we were waiting for government communiqués from overseas. That's how we learned that Kanellópoulos[8] had arrived at Kýthira. From the BBC. That he had landed at Kalamáta. From the BBC and through word of mouth. We heard about Meligalás,[9] we learned about Stoúpas's death. However you look at it, Meligalás was one massive execution. An inhuman execution. But Stoúpas fought at Gargaliánoi.[10] To the last minute. He died with his pistol in his hand. They all died there. Not one of them was left alive. Not one man. Papadóngonas, in order to protect his units, and he did well, opted to bypass Mystrás. Where the Sparta Battalion was, that is. The rebels slaughtered them later on. Using cannons they had taken from us. After the capitulation. Kanellópoulos came to Trípolis accompanied by Tsiklitíras.[11] Kotrótsos came out on his motorcycle to welcome him. Mihális Galaxýdis came out in his truck. Tsiklitíras, a ranking ELAS officer with the PEEA.[12] Something like that. A colonel. The bishop was there. They stayed at a hotel. Aris arrived. In the meantime, and before the people began the manifestations, the organized demonstrations, we were instructed to get ready to go to Spétses. Those of us who chose to. We boarded trucks. With our arms, with our families and friends. And we went down to Ahladókampos, we arrived in Mýloi. We were at our wits' end as to how to arrange our trucks into a defensive system. We bolted our machine guns to the hoods. There was nothing else we could do. Nothing. We finally made it to Mýloi. A small vessel began ferrying us to the other side. In Spétses a British platoon undertook to guard us. The British. In the end they did this and more. They took our pistols away. Officers had the right to carry pistols. Then a group of ELAS rebels arrived by boat from Ermióni. They arrived by boat to parade right there in front of us. Provocatively. Then we routed them. We drove them away, they didn't set foot there again. And that was the excuse for the British to take our pistols away. Then an order came that we would be transferred to a detention camp in Athens. For our own safety. This must have happened around the end of November. I don't remember the date. I won't risk guessing. They were afraid that the Communists would wipe us all out. It would have been quite an accomplishment if they killed two hundred officers down there. Beginning with Papadóngonas. It would have been quite a feather in their cap. I mean in the context of the December Uprising. At the beginning of the Insurgency. They could have pulled it off too. So a minesweeper came. Two minesweepers. And they took us away to Piraeus. About two hundred of us were left. Possibly fewer. The Tavouláris brothers, Stravólaimos, a colonel, and some others. Quite a few officers, anyway. By nightfall we reached Piraeus. There they put us on trucks. They took us to Goudí. Escorted, once again, by the British and the state police. At Goudí, the big brass were housed in the Gendarmes Academy. Lower-ranking officers like us and civilians went to Sotiría Hospital. ELAS rebels were holding Sotiría. That was the company we kept. Garrison commander of Goudí was Manólis Léngourdas. A gendarmes colonel. From Roúvali. An apathetic sort, no interest in anything. Most of us men were from Kastrí. We were all fellow villagers. He showed no interest at all. Perhaps he couldn't. He had a small unit with him, very small, unarmed, backed up by about fifteen Brits. Those Brits played soccer all day. And at night they slept. It was more like we were protecting them than them protecting us. That's when the December Insurgency broke out. We were roused to action. The history of the Uprising is well known. The Gýzi district was across from us, and they fired at us daily. Most of all, those tracer bullets and the mortars drove us half crazy. We were still unarmed, like cattle waiting to be slaughtered. At which point we planned an operation, we stormed Sotiría. In broad daylight. We took them by surprise. We shot a watchman they had posted on a pine tree. A sniper. We took him out. We took control of the Sotiría building with the help of a group belonging to the 3rd Mountain Brigade. We found arms, we took them. Enough for ourselves and for three hundred more men. We took them. We started distributing them. But the British came and stopped us. They confiscated them — the British, again. And so we dispersed. We began moving down toward the center of Athens. The stream of Ilissus was there, and we followed it down. It was supposed to be out of range of the crossfire. But of course it wasn't really. Because there was frequent mortar firing down there. At any rate, we kept moving along. We would go to Kolonáki,[13] which was a demilitarized zone. We'd gather information, and we'd give out information. We'd see fellow villagers there, we'd get the news from home. In the evening we'd go back. Some would stay there, if they had the means. Nikólas Makrís, Nikólas Petrákos. They stayed near the stadium, at Grigoríou's house. Thodorís Grigoríou. Yes, that's where they stayed. I would go back. And the story ended roughly like this. The ELAS troops were pushed back from the greater Athens area, and then the Várkiza Treaty was signed. We were free. We went to Argos. We couldn't go any farther. Later on we went to Trípolis. March came at last. And then we went up to Kastrí.

Chapter 10

The dogs turned on the livestock. Almost got their fangs into my wife too. She calls me, I go over. They had mangled two of my ewes. I tell her, Wait. I go up to Atzinás's storage sheds, I get my rifle. They were away, but I knew where they kept the key. I went in, I took the rifle, I took cartridges from the cabinet. I go back, and *bang*, I shoot one of them, then I shoot the other, they both fall to the ground. My wife asks me, Don't these belong to Askomaídis? I go to the village of Ayios Pétros, I find Askomaídis. His son, the father was away. I ask him, Where are your dogs? He tells me, They were just here. I take him with me, I didn't let on that I'd killed them. He sees them; I tell him, They almost bit my wife too. What could the boy say? He says, Not the bitch, you shouldn't have. Doesn't matter so much about the other one. I tell him, Shut up or I'll kill you too. They destroyed four ewes of mine. They wanted to take me to court. People told them that they'd be the ones who'd end up paying. They compensated me, and we reconciled.

Chapter 11

They kicked him all the way over to the Unknown Soldier. There they walloped him and threw him down into Mákraina's yard. And they shot him full of bullets. And they threw him in Omorfoúla's vegetable patch. For three days they said, If anyone goes to bury him, we'll kill him. We got up, we looked around, no one going there. So I went with Stella, we had a hard time of it, we put him on a ladder. The two of us. And we carried him up to the school. His sisters were waiting there. I don't remember who else. We took him to the cemetery. I tell them, Do whatever you want, I can't help you any more. Do whatever you want. And I got up and left. They dug a hole and shoved him in. Like a dog.

And Mihális, they killed him down near Oriá, on the same day. Petroú was screaming. Maritsoyiánnis's wife went there, and Klaría went there. Petroú went there herself. I couldn't bear it. They went there, they found him, and they couldn't get near him. They washed him there. They tried to put him on the mule to bring him back but they couldn't. So they buried him down there. Just like that. Mihális. Right where they found him. His mother went there, his mother. All that during the big blockade. The village was burned down later. They had taken us in. But before that, before the big blockade. We had put on a play. We'd performed *Gólfo*.[1] As a benefit for the rebels. Then they came looking for Eléni. Eléni had come back from the detention camp. From Orthokostá. They thought she'd helped the Kyreléis women to escape. We found that out later. So in come the rebels, Where's Eléni? She's not here. She was up at Athiná's. I went up and warned her. Rigoúla saw me, she went and told them. They come back, they say, Where's Eléni? I don't know. I left word for her to come back. That's all I know. That's what I told them. Eléni left, she went and hid. It was dark out now. They put two rebels at our house to guard us. My father, my mother, and Phaídros. To guard us. I always had a sixth sense. A voice inside me kept telling me: Go, go. Just before dawn, that voice woke me up. Go to the marketplace, go to the square. I race to the square, I find Yiórghis Haloúlos there. They had put him in charge of the village. How are you doing, Yiórghis? He says, Christina, take your mother, your father, and Phaídros and get out. Because they're coming to round you up and take you to Ayios Pétros. Because of Eléni. I go home and wake them. Get up, we're leaving. The rebels were fast asleep. The two who were guarding us. Sleeping that heavy morning sleep. We get going, we leave. Mavroyiórghis turns off, I don't know toward where. Toward Karátoula. Our mother went to Lambíris's place and started gathering greens. The rebels went past, they called out to her, they didn't recognize her, she kept on pretending. I wonder if she's found peace now. Phaídros and I headed toward Kékeris's mill. Stella was in Astros. I knocked on the door of the mill. There was an Italian there, Petro, one of the fugitives. Petro, I shouted, Petro. Nothing. We left to go to Pródromos Monastery, Phaídros and me. I say, What if there are rebels in the monastery? We find a rock jutting out there, I held on to Phaídros, he grabbed on to a branch and jumped down. He tells me, There's a cave down here. I held on to a branch too and jumped down. We stayed there in that cave. The sun was nice and bright. We could see the village of Perdikóvrisi across from us. We saw the Nikoláous, our koumbároi, on their way to grind their wheat. I tell Phaídros, Go down there and ask them for some bread. Phaídros goes down, our koumbára says, They came looking for you last night. They gave him bread, they gave him olives, and they gave him water. They tell him, As soon as it starts getting dark, go down to the river, we'll be waiting for you. We go to the river. Kóstas was waiting for us, or maybe it was Dimítris. I don't remember. One of our koumbáros Mihális Nikoláou's sons, our uncle the doctor had baptized their daughter Telésilla. He led us along till we came to a certain spot. He says, Follow the riverbed to the end and you'll come out on the far side of Karátoula, just below Bakoúris's house. Knock on his door. He sent us back. Because he got word that our father had stopped there and left a message. We went and knocked on the door. We didn't know if it was Bakoúris's house, but it was the last house. It was nighttime. They opened the door. We went inside. They tell us, Your father's on his way to Atzinás's cattle pen to find you. In Xerokámpi. But here, take this old blanket and throw it around you and go to Spílio. So-and-so will come by to get you. I don't remember who he said. We didn't know Spílio. We went there, we saw a hole, an opening, Phaídros snuggled up to me, I covered him with the old blanket. All night long we heard the ice cracking. It got light out, we waited for them to come and get us, but no one showed up. I told Phaídros, Get up and whatever happens to us happens. We came out from there, the villagers in Karátoula saw us. Two of them tell us, I didn't know them, they say, Don't be scared, we'll take you to your father. They all knew that the poor man was looking for us. And they took us up to Xerokámpi. They tell us, Take that road, it will lead you straight to the pen. We went to the cattle pen, we found our father. The pen was just a hovel partitioned in the middle. The animals on one side, a small room on the other. They had a fireplace, and they slept one next to the other. All of them. They'd milk the cow, we'd churn the milk to give them a hand. We'd make butter. Those people had nothing. They'd mix up some flour with water and bake it over hot coals. Our father told them, Go to Douminá and find Koupadélis. Tell him that Mavroyiórghis is at the cattle pen. And to give you supplies, and ask if he can come here so I can see him. They went and found him. He filled up their shoulder sacks and he tells them, Now go. And tell the man who sent you here that the rebels came through here looking for them. They came back and told us that. We stayed for three days at the pen. On the third day Koupadélis showed up. He tells him, Yiórghis, things have calmed down. You can come to my place. And we left, at night. We arrived at his house. The women had boiled up some coarse ground wheat, and they sat us down to eat. Then we hear a lot of noise outside. Like the trampling of feet. Get up, says Koupadélis, all in a fright. And he squeezes us up against a wall, behind the door. The tramping stopped. We went to sleep. The next day he got us and took us to Melíssi. Chrístos Kapniás was spending the winter there. First time I see this: There was a very bright moon, and all the houses had stone-tiled roofs. Slabs and slabs of stone. A while later he takes us from there. It starts to drizzle. He takes us to the river. To a footpath. That path would take us to Másklina. My father knew it, he knew his way around there. And Koupadélis tells him, Yiórghis, now I've brought you as far as the church, just below it. You'll come out at Másklina in about an hour. And go to Moúdros's place. Not to Yiánnis's place. To his brother's. Yiánnis was in Athens, he hadn't married Vássio yet. We went there. We went to Másklina, we found his house. My father knocks. Who is it at this hour? It's me, Mavroyiórghis. They couldn't believe it. They open the door, they saw my father, and they let us in. Soaked through. They took us inside, we ate, they lit the fireplace, they sat us down on a mattress, all undressed. The women took our clothes, they dried them. We put them back on. In the morning, one of the two brothers goes and finds the Germans. They were the railroad detachment. He tells them, There's a family here, the rebels are after them. And we have to get them out, so they can go to Trípolis. You needed permits for everything. The German says, Bring them at such-and-such a time. And he came to get us. We went to the station, we got on the train, and we went to Trípolis. Chrístos Haloúlos was there, and Kóstas Dránias, all friends of my brother. All of them in the Security Battalions. But where could we stay? Three lost souls. Mavroyiórghis, Phaídros, and me. Our mother down in the village gave and gave whatever she could, and she made it back home. They didn't harm her. Why would they? Yes, well. Then Kóstas Braílas comes in. Or was it Vanghélis? I don't remember. Whoever it was, he says, Uncle Yiórghis, you'll stay at our place. They had got themselves a place near Kolokotróni Square. On the way to Sparta. A low one-story place, almost in ruins. His sister Chrysóthemi was there too. Chrysóthemi. They brought us something to eat, we slept all in a row. Vanghélis, Nikítas, my father, Phaídros, me, and Chrysóthemi. Kóstas didn't come round there much. He had his team, they'd comb the mountains all night long, in the morning they'd come back to Trípolis. We were worried about the rebels. For about a week. Then they sent word to us that Eléni had appeared in Kastrí. And they wouldn't harm us, we could go. I don't remember how we got there, but we made it to Kastrí. We got there. They'd learned that it wasn't Eléni who helped the Kyreléis women to escape. And they lost interest. We stayed there in Kastrí. Then came the big blockade. The Germans arrive. God must have been protecting me from it all. I realized this later. Someone shows up with a pistol, he says something to me. You scumbags. And he drags me down toward Katsandrís's fountain. Just below Kóstaina's house. He was from the Security Battalions. I was scared. But what could I do, how could I go back? Then another man comes rushing over, he says, The Germans want that girl. At Haloúlos's inn. I go upstairs. There was a man there, he spoke Greek. He starts asking me who is this one and who is that one. Wanted information. He says, You took part in a play for the rebels. I say, Yes, I did. What could I do. And I'll take part in a play for you too if you ask me to. Whatever it takes. And his answer to me was: Do you have a friend? I say, I have lots of friends. Kóstas Dránias, Chrístos Haloúlos. They're in the Battalions, they're our friends. Listen, says the German, I didn't mean that kind of friend. We're asking you if you're in a relationship with a man. I say, I'm not. He says, We're going to examine you, and if it turns out you've been exposed to anything, tell us now where and how, or else we'll send you to Náfplion with the whores. I say, I don't have a boyfriend. Then, during my interrogation, a man comes in, I tried to find that man later on and thank him, a man from Tegéa, named Kóstas Karatzás. He came upstairs and he told them, I'll be responsible for this girl, her brother's my friend. Karatzás from Tegéa. Her brother is my friend. And they tell me—they were doctors, the one who spoke Greek too—they tell me, Off you go. Then an order came, for them to leave immediately for Ayios Panteleímonas. They had arrested two girls in Ayios Panteleímonas. Somewhere around there. Two sisters, both pretty girls. They had come to the village for us to sew them some dresses. They were with the rebels but they came to us. And look what happened, they killed them. They arrested them and they killed them. The doctors left. They notified them that they found those girls and they left. They didn't come back. We kept the dresses. No one came asking for them. So we wore them ourselves. The other Germans stayed there for two or three more days. With the Battalions. I went down to the square. And then I see my father. A German was taking him to our uncle the doctor's house to go in and search the place. Mavroyiórghis tells me, They'll come to our house too. I run over to the house. I found a pistol. I had found it under Márkos's bed. Kapetán Achilléas had slept there. During the first blockade, when the Germans arrived on bicycles, and they all ran away. Delivoriás, Broúsalis, Achilléas. We kept it. I take it and hide it. I open the hatch that goes down to the store. I put it behind the stairs. The German comes in. He searches the house. He says, Get the keys, we're going to the store. As soon as we walk in, there's the pistol, in plain sight. Oh, Lord, I say, put a quilt over it, cover it up. A quilt, a quilt. Did he not see the pistol? Did he see it and not say anything? Thinking they might kill us all. Who knows. He left. Then I go and I take it. I put it up against my breast. I was afraid it might go off, I go down to Omorfoúla's vegetable patch and wedge it into the stone wall. Later, when things calmed down there, I went back for it, and it was nowhere to be found. And the year before last some children were playing, and they started shouting, A pistol, a pistol. They picked it up and took it to the police. It was all rusty, of no use. And that was the end of that. The Germans were getting ready to leave. Stávros Karvouniáris arrives. He takes us away, all of us. He came and he threatened us. He took our goat, and our sewing machine, and I think he was the one who took my granny's fur-trimmed jacket. Took everything we had. Whatever the others had left us, he took. Well, anyway. They took us to Trípolis. Márkos's friends were there. Dránias and the rest. They left our old man and our old lady. Mavroyiórghis and Mavroyiórgaina. They went to Athanasiádis's place and he kept them there. They sent Stella to the slaughterhouse. Don't remember where Phaídros went. Phaídros was just a kid. Maybe it was Ménis Kaloútsis's place he went to. They were using it as a jail. Today it's a bank. And Eléni and I were sent to the county jail. By the Germans. Until the beginning of August. Alexandra Boínis was there, she tells me, Let's go peel potatoes. Over here, at the barracks. Go do chores. The barracks were just behind there. They'll give us chocolate, she says. They'll give us cigarettes. We didn't smoke. We'll give them to the men. At least we'll see a few people. Poor woman. We went. I was thin, they had me setting the tables. There were two German women there, worked like machines. While they were cleaning they had on linen aprons and caps. Then they took those off and wore a solid-color cotton dress, spanking clean. And when they were serving they wore white. Bright white uniforms. And they moved so fast. We went back. I tell Alexandra, I'm not going back there. There was a boy in with us, a prisoner. He took a liking to me. He'd come and sweet-talk me. Come on, now, Bábis, cut it out. His name was Bábis. He was from Trípolis, that Bábis. He'd become friends with the guards, and sometimes they would let him go to his house. They'd take him there. Imagine what he was giving them. He'd call me, Come on let's go to my mom's house, so she can see you. I think they executed him later on. I went there once. I went outside and the world looked different. His mother had cooked a meal for me. And what a meal it was. She saw me as a bride, or something, for her son. Then the time came and we were separated. To take us to Germany. About that time they killed ten Germans somewhere in an ambush. They made a list of people to be killed, I was on it. Kóstas Dránias came and erased my name. They took Alexandra. She was also on the list. We were all on the list. And they took the whole bunch of them to Ayios Nikólaos and they executed them. That happened first. Then they put us on the train. I think it was August 2 when they took us. We were wearing these canvas shoes. We'd made them ourselves. We'd made a sole and wound some rags around it and that's what we were wearing. So they took us away. They put us in boxcars, all of us. And Eléni was swearing at them. And off we went. We arrive at some station, and they let us out. As we start walking the rags come off our shoes. We were left in our bare feet. They took us to Haïdári. With the sun beating down on us, on the day of the Feast of the Virgin. Eléni quickly scribbled a message with the address of our relatives in Kifisiá. Saying where they were taking us. They took us from the station on foot and some women were following us, they kept telling us, Write a message, throw us a message, a note. So Eléni wrote one and threw it to them. All that about a month after they'd let her out, from Orthokostá. From the detention camp. She was accused of carrying a rifle, of being a rebel in the mountains. That's what they said. They slandered her falsely. Not all of them. I don't mean all of them. The Galaxýdis brothers and Iraklís. The others, Dránias and Chrístos Haloúlos, they helped us. Chrístos was in love with Steryianí Papaloukás. He was killed because of her. He went to see her and he was killed. In Athens. During the December Uprising. So they took us to Haïdári. Eléni threw them the note, and word got out we were there. They started preparing to send us to Germany. They started sending us to doctors to be examined. I was haggard looking and very thin. Some woman says to me, It's a pity for both you girls to go to Germany. You, you look so bad, tell them you're an epileptic. But I'm not an epileptic. Say you are, because the doctors are allowed to disqualify seventeen patients out of every hundred. And that excuse works, seizures. But another woman from our group had to verify it. Someone did, I don't remember who. There was a girl from Loutráki. Named Evridíki Yero-lymátou. We'd become friends, and we're still friends. She was with her sister Moíra. I think she was the one who verified it. And they separated us. They took me to the sick ward. There I was, all alone, afraid they would kill Eléni. And Eléni afraid for *my* life. We'd meet on the stairs, hug each other, and start crying. At any rate. A few days later they came to get me. They took me to the station to leave for Trípolis. I arrive in Corinth. There I run into the Yiannoúlis brothers. Yiánnis and Yiórgos. By chance. Where are you going, Christina? Well, here's the story. To Trípolis. Don't go to Trípolis because the other side will haul you in again. Go to Athens. I was in Corinth now. I say, I have no money. Yiánnis went and got me a ticket, he sent me back. Don't go down to Trípolis, they'll put you in jail again. I arrived in Athens, I went to some relatives. On Notará Street, near the museum. Yiánnis, my cousin Christina Támbaris's husband, came and got me from there. We went to Kifisiá. Márkos was there in Kifisiá.

He tells me, The Germans have capitulated. And Eléni's getting out on Wednesday. Is this true? Yes, it's true. What's happening in Trípolis? I've been in touch, everyone's fine, we survived. That put my mind at rest. I went and lay down. They gave me some bedding and I slept. I didn't get up for a week. They'd come and check to see if I was breathing. Come have something to eat. I don't want to. And I'd fall back asleep.

Chapter 12

Her father would get himself drunk in Kastrí. The priest. He'd slipped into a drinker's apathetic state. And he'd neglected his family. But my aunt had discussed this with the old man, and she'd put him in charge of their affairs. She'd handed things over to him carte blanche. That all happened in 1925, maybe 1926. I can barely remember it. That's when Stylianós came from Chicago. Stylianós Kalamáris. He was from Karátoula too. Hard times. People were suffering. Wheat shortages, large families, lots of mouths to feed. People didn't have enough of anything, not bread, not oil. Not even wine. Anyone in America was considered to be in the promised land. Should anyone show up from over there, everyone wanted him for a son-in-law. So Stylianós arrived. Someone would approach him, someone else would wine and dine him. He was short and fat, or rather he wasn't all that short. But he looked short because he was fat. Big belly, no neck at all, his head stuck on his shoulders. The old man started working on him too. Diplomatically. I have a girl for you too, he tells him. From a good family. She's my niece. Pretty, upstanding, good housewife. But I'm not sure she'll be interested in you. There was a purpose to all this now. To this manipulative preamble. To lower his hopes as a possible suitor. He talked him up good; in the end he had his way. They arranged for him to come to the house so they could meet each other. His niece was notified accordingly. The old man's second niece. She came to the house, they pulled out a bolt of cloth. Cloth they used to weave on the loom. They unrolled it to cut a blouse for my mother. That was the pretext. After a while the prospective bridegroom showed up. He came in, said good day, they said good day too. An unusual hour for the old man to be there. The whole thing was a setup. Let me introduce you to my niece. The niece was bending over a plane-smoothed wooden chest to measure the cloth. She didn't suspect anything. Today she must be eighty or older. Iríni. She came here last summer. Stylianós isn't alive now. She was plump, heavy. With white hair. But as a young woman she was pretty. At any rate she was thin, and nimble. So let us introduce our niece to you. He doesn't waste any time. You know, your uncle and aunt here have been having a word with me. Do you know about what? Iríni was mortified. He came to the point, that fellow. In medias res. Right to the point. Iríni was so mortified that she dropped the scissors and the tape measure, if she even had a tape measure. I can't remember if she took measurements or if she used a pattern to cut the cloth. Then she found a more convenient place to escape the onslaught. She opened the hatch and disappeared. Stylianós went over to her and leaned over. The hatch was open. You didn't answer me, he said to her. She stopped on the third or fourth step. That's when she realized that a marriage was being arranged for her. Whatever my uncle and aunt say, and my father, she said. The father came last. I agree. He was elated, he considered her response to be, and in fact it was, an acceptance of his proposal. He went out on the balcony—you can still see the bullet marks. He had a pistol on him, he took it out and fired one, two, three, four shots in the air. To proclaim to the world, to noisily trumpet the new-formed alliance. The balcony was covered by a big piece of tin, and he made a hole in it. That son of a gun, said the old man, he shot a hole in the tin cover and now it will leak. And that's how the marriage was arranged. They had their wedding, went off to America, and had a family. And they lived happily for almost half a century. They had four children. Thanks to the old man's clever ploy. Thanks to his sharp-minded strategy. To his telling him, I have a fine young lady, but of course she has no dowry, if you insist on one we'll scrape something together. But I don't know if she's going to like you.

Because you're fat, and all that. He wore that poor man down. Broke his morale. Didn't even tell him they had arranged for him to go to their house, or who the person was. Just told him the person will be at the house, but not who she was. So his curiosity would be aroused. And it certainly was.

Chapter 13

That fall in Athens we had a problem just surviving. When we arrived. That's when we went there—Aryíris Nikolópoulos from Valtétsi[1] took us there. There was a group of men from Valtétsi, with Papaoikonómou and the rest. They cooperated, they all voted for Tourkovasílis.[2] Tourkovasílis, the head of the Bank of Greece at the time. And we went to see him. We explained the situation to him. Thodorís, Aryíris Nikolópoulos said to him. What are we going to do? What's going to happen? Tourkovasílis had supported us in the past. He promised us that soon we'd be able to secure arms. So we could form teams in the Ermionís area. Where there was a sizable EDES[3] organization. In the end the only thing he did was sign us up for the employee soup kitchen. All of us from Arcadia, everyone who had left from down there. To get meals there until we were settled somewhere. They had dining rooms in the basement of the central branch, where they cooked food, and we went and ate for free there. Until October 28. Which is why I said I left Kastrí in October. Until October 28. On October 28, Tourkovasílis was arrested. By the Germans. It happened in the bank's festivities hall, where a ceremony had been organized in honor of Óhi Day.[4] The third anniversary. With the approval of the board of directors, of course. But word of the gathering was leaked, and the Germans burst in and nabbed them all. The board of directors, the employees, everyone. Tourkovasílis was up in his office. He hears about it, he goes downstairs, he says to the Germans, Whatever my employees did was on my order. I'm the only one responsible here. So of course the Germans arrested him. He was court-martialed. They had him in jail in Kallithéa. They cut off his hair. They were going to execute him. And he got off by chance. Because right at that time they killed his brother Yiórghis Tourkovasílis. A former officer of the gendarmes, also a member of Parliament. ELAS caught him and they shot him. I think that this contributed to Thódoros's being let off. He stayed in jail until the Liberation.[5] Tourkovasílis. And later on, when Kýrou[6] accused him in Parliament of collaborating with the Germans, he reacted in the well-known Tourkovasílis style. He had been elected a member of Parliament with the help of Maniadákis. Well, he took care of Kýrou, he waylaid him on Anthímou Gazí Street in downtown Athens, and he beat the daylights out of him.

Chapter 14

—That so-called Recognition for having participated in the Resistance. That's what I just can't stomach.

—Never mind the Recognition. Can you tell me about the old lady?

—Yes, I'll tell you.

—That's what I want. When they caught her, how they caught her, why they caught her. When you found out that they killed her. How old was the old lady when they butchered her. And did they cut her up or did they shoot her?

—Cut her up. They butchered her.

—When did they arrest her?

—They arrested her some time around February. If I remember correctly.

—Where?

—They arrested her here. Right here.

—The old lady worked as a cobbler?

—Yes.

—And how old was she then?

—Fifty-five. Fifty-six. And they didn't just arrest her, they looted her things too. They loaded up two cars, anything they could find. In the house and in the cobbler's shop. They took down the wine and carried it off in goatskins. Loaded up those wineskins.

—Where did the old lady learn the trade?

—From her father. And she made new shoes, all kinds. She was the best cobbler in town.

—Did you learn to cobble from her?

—Yes, from her. And so. They brought her down here. They kept sending us letters to go back.

—Had you gone over to the Battalions?

—We hadn't gone anywhere at the time they arrested her. That's the funny part.

—Where were you?

—We were in Athens, that's all. Trying to protect ourselves, like so many others.

—Yes.

—We were staying there in Athens. The Battalions were formed around March. That is, after things got tough here in the villages. People couldn't take it. Wherever they went, they were killing people, arresting them, and so on. And those actions led to reaction.

—When did they arrest her?

—Around February.

—They must have arrested her earlier.

— Maybe January. And meanwhile they kept sending us letters up in the village. Be back home by midnight and you have nothing to fear—we won't do anything to you.

—Who signed them?

—They just sent them like that. Someone would stop you, for example. The Organization gave me this letter, he'd say. In the meantime the so-called Resistance was formed. The Security Battalions were formed, and people went over to them. And that's when it all happened. The first ten days of June. After the springtime arrests. When the Germans went out on various operations. The big blockade, as we call it. I know that's when they killed her. During the first ten days of June.

—Were you in the Battalions?

—It was at that time the Battalions were formed.

—Yes.

—But when they arrested her there were no Battalions.

—Who told you, do you remember?

—That they arrested her?

—That they killed her.

—Yes. Word got out. Because at the detention camp there were people from Kastrí. Along with the old lady. And when the Germans closed in on them, they had to break up the camp. And execute the people there. Like Polítis, and old Mrs. Braílas, my mother, and I don't know how many others. Someone called Maraskés from Roúvali. Themistoklís Anagnostákos. A man from Trípolis, and a girl. Well, anyway. They killed them. And when they killed that lot the rest of them were scared, they tried to hide. They formed small groups, two here, two there. You know. And those rebels came back up, there was a ravine down below. They say, Just now we executed the traitors. The others all scared out of their wits. They deserved it, they told them. And they were spared.

—You say they arrested her in February.

—Yes.

—Could it have been later?

—No, it was in February.

—But on February 2 the first detention camp was dismantled. They left Orthokostá and went to Mávri Trýpa.[1] On the second of February.

—Ah, the first detention camp.

—And they left. The Germans freed them.

—Yes, right. With the second detention camp.

—Then they arrested her later, not in February.

—Yes, maybe. Maybe around March. Something like that.

—Were you still in Athens?

—Yes, we were in Athens.

—Who else did they capture with her, do you remember?

—From here, Panayótis Polítis. Iraklís's brother.

—Yes.

—There were five, six, seven of them. Five of them were executed.

—Did you ever see Kalabákas, or talk to him?

—Which Kalabákas?

—Yiánnis. The one who escaped.

—Oh, yes.

—He says he dropped down. Just in time.

—And that he covered himself with my mother's skirts. How do you know all that?

—I just do. I heard about it.

—He pretended to be dead, he smeared himself with blood.

—And later when they burned down the village, what do you remember?

—I think they burned down the village in July. In the month of July. That was the big group fire. But before that they burned some down to set an example. The first fire was seven houses.

—Which houses were the first?

—Ours. Braílas's and Galaxýdis's. Who they considered reactionaries. And one or two more in the marketplace. They burned down seven houses in all. To terrorize us, that was.

—And how much later did they burn down the others?

—Much later. Two months, three months. They received an order, the governing committee did. To hold them back you have to set fire to their homes. You have to frighten them. And they went and set fire to the village. A hundred and eighteen houses.

—Don't you remember when exactly that was?

—I do remember. I remember very well. Because on that day we came to see if we could save them. They'd taken them somewhere else, all those people.

—Somewhere else? Where?

—To Ayios Panteleímonas. From Mesorráhi, they had taken the whole of Mesorráhi. Hostages.

—You came from Trípolis.

—We did.

—You heard they were burning down Kastrí, and you came.

—Yes, that they were burning it down. And we tried to get there in time.

—Before they killed the old lady or afterward?

—The old lady was dead. She was dead. They set those fires, that's when.

—So who finally burned down the village?

—They say it was Kontalónis. He got an order from the seven-member committee here. Who knows. He was one of the kapetanaíoi.

—What was the seven-member committee?

—I don't know anything about it. But Kontalónis himself said to Yiánnis Makrís. Who's now my brother-in-law. I don't want you talking politics at the factory. He had opened a lumber factory later, and Yiánnis was a worker there. With those English pounds. He tells him, Find out who was responsible. It wasn't me. I couldn't do anything else. Because if I hadn't burned it down they would have killed me. He told him, Right there, seven of them in your own village. It's true. Kontalónis said that. But it doesn't much matter now. We're not children. That's how things were then. I mean you can see how it all works. If the tornado drags you in one direction, they call you a traitor. And you are one. You have to be taken out. To be killed. The Battalions were formed in 1944, end of March. It was the month of March when Papadóngonas came down to Trípolis. Who couldn't tell that the Germans were losing? Who couldn't see it? But they insisted. You had to be neutralized. To be taken out. To be killed or be labeled a traitor. That's what it was all about.

—Did they burn down Ayiasofiá before or after Kastrí?

—Before. Long before. And I know one thing for sure about Ayiasofiá. They burned a woman, a mule, and a pig in there. A pig. Right in the house. They wouldn't let the woman out.

—I've been told that it was Tsoúkas from Oriá who threw the woman into the fire. She tried to get out, and he threw her back in.

—I don't know anything about that. I don't know about that.

—Was it you who found your mother? Did anyone bring her down?

—No one did. We couldn't. Later on we went there. But they had buried her. They buried her in the bed of a stream, and the stream carried her off in the winter, there was nothing left of her. Some shepherds showed us the place.

—Whereabouts did they execute her?

—Somewhere below Prastós.

—That's so vague.

—I only know what the shepherds told us. They wanted money. At a place where two streams met. Right there.

—All because you'd left for Athens.

—Because we'd left. And because of my brother Kóstas.

—Is Kóstas alive?

—He died last year. In Corinth.

—Alone?

—With Semní.

—What did they have against Kóstas?

—He was in the Organization. And as soon as he left, that's when they turned against us.

—Hold on a minute. Kóstas was in the Organization?

—Yes. As a noncombatant. Not as a rebel. And when they realized that he didn't want to stay with them, they began turning against us.

—I didn't know that.

—They took Kóstas to perform an execution. They'd brought someone from some other village there, name of Nestorídis. They took him up to Zygós. And then Kapetán Kléarhos said to him, Braílas, let's see what you're made of. If you're a fighter. He had a .45-caliber pistol. Hey, what did you just say, he tells him. Me kill people? What did you say? Is this what our struggle is about? Well, anyway. Kóstas got up and left, and they killed that man just like that, those horrid little rebels. He came back and he tells us, Tonight you're leaving, it's finished here. You're leaving tonight. Imagine, telling me to leave that night. With my money, with my store, with my things. You get the picture. And I'll take you there. He knew his way around and everything. But he stayed behind, in resistance to those rebels to collect some money, to take care of some business. And after that he got up and left. He came and joined us. Two months later. They didn't manage to turn him into an executioner, and he became their worst nightmare. Because that was their method. To project an image of power, an image of strength. But of course the others did the same, now didn't they? Absolutely. What else can I tell you?

Chapter 15

That was in 1946. Around then. Ten or so men come down here. I hadn't fixed the house yet, it was just a shack. And right when I moved in there, I hear *tap-tap-tap* on the door. I grab a rifle I had. Who's there, I say. Nighttime. Who's there? It's me, Mítsos. It was Mítsos Fotiás. What are you doing down here in Karátoula at this hour, Mítsos? Is that you, Loukás? It's me. What do you want? He says, Listen, we're looking for Panayótis Laganás. You know, Verémis. And why would you men be looking for him, I tell them. Well, anyway. I moved to the side and I knocked on my brother Tássos's door. He opened it. Tássos, it's me. He opened the door. I tell him, Listen, they're looking for your brother-in-law Panayótis. But they have no right doing what they have in mind, I say. I tell them, Panayótis doesn't live here, let's go to his house. We went there, we knock on the door. Maria was there. She opened up. They want Panayótis. But even if he's here, they can't take him. Maria opened the door. Those men wanted to search through his storage trunk. I tell them, Hey, what do you think you're doing here? Get the heck out before we all get killed in here. And they left. Mítsos Fotiás and Vasílis Kólias, who was still just a kid, God rest his soul. The men from Kastrí tried to get them to take revenge on the men from Karátoula. From Karátoula. And they saw I was strongly against that. For no reason, how should I put it, out of spite. And the next day they gave me a good talking-to. Why was I resisting them? Because Panayótis was in charge, EAM had forced him into it. Shame on you men, I tell them. But Nikólas was the head man then. Konofáos. Who it was that sent them I don't know. But he was the leader. He and the Trýfonos brothers.

—Don't go naming people and things, Loukás. It might stir up trouble again.

—Yeah, all right. But that's the truth.

—It's the truth, but why should people hear it from you?

—Yep, no reason at all. I'm done talking.

Chapter 16

Tzímis Boínis says to me, We have to take part in the Resistance and work for our country. I agreed immediately. The meetings were held in Ayios Vlásis. Beginning of 1943, in March. I called my friends, we went. Hotblooded men. We went to the country chapel. We asked where to find arms. It's easy, Magoúlis tells us. Tzímis Boínis and Níkos Magoúlis. Seems they were the ones in charge. We knew they were Communists. But we didn't know what communism was. They tell us, About the arms, it will all be taken care of. The next evening we went: Thanásis Kosmás, Tákis Pantazís, Mihális Tatoúlis. Lots of men. So we went, we were mostly concerned about getting arms. They tell us, We'll take care of that. They'll bring us arms, there will be drops by the British. On the third night, Tzímis Boínis says, We'll also be working for the Party. What party, we say. We'll be working for the Organization. For EAM, says Magoúlis. That's what we'll call the Organization. At the time we still hadn't heard anything about it. And the party meant the Communist Party. We'll try and bring in as many men as we can. Each of us will bring in two, three, ten men. As many as he can. I listened to this carefully. We left, I was upset. The next night I didn't go. The other men went. They tell me, Antónis, you didn't come. I tell them, No. I came for the Resistance. Not for the Party. When they took over in Kastrí, when they were in complete control, they arrested me. That was the reason. They came to my house at night. They tell me, We're going to Mángas's place. That's where they had their headquarters. Langadianós's brother was there. There were two of them. I don't remember the other one. They took me to Mángas's place. They already had a lot of men there, from Kastrí. And a few from Ayiasofiá. The next day they marched us over to Ayios Pétros. And from Ayios Pétros to Kastánitsa. A few men at a time, so we wouldn't suspect anything. So we wouldn't put up a fight. From Kastánitsa to Prastós. And finally to Orthokostá. To the monastery. And that's where they interrogated us. The charge had already been prepared. We had been linked to Trípolis. To the Battalions that were being organized then. In April of 1944. I say to one of them, You're in control everywhere and you bring us here. Why didn't you interrogate us in Kastrí? And find us guilty, and hang us from the village plane tree? That's exactly what I told him. He stood there, a man named Tóyias from Mesorráhi. He gave me a punch on the back of my neck. I'd never fainted before that. Everything went dark. Then he whacks me again in the face. That was all the beating I got. I don't know about the others. The other prisoners. There were about a hundred of us, maybe more. The camp commander was Tóyias. There was someone else from Kastrí, Stratís Karadímas. The Braílas woman's nephew. Later they said he was the one who killed her. And someone from Oriá, Goudontínos's brother. Níkos. They were our guards. Fifteen of them all together. There were also five or six monks, we never saw them, they stayed somewhere separate. For a month they held us there. Then the cleanup operations began on Mount Parnon. They began letting a lot of men go. They freed them a few at a time. They kept us until the end, thirty-two of us. They took us up to the mountains, up near Ayios Vasíleios. Where a battle took place later on, in 1948. With LOK[1] troops. They took us up to a riverbed, a closed-in space. Good place for a detention camp. We stayed out there in the countryside for three days. It was summer. We had Panayótis Polítis there with his clarinet. He played for us sometimes. Iraklís's brother. We had Braílas's mother there, still alive then, we had Maraskés from Roúvali. We had Themistoklís Anagnostákos. They were all executed. We had Thanásis Kosmás, and Vanghélis Koutsoúmbis. Vanghélis was a butcher from Oriá, our savior. We stayed there three days, we could hear the gunfire in the distance. The sporadic gunfire of an army on the march. Thanásis had been a cobbler on Mount Parnon.

He could speak some Tsakónikan.[2] It was July, ten o'clock at night, we'd gone to bed. We heard footsteps approaching. Army boots. It was Balís and Alímonos. Balís was a big-name kapetánios. Alímonos was an executioner. The most fearsome. They called him the Butcher. Did you hear them, Thanásis Kósmas says to me. Did you hear them? Whispering to me under the blanket. They were speaking Tsakónikan. What did they say, Thanásis? They said that the Germans are coming so they're going to kill us all. That's what they said. They'll kill us and they'll leave. Five minutes later they start shouting, Get your blankets and get up, we're striking camp. And since you don't know these parts at all, our men will take you out. Three at a time to slip through the German noose. We were in the front. These men here, says Balís. Take them and go down to the ravine. He showed them the place himself. Two rebels take us, me, Thanásis Kosmás, and Vanghélis Koutsoúmbis. It was dark out, no paths to walk on. They took us down there. They told us to stop. No one said anything. They were very anxious, those two, we could tell. We waited for some time. Finally they tell us, Stay right here. No one's leaving. We'll go back and see why the others are taking so long. And they went back. Then Koutsoúmbis says, I'm leaving. I'm a butcher, I know every inch of this terrain. There's no road here. And he got up first. Thanásis got up and followed him. I was still hesitant. Don't be stupid, they tell me, come with us. And I went. What happened after that we heard from Kalabákas. He died last year. Yiánnis Kalabákas. They said he was Alímonos's koumbáros. No one knows. They took two more groups of three men down to the gully. And they began killing them. He dropped down and hid himself under Braílas's mother's skirts, pretended to be dead. Meanwhile, they were counting them up, one, two, three, etc. How many they'd killed. They figured out we were missing. Sons of bitches, their chief says to them, where are the rest of them? And they went looking all over trying to pick up our tracks. All that took place in that ravine, and Kalabákas told us about it two or three years later. But we had cleared out. Koutsoúmbis had taken us somewhere up high. He knew those parts well. Because he bought animals for slaughter from there. We spent our first night just outside of Kastánitsa, in the potato fields of someone named Kontoyiánnis. There was a shack in the middle of the fields. Kontoyiánnis was one of us, Koutsoúmbis knew him. We made our way to the shack. We went in, there was a rebel with a gun inside. As soon as he saw us he ran out. They had killed an ox somewhere, and he had a piece of that meat with him. He left it behind and cleared out. A little while later we saw Kontoyiánnis coming. We went outside. He'd come to water his potatoes. We ask him, Where should we go? He tells us, The Battalions are right above us, they've been there three days now. The Sparta Battalions. They had come around looking for a big pot to cook in. Go and find them. And he came with us. Up there to the company of those Security Battalions. It was the administrative division. They had captured fifty men or so and they had them roped together until they could determine whether or not they were rebels. They had captured Sioútos, Goudontínos's brother, with his gun, his beret, all his things. Níkos Sioútos. Our guard in Orthokostá. And they were going to execute him. The captain takes us in front of him. He tells us, You're not to speak. He asks him, Do you know these men? Yes I do. Where did you have them? In the detention camp. And why did you have them there? Because they were reactionaries. Then he let us free. They gave us cigarettes, they gave us food. We went off to get some sleep. There was a big rock off to the side, we slept there, like logs. Around three in the morning we hear shots, *bam bam boom*. We hear shouting. The rebel got away, he's gone. We get up in a hurry. The officers come over, the captain and his staff. What happened? The rebel got away. He jumped down from the rock and ran off. From the big rock. We were sleeping off to the side, the guard was up above us, so was the rebel. It's hard enough to jump with your hands free, says the captain. Even harder with them tied. This here's a very high rock. So you men from his village must have untied him. He accuses us of untying him. And he sends us to the Germans. It was morning now. The Germans were higher up on a different peak. They had put up barbed-wire fences and they put all the men to be executed in there. They close us up in there. At about eleven we see the captain, running up the hill with his cap in his hand. He comes up to us, Listen you men, he says, all out of breath. That's how we learned about Níkos Sioútos's death. A German patrol killed him that night, with his hands tied behind him. Thank God I got here in time, said the captain. Or I'd have you on my conscience too. Then he went to the Germans and they let us free again. From there they took us to Aráhova. Meanwhile they had captured a big fish from Kynouría. The kingfish. Dr. Koúkos from Ayios Vasíleios. He wasn't a combatant, he was a civilian. The cleanup operations were over, the so-called big blockade. They brought Dr. Koúkos down to Aráhova, a man from Corinth arrives. A meek, quiet man. Silent but very strong. Doctor, he says to him. I was there. I didn't want to see all that but I did. My wife So-and-So, he says to him, the teacher at Kosmás, Kynouría, who killed her? You put her on trial and you killed her. Weren't you the judge? With dates, particulars, everything. I've no idea, says Koúkos. A six-month-old child, he says, Doctor, who killed it? I don't know if your wife was pregnant or if she had a six-month-old child. She was against them and they took her and killed her. And she was that man's wife. I wish I hadn't seen all that. At any rate, he hit him. He fell down. He pulled him back up and kept trying to find out who had condemned his wife to death and why. And he hit him again. Over and over. Until the Germans arrived and pulled the doctor away from him. And they sent the man away, so he wouldn't finish off the doctor. A terrible beating. The Germans got rid of him, they sent him away. I don't know if Dr. Koúkos died after that, I don't know what became of him. I don't know the rest of his story. We left. They let us go. And we split up there. Thanásis and Koutsoúmbis went to Trípolis. The Battalions followed. I left for the village. I went down to Yídas's inn, and I arrived at Ayios Panteleímonas. Just below there Tákis Bínis's mother-in-law was watering her vegetable plots. Tsakíris's wife. She was bent over, she was redirecting the water with her hands. She didn't have a shovel. I go stand over her. Good morning, Aunt Kásia, I say to her. It was morning. She stands up, she sees me. Good morning, she says, dumb-founded. And then she says, You're alive. Yesterday they held the ninth-day memorial for you. I went to the village. I went to my house. I stayed there for two or three days. But there was still reason to be afraid. The rebels had started to show up again. My sisters tell me, Get out of here. I left and went down to Argos. We had an uncle there, our cousins were there. They all stood by me. How many months was it? Almost a year. The Germans left. The December Uprising began. Everyone was now heading for Athens. Papadóngonas's cannons passed through. The ELAS Reserve troops came through. I met Panayótis Gagás in a kafeneío. Panayótis was a leftist. He'd gotten out of Haïdári. He was lucky. I was in Argos when the rebels first came there. We heard the church bells. The bells of the Virgin of the Clock tower. All the way from the castle you could hear it: The victors are coming. Panayótis Gagás says to me, Antónis, I know where the tide is heading . . . The ideal system of government has arrived. Panayótis said that. I left. The December Uprising was over now. The ELAS troops were starting to collapse, the British were driving them away. They began coming through Argos again. One night it was raining heavily. At a certain moment I hear Thanásis Drínis shouting. Marínos. Marínos Aryirákis. He was calling my uncle. I was asleep in one of the rooms in the front. I recognized his voice, he stuttered. Marínos. Marínos Aryirákis. Everyone else woke up too. I tell them, He belongs to ELAS. He was in Athens and now he's on his way back. He may be coming after me. My cousins tell me, go hide. Eighteen-, nineteen-year-old boys. My uncle says, Take the carriage out to the yard. They had a carriage, to go around their fields. Take it out, let it get wet, and you can hide underneath. Their house was big, it had a walled-in yard. The boys went down to open the stable, they dragged the carriage outside. I lay down underneath it. The rain was coming down in buckets. The man went inside. He wanted to sleep there, that's what he wanted. Marínos, my friend, he says to my uncle. Can I stay here? OK, you can stay. They made up a bed for him in one of the rooms. He was out like a light. Started snoring straight off. My cousins come in. Hotblooded boys. Let's kill him, they say. Let's kill him and bury him in the garden. I tell them, He left his buddies behind. He left his comrades and he told them where he would stay. And tomorrow they'll come after us, and kill us all. He slept, and he left the next morning. He left them an army of lice and went on his way. Because they'd given him clean clothes to wear. I stayed a few more weeks in Argos. Then I went back to the village. Things calmed down for a while. But not for long. I owe my life to Vanghélis Koutsoúmbis.

Chapter 17

The Germans came to Kastrí. They broke into our house. We were in Koubíla, Yeorghía stayed there. I left to go see what had happened. They had taken two shaggy bedcovers, they had them up at Xinós's place. They were sleeping there too. Then they decided to close up the house. And Pavlákos went and closed it up. And Réppas's old lady was screaming, Not the girls, don't touch their things. God rest her soul. I arrived in Kastrí. Haroúlis comes over, he tells me, Klaría, did you hear, they broke into your house, they took two bedcovers from you. But we had a suitcase belonging to Uncle Periklís in our house, full of things. And they took that too, the whole suitcase. There was a box from America, a metal box, with jewelry in it. My grandmother had brought it from Amaliáda, from the shrines of Saint Dionýsius and Saint Spyrídon. It disappeared. I found one of my dresses, a silk one, left on a fence. It was Diamantís Evanghelíou who took the suitcase. Because they were the ones who slept up there. Pavlákos told them, Who do you think you are, coming here to sleep? But in the meantime the things had been taken. I arrived in Kastrí. They didn't find the suitcase. Pavlákos told me all about it. About Evanghelíou. I tell this to Pítsa. What are you talking about, woman, she tells me, what are you saying? The covers, I tell her, they were ours. Anghelikí, Bisbís's wife, cuts in and tells her, They took those things from the Makríses' house, they brought them up to your place. And that's all she said. Haroúlis arrives, he says to me, Klaría, we have a shelter, get your things and take them there. I didn't know what sort of person he was yet. I went there, it was a small shelter, just a hole in the wall. I carried whatever things we still had over there. Iríni's sister helped me and we took them there. Two trunks, a chest, just like one we still have. We filled up both trunks. The Haloúlos sisters also took some of Old Man Boúrdas's things there. And Lámbros took medicine there, and Yiórgos Yiannakákos's wife took clothes. Just about the whole neighborhood did. The shelter was small but we packed it full up with things. And we kept guard there. Later on the Battalions arrived, our brother Yiánnis arrived, the girls go to him, they tell him, Yiánnis, let's open up the shelter, take our things, and divvy them out. And Yiánnis tells them, What are you saying, you girls, that we should give the hiding place away? Then Harís gave it away later on. It was Harís himself who gave it away. Kontalónis's division arrived to burn down the village. They started setting the fires. Sotiría hid in the clay oven to save herself. And when she came out that night she was all black. They had taken the rest of the people to Ayios Panteleímonas. And Yeorghía came back from halfway along the road. I don't know what excuse she found, but she saved her father's houses. Kontalónis himself was right there in their yard, and their houses were spared. The other houses were reduced to ashes. Harís told them where the shelter was and they went and ransacked it. They broke in, they took anything they could. They took the medicines, they took the clothes. They took everything. Yeorghía went there, she tells them, Hold on, you men, we have things there too. Boúras cuts her off. He's in an old-age home now in Trípolis. He says, Kapetán, she's with the Security Battalions, she can't take things. Because her brother-in-law is in Trípolis. He was talking about Iríni's husband. But Iríni had just married Vasílis and she and her sister weren't speaking, she and Yeorghía. And that's how Yeorghía was able to take a few things and save them. They took everything else. They didn't burn any of it. They took it all. I don't want to mention any names, whoever they were, well, anyway. And that Haroúlis who had set up that shelter and told people to put their things in there, he was the one who betrayed them. And Márkos's wife went there, and they sent her round every which way to find her clothes, to this village and that village. Her daughters' dowries.

They burned the village to ashes. They ransacked the shelter. And the year before last I went into Old Man Yiánnis's store — and we talked very specifically. Spýros Galaxýdis came in. There we were, me, Old Man Yiánnis, Nikólas Diamantís, and Kalamarás from Mesorráhi. Spýros comes over to me, he says, Who set the fire, do you know? No, I tell him, I don't know. And he says, Yesterday I met with Spyrópoulos, who was the section chief here. And he told me, Tell them in Kastrí it wasn't me who burned down your village. My village, Bertsová, was spared, I saved it. It was Yiánnis Velissáris and Haroúlis Lenghéris, they burned down your village. So don't let people from Kastrí go blaming anyone else. That's what he said. Yiánnis Velissáris and Haroúlis Lenghéris. Velissáris was killed. He was court-martialed, they told him to sign a renunciation of his Communist allegiance, he refused. He told all this to Léandros, Tsátsis's daughter's husband. He was the chief guard at the courthouse. Before he came here as a policeman, before he married Anthí. Léandros told him, Yiánnis, you've been betrayed. Impossible, he said. Yiánnis, you've been betrayed, because the others have all signed renunciations. Delivoriás who was the ringleader, and the rest of them. He told him this out of earshot, through the window. They were holding them prisoner in the basement of the courthouse. It's not possible they betrayed me, Velissáris said. To Léandros. Impossible. But even if they did, I'm not signing anything. I'm not having my hair cut off so I can get out. So they killed him. And what about Haroúlis, when *he* was held on that island, he never signed anything and they let him go free. And where do you think he was hiding when he gave the orders? During the big fire. But I heard this from someone else. And he didn't tell me this by chance. Well, Haroúlis was holed up in the sanctuary of the church in Karátoula. All of this back then. And many years later Yiórgos Kambýlis talked about it. I said I wouldn't mention any names. But how can I not give names? The year before last Tasía says to me, It was Haroúlis who burned down your house. Haroúlis and Kambýlis had quarreled, and Kambýlis got sore so he started telling on him. And he told his sister, It was him, he was hiding downstairs in Ayiánnis, and he and Babánis were liaisons, and he was sending messages with the names of people whose houses would be burned down. He was hiding in Ayiánnis in Karátoula. Right there in the church of Ayiánnis. In the sanctuary so he wouldn't be seen, and he was sending out those written messages. Haroúlis.

Chapter 18

In Sítaina they threw people into a pit. They beat them and they threw them in. And you could hear them moaning for days.

—What about Kókotas, Iríni?

—Kókotas, well, it's like this. Kókotas had married a woman from here. From Kastrí, Selímos's daughter. Dionýsius Selímos's daughter. They captured him when the rebel forces were on their last legs. Him, a man named Iliádis, and a lawyer named Tsangáris. Iliádis was a refugee. He had a carpet factory. And they threw them alive into that pit. In 1960 they went down to retrieve their bones, Kókotas's bones were at the top of the heap. He had climbed up, he tried to get out. And everyone said, Oh, come now, didn't they realize what was going to happen? A big, strong man like Kókotas, it wouldn't have taken much for him to get away. In ten days they'd all have been saved.

Chapter 19

They captured me in the beginning of 1944. Between the ninth and the thirteenth of January. Back then the only executions that had taken place were of the county prefect and two or three others. Random executions. In Háradros. Háradros is just below Hantákia. At the bottom of the Háradros River. But I don't know exactly where. When we passed through there they told us, This is where that traitor the county prefect was executed. All this in the month of January. They arrested me in Eleohóri. I had left Kastrí. It was still the olive-gathering season. Másklina. That's probably a Slavic place name. Then Másklina became Eleohóri. The detention camp was there before that. The detention camp where seven of the villagers were sent, the first ones. People who had nothing to do with political movements, simple folk, just poor unfortunate people. And they had no quarrel with anyone either. Most likely they took them to intimidate others. We have them here, we're holding those people. Almost like hostages. Because they'd never been involved in the Resistance or in anti-Communist activities or with the Germans. The Germans were there guarding the railroad lines. They were guarding the bridges, and they would come to the village once in a while when they were off duty to have a drink. And they didn't do anything at all. It was a small group, there weren't many of them. Well that's where they arrested me. At my house. I had a friend, he worked at a bank, a distant cousin, and Iphigenia was grilling some pork chops over charcoal. He was an employee of the National Bank of Trípolis. It was almost night. I didn't expect them to arrest me. I wasn't even afraid. My brother was in Athens, but he wasn't in the Battalions yet. The Battalions were formed later on. As a reaction to everything that had happened. To the arrests and the executions. Various men who had escaped to Athens, like Haloúlos, Nikólas Petrákos, and the rest, banded together under Papadóngonas and organized themselves. In Athens. They didn't come down to Trípolis until the month of April, early April, or maybe the end of March. I don't remember. Three men came to arrest me. They were from Mesorráhi. Tóyias and some others. They turned into butchers later on. I could have taken them out, but I didn't think they would do anything to me. In a hole in the wall under my bed I kept a pistol. I also had a bayonet, a sharp one, behind my coat. They were hanging on the door. I figured I could handle them, they were just a couple of thugs. But I thought of my sister. I was afraid for her. So I went with them. Since I couldn't take my bayonet, I didn't take my coat either. And I left in that cold winter weather. In January, without that coat. Without even my army jacket. They took me to Ayiórghis. We spent the night there. They turned me over to Vanghélis Farazís. Whose house I had stayed at in 1939 for two months. To help combat the olive tree fruit flies. I was working in the area and I stayed at his house. I knew his family, I liked them, and thought highly of them. Look here, Yiánnis, Vanghélis says to me. They had put him in charge of me. I know you can get away. I know you know your way around these parts. He didn't say anything else to me. But of course that was enough for me not to want to get him in trouble. In the morning we headed out on the road to Dolianá. Lower Dolianá. To Loukoú Monastery.[1] That was their transfer section. In a manner of speaking. They had taken over the monastery. There I first encountered the so-called merry evenings. There was a group of men and women from Dolianá. There was a priest's daughter there, and a schoolteacher's daughter. Who had once been a classmate of mine in Trípolis. Merry evenings, you can say that again. In the monastery we ate lentils. We were twenty-one prisoners in all. They put us in a cell. Not all of us were from Eleohóri. I lived in Kastrí too, in two places. Mítsos Karazános from Ayiasofiá. The secretary of the township. The father of Yiórghis Karazános. There were people from Dolianá too. They would put out one of those big pans for us, filled with lentils. There were twenty-one of us and they had some of us sit and some of us stand around that pan. And they gave us one spoon for all of us to eat with. All twenty-one of us with one spoon. Because that way no one could eat more than the rest. A very fair portioning out. The next day they sent us off to Orthokostá. The Orthokostá Monastery. Located on the other side of Mount Malevós. On the road from Ayios Andréas to Prastós. We passed through Astros, through the outskirts of Astros. On our way, in Karakovoúni, we met another column. With an armed escort. They were coming from Koúvli. From Rízes, from Dolianítika Chánia. With Yiánnis Vasílimis among the prisoners. An exceptional man, a progressive farmer, among the best in the area. And that splendid young man was taken to the detention camp by his own brothers. Who executed him later on. But I only know this through hearsay. We arrived in Orthokostá in the afternoon. The guards opened the gate. There was a sudden sense of alarm. Because there were guards there, and prisoners. They pushed us inside like cattle. They lined us up in the inner courtyard. Then, without letting anyone see he was approaching, Yiánnis Koïtsános comes over to me. He was from Parthéni, Trípolis. I knew him from high school, we were friends in high school. But at that moment, because I was so upset and tense, I didn't recognize him. I didn't remember him. I couldn't put a name to his face. On top of it all he had close-cropped hair and looked scrawny. They had cut everyone's hair, in fact. He came and stood next to me and he says to me under his breath, You don't know me and I don't know you. Don't talk in here, don't say anything, don't trust anyone. In other words, he gave me some advice that truly saved me. I found other people I knew in Orthokostá. Old classmates of mine. Níkos Kolokotrónis, but he was a rebel. A quiet man, didn't talk much. How or why he became a rebel is hard to know. There was a waiter there too, Yiórghis Katsarós. He served us coffee in Trípolis, at Antonákos's restaurant. Or up in Athanasiádis's workshop. Waxworks and Distilleries. He would come over with his round tray[2] hanging over his arm. He wasn't a Communist either. How he became one I don't know, why he did I can venture a guess. So they split us up, they put nine of us in one cell. Eight of us from Eleohóri and Mítsos Karazános. I don't remember if they gave us anything to eat. They must surely have given us something. In the morning they got us up to collect firewood. Some of our men were reluctant to go. I was more than willing. I wanted to have as little attention as possible paid to me. To get through whatever was in store for me easily. I had heard, and it turned out to be true, that during interrogations they performed what was called the Torture.[3] I mean beating you on the feet. They beat the soles of your feet with clubs or knotted rope. Just about crippled you. Well, I took the sharpest saw. They didn't give us axes, only saws. We might have found other uses for the axes. We climbed high up, we started cutting the wood. Mostly fir trees. We would cut them down, then cut the wood into pieces, some others would carry it away. Up until noon. Then they'd take us farther down to a clearing. And they trained us ideologically there. They also told us that we would remain there to await trial by the rebel tribunal. In the detention camp there were about seventy prisoners, as far as I can figure. From all over Arcadia, but mainly from the prefecture of Kynouría. Astros and around there. Dolianá. I don't remember anyone else from Kastrí. But there must have been others. And of course there were the ones from Eleohóri I mentioned, those seven. And from Ayiasofiá. From the whole prefecture. We heard there was another detention camp to the north of there. I wasn't able to learn exactly where. Whether it was in Elóna or at the Karyés Monastery.[4] At any rate it's certain that it existed. Because that whole camp followed ours at the beginning of February. When the Communists learned that the Germans were coming. That they were conducting operations on Mount Parnon, expressly to locate and liberate those two detention camps. Then an order came to move us to the Zíreia area. That happened during the third week of our detention. Up until we went on trial we did nothing. Almost nothing. Just the odd chore. We had nothing, we had no life. We were waiting for the arrival of the rebel judges. Anxiously awaiting them. To condemn us and put us to death in order to thin out the detention camp. Their purpose was not punishment but thinning us out to make room for new lodgers. Around that time I also found out what charges had been made against me. In addition to guilt by association with my brother. They told me that on my name day[5] I shouted Long live the Germans. On my name day I was having some wine with Yiánnis Daskoliás, who was also celebrating his name day. Daskoliás was in charge of EAM. We were at his house. As patriots and fellow villagers from Eleohóri. Of course he knew, he suspected that I wasn't a Communist. He knew that my brother was in Athens, for self-protection. And we were talking and discussing things. In fact he had entrusted his heavy pistol to me for a day. He had a heavy Browning pistol, and I had it for almost a whole day. So there we were talking things over. I had no reason not to talk, and he was testing me or something, I don't know what he was doing. Sounding me out. So this German walked in, drunk, and he started shouting, *Partisano, partisano.*[6] He had an automatic Steyr rifle, and he pretended to be shooting, killing rebels. That was the offense, and instead of charging the man whose house this happened at, they charged me with it. And claimed I'd said to the German: Over there, a partisano. A big fuss over nothing. Well, that was the charge. During our stay at Orthokostá we dug various trenches. Some said they were trenches for defense against the Germans, something that was unlikely, foolish, and impossible, others said they would simply be used as graves. We also brought water into the monastery garden. The spring was outside the yard, some ways off, about three hundred meters. And because we all wanted it, wanted that convenience, especially me, we said, Let's do it. We knocked down some old cells, we built ourselves a duct with roof tiles, and we brought water there. And that saved me. I had a habit from before of taking a cold shower every morning. So I would get under the spigot and wash myself. It wasn't exactly a shower, but I did at least bathe my head and my chest. To maintain my body's tolerance to cold. And that saved me, with all that snow, all that dampness. Our cell was damp. It was a dome and it had snow on top, and the cold would get in. And we slept with our bedding on the floor. In the detention camp there were four or five young women. A certain Alíki Maloúhou from Trípolis, she was my age, twenty-six. Alíki Maloúhou. She wasn't pretty, she wasn't particularly appealing, and she wasn't involved in any anti-Communist activities. I never understood why they took her. Why they sent her to the detention camp. Of course she was from a good family. They arrested her in Trípolis and they took her away from there. The Communists were organized, they had connections, they could do anything. And they did, including executing one or two women, if I remember correctly. I can't quite recall, but I do know one, they executed her for selling herself to the Occupation army. There were women then, and everyone knew this, who would do anything for a scrap of bread. So they could survive. And they executed one of them, right there on Taxiarhón Street. In broad daylight. A woman, she was just a girl. It was about that time that they captured Alíki. Alíki Maloúhou. And also Yiánnis Koïtsános from Parthéni. He was a ground air force major, he survived, he had a permanent commission, and he rose to the top, all the way to squadron leader. He was being held at the detention camp as a reactionary, and one of his sisters was with the rebels. The Koïtsános family has quite a history. Thanásis Koïtsános is a story in himself. He went so far as to wear a German uniform. He wasn't in the Battalions, he had nothing to do with the Battalions. He had enlisted in the German armed forces. The third brother, I can't think of his name, a tall fellow, was working for the Ministry of Health. And there were two more sisters, both school-teachers. They were all right-wing in their convictions, in other words anti-Communists. Except for the youngest sister, the rebel. She had spoken out, obviously under pressure, who knows. She had spoken out against her family. Death to my brothers. Death to my father. Death to this, and death to that. We had those women with us in the detention camp. They always slept in a special cell. As for food, of course there was some, usually beans, usually spoiled. Full of insects. Give us better food, some of us would say. Give us meat. They made bread in the monastery. Yiánnis Xinós, a prisoner, was put in charge of baking. A second cousin of mine, a cousin by marriage. One day they brought me a shoulder sack. It had a bottle of oil, a carton of one hundred loose cigarettes, even though I didn't smoke, and a loaf of bread. And olives. Sent from Astros. From a friend. An anonymous one, for obvious reasons. Although I searched repeatedly later on, I was never able to find out who sent those things. Maybe because he didn't survive the turmoil. I could say that we had it quite good in there. If it weren't for the agony over the rebel tribunal. The waiting. At night we used oil lamps for light. Small lamps, they didn't hold much oil. They would last until midnight. Yiórghis Katsarós would take care of them. The waiter. He served people in the detention camp too. One of his duties was to keep the lamps supplied with oil. Every night. And we would ask him — we all knew Yiórghis Katsarós. Everyone from Eleohóri knew him. And especially me. And we would ask him to please put extra oil in our lamp. So we'd have light after midnight. In the cell we all slept on the floor, and the light was a comfort to us. Light from oil. The cell was a dome, as I said before, and there was snow on top of the cell. It wasn't very cold, but it never stopped snowing. And it was very damp in there. The damp and the snow. One evening there was a knock on our door. It was late, it must have been almost midnight. At any rate the oil lamp was still burning. When we heard that knock everyone jumped up. Because it was always midnight when they took people, if they were supposed to take someone. Dránias, I heard Kolokotrónis say from outside. Trying hard to make his voice sound hard and tough. Poor fellow, he wasn't tough or hard. He was just a short, mild-mannered man. In high school he was one of the good students — and a good friend. I jumped up. Come here, come outside. Should I get dressed? No need. Should I take anything? No need. Of course we didn't wear pajamas. We didn't take off anything, not even our shoes. We slept like that, in our clothes. But can I just throw something over me? Come out here. I went outside. There was another cell on the right, and farther along to the right was a door where there were stairs that led to the courtyard. Four stone steps. Walk in front, he tells me. And I did. I walked. And I walked. When we passed the stairs I stopped. I thought, we're not going outside. We're not going to an execution. I'd had a bad fright, so had the others. Midnight. Keep going. I kept going. We came to a corner in the hallway. And we arrived at the guest quarters. The refectory, in other words. The fireplace was also there. I saw the fire. A big fire. I thought, we'll have an interrogation now. Get ready for the Torture. I took a few more steps. I could make out some shadows around the fire. I saw Yiánnis Xinós. He was holding a shallow copper mug. Come here, Cousin, he says to me. I sent for you. So you could have some tea. Tea, I say to him. My knees buckled under me. He slept early. And he had gotten up early to bake the bread. He was getting ready. After a while Kolokotrónis came back. He was standing in the doorway. He might even have been listening in. Let's go, Dránias. Because the others must be scared out of their wits. And he took me back to the cell. As soon as I stepped inside they all breathed a sigh of relief. And I did too. Only then. Horrifying. That game of theirs, Xinós and Kolokotrónis. Xinós was a prisoner, but he knew everyone. He's dead now. As for Kolokotrónis, our guard, I don't know if he's still alive. I never saw him again after that. There were ten other guards. Or fifteen. Three of them stood out somehow. But which of them was the chief and which wasn't, you couldn't tell. They would just strut around. They had good voices too. They said that one of them had graduated the seminary in Corinth. That he was on his way to a career as a clergyman. And he had taught the others. They would chant often. They knew the liturgy. They would chant in jest, of course. But I think there was nostalgia in their voices too. A feeling of loss. But they had no respect for books. They would tear them up and use the paper for cigarettes. To roll cigarettes. Someone had gone to Ayios Andréas and brought back a bag of fine-cut tobacco. Very good tobacco. And a goatskin full of wine. It was just a day or two before we left, no more. Before the order came for us to leave. We still didn't know the Germans were coming. And they let us have tobacco, they let us have wine. Among the prisoners there was an employee of the Prefecture. I don't know what part he played in everything. But he was a communications specialist. He had installed a telephone in a watchtower. To the north, on the upper slopes of the monastery grounds. And later on, farther down, for the villages. And for Astros. Always with an escort. He worked every day. Every day he went somewhere, to connect the lines. He was the one who alerted us. He got the telephone and he said, The Germans are coming. We moved out around the end of January. The twenty-eighth, twenty-ninth, or thirtieth of January. The thirtieth. The chiefs tell us, Time to move. Get ready, take whatever clothes you have, whatever you can take and let's go. They didn't tell us where. But we could tell from what we were doing that we were changing location. That something was up, in other words. The next day we learned that the Germans were really coming. We had left the monastery. There was a road there that we had come on. But we didn't take it. We walked in a different direction. And just at the bend of a large gully we ran into the other detention camp. The one to the north. Now I'm certain that they weren't from the Karyés Monastery, as they said, but from the Elónas Monastery. The rebels always used monasteries as concentration camps. And that one was bigger than ours. Because monasteries suited their purpose. Both for lodgings and for keeping us under guard. It was a larger detention camp, and it had a mixed population. Adults in their prime, of course. But also old people and very young children. They were from the Sparta area. From the prefecture of Laconía. And there were also laggards. A certain Kostákis. Kostákis Mémos, the village alderman of Mýloi. He'd lag behind because of the beatings during the Torture. He couldn't walk at all so they'd put him up on a mule. And so we arrived at Háradros. In the area around Háradros. Places I'd heard about. In this same area they had executed the man who was county prefect at that time. We found that out from overhearing the careless chatter of the rebels escorting us. I think they leaked certain information on purpose. How they killed him, how they pulled out his nails with a pair of pliers. To make him reveal where he'd hidden the gold sovereigns. They had arrested him and accused him of selling food belonging to the Prefecture. He had sold it and didn't give it to the people when the Occupation forces were moving in. I'm in no position to know what happened. But those were the charges, and that's why they executed him. Then we made our way up the neck of the mountain. We bypassed the town of Háradros. By now it was clear that we were heading toward Galtená and Stólos. Our own villages. The winter lodgings of the villagers from Kastrí. We arrived in Galtená at night and ended up at Diamantákos's olive press. Both detention camps. A hundred and sixty-six people, including children and the elderly. In the morning they took us outside. The weather was beautiful. It was the day of the Presentation at the Temple. The second of February. We could see the festivities across the way in the Community of Plátanas, and there we were sprawled out, squashing lice. Out in the sun in the delightful warmth of February. That's when we received notice that the Germans were coming. Then Kléarhos arrived. He came from Astros. He was in charge of that area, and he came to take over as chief of the two detention camps, and to take us to Zíreia. Then word got out that the escape routes were closed and that there was an order for our execution. For both detention camps. On the same day Yiánnis Velissáris also passed by with a small group of men. That reinforced the rumors about execution. Yiánnis, the Farmakídis boy said to him. Stávros Farmakídis. The nephew of Yiórghis Farmakídis, the short one. Yiánnis was like a brother. We had grown up together. If there was a loaf of bread to be had, our families would share it. Yiánnis wasn't a Communist. But he felt he had failed as a lawyer and maybe his disappointment led him to that. Twenty-six years old, just like me. At any rate he came to Galtená. Yiánnis was unarmed, as usual. He hated guns. Even during the Albanian campaign he avoided them. He would tell us stories about the army, about his captain. His reservist captain, also a lawyer. Kalathás. Lots of stories. Yiánnis, Stávros Farmakídis says to him. Let's get Dránias out. They were just passing through. And Yiánnis says, After all he's done, let the son of a bitch die. He called me a son of a bitch, me. They shot him later by order of a military court. He refused to renounce his former allegiance. He was stubborn. He wouldn't renounce his allegiance like his superiors did. Níkos Delivoriás and the others. Sworn Communists. They signed a paper. It was just another foolish government practice. But it gave them the right to ask for a pardon. Because they had renounced their beliefs. And said they were no longer Communists. And Yiánnis, who was never a Communist, refused to sign. Stávros was killed differently. A few months later. Also unjustly. In July of that year. During the big blockade of the village. By some hotheads or other. Not Germans. Hotheads from Kastrí. Well, in any case. We were gathered in Galtená. In Galtená. The execution order had been given. The Germans were approaching. And the villagers from Kastrí started to leave. To head away from there, because they were afraid of the Germans. All the villagers. Lámbros Chrónis, Kourvetáris, Athanasíou. Ismíni Athanasíou. She gave me a bag of raisins. And as soon as he saw me Lámbros started crying. They had heard the news. They knew about the execution. Some other men came through then. Chrístos Kokkiniás, and Thanásis Kosmás. They took them to the detention camp later on. Because the detention camp was reopened. Dínos Pantazís. Lots of men. All the men. They were leaving the village, getting away from the Germans. They came down there. They'd give me cigarettes, they'd give me bread. I didn't smoke. And I had decided to escape. We were approaching Eleohóri, I knew my way around there. My mind was on that. How to get away. In the end the execution never took place. Kléarhos refused to do it. He asked for a written order. They had run telephone lines and everything was arranged by telephone. Kléarhos asked for the order in writing. So the following day we walked across, from Galtená to Ayiórghis. And that's where we spent the night. In Ayiórghis, on Farazís's threshing floors. I had started out from there, and ended up there. In the evening Kóstas Sámbos came by, the German. He had the mill in Koubíla. That was his nickname, the German. Nothing to do with what happened back then. He was simply the German. And he brought us a bucketful of wine. His brother-in-law was with us, Pétros Tsélios. He called us over: Come and drink some water. A bucketful of wine. We pounced on that bucket, we emptied it. Night fell, the rebels disappeared. The cold set in, and they took shelter in various houses. They were sure of us. They had left guards. We would be sleeping out in the fields. With a blanket, or half of one. Someone said the old people and the children should move to the center of one of the threshing floors. Then the women. And then the men, back to back. To make a wall against the wind. Just below the threshing floors was Kóstas Papakonstantínos's house. It had a cement staircase outside. I saw a fire through the window. There was a fire burning. I went up the stairs to go inside. I knew Kóstas. I opened the door. Then I hear Kléarhos's voice. What's he doing here, get rid of him. I turned to leave.

Kléarhos and I were friends. We had no quarrel, no differences. Nothing between us. I knew that, and so did Kléarhos. I turned to leave. He jumped to his feet then, laughing. He came and took me by the arm. Sit down and warm up, man. And the next day, crack of dawn, we started our uphill trek, over the cobblestones of Ayiórghis. Our camp was in front. The road was hard, and the rebels pushed us on. They had information that the Germans were coming down from the village of Korýtes. In two columns. They had passed Kastrí and they were heading down toward Ayiasofiá. We had to change direction. To head for Mávri Trýpa. A canyon with smooth red rocks full of caves. Caves like female parts. At any rate, despite the red rocks the place is called Mávri Trýpa.[7] On the border of Ayiasofiá and Eleohóri. Four kilometers from Ayiánnis. There was a goat trail the first half of the way. After that it disappeared. Alíki Maloúhou was walking in front of me. The poor girl was inexperienced. She had unattractive legs, her shins were abnormally thick. I tried to help her climb over some rocks. Then we heard a shot. Then another one. They told us they had executed Kostákis. Kostákis Mémos, the village alderman of Mýloi. Because he was a laggard. He was up on a mule and they executed him. They shot him twice. He didn't fall down with the first shot, he fell with the second. Afterward we came to a sheep pen. There someone said, Go down to the ravine, go down to the ravine. Then the Germans saw us. They were heading our way, and they started firing. But they fired in the air. We threw ourselves into the ravine. The Germans were shouting something, we didn't understand. We had a man with us named Grigóris Kostoúros. A Reserve officer from World War I. He ran the Boúrtzi fortress in Náfplion until 1940. He used it as a hotel for tourists. And he knew German. Grigóris, Yiánnis Vasílimis says to him. Vasílimis was also from Dolianá. Shout that we're prisoners. Kostoúros shouted. And he took off a shirt, a white shirt. The Germans say, Stand up. And that all happened right there. In the area around Mávri Trýpa. It was getting dark out. Night was falling in that barren sheep pen. We all stood up. Next to me was Yiánnis Koïtsános. He says to me, We can leave them and go to the Germans. No, I tell him. Pétros Tsélios was still there, and another man, and an old woman. I didn't know her, I never saw her again. I tell them, Come with me. I know these parts. We can make it safely to the village. To Eleohóri. But only Koïtsános came over to me. The others had moved out of the ravine. With their hands in the air. They had surrendered to the Germans. We lay low for a while, waiting for them to move farther away. The rebels who were escorting us had also run away. So we walked along the riverbed. Then we came to the Másklina olive groves. There the Germans began shooting up flares. We hit the ground until they stopped. At around midnight we arrived at Liátsis's storage sheds. Behind Ayía Paraskeví, I knew the Liátsis family. They gave us olives and bread. We ate. And they tell us, Now you'd better go because the rebels will be coming round again. They pass through here. We left. I say, Let's go to our vineyard. We went to the top of Mount Kafkalás. It was almost dawn. There were thickets, and the vineyard. My thickets, my vineyard. The vineyard would conceal us. It would save us. It was across from the village. Then it turned very cold. The morning frost. We were freezing. Come daybreak, we saw the activity down below. The prisoners from both detention camps had gathered at the station. Everyone had gathered at the station. The Germans and the prisoners. At about seven a train arrived from Trí-polis and took them away. It was very light out now. I turned to Yián-nis Koïtsános then. What do we do now? I say to him. The Germans were gone. He was curled up from the cold, frozen. Now we can go to our villages, he says. And that's what we did. He left for Parthéni. I stayed in Eleohóri. My sister Iphigenia was there, I couldn't do other-wise. I thought the Communists would look favorably on what we did. Because we didn't go with the Germans. The next day they came and put me in charge of the press and of indoctrination. Me. I didn't want to be connected to them. I tell them, I can't. They tell me, Yes you can. And they sent me to Ahladókampos. Where they had never man-aged to have any influence. The villagers from Ahladókampos were nationalists through and through. Wanted nothing to do with the Communists. So were the villagers from Karátoula. But they never joined the Security Battalions either. There was Yiórghis Baláskas. An artillery officer. A lieutenant. He kept them all close to him. That's why they killed them. No battle, no nothing. They arrested them and they killed them. Just after the Liberation. Right in front of their houses. One by one. About seventy men. I had to go down there then. I couldn't do otherwise. I spoke to some people. They knew me, my hair was cut very close. They knew why it was like that. They knew who I was, what I believed. I tell them, We're like an egg between two rocks. We set up a phony organization. I went back to Eleohóri. Until March when Papadóngonas came down. My brother Kóstas came down. Liberation was coming any day now. Then the whole prefecture, there were no other options, everyone in Eleohóri and in Kastrí, we all joined the Battalions. Approximately the end of April or possibly May. At any rate, except for Kostákis Mémos, as far as I know all the other prisoners from Orthokostá survived. From the detention camp at that time, I mean.

We had stayed there, two families. The Makrís and the Koutsoyiánnis families. Yeorghía had left for Kastrí. Yiánnis Koutsoyiánnis
went there. Who was the village police sergeant at that time. Now he's
retired. He went to get the sprayer from Vanghélis Farazís. On his way
there he finds Themistoklís Anagnostákos. Where are you going, Yiánnis? I'm going to get the sprayer, going to spray. Don't go get the
sprayer, go and tell your family and the Makríses to clear out. Because
tonight they're coming to take us all away. Who said so? Mihális Siou-
rroúnis. Mihális was involved in the Organization back then. Oh, come
on, says Yiánnis, and he keeps going to get the sprayer. You stubborn
fool, Themistoklís shouts. Turn back. You haven't got time. They're
coming any minute to arrest us. I'm locking up and leaving. But there
wasn't time for him to lock up. He was tying his shoes when the rebels
arrived, and they arrested him. The rest of the story goes like this. We
hid ourselves anywhere we could find. I mean the men, our men,
went and hid. Koutsoyiánnis came from Ayióighis. He says, Get ready
to leave because Themistoklís said such-and-such. There's two of you,
three of us, and the Aryírises are another two. We had just baked some
bread. It was Saturday. Nikólas tells him, Who told Themistoklís that?
And he says, Mihális, little Mihális. Siouroúnis. He told him, They're
going to arrest you tonight, they're going to execute you. That's their
plan. They sent a notice from Kastrí. Now who sent the notice, I don't
know. Nikólas says to our mother, Give us a loaf of bread. We're
leaving. They started whispering. And don't you go talking, no matter
who comes here. Of course not, who would we be talking to? Our

parents were protecting themselves too. Out here in the wilderness, who would be talking to us? The men left, they went down along the riverbed. They find Máïnas there. Where are you men going? To catch us some crabs. They came out at the fenced monastery in Mesorráhi, they went and hid in some haystacks. From there they sent word, they arrived outside of Másklina, our relatives came and got them. Máïnas goes back to Ayiórghis. Liás, he says to Anagnostákos. Liás was in charge of Ayiórghis. Liás, those sons of bitches got away. Weren't you on guard? he says to him. And they went up to Kastrí to give them a report. They got away? they asked them in Kastrí. They got away, they said. What do we do now? Burn them down, said Haroúlis. In any case, we knew nothing at all. We were just waiting. They had burned down Ayiasofiá. And as we're there waiting, the next day Máïnas arrives. He had come back from Kastrí. He comes over to us. Do you live down here? We say yes. Yeorghía too? What about Yeorghía? says our mother. Nothing, nothing, Ma'am. They had captured Yeorghía in Kastrí and he knew about that. He says, What are you going to do now? What are we going to do, we'll stay put. He says, If your men don't report to us they'll take you away and burn down your house. They may even kill you. We started shaking. They had burned down Ayiasofiá. Then the Battalions came to Ayiórghis. That's when Kyriákos hit the old lady. He banged the door with the butt of his gun. Trýfonas arrives at that moment. As soon as they saw the old lady, they said, Where's your old man? And Kyriákos gave her a good smack. He pushed her. Why are you hitting the old lady, our brother Nikólas says to him. What has she done? Quiet, he answers. And he smashes in the door with the butt of his gun. The barrel was turned toward him now, it went off, and he fell and died on the spot. In front of Nikólas. Right there in front of him. The others came running, the officer went over, What's going on, Well, it's like this. Did someone else kill him? No, he did it himself. He still had his finger on the trigger. They picked him up, and they stole things off him. They took his watch and his ring. And Nikólas said, He had a watch and a ring on his hand, who took them? They had taken those things themselves. In the end they found them. When we heard that someone had been killed in Ayiórghis we were half crazy. Meantime, two men appear down below. We're sitting on the threshing floor, down near the mulberry tree. How are you, Auntie, how are you, Tseví? They say to my sister-in-law. And we don't even recognize them, we're so confused. It's me Auntie, it's me Tseví, Spýros Yiatrídis. And I'm Nikólas Petrákos. Did anyone bother you? No, we say, no one. We didn't say anything about Maïnas. They say, Get ready, your men are coming now, they're in Ayiórghis. Soon as they said that Nikólas appeared. I'd hidden the rifle, and I'd hidden the shot and the shells. Yiánnis suddenly shows up. The rifle, he says to me, where is it? I say, Over there. And the cartridges are there, he lifts up a floorboard, You'll find them under there. They tell us, Get ready, we're leaving. And we left everything behind. We got out of there. They brought Kyriákos, we all went to Másklina. They'd put him up on the mule. On the mule, like a slaughtered pig. Nikólas put two boards together, they wrapped him in a sheet. And they tied him. We went to Másklina. Then they say, There's a fire in Koubíla. You could see smoke, we could see it rising. They're saying, They burned down the Makríses' houses, they burned down the olive press. And they destroyed the mill. What could we do? We went there, we found everything in shambles. We picked up the broken things and threw them away. They had burned down both houses. They had emptied the winepress. They'd taken the oil, as much as they could. They'd taken the cheese. We found one head of white cheese still hanging, that's what they left. And one earthen jar, it held fifteen okás[1] of oil. They'd taken it to another house. Those things were saved. The rest were useless except maybe to bathe in. The wine all spilled. We found a puddle of oil up in the olive press. And the barrels up above, with holes in them, the oil spilled on the ground. Whatever they couldn't carry off. A complete disaster. They took clothes, they took everything. We had some other things, not ours, from the laundering trough.[2] Things from Ayiasofiá and Tservási. Brand-new blankets and linens for dowries. We'd taken them out, we had them in the lower part of the house. We had a laundering trough at the mill. They told us they'd left them piled up outside on a rock. We didn't find anything. A woman from Mesorráhi told us. Yiannákis Galioúris's mother. Yiannakákis's[3] mother. She told us they were going up and down with lights, all night long. They saw them inside, they saw Yeorghía, Asímos's daughter, coming out all loaded up. Then Kóstas Diamantákos fired a shot. He says, Klaría, I saw the devastation, I saw what was going on then in there and I fired my rifle. I fired a shot and I said, Germans. With the word Germans they ran off every which way. They left. We found out who burned down our houses, we found out years later. They went to Kastrí. Our cousins were hiding in the vineyard. Down below, in Ayía Paraskeví. They were hiding from the rebels. Maria and Olga. Sotíris's girls. And a group of them comes out of Kambýlis's place, with Pótis Lenghéris at their head. The villagers from Karátoula ran into them. They were coming from down below. Where are you going, you men? We're going to burn down Koubíla. And they went and burned it down. That's what they heard, our cousins. A group of them came out of Kambýlis's place, and Kambýlis was with them, Yiórgos himself. He admitted it, he didn't hide it. They took me with them, he said. I did whatever they told me to. He was the one who broke the storage jars. And Kambýlis's wife Evanthía, many years afterward, says to my mother, Konstantína, I'm going to tell you something but you mustn't say another word about it. They had brought some heads of cheese from Koubíla and left them in Tsoúmas's basement. And Rigoúla would go there every so often and cut some, and the whole place smelled so good. But why mention their names now? All they left us was that head of white cheese hanging there.

Chapter 21

I dreamt about Dimítris last night. He was laying the foundation
for a house with Thanásis Yiánnaros and Old Man Bakoúris. Right on
the road, in front of the Biroúlis property. Poor Dína. In the morning she had Martha ask me to go light the oil candles at the Ayiánnis
church.

—Martha? I say to her.

She started to cry.

—Our Yiórgos, he's not well, Marigó.

Her voice kept fading over the telephone. That was the bitter cup
destined for poor Dína.

Chapter 22

When did they burn down the village? It was on Saint Ilías's Day. In 1944. In '44 on July 20. They had burned down seven houses before that. Seven houses four months earlier. In the spring. First off they burned down the two Kyreléis houses. One where Tambákis is now and the other was Anna Kyreléis's. It was their paternal homestead. Seven houses in all and then in July on Saint Ilías's Day.

—When is Saint Ilías's Day?

—July 20. They burned down 170–180 houses.

—Where were you?

—In bed, I was asleep. They came into the house, they broke down the door. Five o'clock in the morning. They took us out and they gathered us at the telephone company. It was an empty lot back then where they kept cars, but there were no cars there, they'd all been requisitioned during the Albanian campaign. Only Galaxýdis's gazo-gene truck was there. Up above was Old Man Boúrdas's house. And right below was Méngos's kafeneío. And on the floor above a hotel, none better in all of Greece. They'd set up their machine guns there and crowded us all into that empty lot. All the villagers. At five o'clock in the morning. Five-thirty. The smart ones began slowly sneaking away. Because they saw the machine guns, they could see what the rebels' intentions were. Seven-thirty, eight o'clock. They kept us there in the sun until ten. And then they took us to Ayios Panteleímonas.

—How many of you were there?

—All of Kastrí. And people from Mesorráhi and from Karátoula and from Roúvali. They had gathered all the so-called reactionaries.

The reactionaries against the Communist Party. All of them. Under the command of Prekezés and Kontalónis. That's right. They took us to Ayios Panteleímonas, in the middle of a pine wood. But their liaisons and the lookout post saw at about twelve that the Germans were coming from Trípolis. And they gave a signal. They set up a committee then and started to pick out who had or didn't have a brother or a father or a relative in the Security Battalions. And whoever didn't they let go. Meantime the houses were burning, One hundred eighty houses. From five-thirty in the morning. It was six o'clock when they started.

—You mean while they were holding you on the phone company lot?

—First they gathered us there. And first they set fire to Panayótis Háyios's house. Used the same broomstick for Strífas's house. Then Horaítis's place. They burned down Méngos's kafeneío. The best hotel in Greece. And from there, with the same broomstick they torched one house after another.

—Were there any local people in their ranks?

—That seven-member committee did quite a job.

—Who was in the seven-member committee?

—Six men and one woman. The most important member was — I hesitate to say.

—Tell me.

—The woman, the one who voted to burn down the village, was Eléni Gagás. Maiden name Eléni Tólias. She was the one. The others had no say.

—What happened to the others?

—They all died. They were killed.

—Haroúlis?

—Yes.

—Who else?

—From what I was told. Because I was thirteen years old then. Yiánnis Velissáris. Yiórgos Velissáris. I'm not sure about Yiórgos. One of the two. There were seven in the committee. They'd managed to persuade them, to scare them into voting to burn down Kastrí. But most of the blame was hers.

—Okay, you said that. Do you know about any others?

—Magoúlis, Haroúlis, Velissáris, three. Eléni four. I don't remember the others. It's been forty years. You start to forget, you say to hell with them.

—Then what happened? After the fire?

—When they burned down the houses. They didn't leave anything standing. A hundred and eighty houses. And every household had two or three girls. All the houses had two or three dowries. If anyone still remembers such things. Because before the Occupation every girl had to have whatever she needed for the rest of her life. And she had to make it herself by hand. Sheets woven on the loom, blankets, towels, everything. They had to make it all themselves. A thousand and one things. Even a sewing machine. So that some day when they married they'd be ready to set up house. That's right. Now some had dowries and others didn't, but I know one thing. From Kastrí all the way to Palaiohóri, Kynouría, they had requisitioned all the mules.

—And they'd carry off the dowries.

—Whatever was in the houses. Burned down or not. The houses were looted.

—Did you see the mules leaving from where you were?

—We saw them. After they freed us. Because a signal came that the Germans were coming from Trípolis. With the local men in the Battalions. That's when they let us go. But when the Security Battalions got here the houses were nothing but ashes.

—And *they* burned the rest down.

—They burned three or four houses. In retaliation. But not the same day. They came back later. To retaliate. Against Velissáris, and Mávros.

—Yes.

—Because Níkos Mávros was also a ranking member.

—Kapetán Foúrias.

—Kapetán Foúrias. The worst, the most barbaric of the lot, here in Kastrí. While the Velissáris brothers, we could say by comparison, they were restrained. One was a lawyer, and the other a soft-spoken type, he had actually finished high school, they kept their distance. But not Kapetán Foúrias. But the thing I remember is . . .

—About the fire?

—About the fire. It's that complete strangers came here, and they had their informants here, and they showed them where my mother or yours or this one or that one had hidden their things, and they'd tell on them, and they went and opened those so-called shelters and took those things. And that's the story of the big looting.

Chapter 23

We loaded up the chestnuts. To haul all through the night. We passed Sourávla, we arrived down outside Ayios Pétros. Was it the devil playing tricks, or was it the smell of blood—three years since Fotiás was killed there, the mules wouldn't set foot there. We couldn't see a thing.

Chapter 24

They arrested me in place of Márkos and our uncle the doctor.
My uncle had left first. Márkos later on. Toward the end of November. There'd been a light snow, about two fingers high. In February,
the seventh or fourteenth of the month. And it had frozen. Two rebels
came by, strangers. Which of you is Eléni? I am. At daybreak. They
took me to Mángas's house. Old Man Dínos Haloúlos was there.
Yiannoúkos's father. And Biniáris I think. And the Bráilas woman.
Aunt Eléni Kyreléis with Kikí. And Kyriákos Galaxýdis. They took us
down to Loukoú Monastery. Old Dínos had a shaggy wool cover. I
don't remember if I took blankets. I must have taken something. They
might have brought me something. At Loukoú we found others.
Eléni Roúgas. Pétros's mother. She was crying all the time, she
wouldn't eat anything. I tell her, Whatever happens to us, we'll get
through it. Mítsos Kapetanéas was there, and Chrístos Panayotoúros.
From Stólos now living in Kastrí. Stólos was nearby, they brought
them food, they brought meat to those men. They'd grill the meat.
As though it were Carnival. One day they let us go out. The rebels
were guarding us, and we went outside the stone-fenced yard of the
monastery. A sunny February day. I thought about running off. About
escaping. But where would I go? My folks were in Kastrí. They had
stayed there. Old Mavroyiórghis and Mavroyiórgaina. They'd be the
ones who would pay for it. In about a week's time they got us up. At
night, it was raining. Get up, we're going. They didn't tell us where.
They just took us. We passed by Astros. I had on some thin wooden
shoes, they came apart, I walked barefoot. My feet were all cut. We

reached Orthokostá at daybreak. Fifty or sixty people. Maybe less. We went into the monastery. Instead of asking for some warm water I put my feet in a water trough. And I fell sick. I came down with a fever. We slept on the same mattress, me, Aunt Eléni, and Kikí. A couple of days later my parents send me a basket, or rather a shoulder sack, from Kastrí. Eggs, walnuts, dried figs. But it all had to be inspected. With a fine-tooth comb. The rebels kept half of it, they gave us the other half. They had nothing either. We found out that Penelope Kaloútsis was leaving, they'd soon be letting her go. So I wrote a letter. I wrote it in front of Kikí. I wrote about how we were doing. I wrote them not to send us things because they kept them. I was planning to give it to Penelope, to hide and take with her. So she could give it to them. But what with my fever and all I forgot in the end. Luckily. They got Penelope in the end. She had a patchwork woolen quilt, they put her up on a mule. And a rebel escorted her. Was it Vasílis Tóyias maybe? I don't remember. Kikí says to me the next day. Kikí Kyreléis. See Penelope's quilt? They'd left it on the stone fence. They'd folded it. We spent our time there in the yard. Walking. Up and down. Kyriákos Galaxýdis was there. Someone named Tálas from Trípolis. Someone else named Krígas, old Liás Krígas, from Rízes. Whose house is on the right as you enter the village. And a young fellow named Yiórgos, I see him in Trípolis, that fellow. He sells gasoline now, I can't remember his last name. Everyone took a liking to me. All of them. Kyriákos Galaxýdis would pace back and forth all the time. A nervous man, with a long face. And all he would talk about was his car. About the tires or about one thing or another. Finally he would stop and he'd look outside. Do you see Mount Malevós? Kastrí is on the other side. When they let us go we'll cut right through the brush, and we'll get there. One day the abbot came over to me. The monastery had a few monks. Not too many. They didn't let them speak to us. Are you Mavroyiórghis's daughter? I am. Do you know I'm a friend of your uncle Ayisílaos? Uncle Ayisílaos lived in Astros and rented the land from the monastery. Olives and the like, he worked the land for profit. On the twentieth of March the rebels get us up. We were leaving. For where, no one knew. The abbot calls me to his cell. He gives me six fresh eggs. Make a hole in them, he tells me, and suck on them. There was no food to take with us. The abbot was getting on in years. I would look around his cell. He had a hand made from bone, he had it hanging, a hand with wood, with a handle. What's that, Father? My child, I have no wife to scratch my back. And that's what it's for. I was downright amazed. The rebels got us up. There was a justice of the peace in the detention camp. From Vlahokerasiá. Kikí and I went to see him. He couldn't stand up. His legs were like barrels, black and blue underneath. They would take him outside the monastery, beat him, and bring him back. They got us up on the twentieth of March, they took us up the mountain. We came to a ravine. The rebels escorting us stopped, they made us stop. And we waited for some liaison. We learned later on that they were waiting for an order, whether to kill us or not. Whether they would kill us all in that ravine. The Germans had learned about our detention camp. They had captured a caïque from Ayios Andréas with army boots that were meant for the rebels. And the rebels were afraid that they would come and free us. They didn't kill us. Night came and went. The next day they took us farther up. We came to a sheep pen. Nothing there but a shed with a small high window. That served as both the window and the door. They put us in there, they cut down some fir trees, they lit a fire. The shed filled up with smoke. There was a prisoner there with us called Bebéka, just a girl. She was pregnant. But she didn't look it. Bebéka was her name, she wasn't married. There may have also been two boys. I think they were from Loukoú. There were about forty of us all told. The shed filled up with smoke, we say, Let's get out, we'll suffocate, and they let us out. We went outside, it was snowing. There were fir trees, the snow would fall, by the time it reached the ground it would melt. And there was a hush in the air, a silence. We saw some lights off in the distance, Kikí says to me, That's Athens. That's how high up we were. Now I think it was probably Argos. In the morning they gave us half a boiled potato. That's all they had. We went outside to urinate. Kikí and I went a bit farther out, and we saw some blood. That Bebéka, her belly gave out. Seems she gave birth to the child in the night and died. Either it was her time or she miscarried, what with all the hardship. I don't know. A skinny young thing, pretty. Two days later they took us back down to Orthokostá. Outside the yard they had dug out a grave. At the edge of the road. They'd covered it up, the dirt was still fresh, they'd thrown some branches over it so it wouldn't show. We never saw the justice of the peace again. Then Broúsalis arrived, a lawyer from Bertsová, and Níkos Delivoriás, I don't remember the rest. They were the Central Committee for the Peloponnese. They were the head men. They put us in the church of the monastery, they talked to us. They asked us if we'd been treated well. We had no complaints. In other words they'd never beat us, they'd never tortured any of us. Whatever discomfort they had, we had too. The men guarding us. They tell us, The detention camp is being dismantled tomorrow. You're leaving. I ask, Can we leave today? Anyone who wants to can leave. It was March 27. Or maybe 26. They got ready. Kyriákos Galaxýdis. Old Liás Krígas. Tálas and that Yiórgos. Maybe Biniáris was with them. Vasílis. It was probably just those four. It was in the afternoon of March 27 or 26. I tell them, I'm coming with you. They didn't want to take me. We'll be sleeping in sheep pens. Then I will too. So I started out. With those four men. We made our way through the brush, we kept pushing forward. When there was a wall they would get hold of my hand and help me over. I was wearing a simple two-piece outfit, made from one of our brother Márkos's suits. I'd burned it with the iron, and he'd given it to me. Right between the wild pear trees and the gorse it began to come apart. In the end I grew tired. Night came. I realized I couldn't go on. I say, Where are we, they tell me, At Asómatos. Old Sotíris Kóllias used to spend the winter there. They had olives, they had land. I say, I'll go and find them. Tálas took me part way down. I reached the village easily from there. I found a woman, I asked her. She showed me the house. And I went there. The girls greeted me with tears. We went to sleep. In the morning Voúla says, We're leaving. We're going back to Kastrí. But we can't put you on the mule. We're taking the animals, we have things to carry. We got up in the morning. With the ewes tied, with the hens on the mule, it took us thirteen hours to get there. Word had got out they'd cut off my hair. They'd cut off Marina's hair then, Aunt Ioulía Velissáris's daughter. The Security Battalions. And Christina would go round the neighborhood crying and saying, They cut off our sister Eléni's hair. We arrived at the village. They ask me about Penelope Kaloútsis. Oh no, I tell them. Penelope left twenty days ago. She hadn't gone to Kastrí. She hadn't gone to Ayiasofiá. They had homes in both villages. And what were the people from Ayiasofiá anyway? Most of them were from Karátoula too. And then someone says, Let's all mourn for Penelope. They understood. Several days went by. It was the time of the Salutations.[1] I went to church. I found Aunt Eléni there, I found Kikí Kyreléis. They had left the detention camp the next morning. After me. Whoever stayed behind, whoever didn't get out quickly, they kept. The Braílas woman and some others. Because a new order came not to dismantle the camp. So I saw Aunt Eléni there, I saw Kikí. We were all hugging and kissing, crossing ourselves, lighting candles because we'd made it home. Kikí didn't tell me a thing. They were planning to run away to Trípolis and Athens. And they left right after church. Next morning in the square I see rebels, strangers, looking at the house. Watching our house. Intently. They were talking, I think Haroúlis was with them, God forgive him. Well, anyhow. I tell my mother, They're going to arrest me again. What are you saying, Child? I tell her, I'm leaving. I'm going to Athens. If they come here tell them I've gone to our koumbároi in Perdikóvrisi. To the Nikoláous. We were their godparents, my father had baptized Dimítro and Uncle Menélaos had baptized Eratosthénis. Uncle Menélaos gave them quite some names. He had a fondness for such names. I go up to Athiná's place. Unfortunately for me Rigoúla was there. Haroúlis's wife. She saw me. Now what do I do? Rigoúla went and told Haroúlis. I put on a kerchief. So, it was them, it was them. They were the ones got our Níkos all worked up. Well, anyhow. I put on a kerchief, I say, Maybe they won't recognize me. And I walk straight through the square, so as not to arouse any suspicions. With my legs shaking,

and me fighting to hold steady so no one could tell. I arrive at Horaítis's house in Lákka. There were some trees up above, and it was very
windy and they were howling. Mr. Manólis, sir, God has placed me
at your mercy. Horaítis worked at the bank up until the war. Before it
closed. He sends word to Yiórgos Haloúlos. Who had seen me. They'd
put him in charge, they were mobilizing at the time. Yiórgos Haloúlos arrives. They were in the dark down there. Two days go by. Then
they send a message to Horaítis to type up a notice that they would
give a certain amount of money to whoever could find me. Or tell
them where I was. So many millions. That's what money was worth
during the Occupation. They went and put it up in all the kafeneía.
Written on his typewriter by Manolákis himself. I stayed for a week
at his house. His girls were there, Póli and Nítsa, and the boys. But I
couldn't stay any longer. We were all in danger. One night Dimítris
Kokkiniás appears, with Antónis Kapniás and Thanásis Vozíkis. Nighttime, midnight. They take me. We crawl along till we reach Kavasális's
place. Aretí came out. She gave us a loaf of bread. There was an empty
house next to theirs, belonged to Eléni, the sexton's sister. The widow
of Yiórghis Kosmás, who was killed in Albania. He had left her with
a young daughter, and Eléni was away in Astros. They had the key. Or
the house was just empty. There was a big crate there, and on top of
it was a mattress, made from burlap, with corn husks for matting. And
that's where I slept. The place was full of rats. I was terrified. It had a
fireplace, made from a large tin pail. So the three sons, they kept
watch every night. They slept next door to me, in the other half of the
house. It belonged to the sexton. And every night they would knock
on the wall to see how I was doing. They'd leave me some bread outside, some water. And I stayed in there. All day long. I'd look out the
window, I'd see rebels passing by. They would shout, Eléni, to find
me. They didn't know me. I stayed ten days on my own. All alone. I
started feeling weak. From hunger and inactivity. And from fear. I say
to myself, Let them kill me, and I decided to give myself up. I got up,
in the early hours, and went outside. Across the way from Thalís
Kapetanéas's house was the Chrónis place. They had a "water-tap"

hung out on the balcony, a makeshift washbasin made out of planks. And next to it a carnation plant. It was dawn. I see Panayótis Chrónis, he was splashing water on himself, washing himself. He looked at me, he didn't recognize me. I went to our house. I went straight to the kitchen. My family had gone off, I didn't know anything. They had gone to Trípolis. Only my mother was there. She was staying down at old Sotíris Kóllias's place. The rebels had taken over our house. I went into the kitchen. It was light out, the sun had come up. And then I hear my mother coming. She had a bag with wheat chaff, she had some hens, she was coming to feed them. She comes inside. She sees me. You're here, my girl? I'm here. Now what will I do with you, what will I do? The whole neighborhood's awake. Where will I hide you? There are rebels in the house. They were still asleep. I tell her, You won't hide me. I'm going to turn myself in, let them kill me, I don't care. But why they wanted me I didn't know. I walked outside, trembling, I went up to Mángas's place. They were all there, with Haroúlis Lenghéris in charge. I turned myself in. Where were you hiding? In our house, in the basement. I'd asked my mother, Did they search the basement? They hadn't. In the basement, I tell them. And what did you eat? There was water outside. I had taken two loaves of bread with me. No one knew me. They wouldn't listen: You were hiding somewhere. I wasn't hiding, I was at our house. That stayed secret for two years. They let me go free. I found out later what the charges against me were. The Kyreléis women had left. That night, after the last service of the Salutations. And because they saw us talking in church, they thought I was a liaison. Vasílis, their eldest son, had gone to Trípolis and he sent them shoes with Nikólas Balahámis. Through Ayiliós I think. Nikólas was their relative. They were barefoot, they sent them some boots. We were barefoot too. In that winter weather. Nikólas brought them the boots and they left, walked all night. They went to Trípolis, Vasílis was waiting for them. And from Trípolis they went to Athens. That's what happened, and that's why they were after me. Later on they arrested Balahámis, they sent him to the detention camp. They had all the people who didn't get away in time, in March.

Then the big blockade started. And to get rid of people they killed some of them. That's when they killed the Braílas woman. I got out in time, she didn't. In the month of June. It was June when we found out. On Saint Peter's Day.[2] The neighbors had come to wish us well for our Pétros's name day.

Chapter 25

Pavlákos was present at the execution of Vasílimis. It was a brother of his who killed Vasílimis. A brother of his, and Bouraímis. Mihális Bouraímis, who now receives a pension for being in the Resistance. He killed the man and he's getting a pension. They captured Yiánnis Vasílimis, a big, tall man. Nice-looking man, good-looking. With young children, a son and a daughter. They arrested him with his father. His father went over to them. He tells them, Hey, you fellows, what did Yiánnis ever do to you? Then someone bashed him, we don't know who, and threw him down in some tall bushes. But the old man lived, he didn't die. They took Yiánnis up a ways, to a place they call Spathokomménoi, it's farther up, on the road from Koúvli. It was Koúvli where they arrested him. His brother, Pavlákos, and the others. And they killed him in Spathokomménoi. The old man got himself out of those bushes, he went to his daughter-in-law. Miliá, Miliá, he shouts to her. They killed Yiánnis, you poor girl, go and collect him. Miliá took my sister-in-law Electra and they went up there and found him. My sister-in-law said he was beaten so bad he'd kicked up a foot's-length of dirt, that's what she told me, he was buried in that dirt. Seems he was beaten a lot before he died. I don't know if they knifed him or not, I don't know about Pavlákos, but that other fellow, the one from Galtená, went to prison for quite a few years. They had him in some prison somewhere. And now they say he gets no sleep, that bloodshed still hounds him.

Chapter 26

Márkos came down to Kastrí in 1943. Just after Saint Constantine's Day.[1] He was older than me but we were both named after the same grandfather. He was trying to put together a group. To start up a skeleton organization. The first of the British had parachuted onto Mount Parnon. The first group of the SMA. And he left to meet them. Of course he never came back. It should be noted here that he was always on good terms with the leftists. During the Metaxás dictatorship he was in contact with them. First of all, he hid someone named Látsis in his house. From Ayios Vasíleios in Kynouría. Later on he made him his koumbáros. He had connections to the Communist Party from way back then. He was also working with Polývios Isariótis. That's not a code name. Polývios Isariótis, a lawyer. They shared the same office. He was a Communist too. Márkos left the army in 1935. He wasn't discharged. He resigned. As a first lieutenant, I think. He graduated from the Army Cadet Academy, he studied, he got a degree in law, he got his license to practice law, then he quit. He brought his brothers and sisters to Athens, he set up house there, he started working. He put the girls in school, his sisters, in some vocational school. 1930–1935. Until that time most everybody else stayed in Kastrí. He struggled. He had a sharp mind, he soaked up everything. He spoke good English, good French. He had also reestablished his connection with the Freemasons, and he was rising. Rising fast. An important and prominent person. Extremely cultivated. Níkos Karvoúnis wrote the battle hymn "To Arms, to Arms" at his house. Níkos Karvoúnis, the leftist writer. Márkos gave him shelter during the early years of the

Occupation. He looked after him. He wrote that at Márkos's house, and Márkos's brother Yiórgos Ioannítzis typed it for him. I have firsthand knowledge of this. And also Polývios Isariótis, when he came down to Arcadia to organize EAM, he sent him to me. He stayed at our house, I helped him make his first contacts. In fact he was the first one from EAM to come to Kastrí. He must have come in November. Early November 1941. EAM was formed in September. It was founded in September in Athens. And the cadres of the KKE who joined up straight away were spread over the rest of Greece. Each of them took a prefecture. Polývios came to Arcadia. We got to know each other. I knew him from Márkos's office. I was a student. He was a short, athletic type. So he came there, he set up his organization, in 1941. The Organization became dormant then but was reactivated in 1943. When the air drops began on Mount Parnon. The first drop took place on May 21, in Megáli Lákka. That's where it happened. Then Márkos came down from Athens. He invited some people for a meal at Haloúlos's taverna. That was his fatal weakness. It sealed his fate. All the EAM activists were there, Magoúlis, Kléarhos, and the rest. As Márkos's guests. He announced that he was going forward, he would form his own cell. A few days later he got up and left. He stayed at our uncle the doctor's. At Uncle Menélaos's house. He went up to Mount Parnon. The third, the fourth, or fifth of July 1943. Until recently I didn't know the circumstances under which he was killed. This past year someone put out a book. One of those self-published books. Stámos Triantafýllis. He portrays himself as a rebel chieftain. A Reserve second lieutenant during the Albanian campaign. The Old Man of Mount Parnon and all that. About himself. And he says that it was Látsis who killed Ioannítzis. Before he met up with the British agents of SMA he met with Látsis. He tried to convince him to leave EAM, to go over to his organization. This discussion took place on the road. From Platanáki to Palaiohóri. Both of them on horseback. Then Látsis took out his gun and shot him in cold blood, from behind. The rebels escorting them were speechless. In the back of his neck. Why did you stop? Látsis yelled at them. And they left, they left Márkos down there. How dependable Triantafýllis's information is I don't know. At any rate, he was there on Mount Parnon. He doesn't say, I saw it. Some eyewitnesses told this to him. I was in Kastrí at the time. And I'd gone to Voúrvoura with Nikólas Farmakoulídas. I don't remember why anymore. On some related business in any case. In the meantime the dispute with EAM was coming to a head. Those bums, Yiánnis Velissáris would say. He'd started out with the opposition. Then he went over to their cell. I knew them all, I was well acquainted with everyone. Aléxis Iatrídis's boys. Old Aléxis. His nephews. My brother Níkos. They also had their friends. Spýros Roúmelis. All of them casualties. Roúmelis, that was his nickname. Selímos. A scrupulous fellow. Roúmelis was his mother's name. After the village of Ayía Roúmeli. Which is in Crete. He had no relatives. Just a sister, she's still living. Someone from Vérvaina married her. Those people had been through a lot. And it showed on their faces. They suffered. And his sister still does, even today. There was another man there. Yiórgos Stratigópoulos. He was studying law. I was good friends with him too. He wrote poems. He came from Kastrí, on his mother's side. And Tzímis Boínis also. Another casualty. Killed. So the rebels set up a blockade. I don't remember the date. They arrested me and Farmakoulídas. In our beds. The others were hiding. They took us to Meligoú. We spent the night there. They left Farmakoulídas there in Meligoú. Seems like the officers were seeing a lot of action. Kyreléis, Dránias, a Reserve officer, Yiánnis Kounoúfos from Karátoula, a squadron chief. From our organization. Me, they kept. Because as a student I was a leftist and because I had no clear involvement in it all. They kept me. And I went up to the mountains. With them. They put me in charge of the Justice sector. I already had my law degree. I was also a good public speaker. I was in my element. I stayed there until November 1943. Working for the committee of EAM of East Laconía and Kynouría. With headquarters in Leonídio. We had the whole area. Up to Yeráki. The secretary was Kóstas Pappás. A code name. For Yiánnis Kouráfas, a *Triatatikós*.[2] In August I asked to go back to Kastrí. On August 15, the Feast of the Virgin. They let me go. I went, I stayed four days, I came back. On my return they immediately placed me under arrest. An accusation was made that I was with the Gestapo.

In the mountains that meant you were executed. I wasn't an agent of the British Intelligence Service, I was with the Gestapo. They placed me under arrest. In Leonídio. Manólis Roúgas was there, working with EPON.[3] My brother Níkos was there. And in Trípolis the secretary of the KKE was Yiórghis Mavromantilás. Mihális's brother. They were from Górtyna, but Mihális had married one of our women. Married into Kastrí. And Yiórghis and I were in school together. I gave Níkos and Manólis a note, to go and find the secretary. To find Yiórghis Mavromantilás. They found him. And he sent a message, I assume, and he vouched for me. So they sent me on a test mission. I went, I came back. The mission was to deliver a highly confidential envelope to the village of Platanáki. Which of course had nothing in it. To check whether I would open it or not. And after that I was escorted by someone known only as Triantáfyllos around the mountain villages to speak to the residents. I was the orator for the whole region. We went to Prastós, we called a monk. He was a KKE supporter. Who is the greater prophet, Christ or Stalin? Christ, who's he? he answered. Why Stalin is. We went down to Leonídio. I started having my doubts down there. Things can't go on like this. I also recognized Márkos's knapsack. A small detachment had arrived in Leonídio. We were eating. They were going to ferry across to Iria in Náfplion in a caïque. They would get to Spétses and from Spétses they would go across. It was there I became convinced that they had killed Márkos Ioannítzis. From the stories told to us by a certain Kapetán Zahariás. He'd go on and on. But there was no mistaking it, I saw Márkos's knapsack. The knapsack he took up to Mount Parnon with him. I gave it to him that morning. Just before he left from our uncle the doctor's house. We had slept there. I recognized it. I say to myself, Now what can that mean? He's finished. So Zahariás went on with his story: And that fellow Karátoulas came along with his knapsack, and so on and so forth. And a rebel said to him. Another version of his murder. What are you carrying that for? And he executed him. Karátoulas was Márkos's code name. Márkos was a protector to all of us in some way. I was overcome by a fiercely intense melancholy. I couldn't live with the idea that I was involved if only indirectly in the murder of my cousin. Kóstas Pappás saw me like that. He took me aside. Because I was a trustworthy associate I had won his friendship. Comrade, what's wrong? I want to go see a doctor. My appendix is bothering me. I need to have an operation. He tells me, I'll let you leave. But you can't come back. You can't come back. I left whatever I had there. We went down to Pláka. A seaport of Leonídio. He put me in a boat himself to get me to Astros. I thought, They'll sink me. At dawn we made it to Astros. With oars—and with sails when there was wind. In Astros I run into Velissáris, right there in front of me. Hey, Yiánnis. He had come down to Astros too. Yiánnis and I were colleagues. He was still practicing law, in fact. What are you doing here? I'm on leave, I tell him. I'm going up to the village. Some things are destined to be. We'll go together, he says to me. Yiánnis had relatives in Dolianá. We went to Dolianá, a crowd gathered. I spoke. We go to Stólos. To Mítsos Kapetanéas. He was Yiánnis's uncle. Yiánnis was his sister's son. We went there, and of course Mítsos put himself out. He got some meat, he got all kinds of things. When it came to entertaining he was a prince among men. In the evening we sat down to eat. He says to me, Márkos, what are you going to do? I say, I'll leave for Athens. And you, Yiánnis? I can't go along. Why can't you, Yiánnis? I haven't the means. Listen, Mítsos says to him. As long as I'm alive you don't have to worry about anything. You'll get on better than anyone. Mítsos not only owned land. He was good at everything. Things came easy to him. Yiánnis didn't answer. Didn't say yes or no. We came to Kastrí. I wasn't afraid he would betray me, that's how much I trusted him. And I'm talking about November 1943. I go find Yiórghis Haloúlos. The clerk. Things are tough, I tell him. They're tough, he tells me. What will we do now? What can we do? I tell him, I'm going to Athens. But I need a permit. Uncle Menélaos had already left. We'll get you one, Yiórghis says. He went down to Trípolis, he found someone from Rízes. He had dealings with the Germans. Black market and all that. My father knew him well. Yiórghis says to him, Márkos, the doctor's nephew, wants to go to Athens. He came down from the mountains. Let's go get him with the Germans, he says. Yiórghis laughed. A permit is enough, he tells him. You don't have to go get him. Kaoúnis was his name, from Rízes. A real chatterbox. So I got ready to leave. I found Níkos Xinós. He was working with his brother Thomás. I knew that a car would be leaving for Athens. Níkos, will you take me with you? I'll pay you. Me, take money for that, Mr. Márkos, sir, he says to me. We'll take you anywhere you want. We'll get the gazogene truck ready. Tsourapélos's truck. Those boys worked as helpers. They were young, had no parents. We arranged for them to come at dawn to wake me. Early that night, Broúsalis, Delivoriás, and Achilléas show up at our house. The entire leadership of the Arcadia branch of EAM. They had passed through Zygós. I think it was about that time that someone called Háris Nestorídis was sentenced to be executed. As a collaborator with the Italians, up around there. They executed him and they came to Kastrí. With an escort of men from ELAS. All the leaders of EAM. They came to our house, they stayed there at our house. We had rooms, the women made up beds for them. At night we had a meal, we talked. I knew I was leaving in the morning. I didn't tell them anything. Around daybreak I hear voices at my window. Mr. Márkos, sir. There are Germans in the square. It was the Xinós brothers. Germans on bicycles in the square. I jump up. I wake the others. I wait for them to dress and collect their guns and all their things. I'm the last one to leave. I jumped down into my aunt Omorfoúla's yard, I put the others ahead of me. The Germans fired some shots behind us. They saw us. They didn't detain us. And come daybreak we had made our way to Koubíla. We went to Koutsoyiánnis's inn. There were others gathered there. Meanwhile, we had come by some information. The Germans had blockaded Kastrí. With a detachment of cyclists in the front guard. A silent front guard. To take us by surprise. We arrived in Koubíla. My brother Níkos was with us. Achilléas says to him. Kapetán Achilléas. Achilléas of OPLA. The terrorist. He tells Níkos and another man to leave for Plátanos. There was an ELAS unit there. To attack the Germans. I laughed. How could they attack, with what and with whom? How long would it have taken them to get to Plátanos? It can't be done, the others tell him. And that heroic decision was quickly forgotten. In the meantime the blockade ended. I went back to Kastrí. The Germans had killed Demosthénis Pantazís and a professor named Panayotópoulos. Not from our parts, from Trípolis I think. There was weeping and wailing of course. Killing was still something unusual in the village. A few days later Níkos Xinós comes and finds me. Mr. Márkos, sir, the gazogene truck is ready. And that's how I left. I went to Athens and left my troubles behind. At first I stayed at Yiórgos Ioannítzis's house. At lunchtime I often ate with our uncle the doctor. With Uncle Menélaos in the Metaxourgheío neighborhood in Athens. Then the Germans left. I went to Kifisiá. I couldn't stay at Yiórghis's place. We had other relatives in Kifisiá. Romylía and the rest of them. Then they found us a room in Ilisós.[4] Just below the Makriyiánni district near the Acropolis. Eléni and I moved in there. I met an old girlfriend of mine there. I'd stayed at their house in Neápolis. As a student. Beautiful girl, like a statue. She was going out with a district attorney at the time. She told me all about him. But she preferred me. She was older than me. I ran into her in Ilisós. Pópi? I say to her. I'm living here with my mother, she tells me. She had a sister. She was living with someone, an old man, he was supporting her. I don't know if he married her. Pópi was down in the dumps. What's the matter? I say to her. Come to my house, she tells me. They were running a gambling racket there. Pópi was one of a group of professional mourners. Which meant that KOBA[5] would send for her now and then and she would go to the cathedral and writhe and swear and wail. The December Uprising came to an end. The official state was reduced to the Palaiá Anáktora.[6] And to Goudí.[7] To Goudí and the Makriyiánni district. Kapetán Achilléas was in Athens. Achilléas, the head of OPLA. He blew up all those buildings. He'd come there as a mechanic, and he blew them up. But our most upsetting meeting took place later on. By the end of Christmas the ELAS rebels had pretty much cleared out of Athens. That's when I went and enlisted. Voluntarily. I still had some time left to serve, from when I was a student. The National Militia was there. It had been agreed at the Liberation to organize certain similar battalions. Manned by Reserve officers, for the most part. I went and enlisted. My thinking was that the sooner I got that obligation over with the better. My thinking was correct. And on top of all that of course there was the problem of survival. The Germans left, the December Uprising came to an end. I had been living off various relatives. So I went and enlisted. I owed that time. But that's what always happens. Where will you get food, where will you sleep? In the barracks. Wherever they give you food. That was the beginning of the enlistments. On both sides. That was one reason to enlist. And the other was safety. In the mountains no one came after you. You went around, you ate, you drank, you got laid. Otherwise you were a reactionary, and you were hounded. You ended up in the Battalions. You found a place to lay your head. I went and enlisted. It was now 1946. The plebiscite was held in September. Shortly afterward I completed my nine months, and I was discharged. I went down to Trípolis. I stayed with my sisters, they were there, they had opened an atelier. I had my law degree, but I had no license yet. I wasn't licensed to practice. The Civil War began. That's when it started. In Litóchoro. And Pontokerasiá. They brought the gendarmes down from Ayios Pétros in their undershorts. They butchered them in their sleep. The revenge killings began. Terrible business. So the KKE could gather its men, all the ones who had run away to Athens, they set up the local guard units. A unit in every prefecture. It was there in the local unit in Arcadia that they captured them all. Velissáris, Kraterós, Broúsalis, Delivoriás. Someone named Dimópoulos. Seventeen or eighteen people. They took them down to Trípolis. A court-martial was held in Trípolis. With Zisiádis as the main witness for the prosecution. Achilléas Zisiádis. Had he changed sides? Had he sold out? It must have been one or the other. And someone named Bouziánis also. Pávlos Bouziánis. In the same line of work. Achilléas Zisiádis, high-rise building construction in the 1960s. An engineer. Offices in Pangráti, in Kypséli, and on Syngroú Avenue, in Athens. The trial went on for days. I would go and watch. Kouráfas was there. One of the accused. When he saw me he became all flustered. Kóstas Pappás. They executed him. Velissáris was there. Kraterós Aryiríou was there. Mítsos Kapetanéas came to Trípolis. He tells me, let's get Yiánnis off. How can we get him off? Go and talk to him. One of the military judges, Alfayiánnis, was from Astros. Mítsos knew him, they were related.

Mítsos, an avowed old bachelor, had married a cousin of his, late in life. Nelly. She's still living. No children. He secured me a permit, I went to see Yiánnis. In the basement of the courthouse. Yiánnis, come on, don't die for nothing. They're going to kill me, Márkos. During his testimony they asked him if he disapproved and all that. He didn't even answer. That trial took place in 1948. In the month of February. Delivoriás and Broúsalis got off. Both of them. They agreed to sign. The whole of Arcadia was mobilized. Priests, bishops. A big thing. They had signed renunciations. But other people also signed and they weren't saved. Diódoros and I would go listen to their defense pleas. And Diódoros would jeer at the ones who signed. In February 1948. Which of them didn't sign: Kraterós Aryiríou. He shook his head. He didn't say a word. Yiánnis Velissáris. The same. He wouldn't talk. Polývios Isariótis. The Iliópoulos brothers. They all refused. Oh yes, and Kóstas Pappás, the Post Office employee, otherwise known as Yiánnis Kouráfas.

Chapter 27

That's how they captured Penelope Kaloútsis. It was Pikinós who got her. I'm not all that certain, maybe Yeorghía knows better. And someone else. There were two of them. And when he got hold of her she told him, Now listen here, you came here after *me*, you came to capture *me*, why, if you scratch between your teeth, my bread will still be there. All this in Ayisofiá, before they burned it down. She was from Kastrí. From the Farmasónis family. Not Farmasónis. Kaloútsis. Farmasónis was her mother's name. Kaloútsis. Anyway, they caught her, they took her somewhere, I don't know where. They said to Orthokostá. And they slashed her up afterward, poor thing. They say she put up a fight, we weren't there to see. Fought for her life. But they beat her down.

—In the detention camp they told me, If you see them taking folks out that door, you know they're taking them to be executed. The monastery had two doors. They took Penelope out that same door.

—She had the flu, that's exactly what they said. And Pikinós got her up out of bed and took her in. Because she might have given shelter to someone there. And they left. They went and burned down the whole village, those rebels. And the people got out, they went across from there.

Chapter 28

The old man had become romantically involved with Leonídas Grigorákis's daughter. Venetsána. They went to school together, to the junior high school. It was a rare thing in those days for a girl to keep on with her studies beyond the second year, or the third year of primary school. We're talking about the end of the past century. Around that time. Eighteen ninety-five. At any rate, that childhood romance ended up in a formal engagement. Rings were exchanged. An engagement party was held, right and proper. In the end, due to some whispering, and perhaps some political expediency, the marriage was called off. Leonídas was the mayor. Of what was then the municipality of Tánia and Dolianá. And the Grigorákis kin had been keeping that office in their family. So the marriage was called off, and not without incident. On Saint Nicholas's Day,[1] after church, the folks from Karátoula were making their way home. At Láni the road forks. The old man invited his fiancée to go to his house. His brother Nikólaos was in America. His only brother. And the bride-to-be was going to make loukoumádes.[2] To celebrate his name day. But her mother didn't let her go. The old man was insulted, he grabbed the girl by the hand and insisted that she follow him. Stubborn as mules, both the groom and the mother-in-law. And Venetsána in the middle. Weak-willed. Finally the rest of her relatives intervened. They attacked the old man. He jumped off the road, down into a vineyard. He took out a pistol from his back pocket, he fired a few shots in the air. His third shot nicked the mayor's wife's long woolen vest. Grazed her hip. An entirely superficial wound. At that point Konstantís Grigorákis, Koufós's father, threw himself at the old man. Who had just enough time to bash him with the butt of his pistol, he knocked out a few of his teeth. And he kept insisting that his fiancée follow him to his house. But the girl refused. Look what you've done to your house now. Believing the mayor's wife dead, and seeing the other covered in blood, she thought he'd become a criminal. After what you just did to your home, where will you take me? She refused. The old man got mad, he took out a pocketknife, and he slashed all her clothes. He slashed them and threw them away. Left her half-naked. He was out of control. They said they found her shoes all the way down in Kokóis's yard. So the engagement was called off once and for all, in spite of the exchange of rings and the much-vaunted announcement of the engagement party, and in spite of the fact that he had made an official trip with his fiancée to Roúvali, where they baptized Zagléras. Who was a small child then. Not only that, when they passed by the house of my grandfather-to-be, my mother, a young girl then, came out and pinned some basil on them.[3] Here, cousin, have a long, happy life together. Cousins, four or five times removed. Cousins. And the old man used to repeat that story. Who could have told me that in two or three years' time the woman you have next to you as your fiancée will have left you and the woman who wished you well for your wedding would be here instead? That *she* would become your true wife, who you would spend sixty whole years of your life with, who you would have children with and acquire property with, who could have told me that? Eventually the old man was taken to court because of that incident. And he was condemned in absentia to one or two years. At which point he absconded to Mount Parnon. And ended up in Sítaina. He had no obligations, he had no sisters,[4] only one brother in America. And he left his mother down there at the mill, she collected the milling fees. Nineteen hundred three or four. He was twenty-five, the old man. He remained a fugitive for several months. Then he initiated some legal action. An objection or an appeal — at any rate this resulted in an indefinite postponement. At which point he gave himself up and was waiting for the re-trial. At that time his uncle, my grandfather that is, was trying to marry off my mother. And he asked the old man to expedite the negotiations. The prospective son-in-law was from the same village, from Roúvali. Today the father-in-law of my brother Aryíris. Vasílis Vavásis. Also called Ayeroyiánnis. They'd go to the taverna, they'd bargain. Raise and lower the numbers. And I want so much, I'm from an upstanding household, and on and on. So the old man says to him. Listen, Vasílis. You know the girl, she's sixteen years old. She hasn't got much to her name. Her brothers will help her from Athens, but she only has so much. No, I need to have four thousand as her dowry. We haven't got four, we have two thousand. That's all we have. Money was very hard to come by then. You could search all of Kastrí, all the villages around there and you couldn't squeeze out four thousand drachmas. At which point the old man exploded. The other old man, my grandfather, that is. Tell me, he says to him, if I have a she-goat, an ugly woman in other words, an unmarried woman, a she-goat. A derogatory term. And I give you ten thousand, will you marry her? The answer: I'll do whatever's best for me. And grandfather blew his stack. Let's go, he said. They paid the owner, this happened in a taverna, over by the elementary school. Where Tákis Zekiós's laundry shop is today. They paid, grandfather grabbed his fez.[5] He used to wear a foustanélla[6] back then. So he grabbed his fez. Even if you give me the moon, he says to Vavásis, after what you just said I no longer want you as a son-in-law. Good day, good day. And they left. When they reached Karamítzias's gas station, the old man stopped short. Hey, nephew, I just thought of something. What is it, Uncle? Why don't *you* marry her? I almost fell over, my father would recount. Oh, come now, Uncle. I'm no uncle, he says to him. They were cousins, four or five times removed. Very distant relatives. Although I looked into it, I could never get to the bottom of things, I never found precise information. At any rate they were fourth or fifth generation. Of course in those days the notion of kinship was different. Social scientists say that the farther south we go the closer the bonds become. In Crete and in Egypt, this was always so, and of course I don't know what part climate plays. But even in our parts, in those years, degree of kinship was a decisive factor. Both in terms of social bonds and of the unavoidable disputes where sides were taken, offensive or defensive, depending on the case. Then again, degree of kinship as a reason to prohibit a marriage is recognized by law. It's also recognized by religion. In the old days the restrictions were more stringent. Today marriage is allowed between fifth-degree relatives or more. Up to four degrees—that is, for first cousins—it's forbidden. In limited cases of course, even that may happen. With the consent of the church. In other words, if you've got your first cousin pregnant, they allow you to marry her. In limited cases. At which point the old man, my father, lost his temper. First of all, he tells him, I don't even know if I'll be convicted. Or if I'll go to prison. I've asked for a reprieve. I've made an appeal, but I don't know what the result will be. Let's agree on it now, says the father-in-law, and whenever, God willing, you are finished with this business, then we can announce it publicly. Taken by surprise, or so the old man claimed, he gave in at once. But I believe there were other things that aroused him. My mother's age, sixteen years old, and a certain feeling, a latent incestuous undercurrent, intensified because it was forbidden. So they agreed, and several days later, when the rejected, as it were, son-in-law returned, having fallen in my grandfather's esteem because of his principles, now remorseful of course, he was informed enigmatically that it was too late. It seems the repentant suitor had his suspicions. Or had found out. So he gets right up and takes himself down to Ayiórghis. Ayiórghis-Douminá. To where my grandfather and my mother were. It was that time of year, they had vineyards and they were spraying. He goes there, he finds my mother in the vineyard by herself. My grandfather had gone to fetch some water. So he finds her in the vineyard. With two or three of his friends. And he tells my mother, I'm from an upright household, and I'm this and I'm that. What does Kékeris have, he tells her. All he has is a plain old mill and nothing else. I have olives, I have other things. With those two or three friends he had probably gone there to abduct her. But my mother said to him firmly, I don't want you. So get out now before my father comes and something bad happens. My mother had the good judgment at the age of only sixteen to sense danger. And with her threat that something bad might happen, he too realized that he had no hope. All because of my mother's good sense. So he took his friends and went down toward the wood. He didn't go on the road, so as not to run into my grandfather. He went through the wood. Some time after that, when my father's acquittal concerning the incidents during his previous engagement came through, they announced the new one. The marriage arrangements were finalized, and a few weeks later the wedding was held. And for sentimental reasons it was held in Roúvali. At the house of his father-in-law. Not long before that Timoléon Bílas had died. The father of Panayótis. The lawyer. And there had been much weeping and wailing in Karátoula. The result of a blow from Kótsios Bílas. They weren't related. Just had the same name. Of course in the villages the same name is never accidental. All because of some little wall over by the threshing floor. Bílas's threshing floor. That too belonged to Bílas. A small protective wall, an abutment for the overlying terrace. And that's the custom to this day. The wall had come down and the owner up above had to fix it. So they were quarreling. Old Kótsios kept telling Timoléon to pick up the rocks. And they had an argument about those rocks and he hit him with his pickax. A small retaining wall, only 50 or 60 centimeters high. Old Kótsios Bílas was tried for that and went to prison, I think for four years. Even though the blow wasn't fatal. Or at any rate it didn't cause immediate death. But in those days there was no penicillin and such things: his wound got infected thirty or thirty-five or forty days later, and he died. And there was weeping and wailing. For that reason my father thought that the wedding should not be held in the village. It didn't hold up ethically because the whole village was in a state of mourning.[7] So they held it in Roúvali. With guests and everything. They got them together, held the ceremony, and went to eat at the father-in-law's house. As a matter of fact, the old man left his bride there for some months. I think it was for a year. Because it says in his day book: The writer hereof was married on March 29 of 1907, and I left the bride at the parental abode. It's written like that, in katharévousa.[8] And when one year had elapsed I received her permanently in my home. And again he invited guests for a meal, even though the wedding had already taken place. In any case he brought

his wife to his house, there was a ceremony for her arrival and install-
ment in the conjugal home. One year later. Because the neighborhood was still in mourning. He was a compassionate fellow, my father.
Which could in fact be borne out by his civic-mindedness. He baptized tens of children. And all those koumbároi ruined him. He would
collect five or six hundred drachmas every now and then. In his
taverna. On Sundays or whenever there was a trial. And by nighttime
there wasn't a cent left in the cash register. He'd given it out in loans.
According to what he thought this or that person needed. That's how
he lived, and when we remarked to him that that money belonged to
the whole family, he would answer with the saying "'Tis better to give
than to receive." By Saint Paul the Apostle. Because those people
were poor, they never gave the money back. I've saved some of his
account books. With credits written in, and all that. From 1905 and
henceforward. Account books where he wrote about the mill and the
taverna. This much for wheat, that much for barley. The Koulioúris
family, all of whom are dead now. Their generation is dead and gone.
So are the others from Roúvali. This much for corn, that much for
rye. The charges. The so-called miller's fee. Lots of account books.
From the taverna too, of course. Wine and tidbits, so much. On the
house, so much, cash payments, so much. I have his diary. Aside from
his marriage, it refers to various other events in his life. In the same
old-fashioned handwriting as in 1907. Until he died. The birth of each
of his children. Perfectly written save for one or two mistakes. First
child, female, born on such-and-such day of the month, baptized immediately, given name Marigó, who died after twelve days. Second
child, male, born on such-and-such day of such-and-such month, in
the year 1909, baptized by Marínos Marinákis, given name Anáryiros.
Third child, male, born October 4, 1920, baptized in Ayios Yiórghios-
Douminá, on such-and-such day of the following year, by Konstantínos Papakonstantínou, given name Konstantínos. And me, after a gap
of ten years. As a matter of fact, it aroused my curiosity because it
refers to Monday as the day. But the "4th" is not so clear. It's not clear
whether it's the 4th or the 6th. There's a smudge there, from the ink
used to write it. Lilac-colored ink. So I made an inquiry to the Athens

Observatory asking if the fourth of October of 1920 was indeed a Monday. And it was. And it continues with the birth of the second child Marigó followed by the birth of Dóxa. A kind of official family record. I also have a small number of his letters. From America. Because in the meantime he emigrated. I have more of my mother's letters. Letters to him. Which he saved and which he brought back with him when he returned. Written by the hand of Yiánnis Bakoúris. He wrote my mother's letters. And he read them the letters they received. Yiánnis Bakoúris, the brother of Yiórghis Bakoúris, of so-called Koútavos. I think he's no longer alive. He had married Sophia Támbaris. Their house was just past the church. That house is a wreck now. Sophia whose name was so respected. And esteemed. Well, Yiánnis Bakoúris was my mother's secretary. There were no telephones then. And correspondence took a month, letters took a month to arrive. Nor was it easy to travel, the way it is today. An emigrant would return, and he would bring five or ten dollars to five, or ten, or fifteen people. And greetings from this person or that person. And so on and so forth. To their families. That's how things were in 1916. In 1917. In America the old man was staying with someone from Oriá. From Bernorí or Oriá. They were living together and they quarreled, for what reason I don't know. Perhaps he didn't pay his rent, perhaps about some loan. I don't know. And the other fellow left for Greece. And one day he arrived back home. He came back. One by one they went to him, women, sisters, mothers, they would ask him about their relatives. My mother started out too. I'm not sure if old Marigó went with her. My father's mother. My grandmother. At any rate my mother went. Perhaps they both went together. And they saw him. He says to them, Your husband back in America, he says to my mother, is a good-for-nothing. That's how he described him, a good-for-nothing. He hasn't got a penny. He plays the horses, he's become debauched. He may even be married, he may have other children. But he has no money. He described him to her in the darkest of colors. Of course the women began to cry. They went back to Karátoula, they put their heads together, and they had Yiánnis Bakoúris, their secretary, write a nasty letter: you did this and this and that. And if what that man from Bernorí told us is true, then our curse be upon you. The old man got angry because it was all lies. The product of the other man's unforgivingness. Because I think that during their argument the old man had given him a good slap. Still quite excitable over in America, he had slapped him. And humiliated, he had come to sow the seeds of doubt. To destroy the family harmony. His wrongdoing was enormous. That man from Bernorí. He could have said, I didn't see him, I don't know. And he was deliberately deceitful because he knew that my father had made money and was doing quite well. My mother had written to him. They had told him not to send money here. Because they had more than enough. They had the mill and they made a good living. There was also the shop in Kastrí. Which later became a taverna. They gave it out for rent. When the old man came back he found the rent in the bank. He also learned that my mother had loaned five or six thousand drachmas with interest, at that time, to Polýdoros Mántis. The father of Mántis, the monk. Money from wheat and various other products she would sell. They had vineyards that were more than five strémmata[9] in size. They sold six or seven thousand okás of walnuts every single year. They had huge walnut trees at the mill. And their own needs were minimal. So she had told him not to send any money. Well, at any rate. When the old man received her letter he immediately thought of murder. Of going back and killing that slanderer. But he couldn't get away from his work. So he goes and sends a large sum of money. Without writing a word. A huge amount of money for that particular time. Through the National Bank of Greece. As evidence of the truth. Five or six thousand dollars. Were we to convert that money, the amount would be equal to at least one hundred thousand today. We're talking dollars. I'm quite conversant with numbers. The money arrived in Trípolis. The postman received the notice from the bank. He went to Karátoula. There was no one at home. He goes down to the mill. He finds my mother up near the woods. She had climbed a birch tree and was pruning it. He gave her the notice. Of course neither she nor my grandmother knew how to read. The postman left, they went back to their house in the evening. Yiánnis Bakoúris was away. They took the notice and went to Papa Dimítris Siahámos. Who was a schoolteacher and a priest. The father of Vasílis who later became a priest. They showed it to him, and he was literally dumbfounded. According to my mother. All he said was, That's a lot of money, Konstantína. The next day they went to Trípolis. With Polýdoros Mántis the muleteer. Because Papa Dimítris was a priest, but mainly because of the large sum of money, the director of the bank received them in his office. Some coffee, Ma'am? Coffee, old man? To gain their favor and all that. And then he says to my mother, Do you want to take the money with you? They might steal it from you there. There was no bank in Kastrí then. A bank was opened later on. In 1929 or '30. At the behest of the Kanglís brothers. Upon their request from Canada to open a branch in Kastrí. And to make their brother-in-law the director. Manolákis Horaítis. In 1929 or '30. And the bank director advised her to leave her money there on deposit as foreign currency. Which she did. Five years later, when the old man came back, he found the money untouched. In other words, a gold mine. But of course that money went out the window in the end. With Protopapadákis's notorious law.[10] It had all been changed into drachmas in the interim. So all the old man's hard work went to waste. His hard work in America. He didn't have time to fix so much as a keyhole in the house. They had Aryíris and he left. He was three months old when the old man left. Four months. He came back in 1920, and he had me. For ten consecutive years he stayed away from Greece. From 1910 until December 1920. Well, at any rate. In that way, with that check the family cohesion was restored. After that they exchanged letters, explanations were given. And of course they understood that that fellow from Bernorí had told them lies. I think he had died when the old man came back. It doesn't much matter. The old man came back in December 1920. With nine trunks in tow. From America: shoes, coats, underwear. Five double-barreled rifles. Nine trunks in all. Some were ours, some were not. Because other people gave him some too. Folks from Karátoula who wanted him to bring them here to their families. He arrived with twelve or thirteen mules from Másklina. Because the train came to Másklina in those days. He had telephoned the muleteers and they were waiting for them. Muleteers from Másklina. They hauled the cargo from Eleohóri to Laconía. There was no road. There were no cars either. And that's why Vozíkis came out against opening a public road. That old Harálambos. President of the Parliament, from the Populist Party. Because dozens of muleteers would lose their livelihoods. From Kastrí and from Másklina. Who received large fees for transporting cargo from the train between Másklina and Laconía. And they meant votes. In any case the road was built later on. There was already one as far as Koúvli. Trípolis to Koúvli. From Koúvli up, the road was mapped out in 1929. But the payment for it was approved under Metaxás's coalition government. With Metaxás himself the minister of transportation. So the old man arrived in Másklina. With two or three others from Kastrí. People heard about it, the children came out to meet them. The "Brooklyds"[11] are coming. That was told to us by Aryíris but mainly by Yiórghis Mantíkos's father-in-law. Who as a letter carrier would transport the mail from Másklina to Kastrí–Ayios Pétros. Aryíris arrived in Mesorráhi. At Ayioi Theodóroi he met Mantíkos's father-in-law. Riding on a mule. Old man, have you seen the Brooklyds? Keep going, they're on their way. Aryíris kept walking. There were other boys with him. They walked about two hundred meters more. There across from him was my old man. Also riding a mule. With the trunks following behind. He saw Aryíris, he didn't recognize him. Who are you? Yiánnis Kékeris's son. Have you seen my father, Old Man? The old man jumped down, he hugged him, he kissed him. He had left him as an infant a few months old, and now he found a grown boy eleven years old. I'm your father. And he immediately took out a gift for him: either a watch or a fountain pen. I don't know if the mules with the baggage came through the marketplace or turned off at Koútselas's water mill. I mean if they took the old cobblestone road below Andrianákos the schoolteacher's house that comes out at Kápsalos. In any event my father wanted to go through Kastrí. To the shop that was the reason for his going abroad. It had been bought with money from my mother's dowry, but it wasn't enough, and it went into debt, and he was obliged to go abroad to pay off the debt. So he and Aryíris were walking toward the main square. But a policeman arrested him there. Before he left for America he had hit a man named Siouroúnis. He had been giving Old Man Kirkís, my old man's father-in-law, some trouble, down along the borders in Ayiór-ghis. They were both dual residents. So he asked to have a word with him, they exchanged views, and in the middle of all this he trounced him with his cane. Whacked old Siouroúnis. The father of Apostólis Siouroúnis. He whacked him one, and he fell headfirst down thirty steps to the basement of Dimitrákis Kasímos. At any rate he wasn't killed. By the time the trial was held the old man had left town. But he was condemned in absentia. I don't know how many years he got. So the policeman arrested him. Oh, come now, dear fellow, come my good man. Nothing. The policeman was adamant. He locked him in the cellar. Vanghelió Koutoúzou took him a roast chicken, and he ate. The next day they escorted him to the state prosecutor. Of course the sentence had been struck from the records. It had been five years since it was pronounced—that is to say, since it was imposed. The judge ordered that he be released immediately. He also reprimanded the policeman for his oversight and the serious abuse of his authority. And so the old man went back to the village. Just days before Christmas. And from that time on he was a slave to the marketplace. He had no other sons, only Aryíris. I arrived one year later. I was born on October 20, 1920. Therefore I was conceived in January. Right after my father returned from America. He had left my mother when she was sixteen or seventeen and he found her when she was twenty-six or twenty-seven. At the height of her maturity and her sexual prowess. During the campaign in Asia Minor. And so as not to join the army, the old man managed to get himself appointed as a grammar-school Greek teacher. In Tservási. As a junior high school graduate. On the first of November elections were held. The elections Venizélos[12] lost. The old man supported Venizélos, so of course they transferred him. To the island of Ithaca along with Yiorghoulís, another schoolteacher. But the old man didn't accept that transfer. He didn't have many children, he had brought his money from America, it was enough for him. He didn't accept the transfer. At which time his military reprieve came through. And he had to present himself to the regiments at the Náfplion Army Headquarters. He was now a soldier. Then came the devaluation of our money, with Protopapadákis's internal loan. The British and the French had refused to reinforce Greece because of the restoration of the throne. Because of the behavior of Constantine, who was considered an enemy of the Entente Cordiale. Because of his sympathy for the Kaiser's brothers and sisters, Kaiser Wilhelm II. So all the money was lost. Then the old man opened the taverna, in the marketplace. The Asia Minor campaign came to an end. At the same time he was also appointed a justice of the peace court clerk. He slowly got back to his routine. With his koumbároi, with those drinks on the house, with meager earnings from here and from there. With the mill, which his mother was running. He made money again. Which he lost once again in 1936 with the Agrarian Reform Law[13] under Metaxás. But the final blow came with the law enacted by Svó- los[14] during the Occupation. Or rather after the Occupation.

Chapter 29

I went back to Trípolis and I reported to Lýras. A verbal report on what I saw during my one and only leave of absence. All that sordidness. In Ayios Pétros the men from Máni and the men from Corinth almost killed each other. We had a battalion of men from Corinth. They'd swiped someone's watch, and he went and asked for it. He was the uncle or the grandfather of an officer. And he asked for the watch, and the watch was found. In the meantime they began fighting in the main square of Ayios Pétros. With the ELAS rebels right there above us. Right above us. Just looking for a chance to cut us up. I went and explained everything to Lýras. He tells me, All this can you please report it in writing, everything, from the time you went to Astros, whatever you saw? I went and wrote up a report. What the general picture was, the unruliness and the corruption. The sordidness. A situation you couldn't control. Because of course various other forces were coming into play. A strange group of people, the down-and-out. Some of them embittered, others on the run, others, like the men from Máni, who have it in their blood, for example. At any rate. The Allied landing came soon afterward, and Kanellópoulos disembarked in the Peloponnese.

Chapter 30

How many were we? We hadn't been issued any arms yet. We were in Trípolis. And they told us, There are rebels in Voúrvoura. Well they gave us arms, since we were from Kastrí. Just the basics, to get ourselves to Voúrvoura. A whole lot of us, I can't remember. Vasílis Papayiorghíou, me, Petrákos, Antónis Biniáris, Miltiádis Mantás, Arapóyiannis.

—Arapóyiannis?

—Stávros. From Koútrifa. A machine-gun operator. We went to Voúrvoura. First we went to Koútrifa. We had information that the rebels had taken Arapóyiannis's wife. But she had gone into hiding, they didn't find her. And they burned down his house. From there we went to Voúrvoura. We spent the night there. We found the rebels inside a small church. I think in Ayía Paraskeví, across from the village. Some of our men got into position once they went up there. We had some men from Ayios Pétros with us, in our platoon. Someone named Fourtoúnis, another man named Lykoúras.

—Who was your leader?

—Our leader was Nikólas Petrákos. I think Liás Vémos was too. As second lieutenant. I don't remember. But I do remember that I was the machine-gun ammo-belt loader. Stávros Arapóyiannis was the operator.

—How old were you then?

—Eighteen. We got them out of there. Out of the church, but they got away from us. We didn't get close enough in time to surround them. They heard us coming. Someone fired a shot inside the village, they realized what was up. And they cleared out.

—Were there many of them?

—About eight of them. Ten. But they got away. Then we re-grouped, and we went back, back to the village. We left from there. On our way to Kosána, on the road to Kosána. Just before Prophítis Ilías, they were waiting to ambush us. It was at Koúbas's Rocks. That's what they call the place. In Kosána, way down low. On the border between Voúrvoura and Kastrí. That's where they set up their first ambush. They fired at us from high up, they didn't harm us at all.

—Was it the same men who got away, or were there others?

—We don't know. In any event, from what became clear later on, there were many rebels in the area. Because on our way to Kastrí, at the mill by the church, they had set up another ambush.

—All the way down there?

—At the church's mill. But we were moving cautiously. And we pushed them back. Then we went down to the village. That's when the villagers left Kastrí. Most of them for the Security Battalions. That's when Papayiánnis left, that's when all the men left.

—Which Papayiánnis?

—The father of Vanghélis the priest.

—Was he still alive then?

—He was.

—When did *you* leave?

—Before that. As soon as the German blockade was over. They were after me, I couldn't stay put.

—Did you go down by yourself, or with which others?

—I don't remember. A lot of us went down.

—And Papadóngonas was already in Trípolis?

—He was.

—So you went there in June?

—End of June, something like that.

—The end of June or July? When did they burn down the village? Were you here?

—They burned it down on the eve of Saint Ilías's Day. Around the twenty-second or twenty-third of the month.

—On Saint Ilías's Day?

—No, later. Later. Saint Ilías's Day is July 20.

—Yes.

—The village was burned down on the twenty-third or the twenty-fourth.

—Had you men in Voúrvoura gone there before or after?

—After. No, you're right. We'd gone there before. Before the fire. Because when we went back, that's when our parents left. When we arrived back from Voúrvoura they left. The house was still intact. They burned it down afterward.

—When they burned it down where were you?

—When they burned it down I had enlisted. So had the others. In the Battalions. We'd been issued arms. At the time I was with a German convoy, escorting them to Meligalás. That's where I was. When I came back Nikólas Petrákos broke the news to me. Gently. He says, Don't get upset. They burned down your house. Well, I didn't care all that much. I tell him, What about my family? He says, They're alive. Well, that's that, I said. If they burned down the house, then they burned it down. So what. Since no one was killed.

—Was the convoy you were with a transport convoy or a military one?

—We were carrying food at the time. There were also buses to Kalamáta. We escorted them as far as Meligalás.

—And you went back?

—We stayed there for a week. We stayed there for backup. Stoúpas was there.

—I think he was in Gargaliánoi.

—He went to Gargaliánoi later. Gargaliánoi and Pýlos. Because I went there also. On a second mission.

—And then you went back to Trípolis?

—Then I went back to Trípolis.

—Which other men from Kastrí were with you?

—Just a few. Because there were a lot of men in the Battalions. A group of us went along with some others from Valtétsi.

—I mean in Trípolis. Had all the men from Kastrí gone down there?

—Yes.

—Do you remember any names?

—How can I remember? They were all there, some enlisted, some not. And they left again, they went back.

—Was Kóstas Karamánis enlisted?

—Kóstas Karamánis? No he hadn't enlisted. He was just part of the group. He went around with us. I don't remember if he'd enlisted. I don't remember him being armed. All those men were serving in the 2nd Civilian Intelligence Bureau.

—What do you mean by 2nd Civilian Intelligence Bureau?

—That's where they worked. They issued orders, they were in constant touch with Papadóngonas. All those men.

—I see.

—From one bureau to the other. That's where they did their informing. In that bureau.

—How did Mihális kill Tsígris? Do you know the story?

—Tsígris was being interrogated at the time.

—Who was Tsígris?

—A major with the Greek Army. They had forced him to join the rebels.

—From down in Yiannakópoulos, from Taygetus?

—I don't know. I don't know about that. At any rate, Tsígris, when he first came to Kastrí.

—He came to Kastrí?

—He did. He gathered all the men in the town square. We were sitting under the plane tree. And he gave us a beautiful speech, about resistance and liberation.

—Was he by himself?

—There were others, but not many.

—Had he already gone over to ELAS?

—Yes, I think so. At any rate, he came here as part of ELAS. He told us we had to support ELAS and join the rebel movement and all that. He had us men all fired up. And there were a lot of us, not like today. He had us all fired up. So at a certain point he says, Whoever wants to go to the mountains, go stand at the Unknown Soldier's

Monument. On your left. Whoever doesn't want to go, stay where you are. And we all went over to the Unknown Soldier. Then he tells us, Go to your homes and talk it over with your parents. To see if they agree. In that way he gave us a chance to think about it. To think it over. No one followed him at that time.

—What happened with Mihális?

—With Mihális. Some men had gone on a raid at the time. To attack the villages down below. Koubíla, Galtená, and the rest.

—And Kyriákos was killed.

—I don't know how it happened. At any rate, he was killed. Mihális had just found out.

—It was his own fault he was killed.

—Yes. He was banging the butt of his gun against a door. As soon as Mihális found out he went up to the 2nd Bureau. Before they even brought his brother to Trípolis. He knew that Tsígris was being interrogated there. And he took out his gun and shot him in cold blood. He settled the score.

—Tsígris, where did they arrest him?

—Tsígris. At some blockade, I think. But I'm not very certain.

—After that the Germans left. Then came the Liberation.

—Yes.

—And you men stuck around. You stayed in Trípolis.

—Yes.

—For how many days?

—Not too many.

—Did you go to Spétses after that?

—No. I didn't go. Papadóngonas told us, Any of you who are with us, who don't have a questionable record, you can stay. We've signed an agreement, they won't bother you. And I believed what he said, so I stayed.

—Then you were there when Kanellópoulos arrived with Aris.

—Kanellópoulos and Aris. Yes, I was there. They spoke from a hotel, in the main square.

—From the Maínalon.

—The Maínalon, yes. And me in particular, for a while, until we surrendered our arms and all that, Dr. Panagákos covered for me. Not only for me, for other men from Kastrí too. He took us to the house of a relative of his. He had left us there. He brought us food until the ELAS men finally arrived. Then a rebel came there, to the house where we were staying. He says, You have to come and surrender your weapons. So the doctor, who's now deceased, loaded up our weapons. Along with Kóstas Yiorghoulís, also deceased. Kóstas was a sergeant.

— How many of you were there?

— About twelve of us. They got our weapons, they took them to the barracks. They surrendered them. But then they asked for us. So the doctor comes back with another rebel. He says, Line up, you're going to give yourselves up. And we went and gave ourselves up. They put us in a room. Someone from Megalópolis arrived, a kapetánios. He talked to us. He told us that they could kill us and all that. But ELAS was sparing us, and we should join in the struggle. And so on. So they let us go free.

— And you went back to Kastrí?

— From the barracks I went down to the square. To the square just when Kanellópoulos was speaking. Well, just then Thodorís Kalamís arrives. I was sitting on the steps of the courthouse. Thodorís Kalamís, from Voúrvoura, comes over and gets hold of me. Are you Anghelináras? I am. Follow me. I followed him. I knew that Kalamís fellow. He used to sing and play the lute at the fairs. He was in Barbátsainas's band of musicians. Before the war, all this. And those same men killed Barbátsainas. So I followed him. And he was leading me down toward Halalás's place. Almost the last house after the grove. But as soon as I saw that I stopped. I ask him, What do you want? Where are you taking me? He says, You're going to tell me where the Galaxýdis brothers have my flock. Let's go back, I tell him. Because if that's what this is about I don't know anything. He scared me for a minute. He grabbed me by the ear. I tell him, Get your hands off me, or you'll have others to answer to. In the meantime, I had Nikotsáras backing me. I'd seen him in the barracks. I knew he was in Trípolis.

— Which Nikotsáras?

— My mother's brother. He was with the rebels. I tell him, You'll have others to answer to. Like Nikotsáras. Dimítrios Selákos was his name. The minute he heard Nikotsáras's name, he says, How do you know him? Go and ask him, I tell him. That's exactly what I said. Now I was getting my courage back. Go and ask him and stop bothering me.

—Had the Galaxýdis brothers taken his sheep?

—Of course they had. Who took them from him? Was it the Galaxýdis brothers? Back during all that unrest, in the middle of all that unrest? Anyone who had the chance would swipe whatever he could. Everyone swiped things from everyone else. I went back. We went back together. And what a coincidence, right there on the steps of the courthouse again, there was Nikotsáras. With Thanásis Fotiás. And as soon as he saw me, he started in. Swearing at me of course. What are you doing with those bums, and on and on he went. I tell him, Now you can explain things to Kapetán Thodorís. And he turns to him and tells him, What do you think you're doing with my nephew? And after that they left me alone. I wanted to come to Kastrí but I was afraid. Nikotsáras gets me, he takes me upstairs. To what used to be the 2nd Civilian Intelligence Bureau. That's where Aris was stationed now.

—In what building?

—In the courthouse. Inside. He takes me upstairs to the 2nd Bureau. He hands me a permit. They fixed that permit for me, stamped it, and I could circulate freely with it. With that permit I saved Panayótis Kouroúnis from a beating.

—Where did they capture him?

—In Hoúria. We were coming down, Vrastós, my uncle, Nikotsáras's brother, me, and Kouroúnis. Not the younger one. Not Tákis. Panayótis. And they mistook him for the other one. As soon as we got to Hoúria. In Hoúria there was a guardhouse. As for me, they saw my permit, there was someone, was it Lyritzís? I don't remember now. Anyhow, he was from Messinía. A major. Or something. At any rate. They let me go. They took Kouroúnis upstairs to the old police headquarters. They started in on him. They had taken Vrastós there too. So I walk into the office, I walk in. I tell them, Who are you beating,

Selákos? Nikotsáras's brother. They knew Nikotsáras. They say, How come one's on our side and the other's on theirs? And they let Vrastós go downstairs. Then we hear Panayótis. They were beating him. They had just started. Nephew, Vrastós shouts. Go up and explain to them. I go upstairs, I tell them, You're barking up the wrong tree. The Kouroúnis you're looking for is someone else. He's young, he's my age. See, it's like this. This one here is a family man, he has children. And with that they finally let him go. And that was the end of it. We went on our way. Continued on foot. I was barefoot. I'd forgotten that. On my way from Trípolis, just before Ayios Sóstis. At the roadside shrine they had a guardhouse. They stopped us, they took my boots away. They asked for my permit. They saw my army boots. They were in good shape, almost new, they tell me, Take them off. And they left me barefoot. After that we came here. They greeted us with insults. The worst ones from Eléni, Karadímas's wife. And listen to this. Five years later they brought her to me. Five or six years. Tried to arrange a marriage between us. I said no. More swearing. You bums, you this, you that. We didn't answer her. My folks were in Másklina, they hadn't come back. We went down there with Vrastós, found our house burned down. We went to the marketplace. Another kind of welcome there. From up on Mángas's balcony. ETA[1] had taken it over, they hadn't burned *that* place down. Chrysoúlis Aryiríou. Nicknamed Kaílas. You dogs, you traitors, what did you think? We'll teach you a lesson, we'll show you.

—Were there any others?

—Mmm, Panayótis Gagás. But it's the other one I remember. Aryiríou. He spit at us.

—And you stayed here.

—Yes, I did. I stayed here. Then they arrested me, they took me to Ayios Pétros. They turned me in, they said I was looting. That I'd taken a sewing machine that belonged to Yfantís. Nonsense. So they hauled me in for interrogation. Still at Mángas's house. It was still their headquarters. There was a man called Yiánnis Spyrópoulos from Parthéni. He asked me about the sewing machine. I tell him, I've no idea. Since you have no idea you're going to Ayios Pétros. There was a superior command there. There were still some prisoners there. Three or four rebels come and get us. They take us to Ayios Pétros. Just ten days after we came back. They keep us there for about a month.

—That long?

—Twenty-nine days. They took us outside, we did chores. We had swept the square of Ayios Pétros. Me, Yiánnis Haloúlos, Achilléas Koútselas. He's dead now. We would go for water. Over at their fountain.

—What did they give you to eat?

—Whatever our relatives brought us.

—Did they come every day?

—Every day. I had my grandmother. She came whenever she could. And she would bring me something—what could she bring me? We had nothing. A potato or two, a cabbage. That's what she brought. Twenty-nine days. Till the twenty-eighth of October.

That was in the fall of 1944.

—In the fall, yes. It was—I was released that day. My other grandmother came, Nikotsáras's mother. They would let her in. She says, so the others can't hear, Listen child, listen here. Your father says to tell you that some pact was signed that's good for you men. It was the Várkiza Treaty. That's when I was released. When the Várkiza Treaty was signed. They called me upstairs. They asked me some stupid questions. About things I didn't know. There was someone named Petsaloúdas there. From here, from Ayiórghis. He recognized me. He knew I was Nikotsáras's nephew. Anghelináras, he says to me, okay, go. Yes. He does me that good turn, he says, You can go. And I left. I left as soon as they gave me my permit. My grandmother was still there. I came here. And I stayed here. I left here again in 1948.

—Did you go to Trípolis?

—I went to Athens. Straight to Athens.

—When did they attack Ayios Pétros? When did they attack the gendarmes?

—That was in 1946. Early on. When the second rebel movement was starting up. Don't ask me for dates. But yes, I went there, and I went there after Trípolis. With everyone from Kastrí.

—When they attacked them, how many gendarmes were there?

—They said ten or twelve.

—Who was police chief then?

—I'm not sure.

—Did they attack during the day or at night?

—At dawn. They killed them at dawn.

—Did they kill them all?

—Not all of them. I remember three bodies. Up on Réppas's truck. Three bodies on his truck.

—And they'd cut off their privates?

—They'd slashed them there, they didn't cut anything off. They slashed them up, all around their privates.

—With bayonets.

—With bayonets. Or with knives, I don't know. Just as they were, in their undershorts.

—In their sleep?

—Yes.

—They caught them asleep?

—They caught them asleep. And if it wasn't for some man named Katsís, Háris Katsís, from the Battalions, he was right-wing. He gave the signal for the others to leave.

—And they got away.

—They got away and they were saved. Some of them. First of all, their officer. A first sergeant, I think—but people were saying things about him.

—What do you mean?

—That he was the one who'd betrayed them.

—I see.

—The gendarmes. Now how true that is, no one knows.

—And they took the dead men to Trípolis.

—Yes, we took them there. A lot of us from Kastrí went to Ayios Pétros. And we got them and took them to Trípolis. Because we were still holding up. So we all went down to Trípolis.

—And you tore the place up.

—Yes, we went to Trípolis.

—How many of you went down there?

—A lot of us. Three hundred. Or maybe one hundred.

—Do you remember any names?

—Where should I start. With Yiórghis Réppas? With Kóstas Goúlas? With Vasílis Papayiorghíou? With Yiannoúkos Haloúlos? All deceased. Mítsos Kokkiniás, Kóstas Boutsikákis? Whose names should I give you? Which ones? Anghelos Katrinákis. There were so many of us. So many.

—And you went down there with clubs?

—We went down there angry. And we got to where we knew the Communists were. We nabbed someone named Babakiás at Panayotópoulos's bakeshop. Up in the attic. Next to Xagás's tailor's shop.

—Down near Ayía Varvára.

—No, at Evanghelismós. It's a museum now.

—Yes it is.

—Panayotópoulos's bakeshop was just behind it. And Kóstas Goúlas had hidden up in his attic.

—Uh-huh.

—Do you remember Old Man Kóstas with the mustache?

—Uh-huh.

—Well, he went up there and grabbed Babakiás by the hair.

—Where was he from, Babakiás?

—From Dolianá. He was a captain. A real captain. Not like Kapetán Thódoros or Kapetán Nikotsáras.

—Babakiás.

—That's right. He grabbed him and dragged him down the stairs. There they started in on him with an automobile crank. There were these imported motorcars back then, they had cranks two meters long. Sarrís and Dimítris Prásinos went to work on him. They put him through the mill. He couldn't move for weeks. Mmm, after that I don't know what happened to him. We were young then. We wanted revenge. After that I left. I came here to the village. I worked until 1948. In '48 I left, on the twenty-eighth of October. A date not easily forgotten, we might say.[2]

—In the meantime the rebels were wreaking havoc everywhere.

—Wreaking havoc all over. Not so much in the day. They were afraid of Kastrí. But back then we would hide. We didn't sleep at our houses.

—Where did you hole up at night?

—Outside. I hadn't slept in my house in years. Not days, years.

—Yes.

—Like animals. We slept in any old hole. We'd fixed up underground hiding places. We had found caves—and we moved around. Right here, behind Houyiázos's place there was one. We once had you stay there too.

—Yiórgos did. I was away.

—Yiórgos. One of you did. I remember. Usually four of us slept there. Liás Andrianákos, and Sofianós's cousin, they're in Australia now; Vasílis Patsiás and me. And whenever Liás didn't come, Vanghélis Koútselas did. He's deceased now. There was a hollow rock. We'd squeeze under it like snakes. That kind of thing. There's no end to the stories. In 1948 I left. I went to Athens. The two girls stayed behind. Maria, born in 1942. In 1948 she was six. And Chrysoúla, a little older. Fourteen, fifteen. Yeorghía was in Athens, the older girl. Yiánnis was in Athens, Kóstas was in Athens. Our uncle tells us. He had flour mills. He owned the Amyla flour mill. He tells us, his nephews and nieces. We were all working there. He tells us, You left something behind for the rebels too. Their portion of the spoils. He meant Chrysoúla. There was no transportation back then. There were no telephones and things. I found someone, and I sent a letter to the old man. I think it was Yiannoúkos Haloúlos I found. Someone, at any rate. At that time there were trucks that went back and forth between Athens and Kastrí. The Galaxýdis trucks. So I wrote that letter to the old man and told him to send Chrysoúla to us. By airplane. There was a Dakota at the time that flew between Trípolis and Athens. You must remember that.

—No, I was away.

—You were away. It was the twenty-fifth of November, the Feast of Saint Catherine. The day the recruits of '47 reported for duty. Everyone was going there, and in Dragoúni the bus stopped. Down near Zoúbas's fields. The rebels stopped it, they had set up an ambush. And they sent them back. You must know about that.

—No, who was in it?

—All the recruits of '47. From Kastrí there was Liás Andrianákos, Grigóris Sítelis, and lots of others. All the recruits in my class. I was away. I was in Athens. I said that. But Chrysoúla was on the bus. With all the others. She was going to Trípolis to catch the airplane. And they sent them back. When they arrived at the square it was covered in snow. Thirty or forty centimeters of snow.

—The twenty-fifth of November?

—The twenty-fifth of November. On the Feast of Saint Catherine. There all the recruits who were able to ran away. Réppas's wife took my sister. And she helped her get away. Took her off the bus. Quiet-like.

—All that happened in 1948.

—In '48. Réppas's wife knew someone. I don't know who. And she managed to get her out. In the meantime the bus started out for Ayios Pétros. To take the recruits there. The driver was Mitsouliás. It arrived in Doúmos. Just before the bridge he runs the bus off the road. Says it skidded on the snow. On the ice. He pretended to be trying to get it out of the ditch, nothing. Get it out, he says to them, and I'll take you wherever you want. So they took some of the passengers and they left. On foot. Where they went I don't know. Four days later Chrysoúla went to Athens. The old man took her to Trípolis on foot. And he sent her on the airplane. We came back from Athens in 1949. By then the rebel insurrection was over. April 1949. It was over for good.

Chapter 31

Someone from Plátanos showed up. He says, Is your name Aryi-ríou? In Koubíla again. I say yes. He'd come to see about the shep-herds. We had shepherds from Plátanos back then. He says, Have anything to do with Kléarhos Aryiríou? We're relatives, I say. You on good terms? We are. I didn't want to be giving out information to any-one from Plátanos. Oh, come on, you're not on good terms, he tells me. You're not leveling with me. I am. Say whatever you want, I don't believe you. I'm sure you're not on good terms. Kléarhos was alive then. He died maybe a year or so later. I'm going to tell you some-thing to tell him, he says to me. I'm called Dimóyiorgas. My name's Dimóyiorgas. If you see him, tell him Dimóyiorgas told you this: I was seventeen and he gave me a pistol, one to me and one to another man, and he told us, Finish your food then go to such and such a house in Koubíla. The key will be under the roof tiles. You'll empty the house, you'll take the mules, and you'll take any men you find there with their women and bring them here to be tried. And have us all killed, in other words. And he was telling me this after so many years. And tell him something else too: When we got here we looked all over, but we didn't find anything. Just a rooster pecking down on the threshing floor. We gave it a whack, and we killed it, and it rolled way down there, and we went and got it. And we took it to Kapetán Kléarhos and he said, So those bastards got away, did they? And that was all—he'd sent us there and that's all we found. That's all he said: So those bastards got away, did they?

Chapter 32

That's who arrested me, local men, from here. Tóyias and Kléarhos. Vasílis Tóyias and Kapetán Kléarhos. They took me to Kastrí.
And then they took me to Loukoú.

— To Loukoú or Orthokostá?

— To Loukoú. They put me down in the basement and started in
on me. First they just slapped me around. Confess. Hey, I tell them,
I never went in the army. And truth is I was a deserter back then. In
1920. 1922. When they were going to Asia Minor.

— What was your year to enlist?

— 1922. And I deserted then and there. When the army came and
the central government was back I joined up. That's when I went and
enlisted. I went all the way to Thessaloníki. So there I was now in Loukoú. They put me in the basement, a filthy old basement. The next day
they make me lie down, and they loop the strap from one of their rifles
around my ankles, with me lying on my back. With my legs up high,
bent. And they would beat me with some sticks and say, Confess.

— On the soles of your feet, is that where they beat you?

— Yes, on the soles of my feet. So there at Loukoú sometimes
they'd give me food and at other times not.

— Who beat you?

— Not local men. They weren't from here. I didn't know them.
And while I was down like that they would kick me. In the ribs, everywhere, my arm's been out of whack ever since. They just kept at it. As
long as I was still breathing.

— And what did they want you to confess to?

—Who, or which organization I was with. But what could I do, I wasn't with any? Well, that's what they wanted. Wanted me to confess. They wanted to make me join against my will, that's all it was. I told you. I wasn't about to join the army by force. So I deserted before I even enlisted, in Náfplion, and I came here and loafed around. Until we lost the war in Asia Minor and the others came and formed an army again, and then I enlisted. That's it.

—How long did they keep you at Loukoú?

—For about a month. Then luckily things changed. They heard that the Germans were coming, and they took us away from there. I was half-crippled so they put me up on some mule. They didn't kill me. They put me on the mule and they took us on a ways toward Ayiórghis, toward the rocks at Másklina. Meantime, the Germans were getting closer. Making their way down from Ayiasofiá, and the rebels left us in a ditch, and they all ran away. They knew the trails around there, they disappeared. All of them. Then the Germans got us, they took us to Másklina. And the next day they put us on the train for Trípolis.

—And you, they never took you to Orthokostá?

—Nope. Only to Loukoú. They had a detention camp there too, but they didn't take me there. They had men from Sparta there. They had a koumbáros of mine from Vrésthena there. But I didn't see them. They took me to Loukoú.

—Who was the chief at Loukoú?

—They're dead now, all of them. Kléarhos was chief. Kléarhos was the top man. The head man. He had his brother there, he was killed too. There's a third one still around, name of Kraterós. That's all.

—How long did you stay in Trípolis?

—A long time. I don't remember. A very long time. I had a brother-in-law there, and I stayed with him. Haralás. I was still limping, I stayed a long time. Those bastards. Well, one of them was my wife's first cousin. And Tóyias, he and I were koumbároi. Vasílis. He was a nasty character, that one. And there were others, too, but those two were in charge. Kléarhos and Tóyias.

—When they burned down Kastrí where were you?

—When they burned down Kastrí. I was here. They burned down Kastrí and they took the villagers to Ayios Pétros. In case the Germans came and found us still here. I was here. In case the Germans came. Well, the kapetánios here, it was him, Kléarhos. There was someone else, Tsítsas, now he's gone. They tell me his son's a doctor somewhere, in Aráhova. He never came back. Their house is here, all rundown, behind the church. Now Saráfis uses it, ties his mule there. Can I get you something to drink?

—No, nothing.

—They weren't good for anything, those men. They were worthless. They were controlled by others. And I'll tell you something else: When they caught me they also caught a certain Hasánis. Remember him?

—Yes.

—Mítsos Hasánis.

—Yes.

—And they caught that Orfanós fellow. Yiánnis. You must remember him too.

—Yes.

—And they had them spying on me. Pretending the others were hounding them too. And on and on it went. Get it? When the Germans arrested us, down in Ayiasofiá, they went along with the rebels. So don't waste any words on them, to hell with them. They've done so many things to me here. They killed one of my brothers, he was a secretary in the County Legal Department. They sent someone named Kaloyerákis, and he stabbed him right in the middle of the street.

—When was that?

—Back in 1943. Or '44. And that's not all. They poisoned my mules, they did all kinds of things to me. They took me to the detention camp, they made a cripple out of me. And I never did anything to anyone, never. I say, the Lord be praised, a clear conscience is everything. If your conscience reproves you, forget it. So, my friend, that's it. And may God forgive them. It wasn't their fault. It was others higher up who were to blame. And I didn't tell you the most important thing. One of Kléarhos's sisters, who was married to my wife's cousin, she had left town. Yes, and they had appointed me the village alderman, since they couldn't find anyone better than me here in the village. They appointed me village alderman, and a paper came directing me to transfer the property of any Communists, etc., to the town. Well, Kléarhos's sister also came here. And I let her, she sold her fields, in Zygós. Someone from down below bought them, from the lower villages. But she did do one good thing for us; she let us keep the water. The big fountain up there, if you know it. She willed it to the town. That one thing. At any rate, I never bothered them, never harmed any of them. That's about it. As much as I can remember.

Chapter 33

The Battalions were advancing toward Astros. Some kind of reconnaissance, something like that. Lýras tells me, You're going with
them. The only time I saw action outside the Bureau. He tells me,
You'll go with the Battalion. My mission was to bring in Paraskevás
Denézos. Paraskevás was a lawyer, a member of ELAS, they'd put
him in charge of ETA. The Rebel Commissary. I think he was Trámbalis's brother-in-law. Trámbalis, manufactured ice and spaghetti. In
Trípolis. At any rate, they were related somehow. Distant relatives
through marriage. And we had to get him out of there, away from the
Organization. Lýras tells me, You'll go down there, you'll get Denézos. He's been notified. He'll go with you. And I had to transport him
safely to Trípolis. It was a way out, that, a setup so there wouldn't
be any retaliation. So he could appear not to be going with them
voluntarily. We went to Kastrí. We passed through Kastrí. The Battalions, hordes of them, were grabbing whatever they could. Kastrí
was already burned down, of course. We went to Ayios Pétros. Same
thing there. We went down to Ayiánnis, and from there to Mesóyeio,
Astros. And all of them barging into homes and looting. As though
they were in enemy territory. In a foreign country. I never imagined
it could be like that. We went back, we spent the night at Koulourás's
inn. For our own safety. The next day we went back up to Ayiánnis.
Paraskevás was there with his sister. They came over to me. I took
them along. Voúla Papayiánnis, Kóstas Vasilópoulos's wife, decided
to come with us. Kóstas and I were colleagues, he was also a schoolteacher. But he was involved with EAM. Voúla came with us to try to

somehow make up for her husband's forced participation in EAM. Of her own accord. We met at her brother's house. Astéris Papayiánnis. Ada was there too. It was summer when that raid was carried out. They'd come up from Mesóyeio. They were spending the summer there. Voúla came with us. They knew us, we were neighbors. She was a colleague's wife. I had her sit in the front seat of the car. Mihális Galaxýdis was driving the car. And he wouldn't stop hounding her. We went to Trípolis. Lýras took Denézos, he took him to Trámbalis. Voúla was staying somewhere else in the beginning. Another man from Astros had come with us, name of Kontákos. A few days later they sent for Voúla, then she went and stayed at Trámbalis's house. Mihális Galaxýdis would keep arresting her, hauling her in to the police station. He'd arrest her and lock her up, put her in jail. Because supposedly her husband was with EAM. They sent word to me. I went over and found him, and I had words with him. I told him, What's going on here? I brought this woman to Astros, she came here with me. Under my protection. And she came here to safeguard her husband, to justify his forced participation in EAM. I would arrange to get her out of the police station, Lýras would give an order, they'd let her go. Then Mihális would arrest her again. He was threatening to turn her over to the Germans. Voúla was staying at Trámbalis's place, I was at the Hotel Grítsi. One afternoon she called me over to the fence. There was an open space between us. She says, What shall I do, how long will this go on? She was upset. And rightly so. I tell her, You're not in danger. As long as Lýras is there I'll take care of things any time you're there. But I couldn't figure out why he was so steamed up, so obsessed with her. And then she told me why herself. A lover's frustration. He wanted her. Even before she was married. And she wouldn't look twice at him. That kind of insane passion was fairly widespread. I just want to point out what sort of thing one was up against then. But we shouldn't speak about that. Voúla was both a fellow villager and the wife of a colleague. May God rest her soul.

Chapter 34

I remember everything. They got me from here. They took me to
Ayios Pétros. Along with Chrístos Kokkiniás. From Ayios Pétros they
took us to Kastánitsa. They had Marínos's brothers there. They killed
Themistoklís. Mihális died last year.

—And Marínos?

—Marínos was in Athens. That's why they caught us. I had Dína
and the boy, they were little.

—Yiórgos?

—Not Yiórgos. I had him later. Yiórgos and Themistoklís.

—Which children did you have then?

—Dína and Dimítris. Dína's almost fifty. She's married to a
miller, in Aséa. Dimítris is in Trípolis. Working for the telephone
company.

—Themistoklís is in Trípolis too.

—Yes, but Themistoklís came later, I had him later.

—Dimítris and Dína, how old were they then?

—Let me think. They must have been four or five.

—And they stayed here when they arrested you?

—My mother took them. My mother married a Perentés. You
remember Mítsos Perentés?

—No.

—You're not very old, you. How old were you back then?

—In the Occupation I was seven.

—You're not old.

—Says who I'm not? I'm fifty-two.

—Then you're older. My children were three or four years old. The girl was born first. Worried herself sick. Bleeding from her ears, you know. And Dimítris started saying, Light all gone, Grandma. Looked at that oil lamp and kept saying, Our light all gone, Grandma. He was so young, I mean he could barely speak. Maybe he was two. And the girl was three. About that age.

—Who took you from here?

—Lenghéris.

—Pótis?

—One of the two. Maybe it was Harís.

—And they took you to Mángas's house.

—Yes. And to Ayios Pétros–Kastánitsa. We were covered in lice, tons of them. Such filth. In Orthokostá we found that poor Braílas woman. They had arrested her earlier. Along with Marínos. I was the one got Marínos out. All innocent-like. I went and saw him.

—In Loukoú?

—No, in Ayiánnis. At Vérvaina grade school. They'd taken them there. I tell him pretend-like, What are you doing here? We've got work to do, why are you still here? Oh, what we went through, he'd say later. And he left for Athens.

—That happened in February, right?

—It was winter. Maybe March. February or March. They arrested me in May. We were still making cheese. Here at my mother's place. With Chrístos Prézas. They came and took me, with my shoes still pressed under my heels. Like slippers. Yes. They were killing me, those raggedy old shoes—when I got to the prison camp my feet were all cut up. In Orthokostá there were lots of people. People I knew. I would cross myself day and night. There were mothers with young children. Day and night, so grateful they didn't arrest me with my children. The children in the camp would gather on the stairs and play. Old stone steps worn smooth by footsteps. And when they said, Come and eat, what did the little ones get? They gave us peas, just pea soup. Except when someone brought us something from outside. Efthymía was there, my cousin Thanásis's sister-in-law. Thanásis Samartzís. She was getting married. She married some older man from down there. And I met him back then. In '39. I was engaged. I got engaged too that day. The same day. They were relatives of my husband, we went to the wedding, and we met them. And he would bring me food. Or send me some.

—Was he from Ayiánnis?

—From Ayios Andréas. Really, he'd send food. To Orthokostá. And not a word to him from anyone.

—How long did you stay there?

—A month. One whole month. And if the Germans hadn't come they would've killed us. They took us out to the mountains.

—Wait a minute. Yeorghía Makrís was there.

—We were together. The two of us. We slept together. All the women did. There was another woman from Ayiasofiá.

—Did they interrogate you?

—No. Nothing. But they did take us out to the mountains. We woke up one morning, they knew the Germans were coming. We saw Tóyias, he had a hand grenade strapped to his waist. A hand grenade. Something's going on, the others were saying. The men. Poor Panayótis Pezoúlis. They killed him. Iraklís's uncle. Chrysanthe, he says to me. We were cousins. Second cousins. He had a dream that night. It's a good dream, I tell him. He was gathering lentils by the handful and throwing them in front of him. It's a good dream, I tell him, what could I say to him? They tortured those two, him and Iraklís. They didn't kill them, they didn't execute them. Just put them through hell. Before the Germans came. And Themistoklís, God rest his soul, could barely move. I went and took him fresh-cut grass. It was May, near summer. Fresh grass to put under him. They'd beat him real bad. To cushion up his body. His back all bruises from top to bottom. That grass gave out warmth, it took away his pain. Chrysanthe, how did you think of that? he said. To ease the pain just a bit, Themistoklís. So you're not flat against cement. Piled-up grass keeps in the heat. Like we used to say about mowed hay that it "heated up." And his back soaked up that warmth, caught that heat. He was seething all over from so many beatings. Then they got us up, they took us out to the mountains. They took us out of Orthokostá when they realized that the Germans were coming. We had all slept together that night. They took us up the mountain, there was a ravine, it could hold us. A hundred, hundred fifty people. As soon as it got dark they separated us and they took us to a shepherd. His son took us there. About ten of us, all women. He says, Father, take care of these girls. All right, says the old man. O-o-o-o-kay, goes his son. O-o-o-o-kay, answers the father from under his cape. The son says, Take care of the girls, I'll take care of them. In the morning at daybreak the father went off a ways. I say to the others, Shall we leave? Shall we just go, I tell them. What are you talking about, they answer me, They'll kill us. They all said that. They were younger than me. Better if they kill us. Shoot us from behind so we don't see them. And we left. We go along some more, down a hill. We see the Germans.

— How old were you then?

— Thirty? Maybe not even.

— Do you remember when you were born?

— I was born in 1912. Twelve from forty-four, thirty, thirty-one years old. And I took those girls, I helped them escape. The Germans saw our white kerchiefs, and they didn't bother us. Back then we all wore head scarves. I told them to. Get a stick and tie your kerchiefs on it, all of you. We tied them on, and we got going. We kept moving toward them. We had to go down a gorge to get across. We meet an Italian man. A deserter. Like someone just stepped out of a washtub, that's how he looked. Covered in sweat. We ask him, Where you headed? he says, Germans. Germans coming. He spoke a little Greek. He was afraid of the Germans now. And we were on our way to find them. We walked on down, a good lot of kilometers, there was a small stream. We found the Germans there, they were washing their feet. They'd captured two rebels. They asked us, Who are these men? Talking with their hands. What could we say? They had them in the sun, and they were beating them. Beating them with canes long as Easter candles. Those rebels had made my life hell, but I felt sorry for them. We left that place. We never saw those rebels again. We went back to Orthokostá. The Germans were advancing. We got away from those Germans there, they let us go free. We decided to go back to our homes. To go up to Malevós, to come back here. They tell us, Rebels ahead, where are you going? So we split up. I left for Galtená. My sister was there. She'd married someone called Kambylafkás. Panayótis Kambylafkás. We walked all day. All day with a woman from Ayiasofiá. Named Lambrítsa. She's married now, down in Mýloi. We got ourselves to Galtená. They bedded us down out on the terrace. We fell right asleep. My sister, her mother-in-law, and the girls. She had six girls. At night I hear dogs. I hear the dogs, They're coming for me, I say. I drag my covers inside. Nonsense, they're not coming for you, says my sister. The rebels are coming for me, I tell her. I get up next morning, no one came. I get up and put on her mother-in-law's clothes. Those old-fashioned dresses. I bundle myself up in her scarf. So they won't recognize me. Where will you go? To Kastrí. I bring myself up here. My mother sees me. You back, my jewel? Come, sit down. I can't, Mama. They'll catch me. What are you talking about, child? I take my girl by the hand, a loaf of bread and the boy on my back. And I go to Másklina. Marínos was there. But I had stamina back then, I was strong. A loaf of bread, the boy on my back, and the girl, I'd have her by the hand, then I'd let her move free for a while. I got myself down there, I found Marínos. After eight months apart. We stayed there. Then we left the place, we went to Trípolis. And that's how we got away. Trípolis was the end.

— How did they kill Themistoklís?

— They took us somewhere else, I told you. No one knows, we never found out. Ruthless men. My mother-in-law went and found him afterward. Two years later. They'd buried him under stones. She found the bones. Was it him, or someone else, well, who knows? So much happened. You get all emotional just talking about it. From Másklina to Trípolis. Terrible years. Especially for me. Bad. Very bad. After the Liberation, I came back here. I wanted to come here. Marínos stayed. I came here. I found nothing. Everything had been leveled. The house burned down. The house here, and the house in Ayiórghis. We had homes in two places. When they set fire to our village Petrákos told us. Chrístos Petrákos. That they burned down the houses one by one. This house here, that house there. And I was left with nothing but the clothes on my back, I swear. We had that shelter, just a hole, we'd hidden our things there. To keep them safe from the Germans. We'd hidden them because of the Germans and the other side took them. They knew the shelter. But now I have shoes. They don't cut into my feet and make me bleed. Back then I'd stamped them down right here. I was setting the cheese to curdle, they didn't let me go inside to change. Thank the Lord.

—All that's over.

—It's over. And later I had children, nice kids with good jobs. I'm not just saying that 'cause they're mine. Everyone thinks so.

—I know Yiórghis.

—Yiórghis—and the others are nice kids too, very nice.

—I've seen Themistoklís once, in Trípolis.

—He's named after his late uncle. We gave him that name.

Chapter 35

That's the way things were. Nothing you could do about it. We'd hear the dog barking at night and we'd tremble. In the spring we'd go outside and sleep five hundred meters from the storage shed. A thousand meters, in any old hole. My old man was afraid someone would come and arrest him. Mostly he was afraid of that Vasílis Tóyias. He was mean as they come. A diehard Communist. Some time later on they got him from Mcsorráhi and took him to Kastrí. To Mángas's place. For an interrogation, they told him. Anyone went there for an interrogation never came back. They got him and took him to Mángas's place. Velissáris was there, and Mavromantilás. Vasílis, what are you doing here? Vasílis was older by then. Maybe forty-five. He pointed at Tóyias. The kapetánios brought me here, he says. You? Yes, me. Go to Doúmos's place, and we'll let you know when you can leave. They sent him to Doúmos's place so the others wouldn't see him hanging around the square. Okay, I'll leave, but I want a permit. To be away for a month. They gave him the permit and he left. Mavromantilás and Velissáris, they arranged all that. He went to Athens, he stayed there for a while, and avoided all the trouble. My brother-in-law Yiánnis was there too. Kalosynátos. Yiánnis, not Yiórgos. They arrested Yiórgos later—in place of the others. Tóyias himself. He was the one that took our animals. He brought them right through the square here. To feed the rebels. I'm taking them to Malevós, he said. He'd take them there and they'd eat. Our mules too, everything we had, food, everything. Everything. They came and took stock, wrote everything down in case we hid anything. They took my mother-in-law to Ayios Pétros, an old woman, eighty years old. Just because Yiánnis and Vasílis had left. That's when they caught Yiórgos. Yiánnis left because he had English pounds, or so they said. And he should have handed them over for the cause. One five-pound note, that was all he had, poor man. And I know that from Vasílis. Like I said, Pavlákos had a bit of decency in him. The Aryíris family had been kind to him. At night when they were about to take in Kalosynátos, Vasílis walked past them. Nikólas Pavlákos and the rest of them. And right away they stopped talking. Good evening, Good evening to you, too. Nothing else. My old man realized that they were on their way to arrest Yiánnis. He hurried past them and went to warn him. By the time he got there, Pavlákos had already been there. He left the others, saying he had to go take a leak. And he went and told him, Yiánnis, get out, they're coming to arrest you tonight. And he upped and left, he went to Kotsóni, walked all night to save his life. And that's how Kalosynátos left and went to Athens. That was how they forced them, one by one, into leaving. He wasn't with his second wife yet. He had no children from his first wife. He had children later on. And the one he's with now is his third wife. I'm telling you that some people were forced into things, then they'd find themselves in over their heads, and once the current pulls you downstream that's it. There's no going back. And later on, much later, when my children were in Athens, going to school there, and Pavlákos got out of prison, he found out that Vasílis was there and he went to see him. Nikólas, why are you staying here, why don't you come to the village? I'd gladly come, Vasílis, he said, but what will I live on? Here I can keep myself fed. If I come down to the village, I'll just fill up on beatings. That's why he never went back. I'm not sticking up for Pavlákos, whatever happened happened, but he wasn't all that mean.

Chapter 36

The men from Karátoula joined the Battalions in 1944. The December Uprising in Athens took place that same year. Because we weren't here for Christmas.

—Don't say anything you shouldn't.

—No, stop it. In 1944 the Germans arrived. In June. The rebels came here, they said, Leave your houses, all of you. Whoever stays in the village will be executed. And the Germans dropped leaflets. Stay in your homes, no one will harm you. We had no choice but to leave. We went to Xerokámpi. All the women and children were there. In Samartzís's storage shed. In Kokkíni. And we were harvesting wheat. The Germans came and arrested us. They brought us to Kastrí. At Kastrí they picked out some men they wanted and let the rest of us go free. Because of the rebels we couldn't find shelter. We went down to Trípolis.

—It was that long before you went to Trípolis?

—Yes, it was 1944. In November the Germans left. They had also come here in June. For the big blockade. There was all that time in between. We went down to the Battalions. Then the head men, Antonákos and Dínos Yiánnaros, sent us away. They say, Go to the village, we'll be coming to form a company there. We came back. We wake up one morning. We hear gunfire. From Ayios Nikólaos. We get up and head for Kastrí, we look around, Mávros's house was in flames. The rebels had set fires, they were burning down the village. Then they come down to Karátoula. Right here to Karátoula. They burn down three houses. Nikólas Konstantélos's house, Sokrátis Marinákos's and Alkiviádis Marinákos's houses. They were in the Battalions, those men, it was for revenge. They didn't burn down Chrysoyénis's place. They looted it. Took everything and left. The next day Pavlákos shows up. I had gone to Oriá with our men. Pavlákos arrests me and sends me to Ayios Pétros, escorted by Voúlis Paraskevoulákos. Voúlis takes me there, they put me in jail. I find four other men from Karátoula there. Vasílis Logothétis, Mítsos Panayotoúros, Vasílis Kounoúfos, Yiánnis Chrysoyénis. In the morning someone comes and shouts, Douénis. I say, Here. He says, Interrogation room. They take me for interrogation. They ask me to hand over my machine gun to them. I say, I don't have a machine gun. They tell me, On the night the rebels went to burn down Kastrí, men from your village were firing at us. We had two old .45 revolvers. We'd make hansa cartridges for them. We'd cut off the tip of the bullet so it would fit into the cylinder, to make it work. And that's what we fired with. It was Vasílis Konstantélos who was doing that. We were together. Vasílis Logothétis, Panayótis's son, me, and Mihális Marinákos. And also Vasílis Pantelís. In the end I never gave anyone away. I tell the interrogator, The Germans captured us, they took us to Trípolis, to the Security Battalions. And we escaped, we came back. We had a little too much wine, we started shooting. That's all. In the end they sent me back to the detention room. The other men from Karátoula were going to leave. They were setting them free. I tell them, Hey, you men, why don't you help me out too? They couldn't be bothered. The next day they bring Kyriákos Bakoúris from Ayiasofiá. He was wearing a Battalions band on his arm. He had sheep, he'd graze them, and when the Germans saw that armband they wouldn't bother you. The rebels arrested him, with his wife and their two children. And they brought him in. They brought someone else in too, man named Thodorís Lambíris. They took them for interrogation. Someone named Nikólas Farmasónis comes to see them, a fellow villager. Nikólas, what about my children, Kyriákos says. And Nikólas tells him, You made your bed, now lie in it. That's exactly what he said. Two days later they take us to be executed. They marched us toward the bridge. On the way we meet Pétros Lagoumitzís. From Ayios Pétros. He sees me there with the others, he says, This one's a goner. And he spread the word that they'd killed me there. A little further along a kapetános from Pýrgos starts hollering. What has this poor man done, what has he done? Talking about me. I don't remember his name. I can't remember it. But the man who was in charge then was Mavróyiannis. In the end they sent me back. That was on September 13. The night before the Feast of the Elevation of the True Cross.[1] We leave at night for Kaltezés. The entire rebel battalion. They took me with them. Next morning another kapetános sees me. He was taken aback. He asks, Why wasn't he executed? And he got into a fight with Mavróyiannis. Then they take me and they send me straight to Stemnítsa. They hand me over to the militia. And they had me free to move about. There was a taverna, the men from the Organization ate there. The taverna was run by an old man. He asks me, Where you from? From Kastrí, I tell him, from Karátoula. What's your name? Douénis. Are you by any chance old man Kóstas's son? Yes, I tell him. I used to tin-plate copper pots and pans, I used to go there. I knew your father. His son comes in. He was in charge of Stemnítsa. He tells him, Take good care of this fellow, he's the son of a friend. The next day Liás Drínis shows up. A cousin of the Pantelís family. Kapetán Liás arrives with some men from Oriá. The Sioútos brothers and some others. He sees me. He tells me, Who in hell's name did you take after? Your brother's a good man. He was talking about Tássos. I didn't say a word to him. And I haven't forgotten that. He goes over to the garrison headquarters, he briefs them. Liás was out to get me. They grab me the next day and send me to Chrysovítsi. They lock me up in the detention camp. Chrysovítsi had a detention camp. A couple of days go by. One of the rebels says, Who's from Kastrí? I say, I am. A company of volunteers is on their way here right now. They had us outside in the yard. It was about five o'clock in the afternoon, the time we were supposed to bring up the food. They prepared it down at some sawmill. Then we hear them down below, singing as they came. It was someone else's turn to do chores. I tell him, Let me go instead, some men from my village are coming. And he did. I take two large tin cans, with the rebel right beside me, we go down a ways. I see a group of men from Oriá. I see

Nikólas Roússos. Hey, Nikólas, I tell him, no answer. Yiórgos Kontós, same thing. Vanghélis Kyriazís, the priest's brother-in-law, same thing again. They pay no attention. You'd think I was a leper. I leave the cans. I walk on a ways. I find Kóstas Logothétis. I find Látzos. I find Vasílis Marinákos. I find Thodorís Kounoúfos. I find Yiannákis Dáskalos. Where you been, they ask me. Here, I tell them, in Chrysovítsi. The rebel had lost sight of me, he comes up behind me, he gives me a good kick. Asshole, I've been looking for you. He kicks me again. The others start yelling at him. They had no weapons. None of them. The men from Oriá were volunteers. The men from Karátoula had been drafted. Forcibly. And they still had no weapons. I take the food, and I went back up. In the morning they call me. Douénis, go to the interrogation room. The men had talked to Vanghélis Kyriazís. They approached him. And he did take an interest in the end. I walk into the interrogation room, I didn't know a thing. What's your relation to Vanghélis Kyriazís, someone says to me. I got scared. None, I say. He's from another village, near mine. How near? We live across from each other. We talk from our balconies. I'm from Karátoula, he's from Oriá. Right this minute, they tell me, you're leaving with an escort to go to Vytína. And you'll report for duty to the company of men from Kastrí. That was that. One of the rebels went with me and took me to Vytína. He took me to the company and handed me over. The company officer was someone named Kolovós, from Trípolis. He'd also been drafted. Later on I found out he was killed in Ahladókampos. In Kolosoúrtis. In 1949 or 1950. He was in the service, a Reservist. A small tank overturned and crushed him. One of those small personnel carriers. The open type. He played right midfielder for Pan-Arkadikós. So he took me there, to the company. The next day they took us back. From Vytína to Chrysovítsi. We had to be enlisted. To be formally divided into units. Kóstas Logothétis goes and writes in as sick. And he left. Látzos goes and does the same. And he left too. I go and write in as sick. The men from Oriá jump up. He was in the detention camp, and we brought him here. We let him out of there so he would come with us. In the end we stayed. Me, Thodorís Kounoúfos, Yiannákis Dáskalos, Vásios Marinákos. Vásios. So they took us away, they gave us a mule. One mule for each of us. They took Yiannákis Dáskalos to another company. The three of us who were left stayed together. With one mule each, close together. They took us down to Trípolis. The Germans had left. They take us to Meligalás. They'd wiped it out. They take us to Gargaliánoi. They fought the villagers there. They wiped them out. Stoúpas was there, he defended himself to the end. From there we go back to Trípolis. Trípolis surrenders, the Security Battalions. They signed treaties. They take us down to Argos, from Argos they take us to Isthmia. Unarmed, with the mules close together. From Isthmia they take us back to Argos. In Argos my only chance was to run into people I knew. People from Kastrí. I go and find Panarítis. Vanghelió's husband. She was married there, Vanghelió, Yiánnis Lymbéris's daughter. I find Yiórghis Tsoulouhás. He tells me, They're taking you to Athens. There's going to be war in Athens. I had decided to escape. I tell Vásios, I tell Thodorís, I tell Yiannákis Dáskalos. They say Okay. We arrange to meet that night at Panarítis's place. Yiannákis doesn't show up. Dáskalos didn't show. We stayed behind too. We were scared and we stayed. The next day I find him. He says, Listen, I'd like to take a blanket or something along. I tell him, Forget the blanket. They'll kill us in Athens. They're taking us to be killed. The next day he showed up. We left, I knew the terrain there. We used to work as gleaners there in the summer. Folks were poor. We head out from Argos toward Kefalári. From Kefalári we go up to Kalamáki. From Kalamáki we come to Platána. It was a six- or seven-hour walk. Vásios's sister and five other girls were there in Platána. Gathering olives. For a daily wage. We knock on the door at night, they opened for us. They made us food and we ate. We come to the village. We say, Let's not tell anyone we ran away. We'll say we're on leave. A week goes by. Vásios tells us, Let's go hunting. We go to Xerokámpi, we shoot four hares. We go back. The next day the rebels show up, looking for us. They go to Yiórghis Látzos's house, the brother of one of our men. He advises us to look out for ourselves. I manage to hide just in time. My brother Tássos comes to see me. I tell him, I can't stay here. Go to your brother-in-law and get an identity card from him. It was Panayótis Laganás, he was the one arranged all those things. And Yiánnis Kapetéris. Tássos went there, they gave him the papers. I get up at night, I leave for Argolís. I reach Kefalári. I find Sophia married there. Vanghelió's sister. Sophia Kefálas, that was her husband's name. She says, You can stay at our house. They had a mill, in Neró. I stayed on my guard. One day her son comes running home from there. Rebels, he tells me. From Kastrí. It was Yiórghis Kontós and Vanghélis Fotiás. They were hunting men down. Looking for Antonákos, looking for Yiánnaros. Full of hate. I go to Sophia's, she shoves me into a trunk. They came inside, they saw the things. They didn't see anyone. They left, I get out of the trunk. If I'd stayed in there any longer I'd have been asphyxiated. I left Kefalári. I had a brother in Koutsí, Leftéris. The old man had spread us out. He had him doing menial work, earning his keep. I go to Koutsí. What are you doing here, Leftéris says to me. This is their hornet's nest. Right here. Get out, he says, go to Kofíni, to Yiánnis. That's my other brother. There was a big plot of land there. The owners had gone off to Athens. They were hiding out there, to stay in the clear. There were five or six dogs on that plot of land. Yiánnis takes me inside. There was a big storeroom, with some sheets of tin lying around. I made a kind of shelter there. As soon as I heard the dogs barking I'd hide. After a few days Yiánnis tells me, I'm going to Náfplion. Yiánnis was hard of hearing and he lived there all alone. I tell him, Bring me a newspaper. I wanted to find out what was going on. It was January. The December Uprising had already taken place, but I didn't know about it. Finally Yiánnis comes back. He went and sold some oranges and he came back. He says, The British are in Náfplion. I tell him, Cut it out, it was rebels you saw. But he knew the Brits. He hid them on his property in 1941 when they were leaving. With their short trousers. He gives me a paper, they had actually marked off a zone up to Mýloi. The British up to Mýloi. And beyond there the rebels. Then I say, I have to get out of here. I asked Yiánnis to give me a sack of wheat. Ten okás or so. So as not to go back empty-handed. He wouldn't give me any. The crop isn't mine, he said. I look around and I see some barley in a corner. I grab some and take it with me. And I'm off. I arrive all loaded up at Dalamanára. At Dalamanára I run into Havdotóyiannis, riding a mule. He gets off the mule, he starts crying when he sees me. He throws his arms around me. We don't know which of our men we've lost, I tell him. Clear out, he tells me, head for Argos. Go to Gonéis's inn, you'll find everyone there. I go to Argos. I go to Gonéis's inn. And it was true, they were all gathered there. The Pantelís brothers. Harís Lymbéris, Antonákos, and the rest, all the men from Karátoula. They were all in there. And we stayed there until the rebels had completely cleared out. By then it was March. Then we went to Corinth and worked. Until Easter when we came back here. There were no more rebels from ELAS, they were gone. And may all that never happen again.

Chapter 37

They brought those boys from Tservási up here. Brought them here, and that was that. One was Nikoláou's, the other Christofílis's. They killed them somewhere in Ayiliás. In Ayiliás. First they had them at Háyios's place, they were holding them there. At Pános Háyios's place. And Lenghéris saw them and he said, Why are you holding them here, why are you holding them? And a short while later they got them and they took them to some ravine in Ayiliás. Dakourélis was there, he saw them. And he climbed a tree and hid. Klaría, who still had all her marbles then—she does now too, but she tells such lies now—she's hard of hearing now, and she tells lies, too. She told me that Eléni, Kyámos's wife, Métsos's sister, was in tight with some kapetános, and he told Vanghélis, Kassianí's husband, he would give him a shirt. And when Vanghélis saw it, he recognized it, it belonged to one of the boys. It had been washed but they hadn't got all the blood out. And he wouldn't take it, poor man, even though he had nothing to his name back then. Yiánnis Christofílis and Kóstas Nikoláou. They killed those boys. The next day those poor women from Tservási went up there and had a hard struggle getting their bodies up the hill, using a blanket. Up to the top so they could bury them. It was God's wrath, all that, there's nothing else you can say.

—A human life wasn't worth much then, that's how things were.

Chapter 38

Kóstas Kirkís was my grandfather's brother. On my mother's side of the family. He died before I was born. A gruff sort of character. He was married, had no children. He was infertile. Could be that's what made him like that. Always angry. He was a hard worker. Even though he had no kids, he struggled with the land. A desperate struggle, one that often pitted him against his brother. They would quarrel over the land. They had plots of land in Melíssi, in Ayiórghis, and across from Galtená. And in Xerokámpi. And they were suspicious of each other. Well, at any rate, each of them thought the other was moving the boundaries. That he was moving it a meter or two in his favor. The problem was in dividing up the land of their forefathers. And what land are we talking about? Just strips of dirt. And every tiny ledge in that confined space was important. But in most cases it was stubbornness that drove people to extremes. To beat others or to murder them. Stubbornness more than self-interest. They divided up the land on the spot, strip by strip, drawing lots. Instead of appraising it as a whole and each one taking something from here or from there. So they could save time. The so-called land redistribution is calculated that way today. So the cultivated land is all in one piece to increase productivity. At any rate. They quarreled, and for most of the year they didn't speak to each other. Once in a while this sorry state would give way to enthusiasm, and then they would go out and eat and drink and shed a few tears together, only to start in again with their suspicions and complaints the following year. Or with violence and threats. So they decided to define the boundaries once and for all. And to do this by sworn oath. Their mutual suspicion finally led them to resort to divine intervention: "Ready are we to be dragged through fire and to swear by the gods," as the ancient tragic playwright[1] says. So my grandfather set out with his brother. And they took my mother along with them. With a holy icon in a shoulder sack, a piece of bread, and two onions. They started out on friendly terms, of course, even though they had quarreled in the past. They made what the law calls a kind of compromise, a mutual promise that by a mutually sworn oath they would delineate and define the boundaries, so that the cause of their differences would disappear. They would mark off the boundaries with stones. They would dig a small ditch and place a rock in it, a long, narrow rock in three or four spots. So that the ends formed a straight line. But that didn't prevent either of them from going and moving them in winter or at night or when the other one was working somewhere far away. Just to gain half a meter. It was precisely to rule out such a possibility that they decided to settle things by sworn oath. Religious sentiment was much stronger in those days than it is today. People were respectful and God-fearing. Afraid of divine retribution. So on they went. They went to Ayiórghis. They went to Melíssi, with my mother beside them with her shoulder sack. At every disputed spot they would stop. The boundary's here, no it's there. They'd take out the icon and swear on it, one or the other of them, depending. By noon they reached Galtená. Across from there, I think the place is called Krampítsa. It's all in ruins now. They were going to leave Xerokámpi for the next day. My mother had stayed behind. They passed by a small watering hole, she sat down to drink. Dying of hunger, exhausted from the heat, she fell asleep. She must have been what, then, about twelve years old? All that was before 1907. In 1907 she was married at the age of sixteen. Before 1905. At the beginning of the century. Poor little thing, my grandfather said. And he wanted to go back. Let's finish first, his brother says. We don't have the icon. We haven't got it. He picks up a rock and puts it on his shoulder. That was another way of taking an oath. That meant he was telling the truth. Otherwise, if he was lying, the weight of that rock would eternally weigh on his soul. They finished. They went back, they found my mother. That night each of them thought he'd been wronged by the other. Both were thinking the same thing. And they didn't continue with the settlement. They didn't go to Xerokámpi. I don't know if they ever divided up their inheritance definitively. In 1923 my grandfather's brother retired to Athens. He came down with partial paralysis there. At any rate, up until his death they were sometimes on good terms and sometimes not.

Chapter 39

They set the big fire on July 24. During the first fire they only burned down a few houses. Then came the blockade, in June. And then the big fire. On July 24. More than one hundred houses. In the morning. And in the afternoon the Security Battalions came. Some hotheaded men, and they burned down about ten leftist houses in revenge. Hotheads all of them. The Galaxýdis brothers. Old Yiannákos Prásinos. Old Man Yiannákos. He gave them a light so they could burn down the doctor's house. Mávros's house. Why should that one be spared, he said. So he gave his flint lighter to someone. Réppas came. Réppas in his truck. He brought them there. All this after the so-called blockade. The Germans had masterminded a plan for operations on Mount Parnon and Mount Taygetus. At the same time, but mainly on Mount Parnon. Mount Parnon could provide cover for troops. And that's what happened during the Civil War. It's a soft wooded mountain. A female mountain. The Germans decided to sweep it clean. But their plan was leaked to ELAS. It was stolen from their headquarters in Corinth. Or so we heard. By the time the Germans arrived here the active corps of the rebels had moved to Mount Taygetus. Without a shot being fired. The Germans arrived there from Platána, from Astros, from Dragoúni. And from Voúrvoura. From every direction, converging at the main bulk of the mountain. It was a well-planned operation. One division took part in its execution. Along with some auxiliary weapons. In the end a Battalion arrived here. They came and set up camp here. With three tanks in the yard of the elementary school. I was in Karátoula. I just happened to be at the mill. With my old man and Aryíris. On the first day we hid in a small cave just above the mill. Above our vineyard. The cave was safe from attack. Nothing could reach us there, neither cannons nor mortars. We could see what was happening from there. We could see the Germans across from there, at Atzinás's chestnut tree. They had a machine gun set up there. Permanently. For twenty or thirty hours. And they kept firing. They were shooting into the dense shrubbery on our left. But most of their fire was toward Stefanákia and beyond. Mainly toward Kavalariá Pétra. Their bullets were well aimed. But there was no one there. At night Aryíris and I left. The old man stayed at the mill. We arrived at Xerokámpi, at Láros's Hole just behind there. In Langáda. We found a lot of people from Karátoula there. And some from Roúvali. At eleven in the morning we saw two Germans passing by. Just across from us, on the other side of the stream. A hundred meters. That stream runs down from high up. It narrows sharply. And Láros's Hole is on the left side. It's twenty meters deep. With a big opening. The Germans walked right by but they didn't see it. There was a maple tree nearby, and by a stroke of luck its shadow hid the entrance from view. Eleven o'clock. The two Germans walked by and kept going toward the mountaintop. We saw them come out at the top. We put a little mirror over to one side, belonging to one of the girls. Marinákos's sisters were there. We set up that mirror, and we could keep an eye on things on both sides. We made sure the Germans had left. Then we decided to come out. To give ourselves up. Someone arrived there and told us that they were letting everyone go free. I had my doubts. I listened but wasn't convinced. And I didn't follow the rest of them. I left with Aryíris and five or six men from Roúvali. We went down to the Langáda riverbed. Tássos Kirkís, and Yiórgos, Marina's husband. I don't remember who the others were. Kyriákos Léngourdas left first with the people from Karátoula. Then he came back to us. Stupid of him. But we didn't know what was happening yet. We kept moving along. I had a blanket over my shoulder. An old blanket to sleep on. The riverbed was hard to walk on, it had small, dried-up waterfalls we had to climb down on all fours. The men from Roúvali knew we'd find some watering holes there. And we found them in the end. Stagnant water, with a film of dust on the surface. We sat down to eat. As evening came on we heard some garbled chatter coming from up above us. The gorge there picked it up and turned it into a kind of echo, and we couldn't understand what if anything was happening. At night I tell the others, I'm going to the mill. Someone has to come with me. So we can find out what's going on. Because the uncertainty was getting to us. Not knowing what was happening. In the end someone came with me, I think it was Kyriá-kos. It was impossible to go down through the watering holes. The trail was cut off by a smooth high rock. So we climbed up along the edge and climbed back down again, and came out on the road to Pródro-mos. We arrived at the mill. The old man was there. What's going on, Father? He didn't know much. Germans had passed by on their way to Pródromos Monastery. And a convoy had passed by with pack-horses loaded with ammunition, going from Dragatoúra to Yerakína. We left. We took some hardtack with us, and a little cheese, and we left to go back to the others. To give them news, to see what we should do. The uncertain information that had reached Láros's Hole about the Germans freeing everyone they'd captured was never confirmed. We went back to the watering holes. In the morning we heard the tramping of feet on the road to Xerokámpi that comes down from the so-called Red Threshing Floors. Sheep and people and bells. All mixed up. And the next day at about eleven my sister Marigó started shouting from up above. Kó-o-ost-a-a-as. And her voice echoed as it bounced from rock to rock. Kó-o-ost-a-a-as. It was terrible. Come out, wherever you are. I recognized her voice, it wasn't distorted by the echo, but I had a feeling she was doing that under pressure. That they had got hold of her and were making her shout like that to trick us into giving ourselves up. As for the tramping of feet we'd heard the day before, we'd taken it to be prisoners marching to their execution. It was nothing of the sort. Finally we left at dusk. We went to the mill. There the old man told us that Panayótis Levéntis and Dímos Koút-sis, Pítsa's husband, had been killed in Xerokámpi. They were harvest-ing wheat, and they saw the Germans passing by. And they raised their scythes to greet them. As a friendly gesture. But the Germans took it differently. And they fired on them from a distance and killed them. Some men from the village went to retrieve them. They had remained where they fell for two days under the sun. We buried them on the Feast of Saints Peter and Paul. July 29, the patron saints of the village. A service was held, but the usual yearly festival was not. We buried them, and I went off to the mill again. The others had to go up to Kastrí. By order of the Germans. They forced them to, and of course they had arrested a lot of them. There were women they found in their storage huts in Xerokámpi, there were people who'd given themselves up of their own accord. They gathered them in Kastrí, in Ayios Nikólaos. Now who are you, and you, and you? They made their selections. That's when they arrested Tássos Kirkís. After a tip-off of course. They had also arrested Annió, Aryíris's wife. And who are you? Aryíris Kékeris's wife. You can go, Chrístos Haloúlos tells her. Then all of a sudden the Germans left. Just like that. And everyone followed them en masse. The noncombatants. People were scared. They had heard about Braílas's mother and the others. Iraklís had found them. And he said they were still warm. Everyone took off for Trípolis. Aryíris put some soft myzíthra cheese and half a head of hard cheese in his shoulder sack. I tell him, I'm not going with you. I call Liás Atzinás so we can put our heads together. He had a good mind. He'd been taken sick in Athens. And he had a paper from Dr. Proestópoulos. He and about ten other men from Kastrí. The paper was in German. *Kranken toubakoulozoum.* It said they had tuberculosis, that the Germans shouldn't bother them. Tássos Kirkís had one of those papers. But Tássos was actively involved in everything. In the end Aryíris got him off. He wrote a note to Nikólas Petrákos and got him off the hook. Aryíris is now in Kastrí. I notify him to come down to Karátoula so we can talk. To come down to the Kouloúros property. I come up there too from the mill. In the meantime the others left. And Aryíris's shoulder sack with the myzíthra, the half-head of cheese, a bottle of wine, and several boiled eggs arrived in Trípolis. Aryíris came to the Kouloúros property. I tell him, We shouldn't go. What should we do? It was all very worrisome. And I was half-crazy, racking my brain to find a solution. I tell him, We need to find a sheltered place. We'll go to Kyvéri. We had olive trees there. And we left the same evening. In Trípolis the men from Karátoula were angry. They were very angry, mainly with Aryíris. Aryíris was a sergeant in the army, they had earmarked him for leadership. And in Albania he'd been promoted to sergeant major. The Kékeris brothers betrayed us, they stayed behind. And then there was our family of course, it was well known that our old man was a supporter of Venizélos, so they thought our political leanings were in the other direction. After several days things calmed down somewhat. We couldn't bear it in Kyvéri. With the summer heat and the mosquitoes. We'd run out of food, we couldn't find anything to eat. We left and came back. Then they ordered us to report for duty to Kastrí. Me and Dímos Aloúpis. With two days' worth of bread. We go to Kastrí. They give us each a mule. They had another five or six muleteers. They tell us, Follow your comrade. Our comrade was Tsoúkas from Oriá. Sarantákos. We had no idea where we were going. Our comrade would consult his map en route. And we made our way toward Zygós. In the end we went to Koútrifa. There was a rebel platoon there. They had looted Arapóyiannis's house. Some of them were from Logistics, they had bagged all the grain. The booty was ready. They put us to work loading it. There was one mule left over. They burned down the house. One of the rebels comes over and says, Follow me. We left. Tsoúkas stayed there. I don't know if he was the one who burned down the house. The rebel was in front of us, saying, Follow me, follow me. We had the extra mule. Aloúpis and I took turns riding it, first him, then me. We kept going toward Ayiliás, then we headed farther out, toward Yídas's inn. To bypass Ayios Pétros and get ourselves across to the place they called Sourávla. Just below Ayios Pétros the Germans had killed Nikólas Fotiás. Mítsos Fotiás's brother. And five other men. In a small vegetable patch on the side of the road. The execution had taken place about ten days earlier. During the big blockade. End of June, or early July at the latest. Just before the Germans withdrew. You could still see the imprint, the outlines of their heads. Three of them had fallen backward and three to the front. Right into the freshly watered potatoes. The blood had dried on the ground. That's what happened, in short. We kept going. We came to

Sourávla. Aloúpis was ready to scream. Where are they taking us, those Turks,[1] those damn Turks. Hey, shut up, they'll hear you. Haven't you figured out where we're going? But he kept at it. The whole way there. Those Turks, those damn Turks. We passed the Malevís Monastery. We arrived in Tarmíri. From there we followed the mule path toward Lepída. Between Tarmíri and Lepída we came upon fresh graves, shepherds' graves. I can't remember the exact number. Anyway, not more than eight or fewer than five. On both sides of the road. Anywhere there was a bit of earth. Earth that their relatives could dig out. In that rocky soil. They'd thrown them in there every which way, with wooden crosses hastily put together. Name unknown. At any rate the people executed in Xerokámpi were a lot more than that. Around forty. The official count was done much later of course. Men and women. They killed them wherever they found them. Or rather no. Because the people they found at the threshing floor in Kokkínis, in Samartzís's storage shed, they didn't harm. This confirmed what had been loudly rumored then. In other words, that a secret line of operations had been plotted out. On paper. It was the carriage route from Ayios Pétros to Meligoú. Anywhere past that route, or the area toward Mount Parnon, was a no-man's-land. That's where everyone was killed. All of them shepherds. Men and women. We kept moving along. We arrived at Plátanos. Some people told us we'd be sent on to Leonídio. Some others would go to Palaiohóri. In the end they gave us something to eat and let us go. They had brought new muleteers there to collect the cargo we had. We went back. And that's when the ELAS rebels burned down Kastrí. In the month of July. On the twenty-fourth. They took up their position in Zygós, set up double patrols, and went down and burned the place. They also burned down some houses in Karátoula at that time. Nikólas Konstantélos's house, Alkídis's place. Alkídis Marinákos. And two or three more. And Kítsos's house in Roúvali. Selectively, to terrorize people. In September the Germans left. In the month of September. And Papadóngonas dug himself in at Trípolis. The countryside remained at the mercy of the rebels. Then a new order came. All men between the ages of eighteen and fifty-five should report for duty to Ayios

Pétros. With bread for three days and so on. We go up to Kastrí. They had their headquarters at Kasímos's house. People with mules and knapsacks and the like. They send us to Ayios Pétros. To enlist, in a large-scale mobilization. Kléarhos was there, he was setting up the 40th Reserve Regiment of ELAS. With no weapons, with nothing. The whole of East Kynouría. It's either all of you or none of you. There he was, Kléarhos with that beard of his, saying, Either all of you or none of you. We were examined by a doctor. Aryíris had hurt his knee. With a sledgehammer. A superficial wound. Dr. Roússos saw him. He tells Aryíris, Posttraumatic arthritis. And he lets him go. Kléarhos says to me. He considered me a colleague. Even though I hadn't finished yet. He says, You're coming along. When we go through Kastrí you'll follow us. And he sent us off. Meanwhile dusk had set in. I tell him, In Oriá they'll arrest us, we need a permit. The men from Oriá had declared war on us. To get to their vineyards in Sayitá, the villagers from Karátoula had to have a permit from the Organization. And they wouldn't give you one. Same thing for the villagers from Roúvali to go to Kápsalos. They were putting pressure on the men from Kará-toula. They had refused to join up. To form a local organization. They were the last in the prefecture of Arcadia. They didn't want to join. They'd also been very disturbed by the execution of Márkos Ioanní-tzis. And they'd been branded as reactionaries. And so had we. We went back to the village. Two days later Kléarhos and some other men arrive in Kastrí. By the time I heard this they had moved on toward Dolianá. I had to go enlist. I go to Dolianá. I find Yiórghis Strati-gópoulos there. A fellow student. Older than me. He would have been a great lawyer if he hadn't got involved. Quick and smart. He came to a pitiful end. His son became a drug addict. His only son. And poor Yiórghis was so disappointed. He had married his first cousin. Married her for love. In 1947 he sold everything he had down here and moved to Athens. I lent him some money. He gave it back to me. He opened a five-and-dime shop. He bought it. He had a seri-ous lung disease. When I left to join the army in 1947 I gave him two gold sovereigns. He was coughing up blood. Yiórghis, take care of yourself. His mother was from Kastrí. Their house was near the Tsoúhlos property. And his father was from Ayios Andréas. Take care of yourself, Yiórghis. Yiórghis was never prosecuted. They never found anything against him. He was never charged with anything, never put in jail. But he cut short his studies. I found them in Dolianá. From Dolianá we made the next risky move. We went down to Rízes. Still unarmed. Where were we headed? Wherever they were taking us. At Rízes the telephone lines were buzzing. We found out that negotiations were taking place in Trípolis. Between Aris, Kanellópoulos, and Tsiklitíras. In the meantime back in the village they were setting up more marching columns with the women and children. Then word got out that if fighting broke out the rebels would put those unarmed columns out in front. The unarmed reactionaries. So that the other side wouldn't fire on them. And finally the shooting started, *bang bam bang*. We said, They've been captured. But nothing had happened. The shooting was to celebrate the agreement, shots of joy. An agreement had been signed. *Bang bang bang*. The agreement was this: Anyone from the Battalions who wanted to go back home could go back. And anyone who didn't want to could follow Papadóngonas. With their weapons, as far as the coast. To Makriyiánnis's mills. From there they would get onto boats that would ferry them across to Spétses. They said that Aris accompanied them up to that point. To prevent any trouble. But that isn't true. Their transferal took place under Kanellópoulos's supervision. They arrived at the mills, they surrendered their weapons and got into the boats. We headed out from Rízes toward Trípolis. Grouped together but in loose formations. And still unarmed. At Ayios Sóstis we ran into the men from Karátoula. The men who'd enlisted. Most of them were going back. Antonákos, Mihális Theodorópoulos, the Pantelís brothers, and five or six more. And about the same number from Ayios Nikólaos. They saw us from a distance, all of us mobilized. But they got scared. They turned off, they went into the fields. To play it safe, just in case. They passed us about two hundred meters to the right. And then someone shouted from the column, They're from the Battalions, the Battalions. But he was the only one. We arrived in Trípolis. The agreement was signed, the ceremony was over. We settled ourselves on an empty plot of land.

I find my brother Aryíris. I find Marigó. And maybe Dóxa, I don't remember. They had brought them down with those unarmed marching columns. To celebrate the capture of Drobólitsa.[2] I find Dínos Yiánnaros. Dínos was in the Battalions, still in uniform. I tell him, Take that uniform off. I ask Aryíris, What do you hear? They had taken them to Áreos Square. It was filled with people, from all the provinces. Kanellópoulos gave a speech. A puzzling one. First Antónios spoke, as the supreme head of EAM in the Peloponnese. Then came the bishop of the prefecture of Helis. Then Tsiklitíras spoke. And Aris. Tsiklitíras, the military commander of ELAS. But Aris had the final say. A woman named Koïtsános spoke, from Bertsová. With her ammunition belts strapped across her breast. Death to my father, death to my brothers. From the balcony of the Hotel Maínalon. On a day of truce she was out to kill people. Kanellópoulos, the minister, the representative of the government-in-exile in Cairo. His speech was puzzling, Aryíris told me. Very puzzling. He had gone to Kýthira with his followers. Then he went to Kalamáta. He met Aris there, they talked. He passed through Megaloúpolis,[3] saw what happened there, he passed through Meligalás, saw things there, too. But he said nothing. He didn't go to Gargaliánoi. Stoúpas was there. They had to fight there. There was a battle. There was no execution. Stoúpas was last. He probably killed himself. Aryíris had his doubts about the way things were developing. Let's go to Kolokotróni Square. The 40th Reserve Regiment had disbanded. And recruiting was now done normally. They had set up some tables on the terrace of the Hotel Semirámis and they were writing down names. Of anyone who wanted to join ELAS. There was no pressure. Kléarhos, known as Aías, Kapetán Aías and his 40th Regiment. I watched. Kapetán Kléarhos sees Vasílis Pantelís. We used to call Vasílis Powderkeg, he was always getting into fights. And who are you? Pantelís, Vasílis says. Antónis's brother? Antónis, Yiánnis, and Liás, all three brothers in the Battalions. Well, well, four jackasses. Isn't there one of you wants to fight for his country? Kléarhos says. I do, Comrade. They didn't pressure him. Only indirectly. And that's how Vasílis joined them. He was killed in the December Uprising that followed. Things calmed down. The 40th

Regiment disbanded itself, so to speak. Without weapons, without anything. Just a mass of people. We didn't sign up. I didn't want to. We spent the night in the Homatá Hotel. We decided to leave. Things would just keep on like that. We went back to the village. Aryíris still full of doubts. I tell him, Let's head down to Kyvéri. Things don't look good. We go to Kyvéri. It was early in the season, no olives yet. Aryíris says, If we stay here I'll send for Annió. So there's someone to cook for us at least. Trípolis fell, the rebels got Papadóngonas's cannons. Thirty-six cannons. At the last minute they removed the bolts from four of the cannons and threw them into a well. Just before they surrendered them. With those cannons they attacked the Sparta Battalion in Mystrá. And attacked Athens later on. During the December Uprising. They began taking them there, we could hear the rumbling. Because the road was in terrible condition. The British tanks had gone over it as they retreated. Those that made it out, that is, and quite a few did. Then the German tanks followed in pursuit. They arrived in Kalamáta. And later after another order from von List, who was in charge of operations in the Balkans, commander of the 17th Army Corps, they left Kalamáta and proceeded north to Bulgaria. And through Bulgaria straight to the Russian Front. So the road was in a sorry state, it was full of potholes. And we heard the cannons, coming from Lykálona down along the Kolosoúrtis mountain road. We heard them in Kyvéri, in among the olive trees where we were hiding out. The thudding and the noisy rumble of those cannons. Cannons being dragged, on wheels without tires. In November, toward the end of the month, I had prepared a barrel of oil to take to Athens. In Argos on the bus we find out that the Uprising had begun. I cancel my ticket, or no, I didn't, it got lost. And I went back to Kyvéri. I found shelter there.

Chapter 40

I saw Sophia in the summer. She came to her nephew's wedding. She came from Kefalári, by herself. I tell her, Do you remember it all, do you remember when you hid Loukás in the trunk? And she started to cry. Poor thing, she's an old lady now, all shriveled up.

Chapter 41

Rebels had come here to Xerokámpi. And some people from
the village went and gave them a list of seventeen people to execute.
From Perdikóvrisi. An uncle of mine had married a woman from
Mánesi. He was also named Nikoláou, a field watchman. Nicknamed
"The King." One day he goes to his wife's village, Pávlos Bouziánis
was there. All of this back in 1944. Bouziánis tells him, Come here.
We have a list here to execute some people from Perdikóvrisi. Perdikóvrisi, used to be called Tservási. Should they be executed, he says
to him, or is it unjust? And the King, the field watchman, tells him,
No, it's unjust to do that. Among the seventeen were two brothers
of Christofílis, my father, and me. The King comes back, he tells us
this. We leave immediately then. We go to Eleohóri. The Battalions
were there. In 1944 I was twenty, twenty-two years old. Just married.
I was born in 1922. My wife was pregnant. I left her behind. We left
for Eleohóri. The rebels come down, as they had planned. They come
down to the village, they don't find us seventeen men there. They find
Christofílis's brother Yiánnis. Yiánnis had been drafted in 1941. And
they find a first cousin of mine, Kóstas Nikoláou. Also about twenty
years old. They didn't find me and my father, they set fire to our
house. Ours and someone named Baziános's. Burned them down.
In the meantime they took my cousin and Christofílis to Kótronas.
Two rebels from somewhere else, strangers. In Kótronas they found
a stream. They were good souls, those rebels. They left the others and
sat down to wash their feet. Our men could have gotten away, but
they didn't. My cousin had a brother-in-law, a man called Kakaviás.
From Ayios Yiánnis, he was a kapetánios. A Party cadre. He felt safe.

My brother told him, Let's go, Kóstas. My brother realized they were going to kill them. Those two rebels were strangers. Men we didn't know. They sat down there by the stream and took off their shoes. As if they were telling them, Make a run for it. But they didn't leave. And they brought them to Kastrí. Haroúlis Lenghéris went there and said, Why are you keeping those vermin? And they took them the next day and executed them. Later two men from our village went there, Nikoláou's brother-in-law and a neighbor, Diamantís Diamantákos, and they found them in some sinkhole on Doúmos's land.

—In a ditch.

—In Ayiliás. They found them there, they'd left them stripped bare. Taken their clothes. The others got them out, they hoisted them over their shoulders. One each. With rebels all around there, and in Kastrí the villagers scared they too would be killed. They carried them up to Ayiliás, they dug out a space right in front of the sanctuary, they put them in. And they came back to the village.

—They had shot them. And Nikoláou, they'd put a bullet in his head.

—An act of mercy.

—Then we men from Eleohóri, my father, a man named Baziános, and another named Karábakas, went to Trípolis. When the Security Battalions were breaking up. And the rebels arrived and arrested us. They took me to the First Police Precinct. Someone named Karamítzas came in, he's a lawyer now in Káningos Square, downtown Athens. Yiánnis Karamítzas from Perdikóvrisi. Same age as me. His father was with ELAS. He came there as a commander, he says, Kill that one, he was with the Gestapo. About me. But they let me go. They put my father and some others in jail.

—They didn't leave for Spétses, that was their mistake.

—Then they took them to be killed. Tied their hands together, about twelve men. They had tied my father to Papahálias, the priest. From Roúvali, Néa Hóra. They took them out a ways, to a small pine grove. The priest keeled over, he couldn't take all the walking. And they beat him with their rifle butts. Then they received a new order, and they brought them back. They didn't execute them. They put them back in jail. In the meantime the Red Cross arrived. And my father was the interpreter. He had spent a few years in America as an immigrant, he knew English. Then Bárlas's wife brought them a pot of boiled wheat. Bárlas was from Bertsová. A lawyer. A good lawyer. His wife took them the boiled wheat, they didn't inspect it at the entrance. And she bent a blade from a metal saw around the inside of the pot. That night they cut through the window bars and left. Bárlas, a fellow villager named Koïtsános, and some others. All of them lifers, they were going to butcher them. Right after they leave the rebels get my father and the priest and beat them to a pulp. Because they hadn't told on the others. Then the Várkiza Treaty was signed, and things changed. We went back to the village. Our house burned down, Baziános's house too. And Karíbakas's house.

— They didn't burn down our house. It was jointly owned by my father and an uncle of mine, so they didn't burn it down. But they looted it, didn't leave us a thing. Some men from Diagálevo came, and they took everything. Sewing machines, my sisters' dowry linens and clothes, everything. Even wires and the nails in the walls. They didn't leave a thing.

— And there was a kapetánios there from Ayiórghis.

— Sotíris, our old friend.

— He was the one who told my cousin, You're going to be executed. Kóstas didn't believe him. He'd put his trust in his brother-in-law Kakaviás.

— They rounded them up right in front of our house. The priest was there too. Yiánnis climbed up a mulberry tree. Just before that. Someone saw him there, he was a smoker. Since they'd seen him he climbed down and asked for cigarettes. And that's how they caught him. They brought him to the group in front of our house. That's where they took him from.

— They arrested him because he supposedly talked about Papadóngonas.

— Unfounded accusations. It was because of my other brother. During the big blockade he made himself scarce. He wound up in

Xerokámpi. Like all the others. The Germans and the Security Battalions left, and the rebels came in. They took everything the others had left behind, cheese and all that. At our house only me, my little sister, and my mother were left. And my brother's wife, she was pregnant. The rebels would leave, and he would come to see how we were doing. He runs into two of them. Where are you going, Vasílis, you traitor, and they began firing at him with their pistols. Vasílis got out of there, he arrived at the village in a fright. He says, We're leaving for Másklina. And he took his wife and went to Másklina. The Battalions were in Másklina. In Eleohóri, that is. Instead of him they arrested Yiánnis. Right in front of our house. They brought the priest there too. He was trembling, the priest. He was not from our village but he performed services there. Now he's in Náfplion, Doukákis. He says, Tell me, Priest, should traitors be executed? What could the priest say? I was very young then but I remember it all. Should the traitors be punished, should they be hanged? They should, the priest says. He was very shaken, he'd gone pale with fear. So they got the men and they took them away. The next day we found out they'd killed them. Yes, it was the next day. Some people from Kastrí came and told us. Then they wouldn't let us bury them. So we sent one of our relatives, with a cousin of Kóstas Nikoláou and one of the Baziános lot, and they took them up to the church in Ayiliás. And they buried them. Without a proper funeral ceremony. We had goats, and we'd hired a young shepherd, the same day we heard the news they went to our sheepfold, they stole two goats. They'd been sent there by Nikólas Pavlákos and a man from our village. They brought them down, they slaughtered them. Right below our house. And they were dancing and singing.

—To make them suffer even more.

—They gave away the liver of one of the slaughtered animals, and someone gave it to my father. Someone. How could he eat anything, my father? With one son killed and his house looted. That Pavlákos comes round, he asks, Where's the other liver? They say, We gave it to the old man. He calls my father. Okay, where's the liver? Comrade, the old man says to him. Your men gave it to us. We didn't eat it. I'll tell them to bring it. Pavlákos gives him a slap. The old man goes tottering and hits himself on an acacia tree we had outside. I remember it, I was young. With my brother killed and everything, just like I told you. I was fourteen, fifteen. And that's why I took care of Pavlákos later on. I beat him for one whole day and one night.

—And word got out that Anéstis Poúlios was also at the execution.

—No. Anéstis and someone called Balátsas. Both from Mesorráhi. They didn't take part in the execution. But they were there. They watched. And they were the ones took their clothes, so it seems. Because later on I spoke to someone called Sarántos. Then I went to Trípolis. Two years later. During the second insurgency. I had started beating people. I couldn't control myself. And I left. They would have killed me. Because I was a documented victim of the insurgency. Well, we were eating one day at Antonákos's place, and that Dakourélis comes in. He sits down there. He says, I have to tell you something. And you have to do it. I say, Tell me. He says, Your brother was killed by a man named Kóstas Harbís from Psylí Vrýsi. I don't waste a minute, I go straight to the public prosecutor. For even the smallest complaint he was obliged to prosecute. And initiate legal action. I told him everything—the whole story in great detail. Dakourélis climbed up a tree, the rebels went past, he saw them, they didn't see him. And he saw the whole execution from up there. How they killed them and what happened. My brother fell with the first shot, he fell over. Died on the spot. The first shot didn't kill Nikoláou, and he was dragging himself along. And one of them went and finished him off with his pistol. That's exactly what happened. We went to Náfplion a few weeks later. The trial date had been set, but Dakourélis went back on his story. He says, It's the first time I see that man. Seems they paid him off. And that was the end of that.

—But we'd beat them to it. We'd tried them ourselves.

—Not them. We didn't know them.

—First we caught Anéstis.

—We caught Balátsas first. Stylianós. From Mesorráhi. Balátsas was his nickname. Everyone called him that.

—Tyrovolás was his name. Stylianós Tyrovolás.

—But he was in prison.

—Well, I used to go to some land we had for grazing sheep. We call the place Bouzouriá. Down in Koubíla. There someone named Fotópoulos tells me, Look up there. Isn't that Balátsas? We thought he was in prison. I tell him, What are you talking about? I go to the sheepfolds. I had the mules with me, I left them with some shepherds. I go back to the village. I get four or five men and we go there at night and we catch him.

—That was in 1946.

—1946 or '48.

—Not in '48. I was in the army in '48.

—Anyway, 1946. I got the men together, we went straight to his house. We knock on the door, they wouldn't open. We break it down. His wife runs out, she started shouting. Stylianós isn't here. He's not here. She was shouting. Even though she could have said that more softly. I tell the others, He's hiding somewhere. Either at Souroúpis's place or at Markoúlis's. By shouting she was signaling him to clear out. We run over to Souroúpis's place, he wasn't inside. We go down to Markoúlis's place. What was his name?

—Kambylafkás.

—He was from Galtená. He'd married someone from Mesorráhi and was living there. He opens the door. I tell him, Where's Balátsas? He says, I don't know. Soon as he says I don't know I smack him. Listen, I don't know, he says again and motions upstairs with his eyes. He had a very small attic—and that's where Balátsas was hiding. Hey listen, I don't know. And he motioned upstairs with his eyes. I think to myself, he's here. I shout, Come down, Balátsas. He comes down. He'd taken out his release papers and he was showing them to me. His release from prison. I take them and I tear them up, I bash him with my rifle butt. And with that my rifle goes off, I could have been killed. We take him outside. I tell the others, Leave him to me. Because I was the one had a beef with him. And then I started beating him. I beat him like an octopus, until the same time the next day. He'd been in prison, stayed there for a year or so, maybe less. And then he got out, when they were ordered to reduce the number of prisoners. We took

him down to Perdikóvrisi. I tell him, Where's Poúlios? Anéstis Poúlios. He says, You'll find him at Kóstas Tyrovolás's place.

—In Mesorráhi.

—We put him in the cellar, tied and bound, and we left. We went
home, we all had something to eat, and then we went after Poúlios.
And we caught him. I started beating him. Then Karelína threw a rock
at me. An old lady, a relative of his. From up behind a wall. Almost
killed me. I go back and I give her two swift kicks. We got Anéstis, we
took him off to Tservási.

—On the way were some vineyards, they'd fenced them off with
pear trees and gorse. We'd pull some up and beat him over the head.

—He could barely walk at that point.

—We take him to the village, I take some scissors, I cut off his ear.

—His ear, his hair. His hair, his scalp, I cut it all. We dump him
in a corner. And in comes Kóstas Nikoláou's sister with an ax handle.
Nikoláou who they'd executed in Ayiliás. Telésilla. She starts beating
him with it. On the head. Trying to break his head open. We carry
him out of there. We go to a deserted house. That lawyer Karamítzas's
house. We throw him in the cellar. There was an empty barrel there.
The top was missing. We shove Anéstis in there, head first. We tie his
hands behind him and pull down his pants. So he can't walk. And we
leave him there. Now if you mention Anéstis and the barrel in Kastrí
they'll tell you all kinds of stories. Like that we screwed him. That's
not true. We left him there. Half dead from the beatings. And what
did he do? He came round little by little. Now they say that a cousin
of Karíbakas, a woman whose brothers were kapetanaíoi, went there
and let him out. And he jumped over some terraces, got as far as Kótronas, and someone named Fotópoulos untied him. Soon after that
we caught him again. We took him to Náfplion, and they kept him
in custody awaiting trial. Then I left for America. I was discharged
from the army, I left in 1951. In June. I had that right. My father was
an American citizen. Twenty-eight years. 1951–1979. The year before
last I was at the bus depot in Trípolis. I was waiting for my daughter,
she's married, in Corinth. I see Anéstis. An old man now. He comes
right up to me, he doesn't recognize me. He asks, Has the bus from

Kastrí arrived yet? I pretended to be American. I say in English, I don't understand Greek. Because I thought to myself, maybe he was looking to get me into trouble again. And last year I saw him again. Again I was on a bus and the bus stopped in Mesorráhi. He was waiting there with a man named Panayótis Tsíkis.

— They're first cousins.

— First cousins, and they were going to get chestnuts. It was October. The bus stopped, I was in the front seat, he put out his hand so I could help him up. He couldn't get up, he was an old wreck by then. I pretended not to see him. And he got up by himself, with Tsíkis pushing him from behind. Well, hello there Nikoláou, he says. Hello, Anéstis, I say. And I thought, now that we're about to leave this life, why did we do all that? For revenge, that's why.

— Revenge, yes. Then from Eleohóri they sent word to us to go after someone named Mathés. An important Party cadre. We left and went to Ayiasofiá, traveled all night. At the railroad tracks Antonákos the doctor was waiting for us. He got us and took us back to Samóni. He was an important cadre, that Mathés. I don't know how that man stayed alive. There were seven men from Másklina and us. He was a murderer. A murderer. Just like those other men who are getting pensions today. Who took part in the Resistance and are getting pensions. Murderers' Resistance.

Chapter 42

And that's how the wife of the justice of the peace lost her things. Manolópoulos was the justice of the peace in Kastrí. Pavlákos let it slip somewhere that they were going to arrest him. Vasílis goes and tells him, Take your wife and get out. I don't remember if they had children, they were both young. They were staying at Horaítis's place. Did I hear you right, Manolópoulos says to him. Don't ask me anything else, Vasílis says, I can't talk to you. They're following me. You didn't dare talk to anyone back then. The court clerk lived right above our house. Konstantinídis. He had a sister named Vasilikí. Manolópoulos's wife called her and said, Come and pack up the house if you can. And I'm leaving a present for you on the table. Take it, I'm leaving. She told her that and she left. She and her husband left at night. She went the next morning, she tidied up the house, and she took a very lovely nightgown the other woman had left for her. She supposedly closed up the house and left. A few days later they supposedly got her things and took them to some shelter. Then Harís arranged things the way he wanted. And later, when he would quarrel with Kouroúnis, every time they had a spat, he'd say: You took those things and you sold them in Megalópolis. All Manolópoulos's wife's clothes.

—Who said that to whom?

—Kouroúnis said that to Harís. Because it was Harís who was going and selling them.

Chapter 43

Our legislature provides for the mutual exacting of oaths. As do all legislatures. A person may establish the truth of all his allegations by the negative process of challenging his opponent to take an oath. I say, You owe me a hundred. You say, I don't owe you anything, because I never borrowed anything. I enter a sworn statement against you. Legally, you can either take an oath or exact one from your opponent. The tug-of-war ends there. No further challenges are allowed. And then, of course, come the penalties for perjury. The process is called the mutual exacting of oaths. It is exacted by one litigant of another, the judge being obligated to administer it. But only in certain kinds of disputes. In trials regarding marital disagreements, for example, the exacting of oaths does not apply. In trials that tend toward the breakup or annulment of the marriage, oaths cannot be exacted for the simple reason that there is a lack of material evidence. In the old days cases of this sort were frequently heard by the Supreme Court. Suddenly the question arose as to whether the fact of *not* being a virgin constituted "lack of material evidence." Because in those days a woman's chastity was given paramount, statutory importance. Which could be proven only by the presence of an intact hymen. Or again in cases of deception concerning a person's identity. I know that that's how they married off the Manavélas girl. Because people in those days were more than just simple-minded. They were sneaky. The bridegroom was only supposed to see the bride at the church on their wedding day. All made up and decked out and covered by a veil. And they usually put the elder daughters there, the ones they wanted to get rid of. They showed me one daughter and they gave me another. That's how that practice came about.

Chapter 44

—I want you to tell me that story.

—No. You ask and I'll answer.

—Fine. When did they arrest you?

—Okay, they arrested me in February. Not February. They arrested me in 1944.

—Do you remember what month?

—That's easy. They arrested me in October. In November to be precise.

—In 1944?

—In 1944. They arrested me in Astros, Kynouría.

—Had the Germans left?

—The Germans had left. I wanted to get out of the country. To go to the Middle East.

—Hold on a minute.

—I wanted to leave.

—Wait a minute.

—So. Triantafýllis tells me. And Matsiólas. Matsiólas the colonel. And Yiánnis the air pilot, Yiánnis Logothétis.

—No, Yiánnis Konstantélos.

—Oh yes, Konstantélos. They tell me, Stay put and see if you can help us, so we can all leave on the *Papanikolís*. The submarine.

—When was that?

—In 1944, in the month of October.

—No, it must have been earlier. In October 1944 the Germans were gone. You wouldn't have left then.

—The Germans had left. They'd gone, because they had to leave. The rebels were in control of everything. The Germans left on October 12. They left on October 12.

—Yes.

—Exactly. And the authorities agreed to say it happened on the seventeenth. But they left on October 12.

—All right.

—They left straight from Trípolis.

—Right. And where were you then?

—I was here. I'd gone up to Mount Taygetus. Then I came back, and I was in Trípolis in 1944. But it was before I went to Trípolis—on February 2, the Day of the Presentation at the Temple.

—In 1943?

—In '44. It was in 1944 on February 2 that the Germans arrested us in Mávri Trýpa. Two hundred fifty-eight prisoners we were.

—In hiding?

—No. Prisoners.

—Tell me about that.

—Yes. Prisoners. But before that I sent those officers out of the country. To the Middle East. I went to Fokianós. In Leonídio. Very rough sea there. The *Papanikolís* arrived, the submarine, it surfaced, and it picked them up, five of them. Matsiólas, Yiánnis Konstantélos, the air pilot from Karátoula, Stámos Triantafýllis.

—Was all that before then?

—Yes, I told you, before.

—They left before 1944.

—They left in '43. In 1943.

—In October?

—Yes. In 1943 I was still on Mount Taygetus. And in 1944 we mounted our major operation. So to speak.

—Wait, you're confusing me. When did they kill your brother?

—On July 29 of 1944.

—In 1944.

—July 29.

—Where were you then?

—The Germans were still here.

—Yes.

—July 29.

—Yes. Where were you?

—I was in Meligoú.

—I see.

—We'd gone on a raid, I was freed in February, on February 2.

—Had they captured you before that?

—Of course, before that. They captured me before that.

—Tell it to me from the beginning. Tell me. It began in 1943. No. It began in 1940. Did you see action in Albania?

—Of course.

—Where did you fight in Albania?

—In all the theaters of operations of the Second Front.

—The Second Front.

—All the way to the lake in Ochrída. To the lake there. That's how far I went.

—And on your retreat?

—On our retreat I was last. The very last one.

—And you came to Kastrí?

—We got ourselves to Corinth. They took my car, outside Thebes. The Germans.

—Were you a driver?

—Yes.

—And you were coming by car?

—I was coming down—and I was bringing some soldiers with me. Stratís Perentés, Yiórghis, Kyriákos Doúmos's boy, Leonídas Méngos, God rest his soul. Polyánthi's son Yiórghis, and Tsarnákos. The Germans made them get out. We started out from Koritsá. I wanted to get my brother, and Vasílis Méghris, and someone named Ilioúpoulos from Kerasítsa. They didn't come with me. I tell them, I'm the last one, the last car. They wouldn't come along, they were blowing up bridges. I picked up a girl from northern Epirus, I took her to Yiánnina. In the front, with me and the captain. The captain didn't want us to take her. At any rate, the bottom line is that we took her. I arrived in Lidoríki. In Ámfissa. And from Ámfissa I went to Thebes. There the Germans requisitioned my car. Then we went across to Peráhóra. In Loutráki. We took the train. It took us an hour and a half to get there. We got off at Eleohóri. From Eleohóri we came to Kastrí. I brought my rifle here from Albania. My automatic rifle.

—What month was it when you arrived in Kastrí?

—April.

—April.

—After the Tsolákoglou capitulation agreement was signed we came here. On April 20, something like that. The twentieth or the twenty-second. I don't remember. In any case, it was April. I arrived in the village. We came back. I'd served about thirty-nine months since I was drafted. And another six or seven in Albania. I arrived in the village in April. I stayed in the village. I didn't stay long. I worked here and there. I was working in the Polychronópoulos warehouse. With fertilizers and whatnot. With Sotíris Tsourapélos.

—Where was the warehouse?

—Just above Kasímos's house. I was working there. One day Níkos Mávros arrives, he takes me downstairs. He says, Kapetán Zahariás wants you.

—When was that?

—In '44. No. It was before the Germans even came to Kastrí. But there were Germans all around.

—You mean in '43.

—Yes, about then. In '44 the Germans were there, not in '43.

—In '43.

—Yes but in '44 they came to the village. They set up the blockade.

—Were you here until then?

—I was here.

—When did you join the Battalions?

—I joined in February. No, in March. It was March when the Battalions were formed in Trípolis.

—Yes, I know.

—In March.

—In March of 1944?

—Yes. Níkos Mávros arrives, he takes me with him. Down to Ayía Paraskeví. Kapetán Zahariás was there, with about ten men from Voúrvoura. They were there. He says, I'll knock your block off. But why, Kapetán? What did I do wrong? Will you become a rebel or not? I tell him, I can't join. I can't join the rebels. He says, You'll join, all right, and you'll do it gladly too. Or I'll knock your block off. Well, I tell him. There are eight of us. And two older folks. Ten altogether. I'm working. I'm earning fifty drachmas a day, enough to buy bread. He says, Will you give us bread? I tell him, I have no bread. I have a little wheat at home, I'll give that to you. And they sent some men and took a truckload of wheat from me. Then Níkos Magoúlis takes me down to Paraskeví's taverna. It belonged to Níkos Konstantélos back then. Before they killed him. Takes me down to the cellar. To buy me a drink. He says, I'm paying. Okay, Mr. Níkos, I tell him. Don't call me Mr. Níkos, don't call me that. Call me Comrade. I tell him, What does that mean? He says, We're part of the struggle. I ask him, What struggle, Mr. Níkos?—I called him that again. I can't join the struggle. There are eight children in my family. My father was ill. Back then I was earning sixty drachmas. One thousand eight hundred a month. Driving Galaxýdis's truck.

—Mihális Galaxýdis's truck.

—No, Kyriákos's.

—Mihális's brother Kyriákos.

—Mihális's brother.

—They killed him.

—He was killed in Ayiórghis. We were on a raid and he was killed. We brought him back dead to Trípolis. And that's when Mihális killed Tsígris. Lýras was interrogating him. They heard shots, a German comes running in. What's going on? Nothing, Some bastard got killed, Lýras said. Lýras was from Karakovoúni, an army captain. And that was that, it was over.

—What was Tsígris?

—He was an officer. An officer in ELAS. We had all agreed in

1943, Tsígris, Vazaíos, and me, and we had gone to Pyramída, just above Ellinikó. When we left Mount Taygetus. I'm talking about 1943 now. When we left there.

—Which of you left?

—Me, Petrákos, Tákis Drínis, and that Mýlis fellow from Karátoula.

—Did you go with Vrettákos?

—We went under the command of Colonel Yiannakópoulos. That rat who sold us out.

—I see.

—He finished us. He's the one who finished us off.

—When did you go with Yiannakópoulos?

—In 1943.

—What time of year, what month?

—Summertime. Yiannakópoulos was out in the mountains.

—Wait a minute, one thing at a time. You were working here, and Magoúlis took you downstairs.

—Yes.

—Tell me one thing at a time.

—He took me downstairs. We ate.

—And he told you all those things.

—Yes. And I tell him, I can't. And then I tell him, This meal's on me, Mr. Níkos. He wouldn't let me. He paid for everything. I tell him, I won't go to the mountains, I won't. He tells me, You won't go to the mountains, but you'll help. I say, What help can I be, I'm as good as dead? With a family of ten, I earn sixty drachmas a day. He says, You'll help us out, and he gave me a note to take to Trípolis. To someone named Nikitópoulos. A cobbler, across from Glinós's shop. Glinós was a shoemaker. And just across from there Nikitópoulos was working in a basement. I take him the note. The Italians were in Trípolis. So I find him, he cuts open a watermelon, he puts a pistol in it. He says, Take it. I tell him, Where should I take it, I'll get caught. He says, You'll take it. And he put it in the watermelon. He had more watermelons. I take a few eggs, and I took them to that bastard Bruno. At the outpost. To that Italian. And I got through.

—The Italians had an outpost?

—Yes, at the train station. And they did searches. I gave the eggs to Bruno, I got through with my car. Pavlákos comes over. Did you bring anything from Trípolis? I say, I brought a watermelon. Oh, I see. I brought the pistol that one time. And after that they were constantly on my back. I say, I'm leaving. Then I went to Kyvéri, on foot. I'd taken some fresh green beans with me, to take to Athens. I got on the train. Some fresh green beans for the black market. I went to Leonídas Vrettákos, the cavalry captain's brother. I tell him, Here's what happened. What should we do? So he took us in hand, he gave us a hundred and ten rifles.

—In Athens?

—Yes. Leonídas Vrettákos. Telémahos the cavalry captain's brother. Rifles to bring to Kastrí.

—Yes.

—We brought them. But Márkos didn't listen to me. Where did he want to unload them? Down at Vatomourákos's place, God rest his soul. He says, Let's take them there. I tell him, What are you saying? What are you talking about, Márkos? That's how I talked to him. We had loaded some wheat, loose wheat, and we put in the weapons and brought them here. A hundred and ten rifles.

—You brought them to Kastrí?

—And Márkos wanted to unload them at his cousin's. At Níkos Mávros's place. I tell him, What are you saying, we can't do that. I say, I'll take them. My responsibility. We had him in Ayiliás in a shack. Márkos Ioannítzis. In a shack that belonged to Yiánnis Baskoútos. In Ayiliás. Four or five days later he comes down to Haloúlos's restaurant. He had invited everyone from EAM there. He pulls out his pistol, he says, Long live the revolution against communism. And *bam bam*, he fires two shots there in the restaurant. God rest his soul. Kapetán Foúrias, his first cousin Níkos Mávros, gets up and leaves.

—Had you unloaded the weapons?

—At the warehouse. We laid out the rifles. Put loose wheat on top, and in Trípolis the Italian poked around with the iron rod, but what could he find? It would just hit the floor. We took the weapons, we handed them out. Vanghélis Mílis took some, we all took some. Well, all right. Nikólas Petrákis, someone named Sakellaríou, a sergeant major from Vytína. A sergeant major. Yiannakópoulos was done for, he signed the pact with ELAS.

—Did you go to Mount Taygetus?

—We did. We went. And after we went there we split up.

—But you're not telling me everything. When you left, when and how you left from here. Did you go with Márkos?

—Márkos fired his pistol: Long live the revolution.

—Yes.

—And then he says, I'm going to meet Látsis, my koumbáros.

—Yes.

—On Mount Parnon. So, when he went up there he confided his plans to them. There were three of them on the road with him. Three rebels escorting him. I don't know the spot where they hit him. Where they slaughtered him. They didn't shoot Márkos. They stabbed him from behind, with a knife. His koumbáros tells him, Keep going till you meet the other men farther down. The three of them escorting him. One of them stayed behind to take a leak, and as they were talking off to the side, they stabbed him. At that time we couldn't get through. We couldn't leave. We wanted to leave. Yiannakópoulos had signed the agreement. Not to attack each other. But we couldn't do any recruiting, none at all. We weren't allowed to. And they gathered us all at Prophítis Ilías, on Mount Taygetus. Just above Goránoi.

—What time of year did you leave from here?

—In the summer, I told you.

—And how long did you stay with Yiannakópoulos?

—Two months. Two and a half.

—Did ELAS attack you after that?

—No. They couldn't attack us. But the English were making drops. They would drop things, and the others would get them. They'd drop arms and automatic weapons, and knapsacks full of sovereigns. The kapetanaíoi pocketed them. We went to catch a caïque in Kalamáta, to leave. Later on we fought the rebels. In Rahoúla. Vrettákos the cavalry captain was there. We split up, to leave. And they got him.

—To leave for where?

—To finally leave the country. Tsirígo,[1] Crete, Africa. Where could we go? And that son of a bitch the boat captain sinks the caïque and leaves us stranded. We got our bearings. We got ourselves to Kaltezés. From there we came to Vlahokerasiá, and we joined the others. Vazaíos and Tsígris. Vazaíos was in charge at Artemísion. With two of the Kokkiniás brothers. Officers in the Greek Army.

—Where were they?

—In Pyramída. Just above Ellinikó. Not the Ellinikó in Astros. I'm talking about Kefalári.

—In Argos?

—In Argos. High up on the left. Some distance away. It's the border, at Pyramída. So the Kokkiniás brothers were there, both of them. Tsígris was there.

—Tsígris, the one Mihális killed?

—Yes, him. And he says, Clear out or I'll order them to fire.

—Order them to what?

—To fire.

—Tsígris told you that.

—Yes.

—Why?

—Because we broke the agreement. Because we wanted to fight. We went there to see what we could do and he told us to clear out. If you don't clear out, I'll order them to fire. I ask Sakellaríou, What should we do, Státhis? What should we do?

—How many of you were there?

—There were about fifty of us. What do we do now? Yiannakópoulos had agreed that we should work together.

—And he'd sent you there?

—No, we went by ourselves. Mílis stayed behind. With no shoes. They kept him. Then Sakellaríou says. Sakellaríou from Vytína. Whoever wants to can stay with me.

—On Mount Taygetus all this?

—Yes, because they had us surrounded. They would have wiped us all out. They would have taken us prisoner.

—Yiannakópoulos?

—Yiannakópoulos was there. Then he left, I don't know where the devil he went. He went over to ELAS, he sold us out. With the agreement he made. He betrayed us. That's why we had to join the others. In Artemísion. And the others were even worse. He had sent word to them. We arrived, they wouldn't have us. Wouldn't have *us*.

—What time of year was it there?

—It was fall. Fall was just coming on. And we went down on foot, me, Sakellaríou, and four or five others. We would tell people we were butchers. Animal traders. We went down to Stérna, above Argos. We got to Koutsopódi. And there we split up. Poor Sakellaríou stayed behind. I came back here. We all split up.

—And you came to Kastrí?

—I came to Kastrí. I came and all this happened. Let me finish, the Germans were still around, after 1944, the Germans were there.

—Wait a minute. You came to the village.

—Yes.

—It's still 1943.

—1943.

—And what did you do when you got to the village?

—What did I do, I went to my car.

—To your car.

—But I was under surveillance. One day they say, Take the car. Mávros's car, God rest his soul.

—The doctor?

—Yes. Kóstas Tsourapélos and the doctor had a car. A Farkó.[2] A truck.

—Mávros the doctor.

—Yes, the doctor.

—Jointly owned?

—Yes. A Farkó. A truck. They come down to Haloúlos's taverna and give me an order. To go to Aráhova and bring back a dead rebel. I tell Tsourapélos, Kóstas, what are we going to do?

—How would you go to Aráhova? Through Voúrvoura?

—Through Trípolis. Trípolis. They would give us passes.

—Yes.

—Kóstas, what are we going to do? He tells me, I don't know what we'll do. I tell him, We're not going. The way things are now, they'll burn our car. He says, Let them burn it. They didn't burn it. We're going. We went and brought back the dead man. And the next day we abandoned our homes. We got up and left, on foot. Finally in March the Security Battalions came. And on February 2, the Day of the Presentation at the Temple, I was freed.

—From where?

—From Mávri Trýpa. There were 258 prisoners there.

—Hold on. The Battalions were formed in March.

—In March. They were formed in March.

—Okay, you were in the Battalions, you joined the Battalions.

—I joined as soon as they were formed. Before that I was with X. From the day I was freed on February 2. In X with Konstanta-kópoulos, who they called Tsékeris. He had an office in Kolokotróni Square. With Thémis Iatroú. On the lower side of Kolokotróni Square, where the pharmacy is today. And they gave me a pistol. A pistol with one bullet.

—The men from X?

—Konstantakópoulos or Tsékeris. But I was half-dead from the detention camp.

—When did they arrest your brother?

—They killed him on July 29.

—In 1944.

—Yes.

—They killed him on July 29. When did they arrest him?

—Five days before. Ten. Something like that.

—When did you join the Battalions in Trípolis?

—As soon as they were formed. I went first. In March. On February 2 I was freed from the detention camp. The evening before, when the sun went down, just after that, the Germans surrounded us. They arrested us all.

—When did the rebels take you prisoner?

—In November.

—In '43.

—In '44.

—But you said you were freed on February 2, 1944.

—Yes. October, November, December. They took me prisoner in November. I stayed in the detention camp for three months.

—In '43.

—Listen.

—In '43. November, December.

—Hang on. ELAS arrested me in November in Parálio, Astros.

—Yes.

—They took me there.

—Tell me one thing: When did they arrest you in Parálio, Astros?

—Three months, two and a half months exactly before February.

—Did they kill your brother before that or later on?

—Later on.

—So they arrested you in 1943.

—They killed Panayótis in 1944.

—In the summer.

—In the summer, on July 29.

—So they arrested you in 1943 then.

—They arrested me—how many months are there before February? In 1944.

—It was after February of 1944. Since it was July when they killed Panayótis.

—It was me in February, it was February when I was freed. On February 2.

—Before they arrested Panayótis.

—Before they arrested Panayótis. They arrested Panayótis instead of me.

—So they arrested you in 1943 then, in Astros.

—It couldn't be 1943.

—It was '43. And in February 1944 you were freed. How did they arrest you in Astros?

—How they arrested me?

—Yes.

—It was—I went to that fellow Kateriniós. The father of Níkos the fishmonger.

—Yes.

—Because I came back half-dead, I'd been shut in a cave without food for eight days. When the officers left. When we left Artemísion.

—Yes.

—I went to that cave, back toward Náfplion. I was tired and barefoot. I went to some house to get bread and had a quarrel. They were sleeping. I quarreled with them. And I got on the caïque to leave.

—To go where?

—To Náfplion. Kateriniós, God rest his soul. At any rate, he was with them. Hanging around with them.

—With the men from ELAS?

—Yes, I tell him. I tell Níkos the fishmonger's father.

—Yes.

—I tell him, Take me to Náfplion. The caïque was at the far pier. And on the other side, at Koutrouyiórghis's bakeshop, Pepónias and Vamprákos had set up a machine gun.

—I see.

—They fire a burst, and they tell the caïque to turn back. I tell him, Keep going, Kateriniós. Nothing doing. He turned round right there. Then they arrested me and took me to the detention camp. I threw my pistol in the sea. If I'd killed Kateriniós I'd have made it to Náfplion. I knew how to take the caïque there. But it never crossed my mind to kill him. Or to threaten him. I knew how to get the motor started. I'd have taken it there. Taken it to Náfplion. And my troubles would never have started.

—Pepónias and Vamprákos were the ones who arrested you.

—Vamprákos and Pepónias. And Kapetán Mavromantilás.

—Mavromantilás.

—Mihális. He was down there. Mavromantilás, Pepónias, and Vamprákos. And Kapetán Pávlos Bouziánis. From Mánesi. He had a brother-in-law in Trípolis, in Dalaína. Who was hanging around with the Italians. His daughters were. He had stolen lots of money from people. He was a big businessman, general foodstuffs. It was down there that they arrested me. They took me to the school in Meligoú. And in Meligoú they tied me up. Tied my feet—my knees and my ankles. And my hands. Kapetán Pávlos Bouziánis arrives and hits me with the butt of his rifle. I fall down, with half my teeth knocked out. I tell him, Why are you hitting me? He says, You're a goddamn traitor. I say, Who did I betray? I went after the Italians, I fought them. You're a traitor. Tell us what officers you were keeping company with. I say, I don't know any officers, I don't remember.

—On Mount Taygetus?

—Yes. The officers I kept company with. I don't remember. You don't remember? And then they gave it to me. They put the rifle through the ropes on my legs, and they turned my legs with the soles facing up. And they started. Thirty lashes with a metal cable.

—At the school in Meligoú.

—In Meligoú. From there they take me to Loukoú.

—Were there other men there?

—Lots of them. They killed a boy, Pátra's boy. Pátra of all people. Such a well-respected lady. Cleopatra's boy. He had a Martelli, a small bouzouki, and he used to play. He'd go begging, have himself a drink. And they killed him.

—In Loukoú?

—Outside Loukoú. They put me in the next day. I slept tied up in ropes. I slept on a board. We didn't all fit in Loukoú. Nikoláou was there, Dránias was there.

—Yiánnis?

—Yiánnis. That son of a bitch Theóktistos was there. The deacon. He calls me a traitor and spits at me. Does the same to Astéris Papayiánnis's sister. Ada. I spit on you, you traitoress. Why am I a traitor, Father? I only just now got back from Albania. At any rate. Then they made me dig my grave. In the yard of the monastery. In the corner. I dug it out with a pickax and a shovel.

—With your feet all swollen?

—My feet still swollen. Open and oozing. At any rate. They put me in, they throw me in there alive. Someone comes over.

—Who came over?

—Someone named Kíliaris. Thodorís Kíliaris. He worked for the Trípolis Electric Company. Down below, at the railroad tracks. Thodorís Kíliaris. And a man from some island. And Vasílis Tóyias from Mesorráhi. They threw me in, they buried me up to my neck. Will you become a rebel? No. Why not, you traitor? And then he hits me with his rifle butt right here, and knocks out the rest of my teeth. My lips were all cut up.

—Kíliaris?

—Tóyias. He hit me with his rifle butt, while I was half-buried. He hit me right here. That was it. They got me out. They gave me a good thrashing. With that metal cable. On my sides, on my kidneys. It was thick. They made it into a club. My skin welted up, they beat me black and blue. Nikoláou and Hasánis, God rest his soul. They tell me, Be patient, Iraklís. Those bastards, they wouldn't just shoot me. I tell Tóyias, Why don't you shoot me, why are you torturing me? What have I done to you? I won't become a rebel. That's it. They take us, and we go to Karakovoúni.

—From Loukoú.

—From Loukoú. On my knees most of the way. So we went up there. Yiánnis Vasílimis was there. The brother of Kapetán Vasílimis, Kóstas's brother. And Aristídis. The one who went crazy and died recently. And Lykoúrgos. The father of Yiórghis Vasílimis, who had the stables over in Koúvli, with the calves. Yiánnis's wife Miliá came there. She brought her husband squash patties. But me, they wouldn't let me eat.

—What month was that?

—Now it was winter. In February I was freed. Twenty centimeters of snow outside. They had me cutting wood in my bare feet. But no, I couldn't eat. Keep going, Yiánnis tells me, take my army coat and put it on. Inside his coat he had four patties, squash patties. Vasílimis. I ate them, like medicine. Someone saw me do that, he starts yelling. Hey, you, what were you eating? I say, Nothing. What did you hide in your pocket and eat? I didn't hide anything. And so a few days later Nikitákis arrives, Dimítris Nikitákis himself, a dairy farmer from Sparta. He brings about sixty prisoners with him. All from Laconía. He brings them, and they join the two detention camps. Ours was under the command of Kapetán Kléarhos Aryiríou. Under his administration.

—Kléarhos was there?

—Of course.

—Now you were all in Orthokostá.

—In Orthokostá. They beat me again there. A lot. Mítsos Nikitákis calls me. The dairy farmer. Who later on had a shop in Ayía Paraskeví, at the main intersection. In Athens. Mítsos's story is very long. He escaped from a group of men the Germans shot in Monodéndri, and he went and joined the rebels. With two twelve-year-old children and his wife. He had his children with him. But he was a good man. A very good man. And he's the one that helped us escape from Mávri Trýpa. We were slow getting out, the Germans arrived, we couldn't get away in time, there was an order to execute us. He got us out.

—So Nikitákis calls you over.

—Yes. He tells me, Come here. Are you hungry? I am. He gives me a piece of pork. A thick piece. Do you have cigarettes? I didn't have any. Money? I had a little money. He went and brought me cigarettes. Then he tells me. Or rather he told them, Don't beat this prisoner any more. And he asked me why I wouldn't join. I tell him, It's like this. What could I say to him? Where you from? From Kastrí, Kynouría. Don't beat this prisoner again. If anyone lays a hand on you, you tell me. All right. What could I do, as soon as he left they'd beat me senseless. They'd already done the worst torture on me. And they'd just finish me off. Like when they locked me in the monastery. Lying on a big table. My feet were bound and freezing underneath. And they had a fire and nails and they'd burn them.

—Who was there. Do you remember?

—I remember the names. That scoundrel from the islands. A serious criminal. His name was Yiorgópoulos. Not the kapetánios, someone else. Not the kapetánios. And there was that nasty old Tóyias, Vasílis. And that rotten Kíliaris. But he wasn't there during my ordeal. Tóyias was there. My feet were tied, tied up to the knees, and my hands like this. They burned them with metal nails. They

pierced them. The pain was God awful. They sent us away from there.
The Germans were coming, and they sent us away. They brought us
to Háradros. To the school. They had killed the prefect at Háradros.
With a pickax. They broke his shins in front. He died like that. They
left him there writhing on the ground. And in one day he died. The
village priest went to the rebel chiefs. He said, Please, I beg you. Put
a bullet in the poor man. And one of them hits the priest with the
back of his hand, knocks his cap off. Shut up, you nasty old priest, or
you'll get the same.

—All this in the school.

—In a ravine farther down. I knew that place. Years later Háyias
the lawyer came there with the prefect's daughter. Antónis. She
wanted to exhume her father. She would pay for it. I tell her, If you
don't find someone with broken shins it's not your father. I don't know
if she found him. I never heard from Antónis again. That's what happened. They took us to Háradros. They took us to the school. There
was a teacher there from Merkovoúni. Dimoyérontas. He's still alive.
Andréas Dimoyérontas. He was a schoolteacher there. After a while
they bring down about thirty more prisoners. From our area. That's
when they brought Kapetán Yioúlis, poor man. Old Mímis Mitro-
máras, from Doliapá. Velissáris tells him, come here, Yioúlis. They
would tease him for laughs.

—Yiórghis?

—Yiánnis Velissáris. Why did you kill the rebels in your house?
Magoúlis was pacing around in the yard. And Kléarhos Aryiríou. He
had a red kerchief, Kléarhos, he had his hat and his shepherd's crook
from Mélana. A staff, not a crook. A shepherd's staff. And Yiórghis
Babakiás was there too. From Doliapá. They were pacing around.
Velissáris says, Why did you kill the rebels? Why you jackass, Yioúlis
answers. You filthy bastard. Those poor men from Sparta didn't know
what to think. They didn't know he was half off his rocker. Now you
listen here, President, he tells Kléarhos. And he goes over to the wall
of the school. Hello. Is this Germany? He starts phoning. Call Hitler
for me. The men from Sparta and the other prisoners were scared out
of their minds. They're thinking, Now they'll kill us all. Listen, Hitler.

At the school in Háradros, Kynouría, there are about three hundred of us prisoners. Being held by the greatest bastards on earth, complete jackasses. Please send troops to free us immediately. Was it a stroke of genius, luck, or what, I don't know. Not half an hour had passed and the Germans arrived. A division had left from Corinth. And they were pressing in on us. Some from Závitsa, others from Dagoúni coming down toward Douminá. They take us away immediately. They take us through the Mántis family storage sheds. They take us to Galtená. Down by Perdikonéri there were a hundred Germans. And because it was dark they didn't shoot at us. They saw us. They would have killed us all. Kapetán Kléarhos shouts, Quick, the Battalion is coming through. And there were Germans. There were Germans down there.

—And you, how did you walk?

—On my knees. I'd drag myself along. I had a shirt, I folded it and wrapped it in some old rags from the olive press in Háradros. I tied them together. And I'd drag myself along from side to side. On my knees. We came to Galtená. Dimítrios Bíris brings an order from Kapetán Achilléas. From Zisiádis. That no-good Bulgarian.[3]

—Zisiádis?

—Yes. He was an engineer at the Agricultural Bank. In Trípolis. The order was to execute the whole detention camp. Both camps. They brought the order at eleven at night. Anyone who can't keep pace with us, step outside. Then Nikoláou comes over. He says, Iraklís, they're going to kill us. They had beaten him badly too. On his legs. Mítsos Hasánis comes over. He says, Don't say you can't go along. Then I go outside. Kléarhos and I were relatives of sorts, koumbároi. Through Manólis, God rest his soul. Manólis Aryiríou. In 1936, when Kléarhos was out and reporting regularly to the police. Under Metaxás. I had taken care of things for him then. In 1937 I joined the army. And he was still reporting to the police. In Galtená I tell him, Listen, koumbáros.

—Was Kléarhos Manólis's brother?

—No, his cousin. Kléarhos's brothers were Kóstas, who they called Kraterós, and Panayótis. Koumbáros, I tell him in Galtená. He tells me, If you can't walk, have a look at this. He pulls a French double-edged knife on me. He tells me, I'm not wasting any bullets on you. With a silver handle. I have it at home.

—How did you get it?

—He threw it away in Mávri Trýpa. Or he dropped it, I don't know. I found it. As soon as the order came they sent us to Galtená. They take us to Ayiórghis. In Ayiórghis I was dying of thirst. Stávros Koutsoyiánnis comes over. I say, Old fellow, give me a little water. He gave me a pitcher of wine, and I drank it without realizing it was wine. That's how parched I was. I didn't realize what it was. And I went off a way and sat down. And it hit me.

—Was Yiánnis Dránias with you there?

—He was with us. Yiánnis Dránias, Xinós, Hayiázos, and Chrístos Bekáris.

—Which Xinós?

—The one from Eleohóri. He died. And Chrístos Moúntros. He died too.

—Because Dránias doesn't remember you.

—No, Dránias didn't come with us. When we went to Eleohóri. When the Germans arrested us. He was in hiding. He stayed behind, and he went into hiding. We gave ourselves up to the Germans. Me and Liás Karzís and another man from Dolianá who works at the hospital now. In the psychiatric ward.

—Were there any women with you, someone named Alíki from Trípolis?

—No, Alíki came later. They had the dye shop, I forget their last name. They had the dye shop down on the way to the barracks, on the right. Next to Kampoúris's pharmacy. Alíki was going out with my brother Panayótis. She thought he died, and it drove her insane. When they killed the others up there. Panayótis, Themistoklís Anagnostákos, Maraskés, Braílas's mother. I forget that girl's last name. The Germans found her, and she was half out of her mind. And she still is, she's alive and half crazy. She doesn't understand anything, she doesn't remember anything.

—Did they take you to Ayiórghis?

—They did. I went to take a leak. They were boiling up beans for the evening. Two rebels get hold of me. Mítsos Nikitákis says to them, Where are you taking him? To take a leak. We're escorting him. For Chrissakes, you bastards. He tells them, He's half dead. Can he run away? Go and take a leak, man. I went and took a leak, I came back. They gave out the beans. I threw them out, they were full of flies. So we start out from there. In the afternoon. They take us along a road with rocks all around. They had the village alderman of Mýloi up on a mule. He was wearing a leather jacket with no sleeves. With his legs hanging down, they'd given him quite a beating. But the mule wouldn't go forward. Fotópoulos's daughter Thýmia from Roúvali was pulling it along, Yiánnis Kaliakoúdis's mother. Poor woman had been pressed into service. She says, Kapetán Kléarhos, the mule won't go forward. Carry out my orders, then send the mule back. Vasílis Skáros from Stólos shoots him with his rifle. My cousin.

—Were you there?

—I was, right there. He fired his rifle at him, hit him up high. The village alderman fell down dead, down among those rocks. Kostákis Mémos. And he went and pulled off his leather jacket and wore it himself. He took it off that same minute, the man hadn't even started bleeding. He must still have it, that bastard. I tell him, Listen, Vasílis. Because he realized the Germans were coming. Listen, Vasílis, let's hide here in Neraïdoráhi. He tells me, Keep going. Keep going, God damn you, or the same will happen to you. And I kept going. We reached Mávri Trýpa. As soon as we got there—Nikoláou, they brought Nikólas over. He was also on a mule. He starts crying. This is the end, Iraklís. Listen, Nikólas, I tell him, they're going to kill us, what else would they do? It was getting dark out. Then I see a German with an automatic rifle. He was coming from the road, from the brambles, from the river of Eleohóri. In the blink of an eye, before we could say boo, there were three hundred flares in the sky. It was dark now. I shout, We're prisoners. When I was in school I knew a little French. I remembered the word *prisonnier* which means "prisoner" in French. I start shouting: Prisonnier of Partisán. Then Kostoúros who runs the Hotel Boúrtzi starts talking, and someone named Grammatikákis from Sparta. In German. The Germans say, Put your hands up. And we surrendered on the spot. They took us to Eleohóri. Dránias didn't come with us. Yiánnis went and hid. And then they took us to Trípolis. As soon as my feet healed, I went and found Konstantakópoulos. And they gave me that pistol. With one bullet. Konstantakópoulos or Tsékeris, from Kalamáta. The head of X. They gave me that gun, they didn't have anything else. Then Kapetán Mahaíras comes down from the village of Stríngos. He comes down to Trípolis. He had to make two hundred identity cards for the Germans. Rebel ID cards. The Germans had their headquarters at the Hotel Semirámis.

—Was Mahaíras a rebel?

—A rebel. A kapetánios.

—And he wanted to make fake IDs?

—To get them approved. So they could come down. But I caught on to him.

—Vanghélis Mahaíras the lawyer?

—No, Mahaíras is dead. He died. Kapetán Mahaíras. Vanghélis was from Bertsová. The other man was from Stríngos. A kapetánios. Mahaíras was his code name. Just like our Kapetán Foúrias. I arrest him down at the Palládio. There was once a gas station there, belonged to Zoúzoulas. So I find him there. I recognize him. I arrest him, I was ready to kill him of course.

—And he left.

—He didn't leave. I had one bullet, I fired it, it didn't go off. I shout, Shoot him, to Konstantakópoulos. They start chasing him, he goes into Papadákos's pharmacy. In the back, where the National Bank is now. It was a basement.

—Yes.

—So he hides in there, they went and killed him. And they found the identity cards on him.

—Did you know him?

—I knew him. He was in the detention camp with us. A kapetánios.

—I see.

—And when I saw him in Trípolis I almost fell over. A big hulk of a man. I grab him, I couldn't hold onto him. He gets away from me. I could hardly stand—could barely stand on my feet. Mímis Athanasiádis had given me a pair of sandals, with holes. With rubber underneath. I couldn't wear anything else.

—What time of year was it then, April?

—Not April. Almost March. And in March, on March 15, the Battalions were formed. I went and joined up. I found Yiánnis Theodorélos. And Koïtsános. And someone called Batíris, last name Yiannoulópoulos. And we went around together, we had our little group.

—Theodorélos from Trípolis?

—A native of Leonídio. They had killed all his brothers. All of them. Yiánnis Theodorélos. He's alive today, he married a woman from Dolianá. His house was burned down, he was from Leonídio. Those men were always on the run. We had our little group and we trusted each other. And we still do. I arrest someone called Kapetán Trákas from Tsipianá. At Kambás's factory. In the plains of Miliá. They'd gone to sleep drunk. Him, someone named Kókkinos, and another man from Tsipianá. The three of them. Some old lady told me about them.

—Were they armed?

—They were armed. When I see him, that Trákas tells me, Do you have my gun? I tell him, I have it, you son of a bitch. Kapetán Yiórghis Trákas. A handsome fellow, he's back and forth to America now. He lives in Tsipianá and he has land in Spiliá. He's bought lots of land.

—But you captured them then.

—We captured them. I hit the ground. I couldn't alert my men.

—Were there other rebels there?

—No. My men were spread out, I couldn't call them. There was a pear tree and they'd had so much ouzo they were out cold. An old woman tells me, Look down there, boy, there are the rebels. Where? I ask her. Down there, in that ditch. Go and hide. I tell her, What are you talking about? Well, I couldn't call out. And as they lay there asleep, I go up quietly with my knife and cut the strap of the automatic rifle. He had a German Steyr, Kapetán Trákas. I take it, I take the other man's gun too. I start kicking them. Kicking them so they'll wake up. That's how drunk they were. We brought them to Trípolis tied up. All tied up. And Trákas kept telling me, Please save me and you'll see how grateful I'll be. I got him off. And I had him with me after that. And we were friends from then on. The other one, Kókkinos, was a die-hard Communist. But somehow he got off too, he made it up until the Liberation. And he was court-martialed later on. Behrákis was the judge. Same judge who pronounced about Kraterós, Velissáris, and the rest. Behrákis. And Yiórghis Stasinópoulos. Military judges. There was no chance they'd give them anything but the death penalty. No reason not to. And he wouldn't have gotten off leniently, he had too much against him. But he didn't say a word. I gambled, Your Honor, and I lost. Now I have to pay. That's all. And we went on from there. And on the fifteenth, no the twelfth of October, when the Germans left, they sent me to Spétses. Toward the end.

—Of October.

—Yes.

—When did they arrest Panayótis?

—In May or in June. I don't remember. They arrested him because of me. Because I was active in the Battalions. And on July 29 they killed him. I told you that before.

—Who found him?

—I did. I went up there. Found him dead. We put him up on the mule, in some sacks. And we brought him back.

—Who sent word to you?

—We were there. We'd been on a raid. We'd come out on the top side of Ayiánnis. We were walking up ahead. Six or seven of us. We sat down near a ravine, we had a smoke. I drank some water.

—At night?

—At night. I drank some water, I had some pills the Germans had given us for thirst. We started off. We went up there. A young shepherd tells us, They just killed six men. Right there. We had heard the rifle shots. Hey, I tell him, where was that? In the ravine. In Tóurkos. Across from Ayios Vasíleios.

—Were you in Ayios Vasíleios?

—No, we were going through Ayiánnis.

—And where did you go?

—We got as far as Karyés, just outside.

—Just outside Karyés.

—Karyés. At the monastery. At Ayios Nikólaos. We go there, we find the well. Here's where they had them, he tells us.

—At the monastery?

—No. Some ways from there. An hour away. Near the mountains of Toúrkos. If we hadn't stopped for a smoke we would have got there when they were still alive. That's how unlucky I was. So we went up there. The shepherd tells us, There, in the ravine. We go down to the ravine, on the left side, nothing. We keep going on the other side. And we find them right where the ravine ends and branches out. Dead.

—How many of them were there?

—Six. My brother Panayótis, and Maraskés, two. Themistoklís Anagnostákos, Braílas's mother, and a man from Trípolis.

—Had Kalabákas left?

—He had.

—He got away.

—Yes, he got away.

—How did Kalabákas get away?

—He must have made some dirty deal. To get away like that. He hid under the Braílas woman's skirts, what nonsense. Such things don't happen. It's not possible.

—Did they kill them with a rifle?

—They killed Panayótis with a knife. He must have fought back. He was a big strapping man.

—They killed them at night.

—Yes, at night. They had drawn some water for them from the well. Panayótis was playing the clarinet before that. That's what they told me. Yeorghía Makrís. And then they killed them. They took them down to the ravine. We put him in some sacks and brought him back. Loaded onto the mule.

—Why in sacks?

—They had cut off his head. They'd cut off his feet, they'd cut off his hands. His torso was a separate piece. So how could we take him? We put him in two sacks. We loaded him into two sacks. Not right after it happened. Three or four days later we went and got him. I didn't do any loading. I couldn't do anything. Then someone told me. I found Yiánnis Makrís, I found Kóstas Karayiánnis.

—Where was Kóstas?

—Poor man had disappeared. Then I ran into him. I almost killed him. He escaped by a hair. Hey, Iraklís, Koumbáros. It's me, Kóstas.

—Was he a prisoner too?

—He was hiding of course.

—A prisoner? From the detention camp?

—No, he left the village. They sent them away. Because of the blockade. And he hid up there. Kóstas, Chrístos Papadimítris and Yiánnis Makrís.

—And then they came to Trípolis?

—All of them. With me. Kóstas, God rest his soul. We went and tore through all of Zíreia, we went through all of Neméa. We went down to Pátras. Yes. We did.

Chapter 45

Ah, those villagers from Tsíveri![1] If a lemon tree wouldn't come up, they'd go plant onions.

Chapter 46

I knew Athens. For four years, while Márkos was a student, I would come there often. I would go to my uncle Kóstas Verétsos, my father's first cousin. He had a shop at 93 Aiólou Street. He sold men's clothing. Socks and the like. He says, Where's your uncle the doctor? My uncle the doctor had left. He says, Go to the Red Cross, where they told you to go. I went to the Red Cross. They put us in a school in Pláka.[1] All of us girls who'd been in Haïdári. We each had a cot. They would give us milk, hot chocolate. They'd give us bread. Bread in those days. We'd go outside, and they'd offer us a sovereign for each loaf of bread. I left Pláka after a few days. I went to my aunt, Yiannoúla Ioannítzis. At 18 Notará Street. Or was it 20? I stayed there, I'd help my cousin Christina. I knew about men's shirts. I'd unstitched one of Márkos's shirts and made a pattern from it. I didn't know much but I learned. Loukía was working at Kaloyiánnis's shop. On the corner of Emmanuel Benáki and Stadíou Streets, back then. We'd go there and pick up a dress or two in the latest style. Christina was an accomplished seamstress. And I was pretty good at it too. I started sewing in people's homes. The woman from Xylókastro I was with in Haïdári—her sister. She'd been adopted by an aunt, a rich aunt. She lived near the museum, on Bouboulínas Street. They'd have me at their house to sew something for them, and my wages were two cans of food. That lady wore her hair high in a bun, and rings on her hands, and she had got her adopted daughter engaged to a naval officer. I was impressed by his uniform, I'd seen it hanging in the closet. Back then he really stood out because there was no navy. I'd work in people's homes, and in the evening I'd go back to Aunt Yiannoúla's. But it had already become like a barracks. Rodópi Ioannítzis had come, and Lítsa, and maybe Loúrdos's wife Evyenía was there too. So many people. And they went through a lot, those folks. Take Loúrdos himself. He had brought oil from Astros. And that was quite something, but we all slept crowded one next to the other. The apartment was on the ground floor. It belonged to Zonar's,[2] and that artist Alex lived above it. He had married Zonar's daughter, and there was also an M.P. living there. They had a piece of property on Spýrou Dontá Street. Not anything much, I mean, just an abandoned old room. It had a bathroom, it had once been used as a small kafeneío. I don't remember if it had a kitchen. We found Andréas Athanasíou, he was staying at his aunt Aspasía's in Kolonáki. His father's first cousin, from Epirus. And Ismíni. They were living there, and we'd meet. Every day at noon we'd go to a taverna called Anoúsi. The owner was from Ayios Pétros. Andréas would bring a sausage, I'd bring my food from Pláka, I was still getting rations, and we'd eat. Márkos too. So let me tell you. Márkos says, Let's go live at Ioánnou's place. Ioánnou was the one who had the property on Spýrou Dontá Street. He let us stay there free of charge. So I took the cot I was sleeping on at the shelter, at the school. I took it on my shoulders and I carried it to Spýrou Dontá Street. Off Makriyiánni Street, after Syngroú Avenue. At the Makriyiánni gendarmes station, just below it. I took two cots. One for each end of the room. With the door in between. Márkos and I slept there. I went to Notará Street, to Christina's, four times a day. On foot. I went and helped her with her sewing, she paid me. And I'd go back there, and we'd sleep. And we had a kerosene lamp, a gas burner, and Andréas gave us a can of olive oil. He owed it to us at any rate, and he gave it to us. Up until December. When the December Uprising started I was at Aunt Yiannoúla's. On a Saturday, I think. Or Sunday. Márkos had come down from Kifisiá to listen to Papandréou speak at Syntagma Square.[3] And he comes and tells me, There's an uprising. We took — or rather I'd taken — two or three loaves of bread from the shelter. I left one at Aunt Yiannoúla's. Back then we had net bags, not plastic ones. I put the two loaves in the net bag, and we left. To go to

Spýrou Dontá Street, to spend the night. By the time we reached Stournára Street the gunfire was under way. And I'd keep my hands held high, with the net bag visible, hands up high, keep them up. And the net bag swinging, back and forth like this. I'd press myself against one wall after another, and how I escaped being shot, I don't know. We went into a basement, through a trapdoor. From there we went to the cathedral. But we couldn't get through. They had started fighting on Makriyiánni Street. I don't remember if we went back. Or if we got there. But we stayed on there, in that room, until Márkos left. They drafted him. He left, and I was left alone. There was a family from Ileía living next door. The Papakonstantínous. A mother and two sons. There was no father. Both lawyers. The two sons. The younger one had a motorcycle. He was a wintertime bather. He'd go swimming and come back. On his motorcycle. Someone who made car upholsteries lived across from me. Lálos. The house is still there. Small world. I asked a koumbára of my husband's niece about them last year. At any rate. She knows them, they're still there. At night alarms would go off, mortar shells would fall, and all of us, the whole neighborhood, would go to his basement. There were no apartment buildings yet. I was there alone, Márkos had been drafted then, but I knew where he was. So I'd take some bean soup, and Ismíni would come with me, and we'd go and find him. Once we met him on Akominátou Street. I saw houses that had been broken into there, with furniture and various household utensils scattered about upstairs. Imagine if the army were to get in there. At Christmastime, I don't know why, there was a cease-fire every day around noon. Twelve to two. I'd managed to get myself five or six passes. There were passes in those days. Back then Maíri Iatrídis, Mítsos Iatrídis's sister, was still alive. She used to come and vacation in the summer at Kastrí. We'd go together to Christina's, we were apprenticing as seamstresses. I had gotten a pass for her neighborhood. A pass for Pláka and one for Exárheia.[4] I don't know how I managed it, maybe the police looked on us with a kind eye. I don't know. I'd be stocking up on food. Stocking up wherever I could, and I'd go to Márkos's place and he'd give us a dab of margarine, and some hard-baked bread. I'd go with Ismíni. On

Christmas Day Aunt Yiannoúla called me—Yiórgos Ioannítzis had been drafted too. Márkos Ioannítzis's brother. He'd been drafted and he was a guard on Heródou Attikoú Street at the palace. I went and saw him and he gave me a can of food. He was an officer. What did I take him? He gave me a can with potatoes, beans, and a piece of meat. I don't remember if I took him something or what it was. He told me, You're too thin. Maybe I took him matches because he smoked a pipe. I was tall and slim. Too thin. I remember him. Maybe I went to see him twice. He gave me that can of food and I took it to Mrs. Papakonstantínou, the lady with the two sons, and we ate it together. On New Year's Day I stayed in. I was in a bad mood, and I'd had a terrible fright the night before. Next to me was another door with the same little stairs, three steps that led up to a two-story apartment. Some Greeks were living upstairs, and British soldiers would come and play cards with them. The Brits would come, and that night they knocked on my door. Maybe they were drunk, or made a mistake. I was shaking. I didn't open the door, but it had a glass pane on the upper half, a pane of glass. And I signaled to them, go next door, next door. They got what they came for, and they left. In the morning I told Lálos about it. He had one son and one daughter. He tells me, If you have an old blanket, bring it, and we'll give it to them, and they'll give you a new one. Trade-offs like that happened, that sort of exchange. I took him an old blanket, and he gave me a new one, a wonderful khaki one. I don't remember the dates, I don't remember when I left that room. I couldn't go to Notará Street to Aunt Yiannoúla's. There were too many people crammed in. So I went to Kifisiá. I had nothing warm to wear. Christina tells me, a different Christina that one, another cousin, a Menglínas. She says, Let's dye this blanket and make it into a nice coat. I had taken it to Kifisiá, and Aunt Magdálo had a tub, and we dyed it brown. A nice soft brown color. But I didn't make it into a coat, I made a suit. People got by like that then. We had the Red Cross, and we had UNRRA.[5] I think. And there was the Athens Archdiocese. They gave out different things, clothes and shoes—hand-me-downs. All those registered with the Red Cross could get one suit apiece. I made that suit, there was a piece of woolen material left at the shop, and Christina from Notará Street made a flared Tyrolean skirt from it. I'd found a silk dress at UNRRA, an evening dress with a cigarette burn just below the waist. And I cut it, made it into a blouse, and embroidered it. I'd wear all those things, and now I was going to get war victims' assistance. Why you smashing young thing, you, Yiórgos Ioannítzis would tell me. You smashing young thing. You look like you just stepped out of a fashion house. I had a handkerchief here in my pocket, I was slim, I was at the height of my youth and beauty. At any rate. I was living in Kifísia, I'd begun to sew. The Támbaris family had a koumbára who was one of the best shirt makers. And she recommended me to various households. People would have new clothes made but mainly they would do alterations. I was good at that, too. I went to a villa in Kefalári,[6] with velvet wallpaper, it was just like being in a movie theater. Impressive-looking furniture — and all that just when I started making money. But I left. There was the problem of what would become of my brother and sister, Phaídros and Stella. They had gotten out of prison, they'd survived, and they'd gone to Kastrí. And something had to be done. How stupid of me, I should have stayed in Athens. Instead of that I began to go back and forth, from Athens to Trípolis to Kastrí. In Trípolis the Salíveros family put me up. Maria was there, we'd become very close friends. And I sewed different things for them, and they were thrilled. I also sewed for the Athanasiádis family. And for Mavroyiórghis. They had stood by his side ungrudgingly. They tell me, Come and live in Trípolis, we'll help you. And stupidly, I did. I moved in September, so the younger ones could go to school. Stella had finished but she was studying English. Phaídros was attending the eight-year junior high school. He was going to enroll in fifth grade. Fifth grade, I think. I went to Trípolis. I couldn't find a house. I had no money. My father had sold some barrel staves, he got 350 drachmas for them. He gave me the money. Voúla Vasilópoulos was in Trípolis, she was pregnant with Maria. Ada Papayiánnis was there. All the men from the Battalions had come down there, Yiánnis Dránias, Iphigenia. They were there then. I don't know why they had moved house again. The Kavasális girls were there. It was a nightmare finding a room, but I found one that fit us. The woman renting it to us had TB, we didn't know it. We stayed there, it had a smaller side room. It was September when we moved in. After that they brought those gendarmes back dead from Ayios Pétros, in their undershirts. I don't remember when that happened. The Galaxýdis brothers came down, they wanted to arrest us again. In Orthokostá they'd taken me as a hostage because of Márkos and my uncle the doctor. They had gone to Athens. I'd been in prison, I'd been in Haïdári. And now they wanted to arrest me again. They didn't let them. I've forgiven them all. But that Mihális Galaxýdis, there was a time when I was ready to throw a grenade under his car. Back when Phaídros was rejected from the Air Force Academy. He was about to become a squadron leader. I was really indignant. Phaídros left for Canada. He made a success of himself there, he has children. We stayed in Trípolis. Our atelier was doing well. I'd go up to Athens every once in a while. I always stayed with Iríni Koutsoúmbis. She lived on Zínonos Street, around there. It was convenient because the terminal for the bus from Trípolis was on Ayíou Konstantínou Street in the center of Athens. So she let me stay there. She had moved to Athens. From Corinth to Athens. Daphne and the younger sister went overseas, they emigrated. One went to Chicago, and the other I don't know where. When Iríni's brother Yiánnis died I was in Trípolis. I heard about it after the funeral. But I went to the forty-day memorial service. Iríni invited some people for a meal. Around 1955. Or was it in the sixties? She had guests, that Mihaíl fellow from Ayios Pétros. Who had a sister called Xáko. Short for Xakoustí. Mihaíl Manousákis. He had dealerships in Trípolis. And another man from Kosmás, a microbiologist, Maístros the microbiologist, at 40 Karneádou Street. They were talking, and they said something. Maístros did. She's Spade-and-Shovel's cousin. About me. Kind of allegorically. And I thought they were being sarcastic. I say, What's up, you guys? Mihaíl says, He's talking about Márkos Ioannítzis. I tell them, Now look. And they talked about my brother Márkos too. I tell them, Márkos Mávros may be my brother, but Márkos Ioannítzis was twice as much a brother to me. I won't allow any remarks from you. Maístros was from Kosmás. His father was a doctor too, a friend of our Níkos.

I tell him, You men must know his story—and how it all happened. Because certain people had spread the word that Níkos had finished him off. He stopped eating. He tells me, I only know what my godmother has told me. Márkos Ioannítzis left our house, and he asked her for a towel and a knife. Alímonos came and got him. This was on June 3. He came and got him from our house. I was just a kid, but I know where they buried him. I say, Go and tell all that to Yiórgos Ioannítzis. Because this is what happened to our family: Níkos got carried away by his ideas, and he made the mistake of writing things against Márkos to Yiórgos. Back then. And Yiórgos told me that very bitterly. I tell Maístros: Please go and tell all that to Ioannítzis. I think Márkos had also left a letter there. At that house. Maístros knew the true Ioannítzis story. And then our Christina said, Since that's how it is, let's tell the girls and go all together and help them dig up their brother's bones. But they didn't agree. They said they hadn't the courage. They hadn't worn black for ten years. For ten years they believed that Márkos was in the Middle East. Because the BBC had said something like that back then. Márkos was betrayed by Kontalónis. He spoke English, and he told the officers, their headquarters liaisons, to stop air dropping supplies to the Communists. He told them, They'll turn against us and against you. And Kontalónis betrayed him. I think that's why they killed him. I was twenty-two years old at the time.

Chapter 47

It's at a depth of 35 meters. Twenty-five cubic meters every twenty-four hours. At 160 meters' depth, it's 250 cubic meters. But I've had it up to here with those villagers from Másklina. I'm not going to let them in on this. Unless they pay me. If they don't, then let the water lie.

The Orthokostá Monastery is situated on the eastern foothills of Mount Parnon (locally known as Malevós), precisely on the road—until recently a mule path and at present a paved motorway—connecting the Ayios Andréas and the Prastós communities, both belonging to the wider Tsakoniá (southern Kynouría) region. The exact coordinates for the monastery (page titled: Dresthená-Asómatoi, sc. 1:50,000, Army Geographical Service, 1938) are K + 290838, and its earliest archaeological remains date back to the times of the Iconomachy.[1] It is dedicated to the Dormition of the Virgin, and its feast is celebrated on August 23 (the Ninth-day Feast), the meaning of the name Orthokostá being unknown to this day. One possible derivation is the mispronunciation of the Tsakónikan place name Órto-Kótsa (the hill on whose northeastern slope it stands). It lies above an impressively steep and narrow ravine, extending from north to south.

Isaákios's mendacious assertions concerning the expansive alluvial plain of the river Mégas, the sea of Náfplion, and the bright-shining vein of silver and lead ought simply to be taken as the poetic escapism of a repressed existence. Isaákios, the bishop of Rhéon and Prastós (1730–1805), after being impeached by the Ecumenical Patriarchate for heretical beliefs and simony, spent the last twelve years of his life under a restraining order at the Orthokostá Monastery.

TRANSLATORS' NOTE

Thanassis Valtinos came onto the literary scene in Greece in the early 1960s with several novella-length prose narratives that heralded a marked shift away from the florid, discursive prose of the fiction of the times toward what was to become a much-imitated and highly respected style of documentary fiction marked by the sparse, unadorned speech of oral accounts. His early works, such as *The Descent of the Nine* (1963), *The Life and Times of Andreas Kordopatis, Book 1: America* (1964), and the later *Deep Blue Almost Black* (1985), are all relatively short first-person narratives that simulate the type of spontaneous communication usually heard among ordinary people.

In the 1990s Valtinos began combining similar first-person narratives with letters or documents into longer, polyphonic works and produced what are most certainly his three major works: *Data from the Decade of the Sixties* (1989), *Orthokostá* (1994), and *The Life and Times of Andreas Kordopatis, Book 2: The Balkans '22* (2000), to be followed again by shorter titles in the twenty-first century. *Orthokostá* can arguably be called the peak of Valtinos's literary career, coming as it does midway between his other two major works. Indeed, its standing in the critical canon of Greece is undiminished today, more than twenty years since its publication.

The subject of Valtinos's novels is not history itself but the recording of history, the way it is remembered and depicted, orally or in writing, reliably or not. What emerges from the seemingly unedited raw footage of his novels is a poignant re-living of history by its participants on a day-to-day basis, regardless of their social circumstances, level of education, or political orientation.

The numerous narrators, be they participants, victims, or innocent bystanders, recount in hindsight, and from many differing van-
tage points, the hardships and atrocities of the conflict portrayed in
Orthokostá, such as the Communist guerrillas' burning of Valtinos's
home village of Kastri and smaller villages like Ayia Sofia; their detain-
ing of combatants and civilians alike in the monasteries of Orthokostá
and Loukou and in local schools; the torture, forced marches, and
executions of many of those detained, and the subsequent revenge
killings by rightist and collaborationist Security Battalions. And while
both sides engage in extensive looting and stealing, German troops
are carrying out their own murderous "clean-up" operations in the
region by arresting, torturing, and executing villagers while imposing
consecutive blockades on the village of Kastri.

It is in the midst of such contrary tides that the human element
begins to emerge. Although the narrators are not clearly identified
initially, they gradually come into focus as their families and fortunes
are pieced together through their own and others' imperfect recollections of the decades-old events. Certain key incidents are told and re-
told throughout *Orthokostá*, each additional telling either contradict-
ing an earlier account or shedding new light on the events in question.

In one of the closing chapters of the novel, at the prodding of
an unnamed interlocutor, a surviving participant pulls together the
different strands of the novel by recounting some of its central executions while also telling of his own travails at the hands first of the
German occupying forces and then of the Communist guerrillas, as
well as the horrific circumstances of his brother's execution by the
latter—the kind of account which today, in 2016, would immediately
go viral on the Internet, but which in 1994, when *Orthokostá* was first
published, was all the more shocking for having been repressed for
fifty years as taboo subject matter.

In practical terms, *Orthokostá* is steeped in references to village customs and linguistic constructions which imbue the narratives with both local color and a sense of verisimilitude. In the original this is masterfully done through Valtinos's frequent citing and
trademark cataloguing of local-sounding names that impart an im-

mediate ring of familiarity to the Greek text, as well as an unmistakable affinity with the epic tradition. To the English-speaking reader, however, Greek proper names are anything but familiar. We have resisted Anglicizing these names (Georgia for Yeorghía, for example) in the interest of preserving the Greekness at the core of *Orthokostá*. We have also tried to make the names and proper names less difficult to pronounce by accenting those that are not already familiar to English-speaking readers and by generally favoring a more phonetic spelling system than that dictated by tradition. Whether phonetic or traditional or a mix of both, individual names are consistently transliterated throughout the novel.

Names and naming, more so than expressions in a specific dialect, are in fact what often distinguishes local parlance in these and other peripheral regions from speech in mainland Greek cities. Whereas oral speech and dialogue are best rendered by equivalents rather than literal translations, names present their own set of problems. In *Orthokostá*, nicknames, diminutives, compound names, and first or last names with suffixes added are all cases in point. Suffixes added onto names in order to denote ownership (as in "Makréka," meaning the house, houses, neighborhood, property, or land of the Makrís family) or relationship (as in "Sokrátaina," meaning the wife, daughter, or mother of Sokrátis) are typical examples of this. We have dealt with these on a case-by-case basis, sometimes through free translation or interpretive interventions in the text itself and sometimes through explanatory notes.

From a grammatical point of view, and again in the interest of simplicity and intelligibility, the variously inflected forms of names of men and women in the Greek have been rendered in a rather unflattering masculine nominative singular that is currently the norm in English.

Our priority was to maintain throughout a balance between the nonstandard or village Greek in most of the narratives of *Orthokostá* and the equivalent constructions in American English. To this end we have flavored our translation with the occasional recognizably rural but not markedly regional expression meant to transpose some of the more common village speaking patterns of the Greek. At the same time we have been careful not to make the villagers in *Orthokostá* sound too much like their Midwestern American counterparts, as they must first and foremost come across to the English-speaking reader as Greek villagers living in Greece.

Valtinos has endeavored to approximate through his punctuation (and frequent, deliberate omission of it) the natural spontaneity of oral speech in Modern Greek. His villagers communicate, for the most part, in short, choppy, sometimes ungrammatical sentences, often interrupting themselves midstream and picking up later on. Like most oral speech, theirs is a mixture of the historical present and the past tense, rendered with great brio and virtuosity in the original. We have tried in our translation to reproduce the effects of Valtinos's prose by adhering as closely as possible to the tense structure and punctuation of the original so as to best reflect its spontaneity within the limits of contemporary English usage.

We have annotated our translation in the minimalist spirit of the novel's author by providing the basic historical data an educated Greek reader would have brought to the book when it first came out in 1994, some fifty years after the events being described. We have also provided the essential backdrop a nonnative Greek reader of the book today would need to make sense of the narratives. This too has been kept to a minimum: too much information would be tantamount to analyzing the individual dots in a pointillist painting whose size, shape, and color are unimportant in and of themselves. It is rather their concentration and distribution that create the overall effect of an impressionist canvas, which is, properly speaking, the aim of *Orthokostá*, and indeed of Valtinos's work in general. To simply index the realist texture of the novel by including excessive biographical or sociopolitical background in the notes would instantly lower the entire work to the status of a poorly researched chronicle. This would be a disservice to the literary dimension of the book and its primary goal of representing the spontaneity and alternating modes of the original accounts: the transcriptions from the Greek killing fields.

"Prologue"

1. Mount Malevós: Another name for Mount Parnon in the southeastern Peloponnese. Much of the action in the book centers on this densely wooded region. During World War II it became a refuge for the Communist Resistance fighters as well as a place where anti-Communist civilians were held hostage.

2. Ninth-day Feast of the Dormition of the Virgin: Like many Greek monasteries, Orthokostá, though dedicated to the Dormition of the Virgin, which is nationally celebrated on August 15, performs its most solemn festivities, or Apódosis, on August 23, nine days later.

3. Tsakoniá: Area in the southeastern Peloponnese made up of villages such as Sítaina, Prastós, and Leonídio, in which Tsakónikan, a descendant of Doric Greek, was spoken as late as the 1970s.

Chapter 1

1. Vigla: A place name referring to a watchtower (from the Latin *vigila*) in the village of Másklina; it was probably built between 1205 and 1432 in the Frankish-occupied Peloponnese.

2. Lioú: The wife of Liás (in this case Liás Tsioúlos). In the provinces masculine first names are often used in their possessive form to denote a man's wife or mother.

Chapter 2

1. Ayiasofiá: Local pronunciation of Ayía Sofía (Saint Sophia), a village in the Arcadia prefecture.

2. Másklina (also known as Eleohóri): A village near the border between the Arcadia and Argolis prefectures. German troops were stationed there at the time the novel takes place.

3. Velissaróyiannis: A local variant for the name Yiánnis Velissáris. This type of construction, where the first and last names are compounded in reverse order, is typical of speech in the provinces, particularly the Peloponnese. Similar constructions include, in this chapter, Kalabakóyiannis for Yiánnis Kalabákas; Stavróyiannis for Yiánnis Stávrou (chap. 6); Mavroyiórghis for Yiórgos Mávros (chap. 7); Mavróyiannis for Yiánnis Mávros (chap. 36); and Havdotóyiannis for Yiánnis Havdótos (chap. 36).

4. Ayiopétro: Local way of referring to Ayios Pétros (Saint Peter), a village on Mount Parnon, in the Arcadia prefecture, and the site of detention camps and fierce battles between rebel forces and gendarmes.

5. The Organization: The Communist Party.

6. "We'll cut off your hair": The Communist guerrillas used to cut off the hair of "enemies" to make it difficult for them to hide among the general population.

7. Antídoron: A bite-size piece of bread that has been hallowed during a Greek Orthodox mass and is left over from the sacrament of Holy Communion. The officiating priest hands out these morsels to the parishioners as they exit the church.

8. Security Battalions: Initially named the Evzones Guard of the Unknown Soldier, the Security Battalions were formed in 1943 by official decree, ostensibly to maintain peace in the Greek countryside. The Battalions were armed by and fought alongside the German Occupation troops, suppressing Communist as well as non-Communist insurgents.

9. Kapetános, Kapetán (voc.): The equivalent of a captain in the Communist Resistance army.

Chapter 3

1. Kapetanaíoi: Plural of *kapetános*.

2. Albania: References to "Albania" by speakers in the novel stand for the campaign of the Greek Army between October 1940 and May 1941 in northwestern Greece and southern Albania to stop fascist Italy from invading Greece. Óhi (No!) Day, October 28, is the annual commemoration of the start of that victorious campaign.

Chapter 4

1. ELAS: Ελληνικός Λαϊκός Απελευθερωτικός Στρατός (Greek Popular Liberation Army), founded on February 16, 1942, as a special branch of the Communist EAM (Εθνικό Απελευθερωτικό Μέτωπο, the National Liberation

Front). Founded on September 27, 1941, EAM was the military arm of the Communist Party, created to resist the Occupation during World War II.

2. Dionýsius Papadóngonas (1888–1944): A politically conservative major general in charge of the Security Battalions in the Peloponnese.

3. Prophítis Ilías: A hill in northern Greece near the Albanian border named after the prophet Elijah and made famous during the 1940–41 Greco-Italian war. The battle that took place there on November 2, 1940, marked the first victory of the Greek Army against the onslaught of two Italian mountain divisions that had recently invaded Greek territory.

4. George Tsolákoglou (1886–1948): A general in the Greek Army who signed the armistice agreement in which Greece capitulated to the German and Italian forces in April 1941. Pressed into assuming the premiership of Greece, Tsolákoglou appointed Major General George Bákos (1892–1945) minister of military affairs.

5. Aris Velouhiótis (1905–1945): Born Thanásis Kláras, he was the leader of the ELAS forces during the Occupation.

6. KKE: The Greek Communist Party (Κομμουνιστικό Κόμμα Ελλά-δας), founded in 1918.

7. Várkiza Treaty: On February 12, 1945, representatives of the Nikó-laos Plastíras government and EAM-ELAS representatives of the Communist Party of Greece met in the coastal town of Várkiza, south of Athens, and signed a nine-point agreement, chief among which was the disarming of the EAM-ELAS guerrillas and their withdrawal from the cities of Athens and Thessaloníki.

8. Antónis Katsantónis (1785–1808): A legendary guerrilla leader who fought against Turkish occupation of prerevolutionary Greece.

9. Grigóris Soúrlas: The organizer of armed anti-Communist farmer bands in central Greece during the Civil War.

10. Plebiscite: On September 1, 1946, the government of Constantine Tsaldáris conducted a plebiscite to determine whether King George II, who had left Greece during the Occupation, could be reinstated to the throne of Greece; 69 percent of the voters favored the restoration.

11. Litóchoro and Pontokerasiá: On March 30, 1946, thirty-three left-ists attacked a gendarmes station in the town of Litóchoro in the prefecture of Piería. On June 5 another group attacked a Greek Army company in the town of Pontokerasiá in Kilkís. These two incidents are generally considered the beginning of the Greek Civil War.

12. Haroúlis: Diminutive of Harís.

13. Napoléon Zérvas (1891–1957): A retired lieutenant colonel and the founder in September 1941 of the right-wing Resistance group EDES (Εθνικός Δημοκρατικός Ελληνικός Σύνδεσμος, Greek National Democratic Union), committed to fighting against German, Italian. and Bulgarian Occupation forces. An anti-Communist, Zérvas openly accused EAM-ELAS of striving to impose a Soviet-style government in Greece following the end of the Occupation.

14. Athanásios Yiannakópoulos: An infantry colonel who, along with army officers Telémahos Vrettákos, Panayótis Katsaréas, and Stámos Triantafýllis, formed a Resistance group that eventually ceded power to ELAS; an agreement to this effect was signed by Yiannakópoulos.

15. SMA: Στρατηγείο Μέσης Ανατολής, the Near East Command Headquarters, which was established in Cairo, Egypt, by the British Expeditionary Forces under Colonels Eddie Myers and Christopher Woodhouse. Their liaisons in Greece pressured right-wing Resistance groups into submitting to mostly leftist ELAS leadership.

16. Metaxourgheío: A poor neighborhood in south-central Athens.

17. OPLA: Οργάνωση Προστασίας Λαϊκών Αγωνιστών (Organization to Protect People's Fighters). The OPLA operatives, commissioned in late spring 1943 and active until 1947, were charged with the protection of KKE members and the extermination of suspected anti-Communists and their relatives.

Chapter 5

1. Voúlis: Short form of Paraskevoúlis, the diminutive of Paraskevás.

Chapter 6

1. "He saw her as a bride": Dreaming of a bride is considered a bad omen in Greek folklore.

2. Panayótis Stoúpas (1894–1944): Army major and commander of anti-Communist Security Battalion units.

3. Ayiórghis: Local way of referring to the village of Ayios Yiórghios (Saint George) in the Argolis prefecture.

4. Gaïdoúras: Nickname derived from *gaïdoúra*, a she-donkey, a jenny.

5. *Koumbároi*: Plural of *koumbáros* (m.) or *koumbára* (f.), a person one has close ties with by having been mutual best men or maids of honor at each other's weddings; *koumbároi* also denotes people who were godparents at each other's children's christenings.

Chapter 7

1. Ioánnis Metaxás (1871–1941): A lieutenant general in the Greek Army who was appointed premier of Greece in 1936, and soon assumed wider dictatorial powers, which brought about strong popular opposition. He is best remembered for the efficient preparation of Greek land defenses and for rejecting Italy's ultimatum on October 28, 1940.

2. Konstantinos Maniadákis (1893–1973): Chief of the State Security Police under Ioánnis Metaxás.

3. Castor oil: Castor oil was used to torture prisoners; it causes diarrhea and rapid dehydration.

4. Sokrátaina: In local parlance, the wife of Sokrátis. Similar constructions where the suffix "-aina" is added to the root of a masculine name to denote a female relative are typical in the provinces. See also in this chapter Mavroyiórgaina (the wife of Mavroyiórghis) and Mákraina (a female member of the Makrís family), and Kóstaina (the wife of Kóstas) in chapter 11.

5. Yiórghis. A variant of the common first name Yiórgos.

6. Petroú: The wife of Pétros (Pétros Tatoúlis, father of Mihális).

7. Saint Paraskeví: A widely venerated second-century martyr and saint of the Greek Orthodox Church. Numerous locations, urban and rural, are named after her. Her feast is celebrated on July 28.

8. Ayiánnis: Local variant for Ayios Yiánnis (Saint John), a village in the Argolís prefecture. "Apáno" designates a community built on a higher elevation than the village.

9. The Feast of the Virgin: A religious and national holiday celebrated on August 15 and preceded by a fifteen-day fast.

10. Mýloi: District on the western outskirts of Athens whose name suggests industrial grain mills.

11. Léla Karayiánnis (1898–1944): Leader of a resistance movement who as early as 1941 and until her arrest and execution ran a network of anti-Axis saboteurs. She is also commemorated in Israel as one of the Righteous Among the Nations.

12. Kifisiá: Verdant, posh suburb north of Athens.

13. *Saltadórissa*: From the Italian verb *saltare*, "to leap": typically an agile teenager who leaped on the backs of occupation supply trucks and emptied them of their contents.

Chapter 8

1. "Like a tax": The owners of an olive press usually withheld one-tenth of any amount of oil it pressed as a fee for the pressing. This payment in kind allowed the press owners to accumulate quantities of oil they could use to speculate, buy property, bribe officials, and so on.

Chapter 9

1. Certificates of "Recognition": In 1982 the Greek government offered pensions to tens of thousands of persons who claimed they had fought against the German, Italian, and Bulgarian occupation armies during World War II.

2. The December Uprising: Known in Greek as Τα Δεκεμβριανά, the term refers to the period between December 1944 and January 1945 during which EAM-ELAS Resistance fighters, on one side, and the British-backed Greek Army, metropolitan police, gendarmes, and the royalist "X" faction on the other, engaged in street fighting in Athens and Piraeus, with thousands of combatant and noncombatant casualties.

3. Mýloi: A seaside town in the Argolis prefecture, not to be confused with the district in Athens.

4. X: A royalist-backed military organization founded in June 1941 by Colonel George Grívas of the Greek Army. Its name was changed to X, the Greek chi (pronounced "hee") in March 1943. The new name was emblematized by the crossing of two Greek capital gammas, one standing for King George II of Greece and one for Grívas himself. Those wearing the X insignia on their berets or armbands were called Heétes.

5. The Feast of Saint Ilías: Celebration for the prophet Elijah ("Ilías" in Greek) held on July 20. Early in the history of Eastern Christianity Elijah, from the book of Kings in the Hebrew Bible, was proclaimed the patron saint of mountaintops and venerated in small churches, often erected on the foundations of former shrines to Zeus.

6. Lighting the oil candles: A service often performed by women in small neighborhood churches that have no sexton. Since the Greek culture has no tradition of a book of prayers, asking someone to light the oil candles (a floating wick in a glass of oil, typically hung in front of holy icons) amounts to asking for extended prayer.

7. Siege of Trípolis: When the flourishing multi-ethnic town of Trípolis was under Turkish administration in the nineteenth century, it was besieged by Greek forces under Theódoros Kolokotrónis. The siege lasted from

the beginning of June until September 23, 1821, and became the subject of a well-known Greek folksong.

8. Panayótis Kanellópoulos (1902–1986): A statesman and historian of ideas who was a member of the Greek government-in-exile during the Axis Occupation. He served briefly as minister of defense and minister of reconstruction, and twice as prime minister. He spent seven years under house arrest during the Colonels' Junta in 1967–74. Kanellópoulos's landing in the southern Peloponnese in 1944 marked the return of the government-in-exile to power.

9. Meligalás: A town in the southern Peloponnese where a well-known battle took place on September 13 and 14, 1944, between ELAS forces, which prevailed, and the Security Battalions.

10. Gargaliánoi: Locality in the southern Peloponnese in which ELAS troops were victorious in the September 21–23, 1944, battle against the Security Battalions under Major Panayótis Stoúpas.

11. Spýros Tsiklitíras: ELAS division commander in Laconía, in the southern Peloponnese.

12. PEEA: Πολιτική Επιτροπή Εθνικής Απελευθέρωσης, the Political Committee for National Liberation, active from March to November 1944; a mostly EAM group created to administer the regions of Greece recently vacated by German Occupation troops.

13. Kolonáki: Upscale residential neighborhood near the center of Athens.

Chapter 11

1. *Gólfo*: A pastoral romance in five acts by Spyrídon Peresiádis (1854–1918) that was a staple of Greek amateur acting companies and a perennial favorite of audiences.

Chapter 13

1. Valtétsi: A mountain village in the Prefecture of Arcadia, the site of important events during the 1821 Greek Revolution.

2. Theódoros Tourkovasílis (1891–1976): A nationalist parliamentarian, cofounder of the Populist Party, minister of education, and founder of teachers academies. As head of the Bank of Greece during the Axis Occupation, Tourkovasílis was jailed by the Germans. Thodorís and Thódoros are colloquial variants for the name Theódoros.

3. EDES: Εθνικός Δημοκρατικός Ελληνικός Σύνδεσμος, Greek Na-

tional Democratic Union, a rightist coalition founded in September 1941 by Napoléon Zérvas to fight against German, Italian, and Bulgarian occupation forces.

4. Óhi Day: National holiday celebrated annually to commemorate October 28, 1940, when Prime Minister Ioánnis Metaxás famously responded no (óhi) to Italy's ultimatum to Greece, thus sparking Greece's entry into World War II.

5. The Liberation: The withdrawal of German occupation forces from Greece in October 1944.

6. Ádonis Kýrou (1923–1985): an influential left-wing activist, son of Achilléas Kýrou, owner of the conservative Athens daily *Estia*.

Chapter 14

1. Mávri Trýpa: A village in Arcadia known since antiquity for its deep geological crevasses. It has since been officially renamed "Trýpi."

Chapter 16

1. LOK: Λόχοι Ορεινών Καταδρομών (Alpine Assault Companies) were special army units trained to engage the Communist guerrillas active in the mountainous terrain of Greece during the 1947–49 Civil War.

2. Tsakónikan: See note 3 to the "Prologue."

Chapter 19

1. Loukoú: A monastery near the town of Astros, in the Peloponnese. It is dedicated to Christ of the Transfiguration, its foundation probably dating to the sixth century. Like Orthokostá, Loukoú was used by the guerrillas as a detention camp and as a center of military operations during the Civil War.

2. Tray: A Greek kafeneío tray, typically of tin or brass, with a handle attached to the rim by three long thin metal strips.

3. The Torture: This practice, known in Greek as *fálanga* (the rod), became particularly prevalent during the 1960s and 1970s when Greece was ruled by a military junta. Allusions to it would still resonate with readers when the novel first appeared in 1994.

4. The Karyés Monastery: Located on Mount Parnon, it is dedicated to the Virgin Mary.

5. Name day: Greeks traditionally celebrate not their birthdays but the feast day of the saint they were named after—in this case Saint John, January 7.

6. *Partisano*: Italian word for "partisan," widely used in Greece to denote Communist Resistance fighter.

7. Mávri Trýpa: Literally, "Black Hole." See note 1 to chapter 14.

Chapter 20

1. Okás: An oká is a measure of weight equaling 1,280 grams or 45 ounces.

2. Laundering trough: Water mills—to this day, when they are not grinding grains—launder heavy fabrics, blankets, rugs, etc., which the mill will also store for the clients.

3. Yiannákis: Variant of the common first name Yiánnis. Other variants include Yiannakákis, Yiannoúkos, and Yiannákos.

Chapter 24

1. The Salutations: The Salutations of the Virgin Mary, sung during the vespers of the first five Lenten Fridays of the Greek Orthodox Church.

2. Saint Peter's Day: June 29.

Chapter 26

1. Saints Constantine and Helen are jointly celebrated on May 21.

2. *Triatatikós*: A made-up word, from the three initial T's in Τηλέφωνο, Ταχυδρομείο, Τηλέγραφος. He was a Telephone, Mail, and Telegraph Service employee.

3. EPON: Ενιαία Πανελλαδική Οργάνωση Νέων (Unified Panhellenic Youth Organization), an extension of EAM. EPON was founded on February 23, 1943.

4. Ilisós: A neighborhood in central Athens named after the stream Ilissus (see chapter 9) that used to run through it.

5. KOBA: Κομματική Οργάνωση Βάσης (Local Party Chapter), a neighborhood-based office of the Greek Communist Party.

6. Palaiá Anáktora: Old Royal Palace, the present-day Parliament building, in the center of Athens.

7. Goudí: District to the northeast of Athens that served over the years as a base for military and gendarmes.

Chapter 28

1. Saint Nicholas's Day: December 6.

2. Loukoumádes: A traditional Greek sweet. Spoonfuls of white flour dough are deep fried until golden brown and served with honey and a pinch of cinnamon.

3. "Pinned some basil on them": Pinning basil on a couple was a sign of public approval of their relationship.

4. "He had no sisters": It was customary for a man to find husbands for his sisters before getting married himself.

5. Fez: A red fez is part of the popular Greek costume worn by National Guards, or Evzones.

6. Foustanélla: A man's white pleated skirt. Part of Greek popular costume worn by Evzones.

7. "State of mourning": A year-long period during which no weddings could be performed in the village.

8. Katharévousa: The purist, archaizing idiom in which all official documents of the Greek state were written. It was also the formal spoken language of conservative politicians, army officers, and educated clergy, among others.

9. Stremmata: Plural of *stremma*, an area of measurement equaling one thousand square meters or a quarter of an acre.

10. "Protopapadákis's notorious law": Pétros Protopapadákis (1860–1922) was a minister of finance who devalued the state currency in 1919–22 to meet the expenditures for Greece's disastrous military campaign in Asia Minor.

11. Brooklyds: From "Brooklyn," financially successful emigrants returning from the United States.

12. Elefthérios Venizélos (1864–1936): An important Greek statesman, supporter of the Entente Cordiale, and opponent of the policies of the Greek palace. A charismatic leader who also encountered fierce personal and political opposition, Venizélos was elected no fewer than seven times to the premiership of Greece in his lifetime. It was during Greece's military campaign in Asia Minor (1919–22) that the Greek Parliament decided to withdraw its support for the campaign and hold elections in November 1920. Venizélos lost and chose to leave Greece. He was elected prime minister again and served from 1928 to 1932.

13. Agrarian Reform Law: Premier Ioánnis Metaxás instituted the Agrarian Reform Law in 1936, whereby large landholdings were redistributed to benefit poor rural populations.

14. Alexandros Svólos (1892–1956): A Greek academic and parliamentarian active—primarily as finance minister—both during the Occupation of Greece and immediately afterward. Svólos is mostly remembered for his 1944 legislation that drastically devalued stock issued by Greek banks from fifty drachmas to one.

Chapter 30

1. ETA: Επιμελητεία του Αντάρτη (Revolutionaries' Commissary).

2. "A date not easily forgotten": October 28 is Óhi Day. See note 4 of chapter 13.

Chapter 36

1. The Feast of the Elevation of the True Cross: High holy day celebrated on September 14.

Chapter 38

1. The ancient tragic playwright: The quotation is from Sophocles' *Antigone*.

Chapter 39

1. Turks: Derogatory term used for Communist guerrillas.

2. Drobólitsa: Folk pronunciation of Trípolis.

3. Megaloúpolis: Colloquial variant of Megalópolis.

Chapter 44

1. Tsirígo: In country parlance, another name for the island of Kýthira.

2. Farkó: Mispronunciation of "Fargo," a vehicle originally manufactured by the Fargo Motor Car Company and produced, under different ownership, until 1972.

3. Bulgarian: Like "Turk," "Bulgarian" was part of the anti-Communist vocabulary to designate a die-hard Communist.

Chapter 45

1. Tsivéri: Local variant for the village of Kyvéri.

Chapter 46

1. Pláka: A picturesque neighborhood on the eastern slopes of the Acropolis in Athens.

2. Zonar's: A fashionable café in the center of Athens, established by the Greek-American businessman Károlos Zonarás in 1939.

3. Syntagma Square: Also known as Constitution Square, it is the central square in Athens, across from the Parliament, and was often the site of demonstrations.

4. Exárheia: A middle-class neighborhood near the center of Athens.

5. UNRRA: The United Nations Relief and Rehabilitation Administration, founded in 1943, was especially active in 1945 and 1946. Forty-four countries contributed to funding, supplying, and staffing the agency, of which the United States was the chief donor.

6. Kefalári: Central square in Kifisiá, a well-to-do northern suburb of Athens.

"Epilogue"

1. Iconomachy: A period of theological and political strife that divided eastern Christendom, from 726 to 842, into icon worshippers and iconoclasts. It ended with the restoration of the icons in public worship and in church decoration.

THANASSIS VALTINOS was born in Kastri, Kynourias, in the Peloponnese. He has written novels, novellas, short stories, and film scripts and translated ancient Greek tragedies for the theater. His work has been translated into many languages and has earned him numerous awards, including Best Film Script for *Voyage to Cythera* (Cannes Festival 1984), the Greek State Prize for Best Novel (1990), the International Cavafy Prize (2002), the Petros Haris Prize conferred by the Academy of Athens for Lifetime Achievement (2002), the Gold Cross of Honour of the President of the Greek Democracy (2003), and the Greek State Prize for Lifetime Achievement (2012). In 2008 he was elected a member of the Athens Academy and served as its vice president in 2015.

JANE ASSIMAKOPOULOS is an American writer and translator living in Ioannina, Greece. Her translations from the Greek and French include novels by award-winning writers as well as poems and stories in literary journals and anthologies in the United States and in England. She is currently employed by a Greek publisher as translation editor in charge of a series of books by Philip Roth.

STAVROS DELIGIORGIS is a University of Iowa professor emeritus in English and Comparative Literature. He holds degrees from the National University of Athens, Yale University, and the University of California at Berkeley. His publications include books and articles in literary theory as well as poetry and prose translations from the Greek and Romanian.

STATHIS N. KALYVAS is Arnold Wolfers Professor of Political Science at Yale. He is the author of, among other books, *Modern Greece: What Everyone Needs to Know*, *The Logic of Violence in Civil War*, and *The Rise of Christian Democracy in Europe*.